A MEDAL FOR DR. MARY

A Historical Novel

Polly Craig

For Jaris
Best wishes!

Polly Craig

ISBN–978–0-9848613–2-3

Printed by Lightning Source

For my kids

Rick, Jeanne, Gary, Carole,
Kevin and Susi

Also by Polly Craig

Situation Desperate: Send Chocolate

Scarlet Acres

PROLOGUE

OSWEGO, NEW YORK, 1919

DR. MARY EDWARDS WALKER'S frail body lay at peace on the dining room table of her family home, awaiting the construction of a simple wooden coffin.

Weathered doors were locked and drafty windows shuttered. No mourners stayed to listen to the creaks and groans of the old house or complain about the moaning of the freezing wind that swirled wisps of cottony snow across the rickety front porch.

Kind neighbors had starched her wing-collared shirt and spit-polished her dainty leather boots before dressing her in her customary black frock coat, close-fitting trousers and black silk cravat. Her opera hat sat beside her as if waiting to be popped atop that proud old head.

The Medal of Honor for Meritorious Service, her most cherished possession, covered the space above her left breast. She'd worn it proudly–even on her nightgown–until the last day of her eccentric life.

Dr. Mary Edwards Walker lay dead after eighty-seven eventful years that spanned a lifetime of uphill battles and exceptional contributions.

Her indomitable spirit was free to soar the universe unfettered by the bonds of convention, bigotry, and chauvinism.

The amazing blue eyes that had intrigued, bamboozled and charmed generals, presidents, congressmen, judges, princes and queens were closed forever.

Gone was the courageous army surgeon who braved enemy fire to treat her patients on the battlefield and single-handedly saved countless Union Soldiers from needless amputations. No longer would the dauntless champion of women's rights and dress-code freedoms argue with the establishment. Stilled was the voice of the daring author who tirelessly campaigned against health hazards unrecognized until fifty years later.

Dr. Mary confronted eternity that frigid weekend in the same solitary manner with which she faced the adult years of her controversial life. Alone. Unsung. Undaunted.

This is her story.

BOOK ONE
1837–1860

*"Train up the child in the way he should go, and,
when he is old, he will not depart from it."*

Proverbs 22:6

CHAPTER ONE

OSWEGO, NEW YORK

FIVE-YEAR-OLD Mary Walker fidgeted, bored with Reverend Philip Willoughby's fire and brimstone harangue. Clad in black cutaway coat, matching trousers and starched white shirt he looked like a penguin out for a waddle.

Spittle exploded from his thin lips, and his glasses nearly flew from his beaky nose as he clutched the sides of the pulpit and berated his congregation.

Shifting bottoms and suggestive coughs signaled the minister had blustered on too long.

Mary sighed as she swung her feet back and forth, and fiddled with the ruching on her Sunday dress. She tugged at the ribbon beneath her chin, and her bonnet went askew, releasing coal black curls. Sister Luna quickly retied it and pinched her smartly. The child winced but knew better than to cry out.

The preacher's ringing baritone droned on, hammering the fear of God into his bored listeners while he did his best to ignore the Walker tableau in the second row.

"I see Lucifer waiting in the wings," he ranted. "I hear his seductive temptations whispering among you, waiting to seduce you at your weakest moments."

Mary's cornflower-blue eyes shifted right and left, searching for the illusive devil Mr. Willoughby had been warning against every Sunday since she could remember.

She sniffed, wriggling in the uncomfortable pew. Finally she shoved a forefinger up one tiny pink nostril.

Vesta Walker's patience wore thin as she monitored her squirming daughter.

"Mama," the child whispered, tugging a sleeve for attention.

"Shh," her mother hushed, pulling Mary's hand away from her nose and inspecting the finger.

"Mama, when can we go?" the daughter insisted even louder.

"Will you please be still, child," her mother hissed, mortified as worshipers in the neighboring pews gawked in their direction. A few old diehards glowered, but most smiled, wondering the same thing.

Mama frowned at her wayward babe. "Behave yourself," she scolded as sister Aurora Borealis, blushing with embarrassment, pushed Cynthia ahead of her down the bench.

The minister raved on. "Hebrews 12, admonishes us: 'Look diligently lest anyone fall short of the grace of God. Lest there be any fornicator or profane person like Esau, who for one morsel of food sold his birthright.'"

"What's that mean, Mama? Fornica? . . ." Mary whispered loud enough to be heard by the preacher. Willoughby halted his tirade, blustering and choking, his face scarlet with anger.

Mama clapped a hand over Mary's mouth and yanked her onto her lap.

Several snickers erupted from nearby children "Don't encourage her," one mother ordered as she tweaked her son's ear lobe.

Thoroughly disgusted, the minister signaled to the half-dozing organist, mouthing the word, "play."

The startled woman struck a loud note followed by several dissonant chords before the music swelled to a crescendo.

Following their pastor's hysterical signals, the congregation stood up, stifled chuckles of relief and struggled to catch the lyrics up to the runaway music. "Now thank we all our God, with heart and hand and voices . . ." The rough-hewn rafters of the meetinghouse reverberated with joy.

Mama snatched Mary in her arms, hiked up her skirts and bolted for the door.

Papa, his four older girls and son, Alvie, sauntered down the aisle, greeting neighbors and friends as if nothing untoward had occurred.

Sitting up front in the wagon on the way home, Papa could barely keep a straight face as his wife admonished their little girl. "You were extremely impolite today, Mary Walker. I'm very disappointed in your behavior."

Luna, looking pleased at the scolding, said, "Good, it's about time Papa's little pet gets called down."

Mary pouted, folding her hands beneath her chin, a suffering and misunderstood cherub. "But you said to ask you when I needed to know a word," she complained.

"Yes, yes, I did," Mama admitted. "But you must wait until after the service, if you don't understand. It's not polite to speak out in church."

The child persisted. "Well, then, explain to me now what Mister Willoughby meant. What is forni . . . forni? . . ." she stuttered.

Aurora Borealis snorted with disgust.

"Oh, for pity sakes, Mama. Will you speak to her?" she huffed. "She is the most aggravating child I've ever seen."

Mary wrinkled her nose at her sister.

The oldest, fourteen-year-old Vesta, Jr., giggled, enjoying the joke. "Go ahead, Mama, tell her what the word means."

Papa usually left the disciplining of the girls to his wife, but female bickering annoyed him. The conversation had gone on too long to be entertaining. It was time to intervene.

He pulled skillfully on the reins, making a hard left turn up the tract toward the Bunker Hill School. "Let's go see how the chimney is coming along at the school," he said, his strict tone putting an end to the squabbling.

"Dinner's baking in the oven, dear," Vesta fretted. The roasting vegetables might cook to a crisp."

"We shan't be long, wife," he said, snapping the rein to urge the horse faster up the rutted path toward the red schoolhouse.

As the wagon rumbled along, Vesta and Alvah discussed the needed repairs that Lake Ontario's harsh gales visited on the clapboard.

After convincing the villagers that everyone should pitch in to erect a suitable building to educate Oswego's children, the Walkers donated the land and construction materials for the first free school in the area,

Both husband and wife taught at the school, as did every Walker girl as soon as she was old enough.

Since no one was left at home to tend them, little Mary and brother, Alvie, were carted along and shifted from classroom to classroom.

Mary was soon reading one book after another.

◈

The little girl inherited her thirst for learning from her colonial ancestors who were listed among the earliest and most influential settlers in Massachusetts.

Papa related their ancestry while she accompanied him on his medical rounds.

As their wagon rumbled over vast distances between farms, she would plead with him, "I know about the elders, Papa, but tell me how you met Mama."

"You should know that story by heart, child."

"Tell it anyway, Papa."

Alvah grinned, romanticizing the details to keep her entertained.

He threw in a few historical facts to tease her. "Among my ancestors were four signers of the Mayflower Pact. One of the most famous was Elder William Brewster. Your Mama's people were very respected citizens, as well."

"I know all that, Papa, but I still want to hear about you and Mama," she persisted.

"I'll get to it, child. Just have a little patience."

He chucked her under the chin. "Now, where was I? Oh, yes. The Walkers came to America way back in the 1620s and they had many, many children."

"More than we have, Papa?"

"Sometimes, ten to a family," he laughed. "They needed lots of children to help with the chores."

"Just like us, Papa?"

"Exactly like us, sweetheart." He clucked at the horse as they veered toward a left fork in the road.

"Anyway," he continued, "they all worked hard and studied hard, and all the children were educated."

Mary knew the story so well she could tell it herself.

"Just like Mama's people," she added, nodding wisely.

"Just like the Whitcombs," he agreed.

Mary wriggled with anticipation.

"Get to the good part," she insisted. "Tell me how you found Mama."

Alvah hugged his daughter. "All right. Now for the good part."

He shifted his seat and relaxed the reins. No need to hurry. They were homeward bound, and he relished the telling as much as Mary enjoyed the listening.

"Your granddaddy, James Whitcomb, believed all his girl children should have book learning just like his sons," he began.

"You believe that, too, don't you, Papa? That's why you're always telling Luna and Vesty to get to their books."

"That's right. Anyway, when I met your Mama she was already a school-teacher. Best in the village, I heard."

"And . . ." Mary coaxed.

Alvah's cobalt eyes twinkled as he dragged the story out.

"And . . . "

"Papa," she wheedled, tugging at his arm.

He laughed aloud.

"All right," he relented. "Your Mama was the most beautiful lady I had ever set eyes on." He paused, savoring her image.

"Tell me how she looked back then."

"Well, she had long, black curly hair like yours, and when the sunshine hit it, it shone like an ebony pearl." He rubbed his daughter's soft cheek with a rough forefinger. "And her skin was like the inside of a sea shell, all rosy and smooth, just like yours."

The little girl clapped her hands and squealed with delight.

"What else, Papa? What else?"

Remembering, Alvah's heart gladdened with the joy of it.

"Your Mama's eyes were as blue as the Atlantic Ocean on a clear summer day, and her smile made my heart jump right up and sing."

Still does, for that matter, he thought to himself.

"Go on, Papa, please," she urged.

"And she was smart as a whip, to boot."

"Did she love you right away, too?"

"That's the strangest part of it all, Sweetheart. I never did know what such a smart and beautiful lady could see in a plain, old fellow like me."

"Oh, Papa," she chided. "But she did love you, didn't she? Right away? I mean right that very minute?"

"Miracle of miracles, she did."

"Then what, Papa?"

"Well, after we married, we moved to Syracuse to set up housekeeping. Strike out on our own, you might say. It was a wild territory then, a rough and scary place to take a pretty new bride. But your Mama was a brave one. Never a complaint."

He sobered, recalling their ordeals through the harsh winters.

"While your Mama was busy with our babies, I was learning to be a doctor."

"Did you always want to be a doctor, Papa?"

"I guess it was always in the back of my mind. I had a knack for helping folks, and they trusted me. Did pretty well, too. Your Mama and I built the first frame house in that wild town. Think of that."

His expression turned melancholy as he told her that not all of their Syracuse years were happy ones. In hushed tones, he said, "Medicines were scarce then and when two of our own babies got sick, I couldn't save them."

Sensing his need for comfort, Mary laid a small hand on his thigh. "You tried, Papa. I know you tried really hard."

"I did, Sweetheart, but losing those little ones just about broke your Mama's heart. That's when I found the farm in Oswego, hoping a change of scene would ease her pain."

Mary, feeling very grown up that he would tell her this part she'd not heard before, began to pat him like a mother soothing a hurt child.

"You did just the right thing, Papa."

Alvah smiled at his serious daughter, so old and wise for her eight years.

To lighten the moment, he forced a chuckle. "That was some trip from Syracuse, I'll tell you."

"Your Mama and your four older sisters and all our worldly goods were packed up and transported on the packet canal boat from Syracuse to the new homestead where we lived in the little cottage that was already there until our real home was ready.

"The neighbors brought food and helped with building us a bigger house."

The new place had a wide front porch, sparkling white clapboard siding, and a wood-shingled roof. The furnishings were plain, but the rooms were filled with books. Visitors noted that the Walkers seemed to value intellectual and spiritual development far more than luxurious surroundings.

The new house wasn't quite finished on November 26, 1832, when little Mary Edwards Walker made her squalling entry into the world she would later confront with her razor sharp mind and caustic tongue.

The family was never quite the same, afterwards.

☙❋❧

Everyone in the Walker household worked. Each member was expected to handle even the heaviest and dirtiest barn and field chores. Mary carried the work ethic learned there for the rest her life.

In his spare time, Alvah experimented with his plantings, creating new strains by cloning or artificially pollinating familiar fruits and vegetables. In between nagging his children about personal hygiene and healthful eating habits, he found time to invent useful household gadgets plus an improved device for moving well water, which he patented.

The community respected the Walkers and rejoiced in their prosperity, but Mary's eccentricities baffled them, and they never recognized her for the brilliant innovator she was.

CHAPTER TWO

OSWEGO, NEW YORK

ALVAH WALKER basked in the crowd's admiration at the County Fair after he'd won the first prize for his new strain of raspberries.

His cross-pollinations had produced succulent berries that puckered the lips with their piquant tartness. The fruit would sell well, but he'd keep his cloning secrets to himself.

Ten-year-old Mary held his hand, relishing her Papa's success.

Mama and the other girls were pricing hand-made quilts hanging along the fence, and Alvie had scurried off to play with the smithy's boy.

Groaning, Papa turned his back when he caught sight of a patient bearing down on him. As the crowd parted to let her pass, Geneva Wilson's strident shouts grew louder.

She yanked at his sleeve. "Alvah Walker, I need to talk to you."

"Good morning, Miz Wilson," he muttered."How are you?"

"I'm no better," she exploded. "I'm still having problems with my bowels."

Mary's hand flew to her mouth, stifling a gasp. Ladies never mentioned such things in public. It was vulgar.

Papa lowered his voice to a whisper. "First off, Madam, this is not the appropriate place for a discussion of your constitution."

He glanced at her tightly corseted figure.

Still keeping his voice low but firm, he leaned toward her. "And, secondly, for the twentieth time, I repeat my diagnosis that your malady would probably disappear if you'd choose looser clothing."

Geneva Wilson smoothed her close fitting silk bodice, directed a haughty glance toward him and hissed, "Not while there's a breath in my body."

Alvah usually maintained his patience, but when he was right, he was right. He was tired of repeating the same prescription to this woman. Judging by her outrageously snug gown, she had chosen to ignore it, anyway.

"Miz Wilson, you are shortening your life by wearing those damn tight corsets and heavy gowns. Simple clothing such as Mrs. Walker wears would make you feel a damn sight better in no time."

"Never." she snorted and stalked off in a huff.

Later, on the way home, Vesta, and four of their girls, Vesta, Jr., Aurora Borealis, Luna, and Cynthia, exhausted from the excitements of the long day at the fair, dozed comfortably in the back of the wagon on a nest of colorful cotton quilts that insulated them from the bumps and jolts of the road.

His youngest child and only son, Alvah, Jr., had permission to spend the night with the blacksmith's boy in a crude lean-to the children had built close to the blacksmith's forge, providing he return home at sun-up for his daily chores.

Mary lay on the seat beside Alvah, her curly head nestled in his lap. Now and then he patted her hair or rubbed her shoulder, unconscious evidence of his special affection for his funny, smart, bewildering child.

He clucked as he adjusted the reins to guide his plodding chestnut, Calley, around a couple of deep wheel tracks in the dirt path that led toward his thriving farm on the outskirts of Oswego. Always something to fix, he thought, making a mental note to return the next day with a load of dirt to fill in the ruts.

He smiled down at his daughter not in the least surprised to find that she was still awake.

The sharp, earthy aroma of fresh horse droppings wafted to his nostrils on the same breeze that ruffled the child's hair.

High in the heavens, millions of stars twinkled around a three-quarter moon bright enough to light the curve of her cheek and brow. He touched one wispy, black tendril lying against the whiteness of her skin. A glimmer of the moon's pearly glow reflected in one visible blue eye surrounded by its fringe of black lashes.

She was so lovely, this tiny replica of himself. How his plain features could be transformed into such beauty was beyond him.

His older daughters, favoring their mother, were pretty as pictures, but

Mary. Ah, Mary. God help the world when this special child came into her own.

His rough hand found the coolness of the bare little arm that rested on his knee, and he gave it an affectionate squeeze. Stooping low, he whispered, "What's on your mind, Mary?"

She swung her legs down and sat up quickly, primly smoothing her striped, cotton dress down over her knees. "Well, Papa, I've been wondering."

"Not unusual," he replied, and thought to himself, what now? His girl was a thinker, all right. Never a dull moment when she started analyzing things.

"You remember when you were talking to that tall lady who was wearing that pretty blue dress?"

"I do," he said.

"Well, you sounded cross when you told her if she took off that damn corset she wouldn't have so damn much trouble with her constitution."

Papa shrugged tired shoulders and shifted the reins slightly to encourage old Calley. Her plodding hooves were lagging. She, too, was feeling the effects of the long day.

He patted Mary's shoulder, fondly. "Don't say damn child. It's not a nice word for a young lady."

Chastened, she ducked her head. "Yes, Papa."

But she could not leave the subject alone. She wriggled her bottom closer to her father, laid her cheek against the scratchy wool of his sleeve and hesitated a moment.

Alvah, delighted at her curiosity, thought to himself, it's only a matter of time. She'll bust if she doesn't ask me about it.

He chirped at Calley who flicked an ear in response but refused to hurry her pace.

Mary waited for what she considered a tactful time. "But you sounded awfully angry with her, Papa."

"I wasn't exactly angry, Mary. Call it frustrated, I guess."

Alvah, who scrupulously protected the privacy of his patients, was not in the habit of discussing them with his daughter, or anyone else for that matter. However, this was a golden opportunity to stress an important lesson.

He snapped the reins and leaned toward Mary's upturned face. Without getting into too many personal details, he needed to explain his position. The words came easily as he warmed to his topic. "That beautiful blue dress you admire so much is probably the cause of Miz Wilson's health problems," he said quietly, glancing back to check on his sleeping brood.

Mary's brow furrowed. "How could that be, Papa?"

How to tell her in simple terms? He pinched the bridge of his nose in concentration.

Finally, he found the way. "You know I refuse to let your mother and the older girls wear tight undergarments to make their waists look thinner."

"I know that, Papa."

"Well, tight corsets are a menace to a lady's health. All that constriction pushes her internal organs out of place, and they can't perform their proper functions. Does that make sense, Mary?"

Puzzled, the little girl pursed her lips and shrugged.

"Think of it another way, child." He tweaked her nose playfully. "What if I were to pinch this little nose together so tightly you couldn't breathe?"

Mary giggled. "Then I'd open my mouth and breathe that way."

The darkness hid his grin. Bright, very bright, he thought.

"All right. Supposing I put my other hand over your mouth?"

"Then I wouldn't be able to get any air at all," she replied, realization slowly sinking in.

"That's right. Now think of the organs inside your body. If a tight corset compresses those organs, they will not work. Just like your nose and mouth couldn't work if I pinched them closed."

"How does that affect Miz Wilson?"

"Miz Wilson's tight clothes depress her stomach and other organs so they can't function the way God intended. She feels sick a lot of the time because her food doesn't digest properly, and she doesn't pass her wastes every day as she should. Does that make it any clearer?"

"Oh, yes," the child replied. "I'll have to look at the pictures in your anatomy book, Papa, so I know exactly which organs you're talking about."

"Good girl," he said, kissing the top her head.

Calley had stopped of her own accord in front of the barn.

"Ah, here we are, now," he said, surprised he hadn't noticed they were home again. "That wasn't such a bad trip, was it?" he asked, turning to wake his sleeping family.

Mary paid them no mind. She was much too busy plotting how she would convince Papa to let her stay up long enough to study the diagrams in his medical book.

His theory made sense, but she had to see the evidence for herself.

CHAPTER THREE

OSWEGO, NEW YORK

BY 1848, Oswego Village was a bustling city with train service and the beginnings of a decent library. Politics was a touchy subject.

Citizens argued heatedly over abolition, and postmasters refused to deliver literature on the subject. Threatened secession of the states advocating slavery loomed like a festering sore.

The Bunker Hill School, now tax supported, suffered the loss of three of its Walker teachers. Luna, Vesta and Aurora Borealis all married suitable husbands and moved away.

Early on, Alvah deeded the Walkers' original homestead and five acres of choice farmland to son, Alvie, who had no penchant for teaching. But Alvie was no farmer, either. His talent for whittling figures from blocks of wood earned him a unique reputation around town.

Responsible adults labeled him as 'queer but harmless,' while children flocked to his wagon, clamoring to see his clever puppets perform in skits he created. He was soon in demand for public appearances at fairs and bazaars. His parents found no fault with his chosen 'profession,' as long as he was honest and happy.

With the older girls gone, and a brother who was no help, it fell to sixteen-year-old Mary to pick up the reins at Bunker Hill School. She gave up her own studies to teach along with her mother and sister, Cynthia, and her father insisted she save her salary for when she went off to college.

Papa stomped the late March snow off his leather boots and threw open the kitchen door. He slammed his heavy knitted gloves down on the table that had already been set for supper. Spoons danced against soup plates, emphasizing his irritation.

Engrossed in the account of the First Women's Rights Convention conducted by Bloomer Girl, Elizabeth Cady Stanton, in Seneca, New York, Mary sat oblivious.

She had already forgotten the fractious youths who disrupted her classroom as well as the visiting minister's snide remarks about the length of her skirt.

How dare he, she'd thought at the time. Why should I wear a long dress that will sweep up the dirt on this messy floor? And what possible harm can the tops of my boots do to young boys? Too bad she couldn't tell him about overhearing their discussion of local ladies' bosoms. That would burn his ears, all right.

Vesta, bending over the stove, tasted her spicy vegetable stew before straightening up. She laid the spoon on the sideboard and tucked a few curly wisps into the bun at the nape of her neck before turning to her husband.

Alvah's face was a thundercloud, his mouth puckered as if he'd bitten into a sour apple. He usually kept a cool head, but not today, judging by his huffing and puffing.

"What is it?" Vesta asked, drying her hands on her apron.

Ignoring his wife, he turned to face Mary. "Daughter," he said, as his stubby fingers struggled with the wooden buttons on his wool greatcoat.

Oblivious, Mary continued to read.

Papa cleared his throat and spoke louder. "Mary!"

She jumped when she heard her name. "Papa," she exclaimed, quickly laying the paper aside and jumping up to hug him. She began helping him out of his coat.

Alvah's face softened at the sight of her pert face shining with welcome. Her dainty hands seemed too fragile to lift the heavy work coat, but he knew those hands could drive a team, or bale hay, or lug water to crops dying of drought.

He sank into his chair at the head of the table. "The new pastor informs me that you argued with him today about the benefits of Spiritualism as opposed to his Methodist teachings."

Mary hung the coat on a hook behind the kitchen door. "I didn't really argue, Papa," she replied, brushing bits of melting snow off the shoulders.

"I only discussed it with him. He was visiting and overheard me telling the children that in the state of New York we are privileged to practice any religion we choose as opposed to the poor Pilgrims who were driven from England because of their dissenting beliefs. I only pointed out the facts to him."

Shaking her head, Mama settled into her own place. "Arguing with the new minister. . . .Mary, Mary, What are we to do with you?"

"I'm sorry, Mama. I meant no disrespect. The children need to understand that they are living in a wonderful country where they are free to worship as they choose."

"She's right about that," Papa said, proud that his girl could stand up for her ideals.

However, he needed to set the record straight. Church was church, and school was school. Bunker Hill must be kept separate from religious teachings. That was the one hard and fast rule he had set down when he donated the property to the village, in the first place.

He glanced sharply at his daughter. "But did you discuss Spiritualism with your pupils, child?"

Mary sat down next to him and leaned forward, forearms on the table. "Oh, Papa," was her earnest reply. "I merely mentioned Spiritualism as an example, but one of the children asked what it was all about. I had to explain."

Papa thought this over. She did have an obligation to educate, and she surely couldn't be proselytizing. It simply was not her way. "Nevertheless," he ordered, "I want you to tell Reverend Armitage that you're sorry you were disrespectful."

"But, Papa, there was no disrespect. I only stated the facts."

"Mary," Papa said in his warning voice that meant his word was to be obeyed.

"All right, Papa, but I'll only say I'm sorry that he misunderstood. Not that I was wrong."

He opened his mouth to contradict her, but the exaggerated innocence of her expression tickled him. He was such a fool where this bright child was concerned.

To avoid further discussion, Mama stood up and headed for the stove.

"Come and wash up, Alvah. It's time for supper," she said, picking up the ladle to stir the stew one last time.

A mouthwatering aroma filled the kitchen, and Papa gave up the fight. Vesta filled the tureen, placed the ladle in it, and carried it to the table.

"Mary, please call your sister downstairs so we can say Grace."

"Cynthia isn't feeling well, Mama. I'll take a tray up to her later. She's resting in bed right now. Probably has a touch of fever."

Papa looked worried. He had remarked on the girl's lethargy, and her color was pale even for wintertime. "What's wrong with your sister, Mary?"

"She got very wet shoveling the snow yesterday. I'm sure she'll be as good as new, tomorrow."

Later, Mama would recall this night and wish with all her heart that Mary's prediction was true.

CHAPTER FOUR

OSWEGO, NEW YORK

A HOT, HAZY SUMMER followed the cold, damp spring, and the school year ended amid joyous shouts of children too long engaged in the battle of the three "R's" fought with a stern Miss Mary who refused to accept less than their best.

The exhausting chores of running the farm now fell to fewer members of the shrinking Walker family. Mary's free time was limited, but every spare moment she studied borrowed anatomy books, making meticulous notes to later supplement her college studies.

The more she read about the human body, the more she believed that her father was right about the waist-binding styles of the times. "I see your point, Papa. Women are torturing their bodies with the barbarous styles that squeeze and pinch and constrict to the detriment of their physical well being."

Cynthia, never recovered fully from her pneumonia in March, could no longer find the energy to tutor students who needed extra help. She still tried to help with small chores around the house, but her pale countenance and halting gait made it obvious that her health was failing.

Weaker and more debilitated, she was unable to assist in the fall harvest, and she fell seriously ill when winter's chill settled into her bones.

Alvah dosed her and fretted over her, but none of his treatments made a difference. Christmas was a sad event quietly observed in the sick room.

By January's end her decline was startling. Deep circles ringed her lusterless eyes. A wracking cough that dredged up a slimy green mucous left her bathed in perspiration and gasping for breath.

Mary took a leave of absence from the Bunker Hill classroom to nurse her. Someone else could tend the children. It was more important that she cool Cynthia's fever and massage her arms and legs to relieve the terrible cramping.

She read aloud anything that might take her sister's mind off her agonizing pain. News pamphlets prompted discussions about Zachary Taylor's zealous Whig Party politics. They pored over anti-slavery speeches by Frederick Douglas and William Lloyd Garrison and spoke of the feminist movement, greatly admiring Dorothea Dix's ongoing battle to improve the treatment of insane patients locked away in madhouses.

They avoided discussions of personal religion and stuck to arguing about novel movements like the Shaker Excitement and the polygamous Mormons.

At times Cynthia's eyes would light up with interest. More often, she nodded in passive agreement to Mary's comments as she sat at the bedside hand stitching new costumes for herself.

"When I become a famous doctor, Cynthia dear, I'll buy us one of these new-fangled sewing machines Elias Howe has invented," she said, displaying a drawing of it.

On a whim, she designed her first pair of pants to be worn beneath a calf length over-dress designed to avoid any constriction at bust and abdomen. Instead of copying the ruffled pantalettes she hated, she fashioned the pants after her father's trousers. That outfit drew the patient's first strong reaction she'd displayed in weeks.

Horrified when Mary modeled the blue broadcloth ensemble, she warned, "You are asking for trouble, Missy. What will the neighbors think?" she croaked, her voice hoarse from coughing.

"Now don't you fret about the neighbors, darling," Mary chided, adjusting the covers under Cynthia's chin.

The warning was prophetic. One glimpse of the outfit and the Oswego Lady Quilters fumed over their patchworks. "If she weren't such a darn good teacher," they sputtered, "she'd be laughed right out of town."

Their husbands, however, chuckled at Mary's shenanigans over meat pies and ale at the local pub. "She's got gumption, I'll give her that," said one, and heads nodded in agreement.

Some of the neighbors ran to Reverend Armitage for guidance on how to tell Alvah Walker that his daughter was making a public spectacle of herself, but the minister refused to get caught up in the controversy. He'd already had one run-in with the sassy little schoolmarm, and, besides, her father was a generous parishioner.

"I don't give two hoots about the opinions of those narrow-minded biddies," she scoffed. "I'm comfortable and modestly covered, and warmer than they are."

The town folk hardly knew what to make of that "loony Walker girl."

On Valentine's Day, Mary handed her sister a card constructed from scraps of lace and fabric left over from her sewing. It contained a prayer for a quick return to health.

Cynthia smiled weakly, rising up from her nest of pillows to embrace her.

"Oh, dear Lord in heaven, darling, you're cooking," Mary blurted as she hugged the hot little body against her.

Covering her alarm, she emptied the pitcher of cold water into the bowl on the dresser and used a small towel to sponge her patient down. Tenderly, she bathed her gaunt back, flaccid breasts, and distended stomach, all the while hiding her dismay at the skeletal appearance of wasted arms and legs.

Afterwards, she dressed Cynthia in a pretty nightgown of softest cotton trimmed with a row of lace around the neck.

Cynthia took hold of her sister's hand as she gently brushed the lank hair back from her wasted cheeks. "Oh, Mary," she cried. "Please don't look so sad. I'm not at all afraid, you know. I'm just so tired, is all. I pray it will be finished, soon."

Overwhelmed, Mary gathered Cynthia into her arms and wept against her shoulder.

Cynthia cried for her sister's pain. "Don't worry, sweetheart," she comforted, "It's going to be all right."

Mary held her until Cynthia fell asleep. She clutched the frail body to her breast, praying, yet knowing that prayers were futile.

Vesta, Jr. and Aurora visited, bringing treats to tempt their sister's appetite. They fled the sick room in tears, unable to bear the sight of her skeletal appearance.

Luna sent long letters of encouragement, while Alvie, grieving in his own way, carved tiny angels that he placed on the bedside table.

Papa and Mama drifted in and out of the sick room, helpless terror clouding their eyes. How could this lovely child who had everything to live for be slipping away from them? Burying two babes they barely knew in Syracuse had been difficult enough, but charming, saucy Cynthia was entrenched in their hearts, an integral part of their family.

For nine days Mary watched at Cynthia's bedside, snatching an hour or two of sleep in a chair nearby. She rarely washed or changed clothes. Exhaustion painted dark smudges beneath her eyes, as her own cheeks lost their rosy bloom. Disheveled curls that hardly saw a brush were carelessly braided into a queue and bound with a scarf.

On the evening of February twenty-first, Mama came to relieve her weary daughter. "Go down and get some hot soup, Mary. You have to eat or you'll be sick, yourself."

Mary protested, but Mama was firm. "Maybe you can get Papa to eat something, too."

She crept down to the kitchen and found her father hunched over the table, staring at his untouched bowl. His cheeks were shining with tears.

He's aged, she thought. He's wearing down, too.

Mary stood behind him, putting her arms around his shoulders, her lips close to his ear. She inhaled his familiar odors of barn and field and clean lye soap. Her throat strangled with fear, she choked out the dreaded words they'd all been avoiding. "She's going to leave us, isn't she, Papa?"

Alvah's shoulders shook with sobs. "Yes, she is," he cried. "The Lord will take her home soon, I'm afraid."

Mary moved to kneel beside him. "Is there nothing we can do?" she begged, dabbing at his tears with a handkerchief snatched from her apron pocket.

Distressed at his own weakness, he gulped back his sobs. He was the father. It was his place to be strong.

He circled Mary's shoulders, pulling her to him. "No, child, her little body is all used up. There's no strength left in her to fight any more."

"She won't fight. She wants it to be over," Mary wept as she buried her face on her father's chest. "I don't want her to go. It's not fair."

Papa roused himself and patted his daughter. "No, it isn't fair, but we don't know enough to save her. Some day, pray God, we will."

On February 23rd, 1849, Cynthia Walker, her countenance shining with graceful peace, smiled at each one of her gathered family, sighed, and then closed her eyes for the last time. She was twenty years old.

∽◌❋◌∾

The church was packed with neighbors, flocking to pay their respects. Preacher Armitage's reverent dissertation eulogized the popular young teacher, decrying the loss of a useful life cut short too soon. Not a dry eye could be seen in the church. There wasn't a person there who did not love the precious young woman whose dedication had worked miracles with their recalcitrant children.

At the cemetery, Mary shuddered as the clods of earth fell on Cynthia's simple coffin. Like a thundering waterfall, her emotions tumbled through a gorge of emotions drowning her in sadness, bitterness, helplessness, frustration, and rage. The most profound loneliness she'd ever felt consumed her.

There had to be a way to keep this catastrophe from happening to other families.

Though her faith was ragged at best, she bowed her head. "Dear God," she prayed. "Please help me be a good doctor."

CHAPTER FIVE

OSWEGO, NEW YORK

"MORNIN', WILL," Alvah said as he removed his hat and entered the bank president's office.

Will Biggers peered through gold-rimmed spectacles perched on the bridge of his bulbous nose. "Come in. Come in. Have a seat. I've been reviewing your mortgage application."

Apple-cheeked with heavy sideburns, cleanly shaved chin and plentiful girth, the prominent banker radiated confidence. From his shock of silvery hair, to his finely tailored clothes, to the solid gold watch lying open before him, he looked every inch Oswego's most successful citizen.

Alvah sat in the visitor's chair before the heavy oak desk while the bank president finished reading the document before him.

Cynthia's absence, never far from Alvah's thoughts, lay like a heavy shroud over his heart. Cruel grief lines dug tracks around his grim mouth. Still, he realized life must go on. His other children were alive and in need.

Finally Banker Biggers shuffled the papers and tapped them together squaring the edges. A large part of his business was extending loans to local clients, and Walker was one of his most reliable. He also knew that expenses for education were the only circumstances for which this client would consider putting himself in debt.

"You know your credit is excellent here, Alvah. Of course I can approve another mortgage on your farm," he said kindly, "but you've just finished paying off the last one."

"I know that, Will, but I've got two more young ones that I'm sending to the academy down at Fulton."

Biggers cleared his throat and smoothed one sideburn. "It's not my place to judge, Alvah, but your Mary seems to be doing a fine job with her teaching in spite of her odd ways. Folks hereabouts are more than willing for her to keep teaching at Bunker Hill as long as she likes. And your son, Alvie . . . well . . . Alvie . . ." Will's face went beet red as his voice trailed off.

Mortified, he shuffled more papers. "Uh, that is, I mean," he stuttered, "Do you really want to mortgage your property for them?"

Alvah bristled. Knowing how his neighbors felt about his two unconventional children made no difference to Alvah Walker. His and Vesta's most important commitment was to provide a higher education for every one of their children.

Sitting up straighter, he squared his shoulders. No explanation was necessary, but he offered one anyway. "See here, Will, my young ones will have the same as their sisters."

He leaned forward and locked eyes with his friend. "My older girls went to Fulton Academy, it's the best school around, and Vesta and I will give the two young ones the same opportunities, no matter what it takes. That's our final word on the subject."

Will Biggers reached for his quill pen and scratched his signature on the mortgage without further comment.

❧◉❧

Fulton Academy, later known as Falley Seminary, located about twelve miles southeast of Oswego, was co-educational, but the majority of its students were males between the ages of sixteen and nineteen.

Anatomy was a compulsory subject. All of the girls and many of the men ignored the requirement, but Mary was excited about supplementing her years of home study.

Wishing to make a good first impression, she fretted over her appearance, finally choosing a black bow to tame her curls into a ponytail that nestled against the shoulders of her fitted fawn jacket. Her white shirtwaist was starched and pressed. Her fawn trousers topped polished, black boots. "Do I look all right, Mama?" She asked, twirling around.

"You look just fine," Papa said. "Now come along or you'll be late for your first day."

⌒◈◈◈◈⌒

The anatomy laboratory was a generous space with a long table at the front. Several tiers of seats held a handful of boisterous young men milling around.

Avoiding the rude stares directed at her, Mary settled onto a bench away from the others and arranged her tunic over her trousers.

All chatter in the room ceased. An arrogant youth clad in brown frock coat and rust-colored weskit squelched the whispers. He swaggered over, inspecting her costume with the insolence of a slave trader checking his purchase.

His left hand smoothed his short, straight hair. Retrieving his silver watch from his vest pocket, he flicked open the case and studied the face as if he were learning to tell time. "Are you here for the anatomy class?" he asked, snapping the watch case shut with a sharp click.

"Yes, I am," she replied in a neutral tone. She turned away and reached into her satchel for writing materials.

Another spoke up, his face flushing with annoyance. "You can't be serious," he spat, staring rudely at her trousers and curling his lip with distaste.

"We can't have 'girls?' in an anatomy class with us," he snapped with a suggestive leer. "Surely, there must be more suitable studies you can pursue—proper attire for young ladies, for example."

A few youths tittered while other voices grumbled agreement.

Mary covered her irritation with a frigid smile. She stared back at him and ignored other frowning faces.

"This is the only anatomy class available," she said evenly, "and it's a required course. I shall stay for the lecture, like it or not."

The second fellow grabbed his books, slapping them together. He marched up to her and stared directly into her face. "You'll do so without me," he snorted. "I'll not study a naked body with a female watching me." He turned and stomped from the lecture hall.

Several others followed, and she watched them leave, her face an unreadable mask. Your loss, she thought, and settled down to wait for the instructor.

Mary threw herself into her studies. Her desire for a medical education had taken precedence over all else, but her decision became doubly reinforced when she read a timely newspaper article by a foreign missionary. He urged that interested young women become doctors and join him to work in the Far East where females could not be approached by men. For a time she contemplated joining the evangelist, but her finances and other more pressing events intervened.

For two difficult years at Fulton, she ignored insults and obstacles placed in her way as she laid the foundation for her medical career. Encouraged by her father, she disregarded the jibes and ridicule that followed wherever she went.

Instead, she conducted her own research. She cut out newspaper accounts of post-mortems and coroners' inquests, poring over them until the yellowed clippings fell apart in her hands.

When classes permitted, she visited sick and feeble patients, making copious notes of their symptoms and progress, while nursing them as tenderly as she had cared for her sister. Sometimes she was paid; more often she was thanked and sent on her way with a small token, a bit of food, or plain good wishes.

Mary convinced the Walker family doctor to lend her his medical books, which she devoured in the privacy of her room away from the derisive remarks of fellow students. Though old Dr. Fortescue knew how stubborn Mary could be, he still treated her request as a girlhood whim. He predicted she would outgrow her ridiculous ambitions and return to teach at Bunker Hill School where she belonged. Little did he know.

Her studies at Fulton Academy came to an end in 1850, the same year "Old Rough-and-Ready" Zachary Taylor, the 12th U. S. President, died in office, and Vice President Millard Fillmore took over to finish out the unexpired term.

"I'll go back to teaching, Papa," she said. "There's no use continuing at a school that thwarts my attempts for medical training. Anyway, there's Alvie's education to consider. I can save my salary for college expenses, if that's all right with you."

"Of course it is, daughter. The town will be happy to have you back."

⊷⊙✿☉⊶

She pretended not to notice when young female students, echoing their mothers' prejudices, snickered behind their hands at her unusual attire, but her nicely rounded figure, though modestly covered with sturdy tunics and tailored pants, provoked naughty thoughts in many a teen-aged boy's head.

An older youth described her. "She's very pretty with her dark curls and piercing blue eyes that can stop you dead in your tracks."

Mary was an autocratic taskmistress, and woe to any disobedient pupils who resorted to nasty tricks in her classroom.

Papa was pleased when glowing reports of her successful teaching strategies reached him. On her eighteenth birthday, he gave her a handsome gold watch. "We're so proud of you, Mary," he bragged as he pinned it to her bosom with the pride of a general rewarding his soldier for bravery in action.

⊷⊙✿☉⊶

Mary ignored the ridicule of Oswego traditionalists encouraged by reports that Amelia Jenks Bloomer was urging women to abandon their voluminous dresses and crinolines for ankle-length pantaloons or "bloomers" topped with short full skirts. Amelia advocated women wear the very same styles Mary Walker had been sporting for years.

She continued to badger the women in town, insisting that shorter, lighter, looser fitting clothing would be beneficial to their health. "If you don't want to wear trousers, at least wear jumpers suspended from your shoulders. Waist-pinching styles are very bad for your health."

Scandalized, they retorted, "No, we'll never wear suspenders, even if they are made of cloth."

In the early 1850s, Mary's costume favored a loose waist called a Jenny Lind, a skirt reaching halfway between knee and instep, though some skirts were shorter than others. With them she wore full-length trousers cut from the same fabric.

None of her critics could be satisfied. When her skirts were shorter, neighbors complained that she was "awfully immodest," though her legs were amply covered. When she lengthened her skirts to six inches from the ground, one mean soul said tartly, "You look like an Indian squaw."

"Why, thank you." Mary replied with an impish grin. "I'll take that as a compliment."

She told Papa, "Since there's no pleasing everyone, I've decided to please myself."

Mama sighed and said nothing.

Late one Friday afternoon, Mary, wearing her favorite cornflower blue costume, strolled home along a path that bordered the neighboring Coolidge farm. The spring thaw had wakened a thirsty earth to the promise of new life.

The sun was low in the sky and the slight breeze blowing across the fields was fragrant with the scent of burgeoning wildflowers. It had rained in the night, and trees and grass smelled lush and well nourished.

Mary's thoughts sped ahead to the weekend that promised extra time for a new medical text she was anxious to study.

Her next-door neighbor, Josiah Coolidge, obese, bulbous-nosed farmer, clad in faded overalls and plaid flannel shirt stood talking with several lanky, teen-age lads whom she recognized as former students. All, save one, Thaddeus Coolidge, quickly turned their backs to her.

A malevolent grin decorated the Coolidge youth's pimpled features. He stared at her like a vulture watching his prey. His insolence annoyed her, but she smiled and said as she strode past, "Good afternoon, boys. Are you keeping well?" No answer but a snide snicker.

She strolled on, her thoughts returning to the medical book she had borrowed from Dr. Fortescue.

Splat went a rotten egg against her shoulder, its sulfurous fumes polluting the air. Hard lumps of horse manure followed.

"You oughta put a proper dress on like a decent lady," one boy shouted.

"You look like a crazy woman in that getup," yelled another.

Stunned for a moment, Mary stopped dead still, turned, and lifted her arms, as if to question why they would hurt her.

The punks continued pelting her with manure and rotten eggs, fouling her hair and clothing with barnyard filth.

"Stop. Stop it," she screamed, covering her face with her hands, but the missiles kept plopping against her. She gagged as the fetid odor of manure and sulfurous rot from the putrid eggs choked her. A few sharp stones struck her head. She cried out in pain and outrage.

With tears of indignation streaming down her face, she took off running, the howling young rowdies chasing after for a hundred yards before they realized they were nearing the Walker property. Fortunately, she sustained only a few bruises, but her clothes were ruined. Her pride lay in tatters.

Papa was working on the porch when he caught sight of his girl, her face smeared with tears, her hair and clothing covered with slime and dung.

"Mary? What on earth?" he spluttered, his nostrils flaring, when the revolting stench reached him.

She gulped back her sobs. "Oh, Papa, it was Mr. Coolidge and a gang of young ruffians, making fun of my clothes, that's all."

"That's all," he shouted. "That's all!"

He came off the step like a whirlwind, his face purple with rage. He threw down the hammer he had been using to keep from doing fatal injury to the nasty villains who had hurt his child. With clenched fists, he headed toward the roadway, a look of murderous determination in his eyes.

Mary was frightened. She had never seen her father in such a state. She flew after him, grasping his sleeve before he could reach the gate.

"Papa, stop," she cried. "I'm all right. Really, I am."

"They'll be sorry they ever set eyes on you, Mary Walker," he swore. "Now let me go,"

"No, don't, Papa, please. Let it rest," she begged. "No need to make a big fuss. They've probably run off by now, anyway."

Her desperate tone stopped him. He was, above all else, a reasonable man.

"I'll give them a piece of my mind, at least," Papa growled. "How dare they do this to you?"

She pulled him back toward the house. "They don't understand, Papa," she replied sadly. "I'm beginning to wonder if they ever will."

She limped over to the horse trough. "Help me rinse this filth out of my hair," she pleaded as she stuck her head under the pump.

His anger gradually subsided as he primed the pump and jerked the handle up and down. "Ooh," Mary squealed as the cold water sloshed over her bare neck. She rinsed and wrung out her hair, twisting it into a rope that she wound around her head.

Drips ran down her cheeks and inside her collar as she started for the steps.

"Let me give you a hand, darling," he offered, grasping her elbow to help her up the steps.

"No, no. Thank you, Papa, I can manage. Don't get any of this filth on you."

Hearing voices, Mama stepped outside. Her hands flew to her cheeks. "Oh, my Lord," she screamed. "What happened to you?"

"It's all right, Mama," Mary soothed. "No great harm done."

Mama pulled her apron over her mouth and nose to filter the stink. "Take off those disgusting clothes at once," she demanded. "I'll try and clean them up for you."

"No, Mama, It's my mess. I'll take care of it."

Alone in her room, wrenching sobs came. "Why is it so difficult?" she mourned. "I mean them no harm. Just because I'm different. . . ." She swiped away the tears. "That stupid Coolidge boy was getting even for the thrashing I gave him. Well, he will not win," she vowed. "None of them will."

She poured water from the ewer into the basin and bathed her face and hands. As she scrubbed the revolting mess from her tunic and pants, she muttered, "Someday they'll all see it, and women will be dressing this way."

In July, 1897, Mary gave an interview for the Sunday edition of a Minneapolis newspaper, during which she related the story.

"Funny thing," she told the reporter, "Mr. Coolidge eventually became a friend of mine. He fell violently ill and was given up by all the physicians in the county. Finally, his wife sent for me. I treated him, and brought him back to good health. He remembered the incident after all those years and actually apologized. I was invited to their home several times." Then she added, "Nobody will ever realize how much I endured for the cause of Dress Reform."

CHAPTER SIX

OSWEGO, NEW YORK

BY 1853, Mary had saved enough to see her through two years of medical college.

The problem was finding an institution that accepted female applicants.

"Remember Elizabeth Blackwell, the first woman in America to receive a medical degree, Mama?"

"I do, dear."

"She was refused by several faculties who vowed to close their doors before enrolling women. Then she was accepted by Geneva Medical College in New York and graduated in 1849. That was supposed to be a breakthrough for women.

"But, because of the hullabaloo over her degree, the administrators decided they couldn't face the controversy. Two years later, Blackwell's sister, Emily, was denied entrance to the school. The vote was unanimous. No female student would participate in their medical courses!"

Mama was optimistic. "That was several years ago, Mary. Times are changing, dear. Perhaps now . . . "

"I'm not discouraged, Mama. Just realistic, that's all."

A missionary society contacted Mary. "We'll pay for your education providing that you serve in a foreign country for several years," they promised.

Playing devil's advocate, Alvah said, "The group exacts a heavy price for their aid. Still your life would be easier. You can save your money, and when you return from foreign duties you can set up a practice here in Oswego."

"Oh, Papa, I don't worry about money. I'm young and strong. I can work on a farm, or teach, or tend the sick. Right now I just want a good medical education, and I'll find the way to do it, whatever it takes.

"Their offer is tempting, but I don't agree with the Society's premise that God can do all things. When I prayed for Cynthia to get well, God didn't heal her, did he?"

"We tried our best with your sister, darling."

"Yes we did, still I kept on praying as hard as I could.

"And where is God when women have to take second place in society? Not you Papa, but most men think that way."

"Give it time, daughter."

"It should be now. Women deserve respect and equality—freedom is written in our Constitution, Papa. It's not a gift to be doled out by men."

"It's not that I'm ungrateful," she explained. "The Society's offer is generous, but I won't tie up my future with a religion I can't follow in my heart. I question their foreign interests while they ignore desperate needs here in America."

She tossed her head. "There is just too much to do in my own country."

Her eyes sparkled. "I know I can make a difference here. I can address the unfair practices against women right here in the state of New York. I don't have to go to the Far East to enlighten men about the burdens they inflict on women. Things need to be changed right here, Papa.

"If I set up a practice in town, I'll have much more influence on my patients. Politics can be changed if enough people work for the same objectives."

"You don't need to convince me, child. I'm well aware of your feelings," Papa said, "and you know that I'll be here if you need help."

She threw her arms around his waist. "I do, Papa," she replied. "I never doubted that for a moment."

Every night over supper, the Walkers discussed the medical climate. "Physiciansargue among themselves," Mary said. "Whose treatment regimens are best? Whose cases are worse? Backbiting and gossip are causing dissension among doctors in neighboring communities. I can't understand why there are no consistent standards."

"It's called competition, dear," said Papa.

"More like ego trips," Mary snorted.

Several weeks after the first queries were mailed Mary settled at the kitchen table and pulled a packet of correspondence from her pocket. With a sniff of disgust she dropped the letters before him.

"Look at these, Papa," she fussed. "I've written to half a dozen schools for admission. Two of them didn't bother to answer. The rest were downright hostile. No women, period!"

She slapped the table. Silverware clinked and water sloshed from glasses. "One stupid man had the audacity to say he must refuse me because 'the necessary education was beyond women's capacity.' Can you believe that, Papa? Beyond MY capacity? Beyond my . . . my . . ." Words failed her.

Mama bent her head over a serving dish, afraid she'd laugh out loud. Her daughter was far too serious, at the moment, for levity of any kind. To hide his own amusement, Alvah pulled out a handkerchief and blew his nose. His daughter was never guilty of modesty when her intelligence was questioned.

Mary's chair scraped the floor as she pushed away from the table and stood to pace the kitchen. Her cheeks flushed with anger, she marched like a soldier approaching battle. Her footsteps emphasized every word as she clumped across the polished wood, thumping her fists against her thighs. Pausing, she picked up a sheet. "Listen to this, Papa. Here's what one dimwit wrote." Her voice dripping with sarcasm, she quoted, "the revolting details of everyday medical practice are totally incompatible with true femininity. I ask you, Papa?"

"Sit down, Mary, and eat your supper," Vesta urged. "Getting all upset won't help your digestion."

Mary looked sheepish as she took her place. "I'm sorry, Mama, I just get so furious, sometimes."

Her mother chuckled. "We never noticed that, darling."

Mary laughed at herself. "Oh dear."

Mama changed the subject.

"If you had your choice, Mary, and could enter any school at all, which one would you attend?"

Mary looked thoughtful. "Difficult to say, Mama," she replied, picking up her fork. "There are so many conflicting philosophies about training, and the differences are remarkable. Some schools teach Botanic Medicine, developed by a retired New Jersey preacher named Sylvester Graham. Patients are permitted no meat, alcohol, tea, coffee, tobacco, or opium. Salt is the single condiment allowed, and then only in miniscule quantities. Every bite of food must be chewed until it's completely broken down."

"Well most of that seems reasonable enough," said Papa. "But I don't like the bit about no meat and opium is out."

"Then there's Thompsonianism, Papa. It was developed by a Dr. Samuel Thompson from Boston. He stresses fewer medications in lesser quantities. He recommends the administration of very small doses of a remedy that would produce symptoms of that disease in healthy persons."

"I'd have to think on that one," Papa observed.

"Dr. Thompson relieves his patients' symptoms with steam baths and claims 'that all diseases are the effect of a general cause and may be removed by restoring the natural heat of the body, making the patient sweat profusely.' That's supposed to clear away canker and putrefaction."

Papa's brow wrinkled. "Well, sweating does relieve fever, Mary. But clear away putrefaction?"

"Some schools still teach the Victorian practices of Benjamin Rush. He defends heroic intervention—bloodletting, blistering, lethal mercury cocktails and debilitating calomel purgatives. His followers practice the same even though Dr. Rush nearly died bleeding and purging himself during the Philadelphia yellow-fever outbreak."

"Remember when well-meaning friends suggested such treatments for Cynthia?"

"Very well, Papa."

"I thought them barbaric and vicious. They're more dangerous and painful to any patient, let alone our darling girl."

Mama said, "I was so repulsed the first time I heard about them I ran from the room and vomited in the kitchen sink."

CHAPTER SEVEN

SYRACUSE, NEW YORK

MARY NODDED graciously as the balding, hazel-eyed Director of Admissions, introduced himself. The small man, stoop shouldered, pot-bellied and pompous, displayed horsy teeth in a grin that stopped abruptly at his bushy mustache. His nondescript brown suit coat topped dun colored trousers, both of which needed the attention of a good tailor.

"Sit down, sit down," he ordered, imperiously indicating the single straight chair before his desk.

He'd kept her twiddling her thumbs in the corridor outside his door for an hour with no place to sit and no excuse for the delay. Since no one left his office before she was invited inside, Mary presumed the wait was a ploy to test her patience.

The permeating odor of smoke suggested this thoughtless popinjay had enjoyed a cigar at her expense. What a maddening waste of precious time, she thought. Poor Papa is waiting outside in the chilly air.

Suppressing her annoyance, she sat gracefully, carefully arranging the folds of her floor-length skirt around her knees.

Determined that prejudices against her unorthodox costumes should not interfere with her opportunity to attend Syracuse Medical College, Mary had temporarily set aside her tunics and pants. For her pre-entrance interview, she had purchased a fetching, traditional gown of pale blue striped silk trimmed with pleated ruffles. The soft shirtwaist that buttoned up to her chin was enhanced by her only piece of jewelry, the gold watch that Papa had given her years before.

No whalebone corset constricted her waist, nor did she choose to balloon her frock with the new-fangled contraption that some misguided idiot

47

had fashioned from steel wires and tape. The cumbersome hoop skirt was one more torture invented for fashion slaves. It was nearly as bad as the horsehair crinoline that scratched its wearer's tender thighs and buttocks every time she sat down.

Mary had gritted her teeth as she paid the dressmaker good money for clothing she thought ridiculous. Already the hems of her skirt and petticoats were grimy with dirt collected as they dusted the filthy streets.

Josiah Pritchard appraised her from head to stylishly booted toes. Her feet were planted flat on the floor, her hands folded demurely in her lap, the portrait of a dignified, respectable lady. Masses of coal black hair cascaded from beneath a blue bonnet that matched her eyes. A crocheted reticule hung from her wrist.

Porcelain skin, a small pert nose and generous pink mouth completed the portrait of a lovely young woman. Pritchard knew from her application that she was barely twenty-one. Why on earth hasn't she married and started a family, he wondered. Modern girls! Who could predict their whims?

Ah well, he had his orders.

Mary forced herself to sit quietly under his scrutiny. He's taking long enough to start his questions, she thought.

The chance for admission to Syracuse Medical College had come out of the blue. While on an errand in Syracuse, Alvah came across an advertisement for the institution's coming sessions. He made a few inquiries and discovered that female candidates were definitely being accepted.

He returned from his trip to the city with the exciting information that a little known medical school had opened its doors in 1849.

"I inquired of the bursar," he told his daughter. The tuition is moderate. It's $55 a term. Board and room are $1.50 per week and there are a few other expenses, as well. There's a graduation fee of $15.00 and laboratory charges of $5.00."

Mary could hardly contain her excitement. "I can handle that, Papa. I have enough saved, and I can get a little job to see me through any unexpected expenses."

She was ecstatic. "Oh, Papa, finally, this is my chance."

Alvah agreed. He and Vesta were nearly as joyous as their daughter.

Later, they discovered the rest of the story. When all the hubbub took place after Elizabeth Blackwell's graduation from Geneva, Syracuse Medical

College refused to yield to pressures from their competitors. Three women were admitted the following semester.

Despite the fact that his female graduates were labeled "quacks," the presiding dean continued to thwart tradition. Also coloring his decision was the school's dire need for equipment and more instructors that year. Though Mary didn't know it, nor would she have cared, the school was only too anxious to accept her money right along with the tuitions of six other female applicants.

Director Pritchard, ever appreciative of a pretty face, silently admired the serious blue eyes that steadily held his glance. No shrinking violet, this one, he thought, unconsciously smoothing his sideburns and adjusting the silk cravat circling his starched wing collar. He was not at all in accord with the school's policy regarding women students, but, at least, this one was a pleasure to behold.

He cleared his throat and reshuffled Mary's curriculum vitae. "Ahem," he said, "I see you've mastered several courses in anatomy, Miss Walker."

"That's correct, sir, I studied it for two years at Fulton and have been reading on my own, as well."

"Ah, good, good." More shuffling as he rocked his ample bottom back and forth on the rear legs of his heavy chair. When they screeched in protest, his face flushed, and he quit immediately.

More throat clearing.

"Now, then, are you familiar with our course of study here at Syracuse?"

"Perhaps you would be kind enough to enlighten me," Mary replied, smiling brightly and pressing her fingers to the button at her throat. A little humility might go a long way, she decided.

What a charming girl, he thought. "Yes, well . . . ahem. You understand there will be three courses of thirteen weeks each."

"I understand, sir."

"In the interim between the semesters, each student is assigned to a local physician for hands-on experience. Is that clear, so far?"

"Oh, yes, sir," came her eager reply.

Mary could scarcely control her impatience. How simple does this blockhead think I am? "We are a very eclectic institution," he continued as he rummaged through a side drawer and drew out a tan handbill that he laid face up on his desk. "We have taken the best of the current philosophies, Homeopathy, Hydropathy, and Botanic Medicine."

"I am familiar with all of them, Mr. Pritchard."

"Yes . . . well . . . hmm . . . "

His forefinger traced the list of subjects as he related them. "Let's see, here is materia medica; anatomy . . . more sophisticated than you've studied, I venture to say. Ah, yes, surgery, obstetrics, diseases of women and children." He paused, watching to see if she was intimidated, as even some of his male applicants had been when they were apprised of the obligatory courses.

Mary simply smiled and waited for him to continue.

"Hmm . . . yes . . . well . . ."

He bowed his head as he dragged his eyes back to the line of print above the finger that kept his place on the page.

"And there are other subjects, difficult ones: pharmacy, physiology, chemistry, pathology, therapeutics." He took a deep breath.

"Are you with me, so far?"

Mary nodded. His condescending attitude was really beginning to rankle. Get on with it for heaven sake, she silently fumed.

"Since we want to send our graduates into the world with a well-rounded education, the course includes the rules of medical practice as well as medical jurisprudence. Let me check. Have I left anything out?"

She was anxious to escape the presence of this supercilious jackass, but her desire for admission far outweighed her testiness. She smiled her prettiest.

"Perhaps you'd be kind enough to give me a copy of your leaflet," she asked sweetly. "Then I can study it at my leisure. I assure you I will be up to any courses the school requires."

"Yes, well . . . of course. Capital idea."

He stood and offered her his hand. "If you feel you are up to the task, we will be happy to enroll you in our Winter Session, Miss . . . er . . . ah . . ." a sneaky glance at the application. "Ah, Miss Walker, if there is anything I can do for you it will be my pleasure to assist you."

Mary was amused that the poor fool had forgotten her name, already, so it took a second for the implication of his statement to hit her. When it dawned on her that she could study at Syracuse, she could scarcely wait to tell Papa.

"Thank you, sir," she exclaimed as she gave Pritchard's damp palm a quick squeeze. She plucked the brochure from the desk, and practically ran from the room.

Outside the door, she leaned against the wall. "Whew," she whispered. She gave a little squeak of delight, gathered up her skirts and raced down the long hallway to the exit.

Papa, waiting just outside, had been dividing his time between sitting restlessly on a bench and impatiently striding up and down the road.

When Mary burst through the door, he didn't need to ask the outcome of her interview. She executed a perfect pirouette then grabbed both his hands in her own and danced him around in full view of smiling passers-by.

Her eyes were brimming with happy tears as she exclaimed, "Oh, Papa. It's beginning. My life is really beginning."

Josiah Pritchard frowned at the frivolity as he watched Mary's antics from his office window. He patted his bushy mustache and massaged his bald spot.

"Be a miracle if that pretty little lady survives the first semester," he said aloud. "On the other hand . . . hmm . . . well . . ."

⟣⟨❀⟩⟢

Mary's tiny room was located a few blocks from the campus. A metal frame, single bed, an oak desk, a battered dresser and wobbly straight chair took up most of the floor space. Her textbooks were stored on a rickety shelf above the simple iron headboard.

If that ever gives way while I'm sleeping, she thought, I'll surely be brained by Anatomy or Physiology. She chuckled as she turned the bed-clothes the wrong way around, pillow at the foot. Fractured ankles were infinitely more desirable than a crushed cranium.

She scarcely paid attention to her meager surroundings. She plunged into her studies, sometimes forgetting to eat, many times working into the wee hours of the morning.

Her kindly landlady, Mrs. Althea Bainbridge, a plump, motherly Irish woman with snowy wisps of hair curling around chubby, rouged cheeks, took to bringing a tray to Mary's room when she failed to appear at the supper table.

Hands too full of food to knock, she'd announce her arrival with the same refrain sung in a gravely voice an octave below normal. "In London's fair city, where the girls are so pretty . . ."

Every time Mary opened her door, Althea greeted her with the same words, "You must eat, dearie. Your mother would want you to keep up your strength."

Mary soon became disgusted with her trailing skirts that constantly needed laundering. She shortened up her gowns and put on pantalettes, which she endured for a time, but their ruffled bottoms were as trying as the voluminous petticoats.

She finally threw up her hands in disgust and sent for her trousers and tunics.

Her unusual costumes became the butt of many jokes, but Mary couldn't care less. If rotten eggs and horse manure did not change her wardrobe, surely insults and jeers would fail to do the trick. Her female colleagues agreed with the basic utility of her clothing but lacked the courage to face the stares and malicious remarks that the crazy lady from Oswego was forced to endure.

Mary shrugged off the slurs and declared, "My life is way too busy to worry about what other people think. I'll dress as I please."

She excelled in all her subjects, but because of her previous education, she was the star of the anatomy course. The practicing physicians who taught the classes considered her a bright spot, her lively participation enriching the proceedings with her astute responses. Legible penmanship made her written work easier to rate than the hen scratchings of most of the young men.

Only three of the six other females admitted for the 1853–54 session returned for the second term. Those remaining never finished the course. Perhaps money was the problem, but, more than likely, the constant pettiness of their male classmates distressed them beyond endurance.

Mary, on the other hand, had encountered as bad or worse during her days at Fulton. Their nastiness rolled off her like rain from a downspout. No one would deter her from her goals.

Her first assigned preceptor, Dr. W. H. Burnham, described her as, "A willing and apt candidate for the medical field and a joy to work with."

During her second session she formed a warm friendship with Dr. S.

H. Potter, an ardent advocate of Eclectic Medicine.

Mary wrote home: "The hands-on training between sessions is my favorite time. I work difficult cases with Dr. Potter and love the nursing duties. Nothing excites me more than watching a patient heal under our care."

Many times, sitting at the bedside of an ailing girl, Cynthia's illness haunted her. She spoke of it to him. "If only I'd known then what I've learned from you in the past months, my sister. . . ." Her voice trailed off, regret stinging her eyes with tears.

Dr. Potter counseled, "There'll be times when you are unable to save a patient regardless of your best efforts." The sadness in his voice bespoke disappointing losses of his own. "At those times, my dear, you must be strong and consoled with the fact that you did everything humanly possible. The rest is in the hands of fate."

As a practicing physician and surgeon, Mary would do battle with fate many times, but she never accepted a loss with easy grace.

☙●❧

Mary's matriculation was not all work and study. In spite of the ridicule of the majority, there were a few intelligent young men who admired her good looks and intellect. They were willing to discuss philosophies with her and occasionally invited her to join them for tea.

Among them was a bright young fellow named Edwin Fowler.

He found in Mary a soul mate, someone to appreciate his talents and share his dreams for the future. Her cheerful disposition and delightful sense of humor tickled Edwin. "I think you are the loveliest woman I ever met," he told her.

And Edwin brought out the best in Mary. She blossomed under his attentions. He was as supportive of her ideas and ambitions as her parents had been, and he saw her for the bright, lovable person she was.

"You remind me so much of my father," she said, letting her guard down. "You're the first interesting man who's looked at me without finding fault with my outspoken views or poking fun at my clothes."

Of medium height and build, with wavy sable hair, ruddy outdoor complexion, and deep brown eyes, Edwin cut a handsome figure in his well-tailored frock coats and close-fitting breeches. His boots were always polished; and, whenever they kept appointments, he gave the impression that he had freshly bathed for her benefit. They had met in the pathology class and an instant rapport was established between them. He seemed not to notice her unusual costumes, nor was he intimidated by her brilliance.

"I don't mind your clothes, Mary. I think you're very brave to stick to your beliefs."

He was her prince. She loved him dearly and hoped for a bright future with him, though she never let him know this.

One drab Friday afternoon in fall, Mary trudged toward the campus, lugging several heavy books in her arms, her sturdy woolen coat buttoned up against the chill.

Edwin was approaching in the other direction. Clinging to his arm was a stunning young girl with slate gray eyes and light brown hair tied up with a bright silk bow. Her smart green gown hugged her voluptuous figure at the corseted waistline, and her voluminous skirts swished around her feet, buffeting Edwin's legs.

Mary felt dowdy and unsophisticated by comparison.

She had no time to change direction, nor did she have time to gather her wits about her. The pang that struck her heart was worse than a physical blow, a totally new emotion for the sheltered girl from Oswego.

"Hello, Mary," Edwin said. "May I present Emily Pershing, a close friend of mine from our childhood school days?"

Mary saw the look of adoration on the girl's face. Clearly she was deeply in love with Edwin.

"How do you do, Miss Pershing," she managed, thankful that her arms were full of books she could cling to.

"Please call me Emily. Edwin has written so much about you that I feel we are friends already."

Mary summoned a sickly smile that flicked across her mouth but never reached her eyes. If Emily noticed, she didn't comment.

Mary gave the couple a lame excuse. "Please excuse me. I'm late," she mumbled and hurried on toward the sprawling granite building that served as Syracuse Medical School.

As she approached the main door, she passed two classmates standing on the marble steps, talking in animated fashion.

"How about old Fowler?" one said. "Where has he been hiding that bit of lace?"

"That's his childhood sweetheart come to visit for the weekend," said the other. "I expect they'll marry once he finishes his training."

Mary's heart seemed to explode in her breast as she bit back tears. Edwin had never mentioned any Emily, but there she was—beautiful, and feminine. Old friend, he'd called her.

Following that fateful weekend, broken-hearted Mary stopped waiting to talk with Edwin after class. When he asked her out for tea, she begged off.

"Mary, why are you avoiding me?" he asked.

"I'm sorry, Edwin, I just have so much to do."

"That's not it, Mary. Have I done something to offend you?"

"Of course not, dear friend."

He stooped to kiss her cheek. "You mustn't," she said.

"Why, dear? Am I not more than a friend?" he begged, his eyes darkening with pain.

"You must keep faith with Emily, Edwin. We are new friends, but she clearly has loved you for a long time."

With that she turned away, hurrying back to her room to fling herself in a miserable heap on her bed. Scalding tears coursed her cheeks, and sobs gagged her as she struggled to swallow them lest another boarder hear her agony.

When Mary failed to appear for meals, or even answer her door, Mrs. Bainbridge began to worry that her petite boarder was seriously ill.

She approached Mary's room quietly and turned the knob, pushing the unlocked door ajar. Waning daylight barely lit the pitiful figure sitting before the small window, head bowed, arms hugging her breasts.

"Oh," she cried, covering the short distance across the room. "Whatever is the matter, child?" she whispered, hugging the girl to her ample bosom.

Mary said nothing.

"It's your young man, isn't it?" Althea asked. "I haven't seen him around for quite a while now."

Mary roused herself from her deep funk. Mrs. Bainbridge meant well, but how could she admit that she had been foolishly smitten with a man who belonged to another?

Still, it might feel good to unburden her soul. Perhaps the older woman could advise where she went wrong. She clung to the kindly landlady. "Edwin loves someone else," she sobbed, swiping at tears. "She's very beautiful, and they'll marry when he graduates. I feel so stupid. Why didn't I realize?"

Althea was incensed. "I might have known. That's just like a man, dear. No thought for a lady's feelings, at all."

Mary defended Edwin. "Truly, we had no understanding between us. He had no idea how I felt."

"Ah, well, then your pride's safe at least. That's the best of it."

She took hold of Mary's arm, urged her up from the chair, and led her to the door. "Come on, a good cup of tea will put a whole new light on things."

Althea Bainbridge became Mary's surrogate mother for the time that she stayed in Syracuse, helping the young student through her sorrow.

"Never again will I give my heart to a man," she vowed. "Edwin is my first and only love, and no one will ever know how deeply I've been wounded."

Mary made many selfless decisions to save others from pain, but most recipients of her kindness never knew of the toll her good deeds took on her own heart.

CHAPTER EIGHT

SYRACUSE, NEW YORK

TO FILL HER LONELY HOURS, Mary applied to The Syracuse Medical Journal for the position of sales representative. She was accepted, in spite of her strange attire and sad little face.

Besides needing the extra money, she must banish the painful memories of Edwin. The newsroom with its jumble of papers and reference books was strangely comforting, and calling on prospective clients gave her contact with interesting people.

Armed with her Certificate of Authorization, she soon became very good at marketing the little publication. She began contributing articles that were well received.

A few months before graduation, she caught the eye of Albert Miller, a popular student, good-looking, outspoken, and worldly. His scholastic achievements were well publicized, and most evenings found him espousing his personal views on the values of Eclectic Medicine to a group of contemporaries in study hall.

Albert was the oldest of the current student body, a smooth talking, arrogant man, with the roving eye of a practiced roué. Tall, blonde, slender and fair as a Viking, he commanded attention as he strolled around Syracuse with some local damsel clinging to his arm. Mary had noticed him on several occasions, each time with a different young lady in tow.

As her reporting duties expanded, it was inevitable that she attend one of the study hall meetings for a possible interview with him. Certain that the school's lone woman scholar would attract Miller's attention, she watched and listened to the self-confident dandy. Beautifully turned out in navy blue, double-breasted frock coat, high collared shirt and red silk cravat, he paced back and forth, holding court like a successful politician.

Albert spotted her the moment she entered the hall. From his position at the podium, he appraised her with the careful attention of a livestock buyer about to purchase a prize heifer. Her tunic and pants amused him, but her winsome figure, flashing eyes and abundant curls gave him pause. A fine looking filly, he thought, as his attention returned to his mesmerized listeners.

When he finished expounding on the benefits of water treatments for the mentally impaired, he dismissed the group and beckoned for Mary to come forward. She stayed where she was.

The audience quickly dispersed, and soon the two were alone except for a few stragglers in the back of hall.

He walked back to her. "You're Miss Walker, are you not?"

"Yes, I am."

"Albert Miller, at your service," he offered, bowing slightly.

I know who you are, Mr. Miller."

"I read your article in the *Journal*," he said.

"Oh, really? And which article is that, Mr. Miller?"

"Uh, uh, the one about . . . ," he stumbled.

She saw through his ploy immediately. "I thought as much," she said and turned away. She had no time to squander on a man so impressed with his own importance that he could not remember an article he supposedly read–especially an article she had written.

His reputation as a ladies' man at stake, or so he thought, Albert glanced about to see if any of the remaining fellows had noticed the rebuff. He wasn't used to being treated in such a cavalier manner by a member of the weaker sex.

He was out of Mary's thoughts the moment she left the room. Still nursing her broken heart, she had no interest in any man. She studied hard, did her job, and kept her own counsel.

Well, Miller thought, who needs to be snubbed by that little minx. Look at her ridiculous getup. Does she know how strange she is?

Still, Albert was intrigued. He knew she was brilliant, her classroom decorum was flawless, and she had developed the reputation of handling her patients with skill and empathy.

For days, her rejection rankled. He decided to teach the little snippet a lesson. He began to appear wherever she was, speaking to her in cool, clipped tones, avoiding the appearance of anything other than a passing acquaintance. More worldly girls than Mary Walker had succumbed to this detached treatment. She would soon fall into line.

During his campaign, he became aware that Edwin Fowler seemed to moon after the girl whenever he managed to be close to her. He noted that Mary was courteous to Edwin, but she always escaped his presence as rapidly as possible.

Something had happened between those two. Albert was sure of it.

Well, well, this strange young woman was indeed a puzzle that his pride dictated he solve.

Graduation was fast approaching. A notice was posted in the study hall, stating that Mary Edwards Walker and Albert Eber Miller, based on their scholastic achievements, had been chosen by faculty and alumni to give the final addresses at commencement.

Mary, the only remaining woman student, had finished second in her class.

Miller jumped at the opportunity. He would ask his cospeaker to meet for a discussion about their speeches. Heaven forbid they duplicate their subjects. Too embarrassing, by far.

Using his formidable charms on the school secretary, a thirty-year old spinster who prayed religiously for a handsome beau all her own, Albert ferreted out Mary's address.

Two days later, he appeared at her rooming house with a notebook and pencil, wearing his best brown frock coat and fawn breeches along with the innocent expression of a dedicated valedictorian. "Albert Miller, here to see Miss Walker."

Althea Bainbridge sized him up as she showed him into the parlor, a room filled with ornate furniture and chairs carefully covered with antimacassars to protect their upholstery from the popular hair pomade of the day.

In her respectable establishment unattached males did not gain access to virtuous young ladies in their boudoirs. Not on your tintype.

"Wait in there," she ordered and pointed toward the parlor.

Althea climbed to the second floor and summoned her perplexed roomer.

"There's a smart looking dandy waiting for you downstairs." But she refrained from adding, a bit too smart if you ask me.

"I'll make some tea and bring it to the parlor when it's ready," she offered.

"Thank you, Mrs. Bainbridge. Please say I'll be down in a moment," Mary replied, quickly checking her hair.

She slipped into her tunic, buttoning it on the way down the stairwell.

A feather in a light wind could have knocked her over when Mary recognized the visitor who stood and ushered her to a seat on the horsehair sofa.

Albert made small talk as he carefully spread his coattails and parked himself directly opposite.

After Mrs. Bainbridge had brought the tea things and departed, Albert broached the subject of his visit. "I'm concerned about the graduation program," he said. "Perhaps we could talk about our topics over lunch tomorrow noon."

Mary poured the fragrant tea into fragile cups and offered Albert milk and sugar.

She had to laugh. He did not fool her for one moment, but she was surprised that he could contrive such an original approach.

It had been several months since her separation from Edwin, and it massaged her ego a bit that such an attractive and eligible bachelor had taken the time to seek her out. His fellow students admired him, and his professors spoke well of his abilities when Mary had questioned them for her article. Perhaps she should reserve her opinion until they were better acquainted.

Despite her initial reservations, she found him pleasant company. Besides looking splendid enough to turn the heads of all the women in the tearoom, he was bright, articulate, and attentive.

During the following weeks, he visited her frequently, and their relationship increased in warmth as they walked out in the evening or shared supper at a nearby inn. His courtly manners and intelligent conversation pleased her, and she became more and more comfortable in his company.

When Miller first called on Mary, her landlady's protective instincts came bristling to the fore. This conceited young rake was a mite too smooth for the old lady's taste. She had seen his type before with his natty clothes and his slicked down hair.

His pencil thin mustache did not raise her opinion much, either. A man should have a real mustache or shave his lip, altogether. Her Mr. Bainbridge, God rest him, had a full bush under his lip that tickled her silly every time he raised her nightie–which was often enough, God bless his randy, black Irish soul.

Pity that that nice Mr. Fowler didn't work out, Althea thought, but I'll give the devil his due. My little roomer seems happy for the first time in months.

When the budding physician examined her own feelings, she admitted, "I can never love Albert the way I loved Edwin, but it's useless to pine for someone I deliberately put beyond my reach."

In one of her newsy letters to Mama, Mary wrote, "There's not much new to tell. Classes are winding down. I've been reading about Florence Nightingale's service at the Crimean War front. Oh, Mama, I only hope I can serve my patients half as well."

Then, almost as an afterthought, "By the way, I've met a man who seems interested in me, and he might come to visit after graduation."

Vesta shared the letter with Alvah over their vegetarian supper of carrots, parsnips, beans and rice flavored with herbs from the kitchen garden.

"I do believe our daughter's finally finding more to life than her medical studies," she laughed as she removed his empty plate. A girlish blush stained her cheeks when she reached across the table to pat her husband's hand, remembering their early romance as if it were yesterday.

"Hmph," Alvah grunted, "He'd better be a decent fellow, is all I have to say on the matter."

As she placed a slice of freshly baked apple pie in front of him, Vesta wondered if he would ever find anyone good enough for his cherished darling.

"Would she choose any other kind, Alvah?" she said, handing him a clean fork.

"She's been in the city a long time, Vesta. The city has a way of changing people."

His wife leaned across the table to gently kiss his cheek. "Surely, not." she said. "Surely not our Mary."

Alvah looked at her fondly, a twinkle brightening his blue eyes. She was still his lovely Vesta, still the light of his life.

"Time will tell," he said, sampling the luscious dessert and chewing with relish.

Albert's commencement speech, titled "The True Thinker," dealt with the premise that all dedicated eclectics were freethinking scholars. His thoughts, delivered in a very practiced and magnetic style, held his audience's attention. Not a cough or a rustle disturbed the silence until thunderous applause followed his final words.

When Mary approached the podium, Alvah and Vesta could barely choke back prideful tears.

No less brilliant than Miller's, the full text of the Walker address was included in the *American Medical and Surgical Journal #7,* published in April, 1855.

Mary's tailored blue tunic and trousers caused a ripple of whispers through the gathering, but once she began to speak, her costume was forgotten. She numbered the obstacles women faced and their rights to learn and produce. Her text included the quote, "Get Wisdom and with thy gettings, get understanding. Know Thyself." At the end, she received an enthusiastic ovation with a 'well done,' here and there.

Mary's final remarks included the following lines: "We are soon to leave and perform the active duties of the profession, and we trust you will never be pained by hearing that any have failed to be successful in, and respected by, the community where we may chance to reside."

Was our usually self-confident Mary nervous about her abilities, or was she reinforcing her own commitment to the dedicated performance of her calling?

In any case, her words turned out to be more prophetic than she could ever imagine.

Mary later spent a hefty portion of her precious financial hoard to have her diploma handsomely framed for her first office.

She also framed two Censor's Certificates, containing the dates, 1854 and 1855. One gave her the legal right to dispense medicine, while the second admitted her to membership in a medical society. Without that she would not have been allowed to practice.

ᔥᘎᗦ

Alvah and Vesta tried their best to convince Mary to practice in Oswego, but Mary's Aunt, Harriet Walker Hall, was also lobbying for her to come to Columbus, Ohio, "because there seemed to be a crying need for a good women's physician."

Mary was cursed with her ancestors' pioneering spirit. New horizons beckoned, and she responded quickly.

While she had no intention of catering to women exclusively, she was convinced that Columbus, Ohio, would be just the place to begin her career.

For a little over seven months Dr. Mary, as she preferred to be called, ministered to patients, mostly mothers and their children. She kept a low profile, quietly carrying on her battle against tight corsets, trailing skirts, and poor hygiene.

Many of her lady patients suffered from ailments caused by street and floor dirt constantly flung up their skirts. Distressing female problems and suppurating lesions on legs and buttocks plagued many of them. They complained of liver and stomach ailments brought on by too constrictive clothing. Still, she convinced too few sufferers that their impractical garments contributed to their ill health.

Albert Miller had hung his sign at 76 Dominick Street in Rome, New York, and his practice seemed to flourish. He wrote Mary regularly. "I have more patients than I can handle. Marry me and help me expand my practice."

Mary went home to talk to Mama.

They sat at the big oak table in the kitchen, the common meeting place where life-altering discussions were always held. The comforting warmth of the room, together with the tantalizing aroma of a sweet bread pudding baking in the oven, created an atmosphere that encouraged intimate discussion.

Here the family hashed over their joys and sorrows while sharing a meal or a homely task in this square room with its paneled walls and cheerful gingham curtains. It was where the Walkers discussed farming strategies, planned celebrations, arranged weddings, and shared their griefs and fears.

Mary fiddled with a tunic she was hemming, while Vesta fitted one of Alvah's worn wool socks over her little darning egg and began to repair a gaping hole in the heel.

"Albert Miller has proposed marriage, Mama, and I don't know what to say to him."

Vesta looked up, her darning needle halfway through the weave she was making with a length of dark yarn.

She remembered the tall, handsome man she and Alvah had met at the graduation ceremony, but she decided not to mention Papa's reservations about him.

"The man's too impressed with his own importance," he'd muttered. "Not husband material, in my estimation."

She'd smiled and ruffled his hair. "Darling, admit it. You don't want to give away your favorite daughter."

"Not true. I just want the best for her."

Try as she might, she couldn't change his opinion. He was an excellent judge of character. Could he be right?

Vesta measured her next words carefully. "He seems a nice enough fellow, Mary, though I don't know him well," she said. "But the question is, do you care for him, child?"

Mary's head was bent over her work. "We speak the same language, Mama. He understands my ambition, and he's not put off by it."

Mama set her mending on the table, leaned over, and raised Mary's chin till their eyes met. "That does not answer my question, darling. Do you love the man?"

Mary sighed and put her own sewing down. "I think so. I admire him, surely. He is very intelligent. He's a good doctor, and he already has a practice in Rome. He wants me to be his partner."

Mama caressed the soft, firm cheek. "Are you trying to convince me, or yourself, Mary?"

The daughter's forehead crinkled, a little frown showing anxiety as she searched out the answer. "I care for him, Mama. I really do."

Her heart whispered, "But not in the way you love Edwin."

She checked the watch on her breast and hopped up. "Heavens. The time." Grabbing a thick towel, she removed the steaming pudding from the oven and set the pan on a rack to cool.

She turned back to Vesta. "Can I ask you a question, Mama?"

"Why, yes, of course, dear."

"Did you love Papa when you married him?"

It was Mama's turn to sigh, but her face showed a special tenderness. "With all my heart," she whispered.

She paused a moment, gathering her thoughts. "After we married it wasn't easy to pick up and leave Massachusetts and the family I loved to settle in a frontier town practically on the edge of the wilderness. If I hadn't loved your father so dearly, I never would have survived that."

"Rome is hardly the edge of the wilderness, Mama."

"Please don't be facetious, Mary. We're talking about your life, about love and marriage."

Sadness colored Vesta's voice as she recalled the three children she had buried.

"It takes a great deal of love to survive the heartaches that life hands us," she advised. "Be sure you understand that loving a man and living out the years with him are not easy tasks in the best of times."

"You're thinking of Cynthia, aren't you, Mama?"

"Yes, yes. Cynthia and the other two precious angels we left behind in Syracuse before you were born."

Mary sat down again, but her sewing remained untouched. "You know, Mama, when I was working with the physicians between school sessions, I thought of Cynthia every time we helped a critically ill girl. I find myself angry over her loss, even now."

Vesta's eyes filled with tears. "I know, child. How well I know."

She brushed at her eyes and returned to Mary's predicament. She hated to sound like a Jonah, but it was important that her point not be missed.

"When adversity strikes a marriage, and it surely does, there has to be unity to share the crises. It takes a lot of compromise, dear, something you're not especially good at."

Mary emitted an embarrassed little chuckle. Her mother was certainly right about that.

CHAPTER NINE

OSWEGO, NEW YORK

LATE SEPTEMBER, 1855, saw giant maples and towering birches crowned in scarlet and gold. Warm Indian summer days and cool, crisp nights had heightened the glorious colors heralding autumn's last bright hurrah before the gloom of winter chased her off. Newly harvested fields, plowed over and tucked up, lay resting till spring planting would waken them again.

The Walker household was all aflutter. That is, Mama was aflutter. Alvah tended to his chores, scowling and mumbling to himself and to son, Alvie, whenever the busy artist put in an appearance to help around the farm. "I'm not in favor of this, at all," he grumbled.

Dr. Albert Miller, the subject of all the dissension, was due for a visit in less than a week.

Vesta argued with her husband, a rare occurrence in the Walker marriage. She fussed and scolded and pleaded to have Albert stay as a guest in their home. At every cunning argument his wife invoked, Alvah set his mouth in a thin line, crossed his arms, and refused to agree.

Vesta attempted diplomacy. "He's coming to ask for Mary's hand, Alvah. We should be polite, dear."

"I'm damned if I'll make it easy for him." he roared. "I don't care for the man."

She tried one last time, appealing to her husband's hospitable nature. "But it seems only common courtesy that we invite him here, Alvah."

"I'll pay for his lodgings in town if it will make you feel better, woman. But the answer is still NO."

Whenever the discussion came up, Mary ran for cover. She saddled Mama's mare and thundered across the fields and through the hunters' trails in the woods. She didn't care whether Albert stayed in the house on Bunker Hill or roomed in Oswego proper. That was the least of her problems. Her own chaotic ambivalence to his visit stressed her to the limit, and only solitude and strenuous exercise seemed to relieve the tension.

Two days before the scheduled arrival, she found herself racing her demons once again, but her headlong flight didn't help one bit. Nor did it allow for her enjoyment of the spectacular weather and the riotous colors of the season.

Edwin Fowler's dear face kept interfering with her common sense. He must be married by now, she thought, and pain squeezed her heart like a vise.

Mary returned to the barn after the arduous ride, breathing as hard as poor Tildie who had responded to the thoughtless jabs from her rider's booted heels by galloping full tilt over fields and hard packed roads, clearing fences and splashing through stream beds.

Distraught, cheeks blazing, hair askew, Mary scarcely noticed the conflicting odors of sweet hay, dry oats, and pungent manure. Her thoughts were still battling one another as she slid the saddle and blanket from Tildie's back and carried them to the storage room. The tumultuous ride had, in fact, added to her doubts and fears.

Her emotions were roiling. Albert was coming to propose in person. True, he was a good choice for a husband, intelligent, attractive, successful, but Mama's question constantly echoed in her heart. "Do you love him, child?"

Papa cornered his daughter in the stable as she wiped down the mare's sweat-soaked neck and flanks.

Running his hand over Tildie's heaving side, he admonished, "Best walk her out, Mary, cool her down some."

"I intend to, Papa. Just let me dry her up a bit."

Alvah leaned against the doorpost and waited.

When she was satisfied that she had dried away all of the sweat, Mary threw the grubby rag over a hook by the door and led the mare out into the early twilight.

Father and daughter strolled together in the quiet gloom. The air smelled of wood smoke and ripe fruit. Tildie's plodding hoof beats echoing on the dry pathway, raised little puffs of dust with each weary step.

Alvah declined to say what was on his mind, and Mary didn't encourage him. Completely comfortable with one another, both remained caught up in their thoughts.

He broke the silence first. "You were late coming back. Supper's almost ready."

"I'm sorry, Papa. There are so many things to think about."

He pulled off a blade of dried cereal grass from a clump beside the path. "I don't doubt that," he said, placing the straw between his teeth.

He waited for her to confide in him, but she said no more. Thoughtfully, he chewed on the stubble then pitched it to the ground. "Are you very fond of the man, Mary?" he asked, his voice stretched thin with worry.

Mary stopped and dropped the halter rope. Reaching up to Alvah's face, she pulled his cheeks downward with her palms in that long remembered gesture he could never resist. She stared directly into his stricken eyes.

Tildie nuzzled her shoulder, and then poked a little harder when she got no attention.

"I have to sort this out myself, Papa," she whispered as if keeping a secret from the mare. "Please don't make it any harder for me than it is."

Gently he took both her small hands in his and pressed them to his chest. "What would you have me do, girl? Keep quiet, say nothing?"

She stood on her tiptoes and kissed him quickly, a little buss on the corner of his mouth. "I guess I just want you to be your own decent self when Albert comes."

His heart melted. "I'll do as you ask, Mary, but you must promise to come to me if you ever need any help. Do I have your word on that?"

Tears stung her eyelids, a lump rose in her throat. He was such a sweet, caring man. No wonder Mama loved him so. "You've always had that, Papa," was her choked reply.

She clucked at Tildie who needed little urging to turn around and head back to the barn.

"Tell Mama I'll be in a jiffy," she called over her shoulder. "I just need to see to the mare, first."

For the hundredth time, Mary reexamined her feelings, counting the pluses while she curried Tildie with the stiff brush. Albert was well read, widely traveled and respected in his profession. His reputation as a physician was certainly rising, though she did feel some of his "free thinking" ideas regarding heavy water treatments were a bit off center.

That was her personal observation, however. She knew that philosophies varied even among long established physicians practicing in the same counties.

Ruefully, she admitted that her own ideas about dress, alcohol and tobacco abuse, along with her outspoken criticism of the mistreatment of women in the modern world were fodder for the fault finders. She and Albert were not in total agreement on any of these issues, either.

She led Tildie to her stall and portioned out some oats in the feed trough, all the while concentrating on the upside of a union with Dr. Miller.

Albert did have a thriving practice. He did seem to understand her career ambitions, and had not spoken out against them.

As she hurried in to help Mama with supper, she decided she really knew very little about Albert's background. Who was he? Where did he come from?

She resolved to have a frank talk with him before making her final decision.

⋘◉⋙

Since Alvah still refused Albert houseroom, he was booked into a local inn in the center of the town, a thriving country hostel that boasted the finest wine cellar in the state of New York. To save face, Vesta offered an explanation. "I'm sorry, sir. Please understand it would be unseemly for you to sleep under the same roof with our daughter when you are not betrothed."

Albert was no fool. He had felt Alvah's antipathy at the graduation ceremony, but he sensed that criticizing him to Mary would not be in his best interest. Her connection with her father appeared so close she could turn against him the moment he opened his mouth.

On the day of his arrival, the hopeful suitor made an appointment to see his future father-in-law. The following afternoon found them in the formal parlor, tea and biscuits set before them on a low table.

Alvah's windblown salt and pepper mop refused to stay combed, but his weathered cheeks were cleanshaven, his best Sunday suit brushed and pressed.

On the other hand, the suave young doctor's blond hair and mustache were slicked down with Makassar oil, and he smelled of bay rum. His new fawn trousers were cuffed and pressed; his paisley waistcoat showed vibrant shades of rust, wine and gold, beneath a beautifully cut knee length frock coat of finest English tweed.

Albert clearly felt this high fashion wardrobe showed him off at his handsome best. Surely the girl's father couldn't fail to see what a good catch he was.

Papa, of course, believed that handsome is as handsome does.

After placing one of Mama's best embroidered napkins across his lap to protect his trousers, Albert helped himself to a fragile cup of steaming black tea.

He chose a small, flaky biscuit, bit into it and sipped the tea to wash it down. He replaced the cup and saucer, finished the last tidbit, and patted his lips dry.

Then he made his first faux pas. His nerve was faltering. Needing something to do with his hands, he removed a long thin cheroot from his breast pocket. "Do you mind if I smoke?" he asked.

"We've never allowed tobacco in our home, Dr. Miller. If you must smoke, we can walk outside."

Damn, he thought, that's where Mary gets her wild ideas about tobacco.

Chastened, Albert stowed the offending cheroot in his pocket and crossed one knee over the other, displaying a boot that had been polished to a brilliant shine.

To cover his embarrassment, he picked up his cup, sipped, and put it down again perilously close to the edge of the table. He cleared his throat and recrossed his legs, then committed his second blunder.

"Ah . . . er . . . sir, I've come to ask for your daughter's hand in marriage," he stuttered, as he fussed with his carefully knotted gold cravat.

Papa was well prepared for the question. He had faced it when his older daughters became betrothed. It was time to tell this ignorant puppy, in no uncertain terms, that his child could think for herself, and he'd better realize that before this thing went any further.

"I do not own my daughter's hand, Dr. Miller," he advised, his features arranged in righteous indignation. "Mary, like all of my children, is free to make her own choices. If you wish to marry her, you must put the question to her."

Then came Albert's worst miscalculation. Thinking to save face by buttering up the old man, he foolishly asked, "But do I have your blessing, sir?"

Alvah's forthright reply did nothing for the young doctor's comfort level.

"No, sir, you do not. But if Mary chooses to accept you as her husband, you may count on the courtesies of my household. Mrs. Walker and I will not interfere, either before or after such a union."

Albert reached over and carefully moved the china cup to a safer position. Hiding his displeasure, he folded his linen napkin and rose to his feet. After all, what did an uneducated country bumpkin know of courtly manners, anyway?

"With your permission, I shall take my leave, sir. I am sorry that you cannot think more kindly of me. However, perhaps when you get to know me, your attitude will soften."

Papa remembered Mary's plea to be his own decent self. He bit back the words that could have caused open enmity between his family and the man that his daughter might wed. Under no circumstances could he be responsible for alienating his dearest child, even though his every instinct told him that Miller was an opportunist more in love with himself than he was with Mary.

Only time would prove him right or wrong, but Alvah prayed that his daughter could cope with the heartache that was bound to come when Albert Miller was no longer on his best behavior.

CHAPTER TEN

OSWEGO, NEW YORK

CLAD IN HER heather wool tunic and grey trousers, Mary patted her raven curls. Her cheeks glowed with good health, and her blue eyes danced with mischief. "Tell me about yourself, Albert," she suggested as the late afternoon sun sank low over the barn. "I really know very little about you."

His brow wrinkled, and the shadow of a frown passed. Her request rankled. What did she need to know?

The air was still, fall's scent pleasantly invigorating as they lingered near the back stoop. The impatient nicker of a mare mingled with the buzzing of a few bees prospecting Vesta's kitchen garden were the only sounds to disturb the quiet.

"Walk with me," he said, offering his arm. "I promise you there are no skeletons in my closet, if that's your concern."

"Don't be silly, Albert, I have no such thoughts. I just want to get to know you better."

He tucked her slim fingers over his arm as they ambled toward the meadow. She glanced up at the attractive man who asked to become her life partner. His profile was patrician, his manner, elegant. He seems to care for me, she thought. So why am I still hesitant about our future together?

Albert strolled on, enjoying the Indian summer weather. Mary removed her hand and scooted ahead. He appraised her figure.

Shoulders thrown back, head high, Mary's restless energy intrigued him. She forged ahead like a gladiator on her way to the arena.

Our wedding night should be very interesting, he thought.

As they progressed, she asked a few questions but kept her reservations to herself.

"My past is really quite ordinary," he began. "I was born in Covert, New York, on July 7, 1831. We moved to Virgil, New York when I was very young, and I have a sister who lives in Cortland." Nothing of his parents. He also declined to mention the disenchanted ladies he'd left behind in the wake of his broken promises.

"I wanted to become a physician for as long as I can recall," he said. "I've worked very hard to get this far."

"I can understand that. I've wanted a medical career ever since I was a child, accompanying my father on his rounds."

Albert talked about his thriving practice in Rome, New York, and his successful lectures to the general public about physiology, the science of bodily functions.

"I get on well with mixed audiences," he bragged. "I can discuss intimate details that might seem odious from a speaker with inferior skills, but I have the gift of persuasion that most people do not enjoy."

Their walk took them by the Coolidge farm where Mary had been pelted with rotten eggs, years before. She stopped at the spot, but said nothing to Albert.

He grasped her shoulders and turned her toward him. The soft evening light brushed her cheeks and forehead with a rosy tinge. She favored him with a beguiling smile that displayed small even teeth behind full red lips.

She is a pretty piece of baggage, he thought. I could do much worse for myself.

He looked steadily into her eyes. "The question is, my dear, have you decided to marry me? You've never answered any of my written proposals."

She started to speak, but he placed his finger against her lips.

"Please don't let that mean that you are not interested in becoming my wife and my partner in practice."

She turned away from him, took a few steps forward and waited for him to catch up. It was the moment she needed to collect her thoughts. "Of course I've been flattered by your letters, Albert. I admire you as a physician and as a friend."

"Do I sense a 'but' there, Mary?"

"Surely you understand such an important subject should be discussed in person?"

He nodded, waiting for her to continue.

It's time to set the rules, she thought. "There are a few things we need to clear up before I agree to marriage."

"For instance?" he asked, unsure where her eccentric ideas might lead.

"Dear Albert," she smiled, touching his face to soften her words. "I hesitate to set unworkable limits on this new partnership, as you put it, but I have strong feelings about certain things."

His impatience began to show. "Such as?"

"I shall keep my own name when I establish my practice. I presume that will be in Rome, where you've already acquired a list of patients."

Albert was flabbergasted. He had expected that Mary would work beside him and attend to his patients while he traveled on his lecture circuits. Never did he envision that she'd want an office of her own.

Well, he could take care of that, after the wedding. Once married, he would become the head of the Miller household, and his wife would obey his wishes.

As if reading his mind, Mary continued, "And there is the matter of the ceremony, Albert. I cannot become a chattel. I refuse to say the word 'obey' when we are joined. That word is simply not in my vocabulary, unless we are discussing the laws of the land."

Albert retrieved a silk handkerchief from his breast pocket. The shiny fabric did nothing to absorb the beads of perspiration at his temples.

Mary concealed a smile behind her hand. That should give him something to think about, she thought. Albert needed to be reminded that she was her own person, not some servant put here to soothe and satisfy a demanding husband. "Papa never treated Mama with anything but respect and deference," she said. "I will not accept anything less from the man I marry. I care for you, Albert, and I'd enjoy being your wife, but not at the cost of my own independence."

He tucked the useless bit of silk back in his pocket. "I'm not sure I understand your aversion to the language of the wedding ceremony," he declared. "Surely you cannot think I would impose my will upon you."

"I'm merely saying that I do not wish to announce to the world that I have put myself in such a position with you or anyone else. And I'm not alone in this matter. I've read the same views from Elizabeth Cady Stanton and Amelia Bloomer," she added, referring to the outspoken proponents of women's rights.

He understood where she was coming from, but he didn't like it. "Very well," he agreed. "I'll try to understand. However, I do wish you would reconsider the use of your maiden name after the ceremony. I want the whole world to know that you are mine."

A small frown creased the space between her eyebrows.

Oh, no, he thought. Wrong choice of words.

Her voice was tight. "Yours, in what way, Albert? If you mean you own me in a literal sense, that can never be."

Her expression softened, as she imagined his quandary. "If you are worried about my being approached as a single person after we are married, you needn't fret about that matter. I believe in conjugal fidelity with all my heart.

"From the moment we speak our vows, I pledge to you that I shall conduct myself with the decorum of a married woman. As such, I will not sanction unwanted attentions from any other man, gentleman or otherwise."

"Still, I ask you to reconsider your decision," he pleaded.

"I shall give it some thought, Albert. That I can promise you."

Just one week shy of Mary's twenty-third birthday on November 19, 1855, the wedding day dawned sunny and clear. Vesta and her older girls had prettied up the family home on Bunker Hill with fall bouquets and satin bows. A wedding supper for the guests was waiting on the sideboard in the kitchen. Neither liquor nor coffee was to be served at the reception, and the fare was strictly vegetarian, as befitted the Walkers' beliefs.

Albert stood before relatives and friends nervously awaiting his bride.

The minister, Thomas May of Syracuse, a stranger to everyone, had been imported at the last minute because he agreed to marry the couple without the use of the word 'obey' in the ceremony. "The noble Reverend would not stoop to such despicable meanness as to ask a woman to 'serve' or 'obey' a man," Mary wrote later. "How barbarous the very idea of one equal promising to be the slave of another, instead of both entering life's greatest drama as intelligent, equal parties. Our promises denoted two intelligent beings instead of one owner and one chattel."

Despite her parents' wishes, Mary angrily refused to have her local pastor in attendance after his scathing rebuke at her 'outrageous' request.

Her pastor had punctuated his objections with admonitions about the obligation of a wife to obey her husband. In a booming voice, he quoted chapter and verse from The Book of Proverbs. "An excellent wife is the crown of her husband," he roared, "But she who causes shame is like rottenness in his bones."

What that had to do with obedience was beyond Mary's imagination, but she had been careful not to insult the old man to his face. He was, after all, their pastor.

The bride was exquisite. Her older sisters had carefully arranged her hair in ringlets to frame her sweet, round face. Her porcelain skin was complemented by a band of seed pearls and lavender lace that graced her forehead.

Albert's heartfelt pleadings (and those of her sisters, as well) that she wear a traditional gown for the ceremony, had gone unheeded. She refused to kowtow to the fashions of the day. Her tunic of white silk was lavishly trimmed with the same imported lace that made up her headband, while her trousers matched the white silk of her calf-length overskirt.

Albert did a double take as Mary approached on her father's arm. Though he was incensed that she had not acceded to his wishes, he felt a grudging admiration that she had stuck to her guns. No silly will-o-the-wisp this strong-minded slip of a girl. Her revolutionary ideas were written in stone.

Oh, yes, his headstrong bride would take some careful handling in the future, but he had no doubt he could bring her to heel.

The wedding was allotted considerable space in local papers, as well as in The Lily, a small journal published by Amelia Bloomer. Its format was devoted to the premise that women held the same rights as men. An admiring female journalist proudly reported, "Dr. Mary Walker, a staunch advocate for women's rights and Reform Dress, had declined to sacrifice her clothing policy, even on her wedding day."

Truly, Mary believed that statement with all her heart. Dr. Albert Miller's private ideas on the subject were quite different.

Once married, Mary never used the Miller surname, though there were a few instances when she signed herself, Dr. Mary E. M. Walker, or Dr. Mary Miller-Walker. Faced with her unbending will, Albert tolerated the situation, but her stubborn rejection of his name irked him their whole married life.

Whenever he threw it up to her during an argument, she quietly replied, "But, Albert, you agreed before we were wed."

CHAPTER ELEVEN

ROME, NEW YORK

BECAUSE ALBERT SAID his patients needed his attention, and Mary was in a hurry to start practicing medicine again, the newlyweds decided to go straight to Albert's bachelor apartment.

Their wedding night was spent in a small inn halfway between Oswego and Rome, New York. Albert, rough and impatient with his virgin bride, doused Mary's expectation of a tender, romantic experience. She was left with the feeling that she'd missed something precious that would never come her way again.

Albert's place in Rome was much too small, so the busy physicians leased larger quarters. The new location provided ample living space and room enough for both medical offices.

Their apartment was sparsely but tastefully furnished with comfortable chairs in the parlor. A four-poster bed covered with a beautiful patchwork quilt–Vesta, Jr.'s handmade wedding gift–graced the bedroom.

Mary prepared nutritious vegetarian meals, occasionally supplementing Albert's fare with beef or lamb.

Mary, determined to make a success of the marriage, hired a housekeeper and took charge of their private lives while maintaining her own practice. Anxious to please, she treated Albert with deference and affection, and their relationship appeared ideal to outsiders.

Because of her sympathetic manner and willingness to sacrifice her time, her practice grew. Still, she found time to lecture on temperance, dress reform, and equal rights for women.

Since it was unusual for a woman to take the podium, especially one in trousers, she created quite a stir.

Comfortable with her pants—Mary's favorite word—she already had developed a thick skin. "I design my clothes for comfort, and I don't care what others think," was her answer to critics.

A column in the *Black River, New York Herald*, reported that "The lecturer acquitted herself in a graceful easy manner, and exhibited familiarity with the science connected to her profession." It quoted the mantra she preached over the years: "Woman should make herself better acquainted with her physical organization so she might preserve her own health."

The article also mentioned Mary's aversion to the "tight and cumbrous" clothing that dominated the fashion world. To his credit, the author recognized Mary's noble motives and abilities when he wrote, "She manifests a great desire to be useful to her sex and undoubtedly has it in her power to do much good."

However, equal space negated all his previous remarks with a derisive description of Mary's "bloomers."

Mary thought the man an idiot. "What responsible journalist could possibly think a speaker's wardrobe more important than her message?"

When Dr. Lydia Hasbrouck, another outspoken proponent of dress reform, read the disparaging remarks, she attacked the editor of *The Herald* for publishing the insensitive paragraphs and wrote a heartfelt article begging publicly that "Dr. Walker not become discouraged and give up the good work she's doing."

Such public discussion aggravated Albert because Mary was getting more attention than he was. His lectures were well attended, but Mary's audiences filled the halls to standing room. True, some came to see the 'funny outfits' she wore, but they left with a greater understanding for her causes.

Albert stayed away from home, neglecting marriage and patients alike. He accepted speaking engagements in small towns on Cape Cod, Nantucket, and Martha's Vineyard, in addition to his usual tours around the counties of New York State. Most were far enough away to warrant overnight stays.

Mary took up the slack in his office whenever she could, making house calls till late into the night. Meals were missed, and she ignored her constant fatigue. She lost weight and dark circles bruised the areas beneath her eyes.

With her parents a hundred miles away and no one she could confide to in Rome, she faced her heartache feeling lonely and discouraged. Her dreams of a satisfying marriage merged with a successful dual practice were fading with each passing day.

A deadly pall washed over her when reports from well meaning friends disclosed Albert's peccadilloes—an intimate supper here, a tête-à-tête there, all with much younger, and, Mary agonized, much prettier girls.

One blustery evening in early March of 1858, she swallowed her tears and confronted her husband. As he removed his greatcoat from its peg in the hall, she begged for his attention. "Will you please talk to me, Albert? You're hardly here, anymore."

"I'm late for an appointment," he said shrugging his arms into the heavy sleeves.

Determined not to sound like a whining female, she kept her tone neutral and her words reasonable. "You're always rushing off to an appointment. You're out every night, and you've been skipping your office hours. We need to at least discuss your patients."

"What do you expect, woman?" he demanded viciously poking buttons through buttonholes. "You are always away somewhere, yourself, trotting off to see patients or talk to some group of babbling females who haven't the good sense to stay home and take care of their husbands."

"That's not fair, Albert," she cried. "Many of the patients I see at night are people you began to treat and then abandoned. By that I mean you haven't followed up on them—your own patients, I mean . . ." Her voice trailed off at his livid glare.

"You and your outrageous ideas about freedom and equality are driving me away, Mrs. Miller. When we married, I thought you'd be my helpmate, complement my career. If you'd stay home and see to my needs, we wouldn't be having this discussion."

"Albert Miller, you knew full well what my intentions were long before we married. We talked about my career and you were perfectly agreeable then."

"That was before I knew that you would put everyone else ahead of me. And you never said a word about any lectures you planned to give. I'm getting short shrift here, Mary, and I don't like it. I don't like it one bit."

Mary was stunned. She took hold of the lapels on his coat.

"How can I minister to your 'needs' when you're never here?"

He pushed her hands away in disgust. "There's no reasoning with a woman whose head is made of stone."

With that he clapped his derby on his head and flounced toward the stairs.

She called after him, "Please don't go, Albert. Surely, we can work out our differences."

He stopped, turning slowly to face her. "Why would I want to stay?" he asked, a malevolent scowl altering his attractive face.

His eyes swept over her dark serge tunic and trousers. "It would be nice to come home to a wife who looked like a woman instead of some circus freak wearing that ridiculous getup."

Stubborn pride refused to allow tears as she blinked against their sting.

"Wait," she said, extending a trembling hand toward him.

He bolted for the stairs.

"Where are you going?" she shot after him, her voice tightly controlled.

He was nearly at the bottom when he growled, "I told you I have an appointment."

The door slammed behind him. Mary sank to the floor. With her face against her knees, she cried till her head pounded and her eyes stung like fire. Then she crept off to their bed, dropping fully clothed on the coverlet to weep some more.

When he hadn't returned several days later, Mary consulted a lawyer and explored the possibilities of a separation. The case was brought before a magistrate, but Miller thwarted it by whining over his lot. His handsome, broadcloth suit, spotless linen, and polished leather impressed the judge who was aware of the noted physician's reputation.

"I am a man of forgiving nature, Sir," Albert pandered. "I am perfectly willing to live with my wife as a good and dutiful husband even though she left me without just cause."

Mary was too astounded to speak. The man was actually lying in court without a modicum of shame. She stood before the bench waiting for the judge's decision. Her hair was neatly curled, and a pretty lace jabot rested against her dark tunic. Her whole demeanor and delicate appearance left no doubt of her femininity.

The magistrate, a corpulent, red-faced fellow with flyaway locks and bushy sideburns, peered through his pince-nez. He snorted with distaste at Mary's trousers and tapped his gavel once. "Go home to your husband, madam," he ordered. "I see no cause for divorce at this time." As an afterthought, he pointed to her pants and said, "Perhaps, you would have an easier time keeping your husband at home, if you put on a gown and acted like a lady."

He couldn't resist meddling further. "For heaven sake, woman, develop a hobby. Take up Faro or needlework like other respectable ladies of the community."

Albert gave a triumphant snort. "Thank you, sir. My sentiments exactly."

Furious, Mary shot back. "Sir, as my husband well knows, I'm a practicing medical doctor, and I assure you both that it never has been, and is not now, a hobby!"

"Hmm . . . yes . . . well," the judge replied, flicking his wrist to shoo her from his courtroom like a nuisance insect unworthy of his attention.

She was utterly disgusted but knew she was faced with two choices. Either submit to Albert and obey the order or face charges of contempt of court.

"The court is wrong," she hissed, shaking her fist as she vowed, "I will fight till my death for a woman's right to be fairly treated in court. We are not chattels."

The couple returned to 60 Dominick Street, where an uneasy truce developed between them, made somewhat more palatable by the fact that Albert was away a good deal. His needy patients along with her own kept Mary too busy to think.

಄ೄ⊛ೄ಄

September, 1859. One of Albert's patients came to Mary with startling information. He wept as he told her, "Your husband is carrying on an affair with my wife during the week while I'm travelling my sales route."

Once again, her ideals concerning duty and fidelity to the marriage contract were put to the test. Outraged that his promises to the court had been broken, she confronted him.

"You're sleeping with a patient's wife."

He made no apology, smirking as he admitted, "Just a small dalliance, my dear."

"I can't countenance such behavior, Albert," she choked, "I refuse to live with you one minute longer, no matter what the court has decreed. I'll find another lawyer and sue for divorce, immediately."

"You can't do that," he roared, fearing for his reputation if a scandal erupted. He proposed another solution. "If you stay with me you can have the same privileges, yourself. As long as you are discreet, you'll be free to see whomever you choose, whenever and wherever you like, without recourse from me."

Mary was livid. "That's disgusting," she screamed. "Get out. Get away from me before I . . . before I . . ."

Words failed her. She grabbed his medicine case and flung it at him. Pills, bandages, instruments, clattered across the floor.

Albert retreated hastily, nearly knocking a patient off the doorstep. Without apology he exclaimed angrily, "I'm going away, Pettigrave, and I won't be back for a long time."

Shocked, Pettigrave called after him, "Albert, what on earth? . . ." But Albert had disappeared around the corner.

Close to hysteria, Mary fled when Pettigrave entered. He waited in the parlor unable to understand such irrational behavior from two people he considered pillars of the community. The myth of the happily married couple disintegrated, leaving him disenchanted and perplexed.

❧❀❧

Later that month, Mary made a painful visit to Oswego.

Without revealing gory details she found too distressing to discuss, she informed her family of her decision to divorce.

Both parents hugged her tightly, asked no questions and expressed immediate support.

Alvie felt sad for Mary, but declared it was her own business. He brought a little smile to his sister's lips when he adopted the squeaky voice of one of his puppets and vowed to love her, short or tall, fat or skinny, married or single.

In the privacy of their bedchamber that first night, Alvah comforted his wife. "I hate to say it, Vesta, but their union was bound to fail. It should never have happened in the first place."

Underneath his calm demeanor, Vesta sensed a boiling rage that frightened her. His controlled whispers made his statements all the more menacing.

"I know she has good reason, Vesta. Our Mary would not take such a destructive path on a girlish whim. Her ideals are much too noble for that. Something terrible must have happened between them."

Fearful for his health, Vesta nestled against him, hoping her warmth would calm him.

"I know that, darling," she whispered close to his ear, "but if she chooses not to tell us about it, we haven't the right to pry."

"I have never seen our Mary look so defeated."

"Nor I, Alvah. Nor I."

"I should take the buggy whip to him," he hissed. "If he were here, that's exactly what I would do."

"Be calm, dear. It's strength she needs right now. Try to get some sleep. Maybe we'll hear more when the girls arrive tomorrow morning."

"They won't give her much sympathy, Vesta. You can count on that. They were never in favor of her going away to medical school, and they have never been comfortable with her free thinking either."

His words were prophetic.

Mary's sisters constantly criticized her outspoken views and unconventional ideas about clothing, suffrage, and health issues. They destroyed literature Mary sent them and went about their gardening and quilting. Because of their upbringing, they eschewed tightly corseted bodices in favor of looser, more comfortable gowns, but they never approved of trousers for women.

"It's not for them to decide about Mary's life," Vesta murmured. "I'll make that clear to them if they try to interfere."

The 'girls,' Vesta and Aurora Borealis, came for breakfast, and the advice began the moment they hit the dooryard. Fortunately for Mary, Luna was still in Scriba with her husband, or she probably would have had to contend with three naysayers.

While forking mouthfuls of scrambled eggs and crispy potatoes, both sisters advised her. "Go back to Rome and work things out with your husband."

A vision of the arrogant court magistrate flashed before Mary's eyes, but she sat with her hands clasped tightly in her lap and said nothing.

Between bites the sisters dabbed their lips with linen napkins while continuing to pick away at her—two well-meaning busybodies dispensing unwanted advice.

Aurora condescended. "My own marriage is successful, Mary, because I know how to compromise. That's the secret, you see."

Vesta, Jr. spoke with disdain. "Career and lectures, that's all we hear from you, Mary. When will you take the time to behave like a married woman? Be patient in your home and cater to your husband's comforts. Raise a family." Look at me, she seemed to say, my husband gets his meals on time, his comforts are accommodated, and I don't pry into his private affairs.

Too sick at heart to eat, too weary to argue, Mary let them think what they chose. She would not humiliate herself by exposing Albert's true colors.

Mama had had enough. "Leave her alone. Your lives are not hers. Your husbands are your own responsibility. If you cannot support your sister, then kindly keep your criticisms to yourselves."

Papa laid his fork beside his plate and gave his mouth a vicious swipe with his napkin.

"I'll say this only once, and then I shall listen to no more about it. Mary is a grown woman. Her decisions are her own, and I feel sure she has made them for good reasons. Those reasons are not our affair, and we have no right to advise or criticize when we have no information about the subject. That's my final word at this table."

He picked up his fork and helped himself to more potatoes from the serving plate.

Vesta, Jr. went red in the face, but held her peace. Aurora Borealis bent her head close to her food and said nothing. Neither sister apologized, but the point was made.

Mary sipped at the glass of milk she had hardly touched. Thank you, Papa, she thought, as she tried to eat a bit of egg to keep Mama from worrying any more than necessary.

❧❀❧

Mary returned To Rome, exhausted and dispirited. When she unlocked the door she found a note from the housekeeper on the refectory table. Succinct and to the point it read:

"Dr. Miller has relieved me of my duties. I can be reached at my home, if you need me.

Yours faithfully,
Margaret Doherty"

She hurried to the parlor. Most of the furniture was missing. The other rooms had been similarly stripped. A few scraps of paper littered the floor in Albert's office along with gray dust curls scattered in the corners. He had taken his medical equipment, lecturing apparatus and library. Everything was gone. Bewildered, she sank to the floor and wept.

Later, she discovered he sold their furniture at ridiculously low prices to keep her from having it and then rushed out of town.

He settled in Cortland, using his sister's home as a base of operations. Most of his time was spent on tour, and he never practiced medicine there.

He presented a riveting seminar whenever he spoke. One report states, "He had honed his skills till he could fill an auditorium for nights in succession and could discuss intimate matters unmentioned by respectable people."

The Millers had gone their separate ways, but their battles were far from over.

CHAPTER TWELVE

ROME, NEW YORK

WITH ALBERT no longer contributing financially, expenses for the chambers at 60 Dominick Street became unmanageable.

Unwilling to settle too far from her patient base, Dr. Mary secured smaller quarters just down the street. The following advertisement appeared in the *Rome Sentinel*:

FEMALE PHYSICIAN

Dr. Mary Walker has removed to
No. 48 Dominick Street
opposite the arcade over

Messrs. H.S. & W.O. Shelley's Clothing Store

Between March and August of 1860 her bookkeeping showed office expenses of $35.00, plus $7.69 for medicines, while her board and rent were listed at $63.00, far lower than her former quarters would have set her back.

She continued to see a few of her husband's patients, but her own practice had already grown. Generally, she confined her ministrations to women and children, but occasionally she treated a grown male at the behest of a worried wife or mother.

Early on, Albert ordered her to stop treating men. "Well, Albert," she said, "I'll stop seeing male patients the very moment you cease to treat women." They'd argued about it constantly. He'd thrown that up to her along with his disapproval of her dress code every time she brought up his unexplained absences.

Albert was a competent doctor, but he lacked the commitment to his patients that a dedicated practitioner needed to be truly involved. He enjoyed the freedom of the lecture circuit rather than the confinement of regular office hours and home visits.

⨳

The doctor refused to negotiate when charges for her services became an issue. If patients demanded lower fees for treatment, she quickly put them in their places.

"Why would you think I should be paid less?" she asked one churlish husband who protested the amount of his wife's bill.

"You are a woman," he answered, "and the work of a woman is always cheaper."

She could barely refrain from showing him the toe of her boot, but violence was not her game. Besides, he was well connected in town, and consequences could have been severe.

"My education has been quite elaborate and occupied the same time and cost as a man's, sir," she told him. "I can treat a patient as well as any man. The obstacles I face are far greater. Therefore, I am justified in charging not only as much, but more."

The man gasped at the thought.

Then with her most engaging smile she let him off the hook. "But you are fortunate that I shall be happy with perfect equality only and will not exceed the going rates."

Scarlet with anger, he slapped the money down and departed, grumbling about upstart females wearing britches, no less.

Dr. Mary treated everyone who came to her. Their illnesses included the usual female complaints, stomach ailments, childhood diseases, skin eruptions, and dental problems.

An entry in her ledger indicates that she extracted a patient's tooth for the grand sum of twenty-five cents. She stepped in to help when midwives encountered difficult births, and treated premature babies by placing them in warming beds made from padded metal washtubs placed close to wood burning stoves. She saved underweight infants, too weak to suckle, by having them fed warm breast milk patiently infused into their tiny, bird-like mouths with medicine droppers until they grew strong enough to nurse properly.

Once ether came into general use, she used it to surgically remove appendices, gall bladders, and tonsils.

Because of ill-fitting shoes, the removal of calluses and bunions was common while the lancing of boils and carbuncles elicited more than a few screams of pain when Dr. Mary applied her sharp instruments to hot red pustules on offended bottoms.

In some cases payment was made by barter. Her ledger states that she treated the local hostler for an ongoing case of painful gout in exchange for the use of a horse and buggy that she used to make her rounds.

Distressed women were more than willing to consult her about marital problems, painful coitus, and sexual abuse, complaints they would never dream of discussing with a male physician.

About this time, Dr. Mary declared war against high fashion for another more dangerous phenomenon. Two of her patients were severely burned about the legs and buttocks when their voluminous hoop skirts caught fire as their owners swished against small tables, dousing their clothing with oil from the lighted lamps seated precariously atop them.

Scalp problems developed from the "waterfall" coiffure, an intricate arrangement of hair drawn over a horsehair frame. The hairdo was so elaborate and time consuming that women declined to redress the style for weeks. Discomforting itches and sores appeared, but when Dr. Mary ordered the patients to scrub their heads and redo their coifs at shorter intervals, many suffered the consequences in favor of fashion.

Busy as she was, Dr. Mary found time to write for Lydia Hasbrouck's *The Sybil*. In the May 15th, 1859, issue she contributed an article referring to the Sickles/Key case, a current Washington scandal involving a wife's adulterous relationship. Her argument: "The wife is no more blameworthy than the lover who seduced her. . . .The cuckolded husband's well-known peccadilloes made him as guilty as his wife."

The article continued, "Never, until women as a mass are better educated physiologically; until they are considered something besides a drudge or a doll; until they have all the social education and political advantages that men enjoy; in a word, EQUALITY with them, shall we consider vice in our own sex any more culpable than in men!"

She continued, "I wish that ladies who have no time to read had sense enough to throw aside their embroidery and read Mental Philosophy, Moral Science and Physiology, and then go forth as free, sensible women."

Because of her own experience, she wrote, "Why is there no law to imprison adulterers? Are all our legislators too pious and too devoted followers of the Bible to condemn in others what they allow in themselves?"

To the consternation of her guilty male readers, she exposed venereal diseases transmitted from fornicating husband, to unsuspecting wife, to innocent child.

Lydia Hasbrouck willingly published her remarks: "Women must have the right to vote, to be paid equally for similar jobs; and, most especially, to enjoy the same prospects for higher education as their husbands and brothers."

As a champion of the underdog, the plight of "fallen women" became one of her crusades. In that same year, Dr. Mary issued an appeal through the little paper to establish a New York State Foundling Hospital. "Such a refuge was needed as sorely as institutions for other grossly handicapped members of society." (Years later, similar institutions were created in several large cities.) "Anti-abortion laws should be abolished, and the men who contribute to the fallen morals of unfortunate females are equally as guilty as the women charged with the crimes. We must have compassion for prostitutes, and shun the men who solicit them."

Dr. Mary watched the escalating abolitionist movement. In Oswego she helped a runaway slave from the Underground Railroad to escape to Canada. "Enslaving Negro families is an evil sin against human rights on par with the enslavement of women in a male driven society," she preached.

At the Dress Reform Convention in May 1860, in Waterloo, she was elected third vice president of the National Dress Reform Association. By the time she returned to Rome, she'd made the decision to divorce Albert. The state of New York recognized one reason for divorce, but Mary refused to trot out her dirty linen in front of a second judge who'd probably treat her as shoddily as the first.

In June, she referred her patients to a colleague and left for Delhi, a bustling Iowa town where divorce laws were more lenient, but she had to establish a year's residence. A long time friend, Judge House, invited, "Come to stay with us for as long as necessary."

Once settled, the good doctor needed to find something to occupy her time.

CHAPTER THIRTEEN

DELHI, IOWA

THE BOWEN COLLEGIATE INSTITUTE (later, Lennox Junior College) in Hopkinton, Iowa, accepted Dr. Mary's application for entrance into its third-year curriculum. Her aim was to learn the German language and also participate in their debating society to polish her public speaking skills.

Petite and slender with a tangle of waist length curls she appeared dressed in trousers under an over dress that reached to her knees. Dainty in manner, she was lovely to behold despite her unusual costume.

Her tunic and pants caused the ninety undergrads as well as the faculty members to consider her a mite peculiar. Mary took small notice of their rude stares and whispers. Others' opinions never troubled her.

Miss Isobel Cooley, Bowen's counselor to female students, was in charge of all classes. Mary sought her out and asked, "Could you please give me information on German classes and Public Speaking Courses?"

Cooley, a middle-aged spinster, tall and stout, with a prickly expression that could curdle cream gazed down her nose at the new student.

Her mousy brown hair was parted in the middle, drawn straight back to end in a tightly twisted knob that sat on her collar daring one stray hair to rebel. A cumbersome ugly, brown gown corseted her plump figure so closely her breathing was shallow and labored. Her numerous petticoats under the heavy material, coupled with the warm afternoon sunshine, caused a line of shiny perspiration along the bristles that shadowed her upper lip.

This woman is about to burst, Mary thought, and I hope I'm not in the vicinity when the blast occurs.

"Can you help me with the locations of these classes?" Mary asked again, handing over the receipt the bursar had given her.

Cooley stared an extra long moment at Mary's sea foam green tunic and lace collar. When her eyes reached the trousers her nose wrinkled as if she smelled dead fish too long in the sun. "We regret to inform you," said the officious woman, dragging her eyes back to the sheet in her hand, "we have no facilities here for the instruction of the German language."

Mary frowned. "But your curriculum notices advertise such."

"We are sorry," Cooley offered, lowering her voice as if it were privileged information. "It's the war, you know."

Mary gritted her teeth. Give me patience, she thought.

"That is most disappointing, Miss Cooley. Then I shall content myself with the rhetoric classes."

The counselor, who believed proper young ladies should be seen and not heard, puffed up, worrying Mary further of a precipitous explosion.

"That will not be possible," Cooley announced as her steely eyes raked Mary over, resting on her pants. "Those classes are limited to gentlemen, of which you are not one despite your costume."

All right, Miss Cooley, war it is, Mary thought. We shall see what I can and cannot do.

She dashed off a letter to the faculty, "Sirs: If you do not find a German teacher, I shall publish far and wide that the university advertises what they did not, and could not, perform."

The school never was able to produce a German teacher . . . the war, you know!

Mary was not unreasonable. She accepted that, but the debating society was another matter. The members met regularly in one of the auditoriums, and she saw no reason why she should not join them.

She appeared at an evening session where students, along with youths from Hopkinton, were debating current issues. Mary bided her time, and during the break, she turned on the charm and petitioned the attendees to give her a turn on the rostrum.

"I have alternative views that are guaranteed to rebut your arguments about the Constitution. That is, if you dare," she challenged, softening her words with a merry wink.

Either the novelty of her costume, her impish smile or the twinkle in her eyes won them over. They elected her a member and promised her time at the next meeting.

When Miss Cooley received the news, she was livid. A student had defied her!

She summoned Mary to her inner sanctum, a sparsely furnished, unwelcoming room, innocent of drapery and stuffy with the odors of floor oil and book dust.

Standing behind her uncluttered desk, fingers entwined so tightly her knuckles were white, Miss Cooley issued her order. "You will cease your foolishness, at once," she hissed. "You have already been warned away from the debating classes which are strictly for males."

"I am sorry, madam," Mary replied, "I have already been elected to the body, and I intend to exercise my membership privileges."

The counselor seethed with rage, but she stuffed her feelings down enough to whisper between clenched teeth. "We shall see about this." She pointed dramatically at the door. "Leave this room at once."

Mary sauntered out of the office, trying her utmost not to laugh at the sight of the woman's heaving bosom straining against the bodice of her snug frock.

The school administration was put on notice that a rebel was in their midst.

The following week found a delighted Mary up on the podium against several male debaters. She exchanged argument for argument, reason for reason, enjoying herself immensely. The audience was having almost as good a time as the group on the stage.

Miss Cooley—furious because a snip of a girl wearing trousers had thwarted her—rushed to the faculty and spat, "Either this upstart goes, or I go." Since Cooley's father was a generous Bowen contributor, there was no doubt which way the wind blew.

But Mary had worked her powers of persuasion on the debaters. When she was expelled from the next meeting, all except two of the men walked out right along with her. They formed a picket line and marched through the town with Mary leading the parade. Laughing gentlemen carried signs reading: FREEDOM OF DEBATE FOR WOMEN. REINSTATE MARY. FREE SPEECH IS A RIGHT.

Local citizens, enjoying the controversy, argued the merits of the strike among themselves. Most agreed that one fine day that little fireball from New York would make her mark on the establishment.

Isobel Cooley would not be outdone. Her revenge was swift and devastating. Every one of the sign carriers was suspended, with prejudice. They immediately petitioned for reinstatement with the stipulation that Mary be included along with them.

The faculty refused to be swayed. Rules were rules. Otherwise anarchy prevailed. The men could return, but the female instigator was out.

One by one, the third year students drifted back to the fold. Some even apologized to Mary, declaring they had no choice but to comply since their careers were in jeopardy.

When Mary received the news that all her former supporters had given in and returned to classes, she closeted herself in her bedroom and pounded her pillow. Tears of futility soaked the bedclothes as she buried her face and wept. Despite her frustration, she couldn't expect her friends to lose their school status on her account. But the hurt cut deep.

"When will the world recognize that a woman is as smart as any man," she cried? "What will it take to wake stubborn men up to the fact that we have minds, and feelings, and hearts that bleed when we are demoted to second-class citizenship?"

To combat the dreadful emptiness that followed her banishment, she appealed to several local physicians, offering to fill in for them, or assist with extra cases. Several accepted on the spot.

Working at what she loved kept her from falling into depression, but the indignity of her treatment rankled. "I shall never give up the fight for freedom of education for women until ignorant people accept the fact that the United States Constitution guarantees equal rights to every citizen, male or female."

⌒◈◯⌒

Her mandatory year's residence in Iowa completed, Mary returned to Rome to collect her belongings and close her apartment permanently. She notified her colleagues and patients, "Please be advised that I will not be returning to my practice. I wish you well."

At the same time, she put aside her revulsion and applied to the Madison County branch of the Supreme Court of the State of New York, for a divorce.

Her decree, awarded September 16, 1861, charged that "all facts of her petition are true." Referee D. D. Walrath, Esq. found, "the defendant, Albert Miller, is guilty of several acts of adultery. The marriage between said plaintiff and said defendant is dissolved. It is further ordered that . . . the plaintiff may marry again . . . but it shall not be lawful for the defendant to wed until the plaintiff is actually dead. . . ..

"And it is further ordered and adjudged that the defendant pay the plaintiff the sum of $100 for her costs and disbursements in this action."

William W. Campbell, Justice of the Supreme Court, signed the decree and the official seal was duly affixed.

Albert was beyond livid. "She won't get away with this."

Mary had her divorce. She now felt she could put the past behind her and forget the disrespectful and despicable treatment suffered at the hands of Albert Miller.

She was wrong.

CHAPTER FOURTEEN

OSWEGO, NEW YORK

MARY DROOPED in her usual place at the Walker table, looking small and vulnerable, her cheeks bloodless above her white shirtwaist. Lusterless black curls tied back with a scarf contrasted with her alabaster complexion, making her appear more ghostly in the soft evening light. Underweight and depressed from the ordeal of the divorce proceedings and the close of her practice, she struggled to exhibit an optimistic front.

August, 1861, found the Walker kitchen the scene of the last critical family discussion ever held there. Parents and daughter had a good deal of catching up to do, and Mary was about to inform them of the most momentous decision of her life.

Their supper of roasted vegetables, baked beans with molasses and apple-pan-dowdy drenched in thick clotted cream was finished. Alvah poured himself a second glass of fresh milk from the pitcher on the table, and waited while dishes and pots were scrubbed, dried, and stored away.

Finally Mama's flowered apron was hung on its hook beside the stove. While he waited for the women to finish their chores, Alvah rolled the sleeves of his work shirt to his elbows and loosened the laces of his heavy leather boots to ease the arthritic aching in his ankles. Long, hard seasons in the fields were exacting their toll.

Idly, he ran his fingers through the moisture on the glass in front of him, watching his daughter with a physician's appraising eye.

The girl is too pale and undernourished, he thought. She doesn't look well.

His palms itched to administer a few lashes to Albert Miller's backside with his buggy whip.

Mary had likewise noted changes in her parents. The Walkers had aged since her last visit. Mama's middle had thickened, and Papa's step had slowed.

Vesta's dark tresses, though still abundant, were shot through with silver strands, while Alvah's hair, sparser now, had turned completely white. Fine lines creased their faces, and both seemed infinitely wearier than Mary had seen them since Cynthia's illness and death.

During supper, the family's conversation was dominated by news of war, a topic that filled Mary's mind from the moment the Iowa newspapers reported the April 12th shelling of Fort Sumter by Confederate patriots angry that Federal troops occupied "sovereign territory" in the seceded state of South Carolina.

She told her parents about the mood she'd found on the Bowen campus once the attack was announced. "The students were a mixed lot," she reported, "Some were southern, many more from the north. Arguments broke out. Unhealthy suspicion was rampant. Many of the South Carolina boys quit classes and hurried south to join their fathers and brothers in the Confederate ranks. I tell you, Papa, tempers ran high."

She didn't need to say that her own temper had been roused at the thought of war and what it meant in terms of casualties.

Though the only fatality at Fort Sumter had been a handsome Confederate stallion that took the brunt of a Federal shell, she was certain hostilities would escalate. "The next time around," she predicted, "there'll be mutilated human bodies on both sides."

That knowledge had made the last month of her stay in Delhi almost unbearable. She could hardly wait out the year before she collected her belongings, bade farewell to her hosts, and hastened back to Rome. A plan was hatching even then.

As she followed the reports of the North/South conflict, the idea of serving in the military took shape.

During May and June, Arkansas, Virginia, North Carolina and Tennessee seceded to join their sister states, South Carolina, Florida, Georgia, Alabama, Mississippi and Texas, in their rebellion against the Union. Ports were being blockaded, garrisons armed, and the ranks of both armies were swelling daily. It did not take a military genius to know that an all out war was inevitable.

Surely, capable surgeons would be needed to care for the wounded. But Dr. Mary's motives were not entirely noble. The experience gained on a battlefield would be invaluable, and an exemplary record in the service of her country was sure to advance her career.

She was determined to be ready to go, if and when she was needed.

Suffocating July weather coupled with the emotional memory of the divorce proceedings, further debilitated Mary, stealing her appetite, wearing her down. Worst of all, the specter of war kept eating at her soul. The Constitution she revered was being shoved aside, its essence lost in endless arguments about states rights, economy and slavery. The plantation system was in direct conflict with the free labor of the agricultural and industrial north. Greedy self-interests ignored the good of the country.

The *Rome Sentinel's* continuing accounts of the fighting at Bull Run in mid-July had sent the outraged doctor's heart into a tailspin as she pictured more than a thousand union soldiers lying on the Manassas hillsides, soaking the soil with their lifeblood. "Why am I not there helping to ease their agonies?" she wailed.

Her own troubles became less and less important, as she fretted about the escalation of the war. Men were dying, for God's sake.

Grieving for the sick and injured Union soldiers and the families left behind, Dr. Mary finally came to the vital decision that would have a profound effect on her life for years to come.

Meanwhile, the Yankees demanded revenge at Bull Run. Another vicious battle had raged for the same territory around Manassas, and the reports in the Oswego Weekly News that lay on the table before Alvah were devastating. Grisly descriptions of bodies maimed and butchered by Confederate shells horrified the Walkers.

It was obvious from the article that when the Confederates emerged victorious in the last days of Bull Run, the morale in the north hit rock bottom. Nevertheless, Abraham Lincoln refused to take the advice of Horace Greeley to "make peace with the rebels." Instead, he appointed new generals and issued orders for 100,000 conscriptions for a three-year tour of duty. The war would be fought. "The Union is everything," said the President. "The Union must prevail!"

Mary agreed.

She took her father's gnarled fingers in one hand and her mother's callused palm in the other. Sitting quietly for a moment, she thought of Florence Nightingale's selfless dedication to British fighters on the battlefields of the Crimean War. How to convince her parents that she could contribute as good or better treatment to American soldiers? She had the education and skills to save lives.

Mary took a deep breath and exploded her bombshell. "I'll be leaving for Washington to sign on as a surgeon in the Union Army as soon as my health permits," she stated in a manner that made her decision irrevocable.

The senior Walkers were thunderstruck. Hot protests spilled out like flames spewing from an over-stoked stove.

"Please understand," she begged. "I cannot sit by when I'm capable of caring for young men who need me. I can put my expertise to good use. Helping sick and wounded soldiers seems the best way to do that, right now."

She released Alvah's hand and picked up the little newspaper and held up the report. "The Federal Army has suffered overwhelming casualties—thousands of men and boys felled by the guns and bayonets of General Robert E. Lee's rebellious renegades. The Confederate forces are already advancing into northern territory," she read.

Instead of sustaining her argument, the disastrous figures reinforced her parents' opposition.

For the first time in her life, Mary encountered a stubborn reluctance to support her intentions. She appealed to her father. "You're a medical man, Papa. Surely you understand my compulsion to save the sick and wounded."

Placing the newspaper back on the table, she reached for his hand again.

"Don't you see, Papa, there's a desperate need for skilled surgeons to take care of those poor men? My experience could be of enormous help."

"The battlefield is no place for a woman, Mary," he cried, his heart constricting in light of his determined daughter's resolution. "Knowing you, you'll be in the thick of it, without regard for your own safety."

"Papa, I'm a doctor," was her vehement reply. "My gender has nothing to do with it. Don't you see that I have the training? I can help those pitiful souls."

Vesta was crying softly, shaking fingers covering trembling lips.

Mary drew both their hands to her breast. "Please don't cry, Mama. Papa, please, just help me do what I feel I must. I promise I won't take unnecessary chances, but I have to be there."

Tears streamed down Vesta's cheeks to end in hot droplets against their hands. "You're not asking for our advice, darling. You've made up your mind without considering us. Haven't you?"

Her words struck Mary like a blow. The disappointed tone left the daughter shaken.

"Yes, yes, that's true," Mary admitted, "but I need your help and support to see me through this. I have to build myself up to be ready for duties out in the field. My body must be strong, and my will even stronger." A sob caught in her throat. It was time to garner all the help she could muster. "More than that, I need your prayers," she begged, reaching out to him.

Alvah took a hard look at his daughter. "Prayers? You're asking for prayers?"

Mary hesitated, waiting for one of them to offer the supporting words she desperately craved. "You want us to pray over your grave, Mary? Must we bury another child?" Vesta croaked, barely able to string the words together between sobs.

Mary understood her mother's distress, but refused to let it sway her. "If I don't have your blessings my task is harder, but I will do it anyway," she vowed, squeezing their fingers with her own.

Papa kissed the hand that clung to his. "All right, child. I see there's no changing your mind. What can we do to get you ready?"

Feeling alone in her grief, Mama extricated her fingers from her daughter's, placed both hands over her face and rocked back and forth, wretched with fear for the safety of her precious girl.

❧⊶❀⊷❧

Alvah worked Mary heartlessly, lugging, hauling and shoveling to strengthen her limbs for the grueling requirements of a soldier in the field.

"If you must go forward with this damnable plan of yours, we'll see to it you go prepared." By God, he'd send her to war as strong as she had been as a young girl working by his side, or he would die trying.

He shuddered, thinking of the perils she would encounter. He knew his daughter would never be far from danger. She'd jump right in with both feet, just like she did everything else in her life. God help my child, he prayed, as he pushed her even harder.

While Alvah drove her like a field hand, Vesta plied her with nourishing meals to build up her weight. Ninety pounds was not enough flesh for her five-foot frame. Muscle and a little more body fat were needed if her daughter's resistance to sickness and fatigue was at stake.

Recognizing her resolve, Alvie encouraged his sister. "Go for it, Mary. I know what it's like to suffer criticism for being 'different,'" he said. "Being an artist and performer has its joys, but the world's not always kind."

Mary's heart went out to him; her gratitude could not be measured in words.

Vesta, Jr. and Aurora Borealis came by weekly to talk Mary out of her 'ludicrous' plans. They were careful to confront her when neither parent was within earshot. "It's just like you, Mary. Embarrass us all," Vesta, Jr. said nastily. "I think you take pleasure in making this family the joke of Oswego."

Mary declined to fight back.

Aurora Borealis added her two cents' worth. "It was bad enough you couldn't make a success of your marriage, but this is the limit, *Doctor Walker*." She spat the words like a barn cat hissing at a threat to her litter.

Mary shrugged her shoulders. "You'll never understand, sister. Never."

Luna traveled all the way from Scriba to try and knock some sense into Mary. "Why put yourself in the position of handling all those men, stinking and lying about with blood and dirt all over them?" she asked, her face screwed up at the very thought of such filth and gore.

The disgusted young doctor shook her head and made a beeline for the barn, a place she knew her fastidious sister deplored.

Mary practiced her riding skills, urging poor Tildie across the fields, jumping the willing mare over dead logs lying on the forest floor. She cantered along the back roads for hours, strengthening her thighs and leg muscles, improving her balance. God alone knew whether she would walk or ride into battle, but she would damn well be prepared for it, either way.

She followed a Spartan routine, working in the barn and fields with Papa, sleeping on a single blanket spread on the floor, and forcing herself to wash thoroughly while allotting only one basin of cold water per sponge bath.

A troubled awkwardness clouded the relationship between Mary and her mother. Vesta did everything outwardly to help, but her heart beat a measure of doom inside her chest. At her husband's behest she put on a good face, but her depression deepened as the time for her daughter's departure drew near.

One day Mary approached her while she worked in the dooryard hanging freshly scrubbed laundry over a line stretched between two poles.

"Mama, talk to me," she said as she bent over the half-empty basket and handed Vesta a pair of Alvah's drop-seated long drawers.

Vesta arranged the underwear over the line before she answered.

"Oh, Mary, what can I say to make you understand? I'm afraid. I can't lose another child. Cynthia's death just about killed me."

"I have no intention of dying, Mama."

The wash was forgotten for the moment. "That's just it, darling. You have no conception of how fragile life is. You think you are immortal, that nothing can touch you."

"Not really, Mama. I don't feel that way, at all."

"I watched you endure insults because of your unusual opinions, I saw you struggle for your education, and I saw the dreadful results of your failed marriage. I know how strong you are, but . . ."

"I am not strong, Mama. I have doubts and fears, but if I don't follow my heart, I'll regret it the rest of my life. I am more afraid of that than anything."

"Better regrets than a maimed body or a cold grave."

"Please trust me, Mama. Just trust me."

Vesta reached for another piece of laundry and shook it out. "Bullets do not respect medical degrees," was her sad reply. "Bullets do not respect anyone."

Mary had no answer for that. She took the wet petticoat from her mother's hands and pegged it to the line beside her father's union suit. Then she took her mother in her arms, holding her gently while they both wept.

On the last day of September, Mary determined she was ready to go forward.

Papa examined her and found her heartbeat steady, her muscles firm and taut, and her general health excellent. The roses had returned to her cheeks, and her eyes sparkled like old times. He declared, "You're as healthy as any soldier should be, Mary."

She put together a wardrobe of her favorite tunics and trousers, along with extra underwear and heavy stockings. Two pairs of boots also went into the bag.

She packed her surgeon's kit with all the medical and dental instruments she owned, and some she begged from her father's and old Dr. Fortescue's supplies. Now retired, the feisty physician finally conceded that "little Mary Walker" was indeed the doctor she always vowed she'd be.

As they outfitted her medical bag, Mary seized the moment alone with Alvah. She placed a palm on each cheek and forced him to look directly into her eyes.

"I don't want you fretting about me, you hear? Mama needs you to be strong. So you just remember you raised a sturdy, resourceful daughter, you provided a wonderful education, and now you must let me go in good faith. I need to do this as surely as you needed to leave Massachusetts and strike out on your own. Remind Mama of that when she gets blue. And remember, nothing is going to happen to me."

Alvah's eyes shone with tears of pride. He hugged his daughter close, smoothing her hair. "How can I argue against such relentless dedication? I'm so proud of you, child," he whispered. Then louder, "You've already seen more than your share, but I send you off with my prayers and my faith that you will come back to us safe and well."

One more hug, and he held her away until he looked squarely into the serious little face that he feared he might not see for years, if ever again.

"I'll take care of your mother. Don't you worry about her. You go with an easy mind, and know that my heart goes with you."

And so it was on to Washington and enlistment, but it was still a man's world, war or no war. Mary's willingness to serve would not be enough. Her army commission must first be approved by men who would be scandalized at the audacity of the proud little Oswego surgeon who appeared before them in the strangest outfits they'd ever seen.

BOOK TWO
1860–1865

"A terrible darkness has fallen upon us, but we shall survive it. We must lift the lamps of courage and find our way through to the morning."
French Resistance
Anonymous

CHAPTER FIFTEEN

WASHINGTON CITY

AUTUMN of 1861 found the nation's first city teeming with activity. The pulse of the Capital beat erratically. America's broken heart was fighting to preserve its life.

Appalling stinks nauseated Mary as she entered Washington City. Alternately fascinated and repelled, she held a handkerchief to her nose as she picked her way over decaying horse droppings and scooted around scavenging pigs rooting in the garbage-strewn gutters.

Frightened Negroes—escaped slaves—shuffled along, lugging their worldly goods strapped to their backs and their mewling pickaninnies clutched to their chests.

Ravaged survivors of Bull Run shuffled through the streets, desperately struggling to understand why their peace and security had been scattered like chaff in the wind.

Pity for the walking wounded, victims of the Confederate thrashing at Manassas, made her itch to change dirty bandages. She ached to comfort dazed, exhausted boys, hobbling along in the muck and wanted to thrash the heartless civilians who avoided their gaze and hurried away.

She watched despairing mothers dart about, searching blank faces for missing sons.

Young women, many heavy with child, swallowed their fear and apprehension as they peered into the guarded eyes of bearded derelicts who might have a scrap of news about their war-ravaged husbands.

She listened with disgust to pompous politicians and businessmen who stood on street corners vilifying General McClellan's reticence to attack the Confederates after "Stonewall" Jackson's regiments had humiliated and decimated McDowell's divisions during the battle of Bull Run.

The Yankees dubbed the hoard of fleeing soldiers racing away from the screaming rebels the 'Great Skedaddle.' They overran the civilians gathered on the hillsides, sanguine voyeurs enjoying picnic lunches while they waited for a bloody contest to begin.

"Go back and kill the rebel maniacs," one stocky, red-faced dandy shouted, brandishing his walking stick like a sword.

What did that fool in safety behind the lines know about killing the enemy?

"String up the bastards," cried another, his manicured fingers clutching his own throat in mocking contempt.

Other voices joined them, vehement in their shame and hatred for the demoralizing defeat of Federal troops by a rebellious band of ragtag southerners advancing in droves, yelling up the hillsides like banshees from hell.

Mary, her face red with rage, finally spoke up to one group. "How easy for all of you. Why don't you put courageous deeds behind your foolish talk? You jabber on with your criticisms safely distanced from the deadly cannons. You spout hearsay information while you pose as paragons in the art of war. Get into the fray yourselves, and then criticize."

Although it was common knowledge that 'Little Mac' McClellan had bullied, and threatened and cursed his conscriptives, whipping them into the well-equipped and decently trained Army of the Potomac, no credit for that incredible feat was forthcoming. It was much more fun for the pseudo-experts to savage his good name.

Though General McClellan had turned the disheartened troops into a mighty fighting unit, totally prepared for battle, he procrastinated, refusing to engage the enemy without a formal written command from President Lincoln. He would not be forgiven for this grievous decision.

"Replace the coward," one bystander spat. "Send a man who will attack instead of twiddling his thumbs while our soldiers grow stale playing a waiting game."

"Who?" others asked. "Who do we send?"

"How do I know?" came the defensive reply.

"Check with Horace Greeley from the *Tribune*," another advised. "At least he has an opinion."

She wanted to ask what possible expertise Greeley could bring to the table, but she held her peace. She walked among them, listening, gleaning bits of information that she might use to argue her cause.

She held her own opinion in abeyance, willing to give the General the benefit of the doubt. She was not a military strategist any more than those loud-mouthed dissenters were.

❧❀❧

Secretary of war, Simon Cameron, glanced up from his paper work and scowled as an assertive knock preceded the entrance of an unannounced visitor. His aide would catch hell for this intrusion, he could bet on that.

A handsome young lady stepped into his office, displaying a smile that would enchant a gaggle of suitors at a drawing room soiree. Without invitation, she walked directly to his desk, one gloved hand extended in greeting.

Cameron's initial impression was that of a lovely girl, elegantly turned out, her attractive gray hat perched amid ebon curls that sprang forward in wiry ringlets to cover her ears. Dainty pink ruching graced her shirtwaist, filling the opening of a handsome tunic that was the exact color of the breast feathers on a female dove.

He noted with pleasure that the coat molded itself to her slim waist accenting her pleasantly swelling bosom and rounded hips.

He half rose from his seat, but chivalry won for only a moment.

Suddenly his mouth dropped open. Awkwardly, he plopped back into his chair at the sight of the intruder's dove gray trousers peeking from beneath her knee length frock coat. His grunt of disapproval could be heard in the offices at the other end of the hallway.

He stifled a groan. The effort puffed out his thin lips and inflated his gaunt cheeks, giving him the appearance of an underfed guppy. "Good Lord, who are you?" he sputtered. "Where on earth did you come from?"

Mary pretended he had just greeted her with all the grace of a charming prince.

"How do you do," she said, still smiling and offering her hand. "I'm Dr. Mary Edwards Walker from Oswego, New York, Mr. Secretary, and

115

I'm here to offer my services as an Assistant Surgeon in the Union Army. I'm requesting assignment to treat wounded soldiers in the field."

Cameron, a short, spare man with an elongated nose and deep-set eyes beneath heavy brows, leaped from his seat as if he'd sat on a pitchfork. Above his receding chin, his overshot upper lip clamped down on the lower to stem a snort of disbelief.

The former Republican Senator from Pennsylvania, whose appointment as Secretary of War had been political payback for his help in Lincoln's election campaign, ignored Dr. Mary's friendly hand, while he rudely inspected her from head to foot.

His upper lip curled in disgust. Who did this upstart think she was addressing? Surgeon in the Army, indeed. And where the devil was his aide?

"See here, Miss Whoever You Are, we do not induct females to battlefield positions," he stated, his eyes clamped fixedly upon her impeccably styled pants. "If you are female, that is," he added under his breath.

Damn. Who was her tailor, he wondered. Her trousers were a better fit than his own.

His eyes strayed to her pretty face, as she repeated quietly, "I'm Dr. Mary Walker, Sir."

He relented a bit, offering a lame explanation. "Why, Miss . . . Miss . . . the newspapers would have a field day with us, if we sent ladies off to war," he huffed. "Women are much too delicate. Why, you couldn't possibly cope with the terrible conditions on the battlefield, let alone the ugliness of all those disfiguring wounds."

Struggling with her temper, she pretended not to have heard his mumbled insult questioning her gender. How to handle this bigoted jackass? Her smile remained pasted in place. "Really?" she said, lowering her extended hand.

Stuffing her impatience down, she asked in her most reasonable tone "Have you ever been on the battlefield, Mr. Cameron?"

"No, I have not, but I've read the eyewitness accounts of reporters who covered Bull Run and they leave little to the imagination. There are cruel evidences of the war on every street corner here in the capital. Even the Patent Building has been turned into a hospital for the dying."

Studiously controlled, Mary's voice came across soft and sympathetic, but there was no mistaking its firmness. "You are right about the poor victims in the streets," she said. "All the more reason to let me help with their care."

She placed both hands on his desk and leaned forward. Her whole demeanor exuded an aura of self-confidence and pride in her own accomplishments. "But, first, let me enlighten you about my own experiences, Mr. Secretary. During my courses at Syracuse Medical College, I undertook the study of anatomy, pathology, and physiology, and I assure you there is nothing genteel about a two-day-old corpse lying naked on a cold wooden slab in the morgue. And there is nothing ladylike about using a saw to remove the top of a cadaver's head to study his brain, or opening an incision from his sternum to his pelvis to study his internal organs."

Cameron whipped a handkerchief from the pocket in the tail of his frock coat and crammed it against his mouth, squinching his eyes tightly for fear he might make a complete ass of himself by vomiting up the lamb stew he'd wolfed down at noon.

Mary struggled to conceal her amusement as she waited for him to regain some composure, but the sight of his twitching nose summoned a tiny smile that turned up her lips.

Good, she thought, eyes twinkling. This arrogant fool might get the message after all.

Cameron mopped his brow and stuffed the handkerchief up his shirt cuff to keep it close at hand. He sniffed and swallowed and fiddled with his buttons, playing for time.

Finally he issued his decision. "Your experience does not impress me, I'm afraid. My statement stands. Females do not go to war. Not during my tenure, at any rate."

Mary hid her irritation, framing her retort in the politest terms she could muster. "There is nothing in the law which denies a woman surgeon's admission to the Union Army, sir. I've done the research, myself."

Cameron shuffled the papers on his desk, avoiding her eyes as he shot back, "That's because we've never had such a ridiculous request, Madam, but I assure you that we cannot allow you a commission as an Army Surgeon."

Her expression turned grim. "Cannot? Or will not?" she charged.

He looked up at her, finally. "Whichever. It will never happen. Never. That is my last word on the subject."

He rearranged his documents before he came up with his counter offer.

"Miss Walker, let me tell you this. A Miss Dorothea Dix from Massachusetts convinced me some months ago to appoint her Superintendent of Women Nurses in the Union Army. I believe she's still recruiting volunteers for military hospitals. Nurses are not generally assigned in the field, but I suggest you search her out and make yourself available for service in that capacity."

"I'm a DOCTOR, Mr. Secretary, and while I feel nursing is a noble profession, my abilities as a registered surgeon far surpass the potentials of untrained women with superficial skills in patient care."

She started to leave, changed her mind, and turned back to him. Stepping closer to his desk, her firm chin jutting forward, she stared at Cameron for several seconds before she spoke. "I shall get my commission, sir, with or without your help. You have my absolute word on that."

She wheeled around and stomped from the office.

Cameron smirked after her as he pulled the handkerchief from his sleeve to blot away the sweat on his forehead and upper lip.

The Secretary heard the heels of her boots beat their sharp tattoo down the corridor, punctuating her commitment with every step, but he was too far away to hear the words she threw at his startled aide as she blinked back tears of frustration and disappointment.

"I'll show that pompous ass he's wrong, if it's my last act on God's earth," she threatened, slinging her reticule over her shoulder like a miniature gunnysack.

There were lots of ways to skin a cat, and, by heaven, she would try every last one of them before she was finished.

CHAPTER SIXTEEN

WASHINGTON CITY

THE UNION ARMY entered the war dangerously unprepared for battle and woefully deficient in personnel and inventory to properly treat the sick and wounded.

In 1861, Thomas Laws, tyrannical head of the military's Medical Department, was over eighty years old and dying of cancer. His appointment dated back to the War of 1812, and, by God, he would hang on to his title until the day he died!

Penurious to a fault, he maintained a ridiculously low bottom line on his budget reports by stinting on medications, bandages, surgical instruments and other critical equipment. One would think his own fortune depended on the savings he gleaned for the government.

Throughout his entire tenure, officers under his watch were grossly mistreated. Long-term veterans were discharged without cause, and substandard practitioners were advanced in rank for frivolous reasons unrelated to the military.

Lawson kept doctors stationed in remote frontier posts for ten years or more before allowing them inadequate sixty-day furloughs.

With their morale in tatters, physicians and surgeons were abandoning the Medical Corps by the dozens. The moment the war began the Corps lost twenty-five percent of its men, some to the Confederacy, many to private practice. They'd had enough of Thomas Lawson's dictatorial management.

The Union Army was left with approximately 90 medical officers to serve 16,000 men. It fell to states and individual regiments to take up the slack. Stuck with the concept that a poor doctor was better than no doctor, unskilled medical personnel created dangerous problems.

❦

Although she was seething when she left his office, Simon Cameron's remark about wounded soldiers billeted in the Patent Office gave Mary an idea. She would start with the local hospitals.

"If I can convince an Army Surgeon to speak up for my cause, that idiot Cameron will be forced to rethink his obstinate position," she muttered.

The next few weeks were spent wandering among bewildered throngs, roaming the capital searching for answers. She haunted government offices and military hospitals, but the negative information dispensed by well-meaning contacts was not what she wanted to hear.

She was flabbergasted. Her degree from Syracuse, considered a "non-regular" medical school, was not recognized by the Army as a legitimate license to practice.

The newly installed United States Sanitary Commission, (USSC) formed in June, 1861, for the aid and comfort of volunteer soldiers and their families had already begun to drum out male 'quacks with questionable credentials.' Read as: diplomas from non-regular schools.

Many of these doctors who had been improperly vetted were employees of their own states or the individual regiments they served. Regulations were often ignored when military needs surpassed the number of qualified physicians applying for positions that paid a scant $80 a month.

A leading medical journal decried the current policies: "We may estimate by hundreds the number of unqualified persons who have received the endorsements of these bodies (medical examining boards) as capable surgeons and assistant surgeons of regiments. Indeed, these examinations in some cases proved to be a total farce."

The politically motivated USSC adopted tenets forcing the replacement of so-called incompetent surgeons with younger, less experienced personnel just because they'd graduated from recognized colleges. Even if Mary had been a man, her unorthodox, eclectic education had reduced her chances of acceptance from slim to none.

In the eyes of the Victorian establishment, Dr. Mary's gender constituted an insurmountable barrier. A female 'quack' was surely the lowest pariah on the list of eligibles.

Hoping that she could come across some useful help or information, Mary crossed the Potomac to tour the forts strung along the Virginia border from Arlington to Alexandria. If she were going to serve, she might as well check out possible venues where she could be posted.

At every camp, she found the medical accommodations horribly deficient. Clearly, there was desperate need for qualified personnel. She pocketed the knowledge, and her spirits filled with hope.

Back in the city, she visited hospitals that were overflowing with sick and wounded. She interviewed officers in command of the units, pleading for acceptance of her services. They either laughed at her or ignored her altogether.

But Dr. Mary refused to waste her time.

Wherever she went, she comforted patients stricken with melancholy as they lay on dilapidated cots so close together that communicable infections were transferred back and forth among bedridden neighbors. Filthy bedclothes, lice, unwashed bodies, and bloody wounds contributed to an unrelenting stench. The moans of the afflicted plucked at her heartstrings until her nerves hummed along in a symphony of pity for the victims.

Outbreaks of moist gangrene were precipitated by the use of dirty instruments. Suppurating exudations from one patient's open sores infected the ulcerated limbs of his bedfellows because lowered resistance and lack of hygiene could not combat the gangrenous mortification of compromised body parts.

Some wards suffered epidemics as critically ill smallpox patients were confined among the non-infected.

Screams of pain-ridden amputee victims sent shivers up her spine.

Frightened nurses cornered her, whispering, "Comatose patients are being mutilated, and some of the surgeons operate on them for practice or to bone up on their anatomy studies."

Others complained, "Alcoholic and drug-addicted doctors leave the wards unattended and dying patients are left untreated."

These dedicated, exhausted nurses did what they could, but it was never enough.

Dr. Mary began to fear that she'd rushed into an impossible situation with romantic expectations that might never materialize. Armed with her education, experience and a grandiose idea of snatching brave Federal soldiers from the jaws of the grim reaper, she had expected to be welcomed into the bureaucratic structure with open arms.

Instead, she faced terrible conditions she could not combat, along with a rigid prejudice against her gender that would take several sticks of dynamite to dislodge.

Understaffed hospitals, feckless practitioners and inadequate supplies were some of the ills that killed her lofty dreams. She found the whole weighty system disintegrating for lack of leadership and dedicated help. Still she persisted. She told one nurse, "If this war continues for any length of time, thousands of men will die needlessly. Someone must speak out in their defense."

How fortunate for them that a tenacious little doctor from Oswego, New York, finally took up their cause.

Dr. Mary continued to visit facilities, watching and listening, counseling patients, checking their progress. When obvious neglect or inferior treatment presented itself, she opened her mouth, offering alternative solutions to relieve patients' sufferings.

She became a troublesome glitch in the network of the establishment. Hospital directors dreaded her visits, absolving their deficiencies by citing time constraints, "We have inadequate materials, too little help and no time."

"Excuses, excuses, excuses," she replied. "At least clean the men up. Soap and water and adequate food could not cost all that much."

To prove her point she garnered donations from patriotic civilians.

While her blatant interference endeared her to the patients, many Medical Officers took to hiding the minute the grapevine announced her arrival. The commander in charge of one hospital spotted Dr. Mary as she approached the cot of a comatose amputee. Hiding behind a full beard and heavy sideburns, he peered through pince-nez glasses perched on a bulbous, spidery veined nose. The thickened glass lenses enlarged his froggy, gray eyes, magnifying their bloodshot condition. He reeked of essence of peppermint he had dropped on his tongue to disguise the fumes of his lunch-time brandies.

"There goes that little devil in britches," he said, not bothering to lower his voice. "She's been a boil on my backside for days, now."

Dr. Mary turned and faced the officer, hands on hips and feet firmly planted. "Ah, yes, sir," she said, grinning coyly as an ingénue, "but you should have said, 'there goes that little DOCTOR in britches.' I'm here as a physician and not a demon. I'm only trying to help these poor men."

She stooped to rearrange the blanket of the unconscious patient.

"Madam," he carped, "This is my hospital, and I don't appreciate your interference or your interminable suggestions for reform. I find your meddling increasingly insufferable."

She patted the soldier's pillow before she turned to him again.

"Sir," she answered, "this is a military hospital owned by our sovereign country of which I am a proud and loyal citizen. My recommendations for improvement of patient care come from my own expertise, years of training and plain old common sense. You would do well to take heed. It might improve your success rate with curing the injured."

She bowed saucily at patient applause, smiling like a diva accepting her accolades from an appreciative audience.

The officer sputtered, and stomped off, muttering curses. "Impertinent little piece of baggage with the addled brains of a simpering milkmaid."

Their spirits temporarily lifted, every man in the ward had a grateful word for the pretty doctor as she passed among the beds dispensing her own brand of tender, loving care.

In the days to come, it became increasingly impressive how often this 'impertinent little piece of baggage' chopped the knees out from under some arrogant brass hat overly impressed with his own importance.

❧❦❧

Still convinced that voluntary service attending the wounded would ultimately gain her an Army Surgeon's commission, Mary doggedly solicited every hospital commander, begging for a temporary posting

After half a dozen failures, she arrived at the Indiana Hospital, a surgery that was crowded into the unused rooms of the United States Patent Office in Washington City, its burgeoning wards crammed with pitifully afflicted military casualties.

Dr. J. N. Green, whose predecessor died unexpectedly from stress and exhaustion after operating the facility for months without an assistant, administered to his patients without regard for his own health.

Here was a golden opportunity for an official Union billet while finally providing hands-on surgical attention to many needy soldiers. Surely, if poor Dr. Green was to survive, he must have a good right-hand to relieve the pressure.

Mary backed him into a corner to argue her case. "I'm Dr. Walker, a qualified surgeon come to help," she told the harried director.

Her eyes lit up as she described her theories for handling infectious cases. "I've been observing facilities for weeks, and I've figured out better ways of triaging incoming wounded. I have no fear of contracting small pox or typhoid, and I can work for as many hours as needed."

She presented him with a letter from Dr. J. M. McKenzie, addressed "To Whom It May Concern." It contained the paragraph:

> *"I am happy to bear testimony to the moral worth of Miss Walker who is a graduate of Syracuse Medical College and is well versed in the science of medicine, and whose unbounded patriotism and love of humanity prompts her to seek a position where she can be helpful to our soldiery."*

Dr. McKenzie's emphasis on Mary's "moral worth" was prompted by the concern that his protégée' might fall under adverse scrutiny—the contemporary misconception being that females applying for military duties undoubtedly had 'questionable virtues.' Chaste, gentle women would never subject themselves to a bloody, disgusting atmosphere populated by unkempt, cursing, morally diminished men in varying states of undress.

The letter settled it. Dr. Green said, "Your credentials seem impeccable, doctor, and it doesn't matter that you're a woman. I need all the hands I can get."

He penned a recommendation that demonstrated his desperation for Mary's help. In it, he neglected to mention the name of her alma mater, nor did he report that her training was from an unrecognized medical school.

He wrote:

> *"Miss Dr. Walker from N.Y. has come to Washington seeking a position as Asst. Surgeon in some hospitals or regiments. I need and desire her assistance here very much believing as I do that she is well qualified for the position. She is a graduate of a regular Medical College, and has had a number of years extensive experience and comes highly recommended. If there is any way of securing to her compensation, you would confer a favor by lending her your influence."*

When she arrived at the War Office, letter in hand, Mary discovered that her old enemy, Simon Cameron, had been dismissed because of his flagrant misuse of patronage. She resisted the urge to kick up her heels in the hallway.

Clement A. Finley who held the grand title of Surgeon General had replaced Cameron. Unfortunately, he turned out to be a spit and polish man as hardheaded as his predecessor.

Dr. Mary, ushered into his presence by a reluctant sergeant, barged in and began to pitch her case. Finley wasn't having any. He held up his hand to stop her. Could he have been forewarned about the persistent little doctor?

He flicked an imaginary mote of dust from his sleeve and adjusted his cuffs. "I cannot possibly appoint a woman," he said, peering down his nose at her. "I don't believe females have any place in the military."

Dr. Green's deception had done no good at all.

Mary opened her mouth to argue, but Finley walked around his desk and stepped behind her to the door. "That is my final word on the subject, young woman." Opening the door, he ordered, "Sergeant, please escort this woman from my office."

"Wait," she said, folding her hands in supplication. "Wait, please."

He pointed his finger into the hallway. "Out," he commanded and nodded to his aide.

The sergeant seized Mary's elbow and gently urged her forward.

She planted her feet and drew herself up tall. "Unhand me," she spat. "I shall leave on my own."

She stepped close to Finley who retreated a step in surprise. She grabbed the letter from him and snapped, "I'll be back, sir. I promise you, I'll be back."

She turned on her heel and stomped down the long empty hall.

"Cheeky little hussy," said Finley, winking at the sergeant.

"Yes, Sir," the man replied. He did not wink back.

Refusing to lose heart, Mary took a grand chance. She approached the Assistant Surgeon General, Robert C. Wood, and showed him the letter. "Can you somehow overturn Finley's refusal?"

He beckoned her close and lowered his voice. "I'm sorry I can't help you," he whispered, afraid of being overheard. "Your credentials are impeccable, and if the Surgeon General were away, Dr. Walker, I'd be happy to appoint you. However, since he is in the immediate vicinity, it is not within my province."

Without her appointment, Dr. Mary could not be paid.

She reported her failure to Dr. Green who was desolate. "I have no way to pay you. I'll be sorry to lose you."

She refused to waste her valuable training. She could still do volunteer work until her luck changed. God knows, she thought, every willing hand is needed to help with the constant stream of wounded veterans. At least Dr. Green appreciates my help.

"No matter, doctor. It has never been about money. I'm here to help."

⊱⊰⊱❀⊰⊱

One frigid day in November found Vesta Walker, clad in a gingham housedress and knitted shawl, hurrying out to the barn, waving a letter. Her husband sat on a milking stool in the storage room, his head bent over some tack he was mending.

"Alvah, darling," she shouted, "I have good news."

He looked up from the faulty harness. "What is it, wife?"

He frowned and clucked his tongue against his teeth. "Why aren't you wearing your coat, Vesta? It's freezing out here."

He set aside his work and stood, opening his mackinaw to cuddle her close. "Now, what is it that's got you so het up, my dear?" he asked, kissing the tip of her chilled nose.

She huddled against him, enjoying the heat from his body. "I have news from our girl. News from Washington," she cried, her voice cracking with emotion.

He removed his coat and placed it around her shoulders. She inhaled the familiar scents of leather and oil and just plain husband.

"Come inside, wife," he said, leading her back to the house. "You'll catch your death out here."

He sat her down in front of the hearth and poked at the fire until it was burning merrily.

Vesta stretched forward, gratefully soaking up the warmth.

He folded his rough, chapped hands and cleared his throat. "Now, what's all this commotion? What's so urgent it could not wait?"

Smiling widely, she leaned forward and handed him the letter.

He patted his pockets and glanced about the room. "I don't have my spectacles handy," he fretted. "Will you read it to me, please."

She unfolded the sheets and proudly pointed at the stationery with the letterhead of the Indiana Hospital. She cleared her throat and smiled as she read:

"I suppose you all expected me to go to war, and I have thought it too cruel to disappoint you, and have accordingly made my way to 'Dixieland' . . ."

Vesta paused and glanced at Alvah. "She's pulling our leg, isn't she?"

He waved impatiently. "Yes, yes, go on, go on."

Vesta read further, ignorant of the fact that Mary had stretched the truth about the extra help. "I am Assistant Physician and Surgeon in this Hospital.

We have about eighty patients now. We have 5 very nice lady nurses, and a number of gentlemen nurses. We have several cooks; and a dispenser to put up and prepare medicines, after our orders."

Mary described the marvelous glass showcases that housed thousands of U.S. patents issued over the years. Delighted, she reported that hundreds of General George Washington's personal effects were proudly displayed on the first floor of the facility as well.

The letter continued:

"Every soul in the Hospital has to abide by my orders as much as though Dr. Green gave them, & not a soldier can go out of the building after stated hours, without a pass from him or myself . . ."

Alvah laughed out loud. "That's my Mary. Bossy, bossy, bossy."

"At least she's safe, for the time being," Vesta said, reaching to hug him.

Her husband sobered at that. He pulled his wife onto his lap and settled back in his chair. "For the time being," he repeated, sighing with relief.

He circled her shoulder and pulled her close, staring over her head into the dancing flames. "When will this madness end?" he whispered, as he buried his face in her soft, graying hair.

CHAPTER SEVENTEEN

WASHINGTON CITY

H EARTSICK, MARY TRUDGED UP the flight of stairs to the wards of the Indiana Hospital.

Catching sight of Dr. Green across the row of cots, she took a deep breath and strode toward him. His shoulders sagged with fatigue; his skin seemed gray from lack of sunshine. Poor fellow, she grieved.

An angular man with kindly eyes, he personified the demeanor of a physician strained to his limit with the overwhelming task of caring for too many desperately ill patients.

Her throat tightened with despair as she dug deep inside to dredge up a few words of cheer for him. "I'm back from the wars," she sighed, struggling to rearrange her downcast expression. Her lips refused to cooperate. The elusive smile she sought remained buried under the weight of her painful disappointment.

He took her by the shoulders and turned her face to the light, searching for some clue that things would be all right.

Her cobalt eyes swam with tears. A salty bitterness flavored her speech. "That fool, Finley, turned me down flat," she said, dropping her chin onto her chest.

Aghast, he shook her harder than he intended to. "Why . . . How in God's name could he possibly do that?" he demanded.

She gently removed his hands, and took off her floor-length cloak. She folded the garment over her arm.

Her mouth twisted in anguish. "Same reason as all the others gave," she sighed, smoothing the wrinkles in the wool. "He doesn't believe in women in the military."

Dr. Green led her into his tiny office, a dingy, windowless room with a rickety desk and a useless, top-heavy alcohol lamp. The uneven base sat on three spindly feet fashioned from beaten tin. "What about a civilian appointment paid by the military?" he asked, guiding her to the only chair in the room.

Mary threw the bulky cape over the back of it and slumped into the seat. For a moment, anger got the better of her. She pounded the arm of the chair. "That idiot's too prejudiced to believe that a female is bright enough to even be a doctor," she sneered.

"That's rubbish, Mary. Your references are beyond reproach. I've never seen better."

His kind words soothed her, but she shrugged as if to say nothing ever changes.

"Yes, it's rubbish," she muttered, "but it's his rubbish, and his word is law right now."

Dr. Green sank down on the corner of the battered oak desk and massaged the creases on his forehead. Despair roughened his voice as he responded, more to himself than to Mary, "Whatever will I do? I was counting on having your help. We're short of nurses, there are over a hundred patients now, and I'm only one pair of hands."

She spoke up quickly to comfort him with the decision she had reached long before she arrived back at the Patent Office. "No need to worry," she said, standing quickly to take his hand.

The hasty movement was too much for the tippy lamp. It wobbled and toppled off the desk with a crash. Both doctors jumped at the racket, then laughed uncontrollably at the foolishness of the situation. Mary groaned. "The Army wouldn't even provide us a decent lamp for this stupid supply room." Another wave of giggles seized her.

He picked up the lamp and chucked it into the rubbish bucket. "Good thing there was no fuel in the base," he said. "One more mess might be one too many to deal with at the moment."

Wiping away tears of laughter, Mary gasped, "I was about to say that I'll work with you in a volunteer capacity. No one can find fault with that."

It was Dr. Green's turn to gasp. He knew that Mary was self-supporting. He wagged his shaggy head and put one hand against her cheek.

"You can't do that," he objected. "How will you live?"

She thought a moment then looked up brightly. "You let me worry about that. Besides, all I really need is an alcove with a screen. I can sleep there, and I'll eat hospital rations. It should work fine for a while, if we keep it between ourselves."

Dr. Green hesitated, considering her offer, thinking it wasn't exactly legitimate. All he needed was some stiff-necked officer from the bureaucracy bringing him up on charges for a breach of regulations.

Finally, he agreed. "Very well, but you must let me share my wages with you."

Dr. Mary, insulted at the suggestion, became indignant. "Absolutely not. You have a wife and several hungry little mouths to feed, do you not?"

"Yes, that's true," he admitted. "What they pay me is barely enough as it is."

She nodded. "I thought so. Every cent you earn should go to them. Now let's hear no more about it."

Green appraised the petite doctor, neat as a pin in her tunic and trousers, feminine to her bootstraps, but stronger than any woman he'd ever met.

"How will I ever thank you, Mary?"

"No need," she said reaching for her cape. "I'll just go for my things and be back in a jiffy. Meanwhile, you'd better scare up a place for me to lay my head tonight."

He thanked her again and promised to make her comfortable.

"Think of it," she said brightly, "I'll be here at night so you won't have to leave your family if there's an emergency."

With that she hurried off, swirling the heavy cape around her shoulders as she rushed down the stairs.

Dr. Green looked after her, astonishment chasing the exhaustion from his features.

"Amazing," he whispered, shaking his head. "Absolutely amazing."

And amazing she was.

Her volunteer status gave her unlimited leeway a formal job description would never allow. She saw what needed to be done and attacked each task with the supercharged energy of a whirlwind. Her twenty-ninth birthday skated by unnoticed, her attention riveted on more important things.

The moment her professional title was revealed to the patients, the morale of the wards took an upswing. One patient observed, "With two doctors around we'll get quicker attention, night and day." Having a pretty woman care for them did wonders for their morale.

A paragraph from a letter to her parents summed up their hopeful attitude perfectly:

> *"As soon as the soldiers learned of my being a physician, they were very pleased and whenever they felt worse in the night so that they wished to have a surgeon called, I was the one they sent for."*

In her limitless empathy for her suffering patients there wasn't a thing Dr. Mary could refuse them, whatever the time.

During the slower hours of early evening, she penned letters for young men too illiterate or too badly injured to write their own. Some nights she simply sat and held a hand or stroked a forehead until sleep temporarily delivered the patient from his pain or loneliness.

Besides treating dreadful injuries and diseases, she quickly assumed the role of general administrator, organizing stewards' schedules, ordering supplies and establishing a patient book that recorded daily care and treatments. It was the beginning of the hospital chart system as the world knows it.

Each time ambulances arrived with their pitiful cargoes, she set up a triage to prioritize medical and surgical emergencies while weeding out smallpox victims to be quarantined. Again and again she raced up and down the long stairwells without complaint about the work or the exposure to deadly illnesses. Indeed, she thought herself immune and too busy to succumb to mere disease.

Besides operating on casualty cases, she counseled terrified youths who faced amputation of damaged limbs.

Her physical therapy sessions enabled the wounded to become stronger while her emotional support snatched depressed youngsters from their quagmires of despair.

Believing that patients required diversion to fill their empty days, Dr. Mary requisitioned checkerboards for them. Her motto was, "Working minds and busy hands hasten recovery," She lobbied tirelessly. "If we give convalescing patients something to think about other than themselves, their mental and physical well-being must improve."

The checkerboards were sent, and occupational therapy was born in a ward at the Indiana Hospital.

Espousing the healing properties of fresh air, she issued day passes for soldiers who were well enough to walk outside.

One day a vigilant sentry on the steps outside the capitol halted a slender young patient clad in nondescript clothes and sporting bandages on both his arms. The lad offered his signed pass as proof of permission to be afoot.

A robust guard with thighs like tree trunks and arms to match squinted at the slip of paper then crumpled it up in his fist. It hit the ground at his feet.

"You are under arrest," he said, taking hold of the scrawny lad by the scruff of his neck.

"But I have a pass," the frightened boy wailed.

"Impossible. This is signed by a Dr. Mary Walker and there are no women surgeons in the Army."

At the mention of Mary's name, the soldier's courage returned. He adjusted his jacket, indignant that he had been unjustly accused. "Oh, yes, there is too," he insisted, growing braver with right on his side. "You come with me upstairs to the Patent Office and you'll see her. She's there every single day."

The guard picked up the pass and smoothed out the wrinkles so he could read it again. After a moment, he handed it back to its owner. "All right, then," he said grudgingly. "Go on. Be off with you before I change my mind."

As the lad limped away in his poorly fitted, borrowed shoes, the sentry smacked the side of his head, muttering, "A woman in the Army. What will this crazy war bring next?"

Bossy and driven by her own strict standards, Dr. Mary still comforted the boys who begged for their mamas, and counseled husbands who cried for wives, consoling them and promising help in the form of furloughs or outright releases.

But she didn't stop at promises. She petitioned for passes and secured transportation home for them. Word circulated throughout Washington that she was a champion of the needy, and she was soon getting requests for aid from desperate wives and mothers. She did whatever she could to help with no expectations of reward or recognition.

She personally accompanied one critically wounded soldier to his family in Rhode Island. Another patient was escorted to Ravenna, Ohio.

Before hurrying back to her duties from the Ohio trek, old friends persuaded her to speak at a benefit for the Soldiers' Aid Society. She described the horrible conditions in Washington. "There's an overwhelming need for financial aid as well as food and medical supplies for these wretched souls who gave so much," she begged. Her eloquence was rewarded with large donations from the audience.

Mary learned through the grapevine that many of the inmates in the Federal Deserters Prison were not deserters and did not deserve to be incarcerated. She persuaded the captain of a steamboat to give her passage on his next trip to Alexandria. "For the good of our valiant boys," she said.

And who could refuse her?

On November 13, 1861, a blustery day with a wintry sun barely breaching the overcast, Dr. Mary, clutching her precious medical kit, marched up to the sentry patrolling the space before the wide front gates of the stockade. She was warmly clad in her circular cape and a dark felt hat with a pheasant feather swirling around the crown. Her cheeks and lips, rosy from the cold, accented the bright blue of her eyes.

"Halt," bawled the guard, spreading his legs and bracing his bayoneted rifle across his chest. Two of his companions ran quickly to his side, obviously more amazed than threatened by the small, curly-haired female staring brazenly back at them.

Mary stopped as ordered and placed her bag at her feet.

"You can't go inside, Ma'am," the corporal said, and both his companions, lowly privates, nodded their heads in vigorous agreement.

Dr. Mary stretched to her tallest, and placed her hands on her hips. One corporal and two privates did not a deterrent make. "I am Dr. Walker of the Union Army. I command you let me pass or you will suffer severe consequences."

Three mouths dropped open in disbelief. The first sentry said, "The sergeant never gave me no orders about no lady doctor. And when did they let females into the Army, anyway?"

A short, whispered consultation with his buddies followed as they huddled out of earshot.

"Shall we git the sergeant?" asked one private.

All three glanced Mary's way.

"Naw. She's a bitty woman. She can't do no harm, can she?" said the second private.

A small boot tapping loud enough for them to hear, hastened the sentry's decision. "Well, I'm not gonna argue with her."

He shrugged his shoulders and ushered her through the small Judas gate in the retaining fence.

She secured grudging permission from the commander and interviewed every prisoner in the camp before hurrying back to Washington on another crusade. "I want pardons for all the innocent men billeted at the prison for lack of space elsewhere. And I shan't take no for an answer." She got her pardons.

⚜

Christmas came with an invasive cold and damp that sapped the strength of the caregivers. It was an even grimmer time for Indiana Hospital's charges who openly pined for their loved ones.

Determined to lighten the depression of the lonely men, she pleaded with local merchants, "Please help me create a little holiday cheer for my boys."

Offers of help and donations of medicines and supplies were forwarded to her attention, and the whole hospital celebrated.

Despite her strict, autocratic rules, the patients loved her. Dr. Green told his wife, "She's a wonder. She's like a female drill sergeant, and I feel truly vindicated in the deceit I helped to perpetrate."

Abby Gibbons, a renowned volunteer nurse at the time, visited the Indiana Hospital and followed Dr. Mary on part of her exhausting schedule. Later she wrote:

"Dr. Mary Walker is a character with a keen eye and a cheerful manner and the patients believe in her. I can't fathom how she keeps up such a pace."

That was all the little doctor in pants really wanted.

⸎✿⸎

Dorothea Dix failed to show the same appreciation for Mary's efforts.

The woman that Secretary of War Cameron had appointed as the Union Army's first Superintendent of Women Nurses paid an unannounced visit to the Indiana Hospital.

Dix's reputation for efficiency was well known, and accolades for her wonderful pre-war work to improve the plight of the institutionalized insane had preceded her.

Like Mary, Dorothea had encountered jealousy and prejudice among Army Surgeons who resented female intrusion into their domains. There should have been instant rapport between them; instead, they bonded as uneasily as oil mixed with water.

She was thirty years older, not much taller than Dr. Mary, plain-featured and slight of frame. Wide set, penetrating eyes beneath heavy brows pierced her adversaries, dissecting their weaknesses and capitalizing on them.

The heavy, dark hair framing her solemn face was parted in the middle and drawn up in a pug above the nape of her neck. The thick knot was fashioned from a long braid coiled round and round and secured with tortoise combs. She wore numerous petticoats over a brown, full-skirted dress that swept the hospital floor collecting bits of debris that had fallen from the men's cots.

This humorless woman was the only one who could approve female nurses for duty, but her unsympathetic nature and carping attitude destroyed the patience of nearly every hospital administrator in the city. Despite the fact that she had acquired an awesome reputation for procuring donations of money and vital supplies from private citizens, her poker face and acid manner made her inspection visits bleak. Because she seemed devoid of compassion for male patients and their caregivers, her dour personality was far better suited for administrative duties than nursing could ever be.

Dorothea's rigid standards for volunteers prohibited any attractive, well-proportioned woman to pass muster. Her idea of the ideal nurse volunteer was a plain woman, simply dressed and devoid of personality. In other words: only skinny, ugly women with warts need apply.

"Dragon" Dix, as a young volunteer tagged her, took one look at pretty Mary Walker winding her way among the beds in the Indiana ward and nearly split a gusset. She was positively scandalized to discover a lovely, single woman ministering to lascivious young men who lusted after her like dogs in heat. That most of the men were too sick to care whether Mary looked like a Madonna or a witch made no difference to the formidable Miss Dix.

Mary was immediately relegated to the top of the hit list.

Before her arrival, the hospital gossipmongers discussed Dorothea's biased proclivities, but Mary was not intimidated. She graciously accompanied the head volunteer around the wards, carefully skirting Dorothea's questions. When she was asked to see her appointment papers, Mary skillfully changed the subject. She proudly described the strides that had been made since she came aboard, and quoted from memory the difficult cases that had been healed and sent back either to their regiments or their homes.

Later, Mary commented, "When she saw a patient who was too ill to arrange the clothing on his cot and a foot was exposed, she turned her head the other way, seeming not to see the condition. I was so disgusted with such sham modesty that I hastened to arrange the soldier's bed clothing . . . I was not able to understand what use anyone can be who professes to work for the cause and then allows false modesty to prevent her from doing little services that come her way."

Even so, in the face of behavior she considered unbecoming to the medical profession, Mary was careful to soften her comments with a compliment.

She tempered her criticism by praising Dorothea's marvelous work in the insane asylums. But she breathed a sigh of relief when Dorothea's inquisition was over. She worried for weeks that Cameron's watchdog might launch a full-scale investigation. Please let her be too busy with other things, Mary prayed.

＊

Late one evening, the heartbreaking sights and ugly smells of the Indiana wards became overwhelming. Mary had reached the end of her tether as her old enemies, illness and death, seemed to be getting the better of her.

Although she loved her work, her mind could handle only so much misery. Her back ached from lifting and tugging and turning patients, heavy with their own helplessness. Her arms felt leaden and useless.

She ventured into the Washington streets to walk a bit, and gather the emotional strength that would see her through to another dawn.

Bundled against the cold in her voluminous cape and feathered hat, she strolled along, savoring the silence and the freshness of the pearly night air. Her breath formed smoky clouds, and her toes tingled in her boots.

Vying for mortal attention, a three-quarter moon floated among the myriad of stars that sparkled in the Milky Way. Besides her soft footfalls the only sounds Dr. Mary heard were the sputtering gas lamps casting elongated shadows before her.

But her thoughts were far from her surroundings. Her attention was focused inward as she contemplated the desperate plight of a pitiful sixteen-year-old whose left leg had been blown away at the knee. The boy fretted because his father had been killed at Bull Run, and he was now the sole support of a mother and two small sisters. He pleaded to go to them right away, because they were already in dire need. "How will he manage with only one leg?" she mused aloud. "I know where I can get him a peg leg, but the leather casings and straps will put too much stress on his shattered joint if we attach it before his knee heals properly. Perhaps we can get his family some help in the meantime. Maybe then he will settle down and give Mother Nature a chance to do her work—with my help, of course."

Suddenly Mary was startled from her reverie. The hair on the back of her neck prickled as sharp adrenalin needles warned her to proceed with caution. Something evil was afoot!

Her heightened senses picked up a foreign sound, the scrape of a boot on a loose stone. A shadow fell across the path in front of her. Someone was sneaking alongside the building ahead.

She did not hesitate. She did not cry out.

As she passed the front of the Treasury Building, a 'dude'(Mary's word) stepped out into the lamplight with his arms flung wide.

"Where ya goin', Missus?" he demanded, a malevolent leer plastered across his whiskered face.

He was at least a foot taller than the diminutive doctor, his wide shoulders stretching the limits of his threadbare coat.

Menacing hands reached toward her. She could see tiny flame-like reflections the flickering street lamp cast in his bleary eyes. She flinched from the rancid odor of old liquor and stale tobacco.

Stepping back, she assumed the stance of Alvah's prize bull, shoulders hunched, both feet planted firmly. She flung back the front panels of her cape and scowled up at him. "Get back," she ordered. "Get back."

Instead the dirty vagrant hawked up a gob of phlegm, spat it near her feet and shuffled toward her. "Whatcha gonna do about it?" he leered.

Mary stepped left and pulled a small pistol from the folds of her cloak. The metal glinted in the half light. In one swift motion she trained it directly at his chest. The thug's look of complete surprise might have been comical had he seemed less threatening. He spread his hands in front of him, a defensive reflex.

"Whoa, Missus," he gasped.

"Mister, get away from me this instant," she commanded in a firm voice that echoed in the midnight silence. She raised the pistol and aimed at his face. "I can kill six dudes just like you, before you can blink an eye."

"Whoa," he repeated, splaying his fingers in supplication. "I don't want no trouble, lady," he choked and turned away, quickly scuttling off and disappearing into a nearby alley.

Mary watched after him feeling her chest swell with her own power. She laughed out loud and danced a little jig right there on the sidewalk. Her cape swirled around her, her hat went flying. She stopped then glanced around, saw no one was looking and fired a shot into the air. Thank you, Papa, for insisting I arm myself!

A policeman raced up to her and demanded, "Just what the devil do you think you're doing?"

She restrained from asking where he'd been when she really needed him. Her accounting was kept totally factual. It was bizarre enough on its own.

She explained, "I fired the ball to give those dudes an understanding of where I stood. Those of his class who believe that there are no young women capable of taking care of themselves better inform their friends that they might be in danger of their lives if they ever approach me."

Her hands shook with fear, and her stomach turned queasy when she thought about it later. However, she was proud that she'd been absolutely calm during the emergency. Please let me be that way when I get on the battlefield, she prayed.

Though she took her lonely constitutional on many a dark night around that same neighborhood, she was never approached again. Once the story got around, those who knew Mary were not surprised: those who did not congratulated her courage.

Most important of all, the word had spread like wildfire among the riff raff: "Watch out for the crazy lady from the Patent Office. She'd just as soon put a ball in your gut as look at ya!"

CHAPTER EIGHTEEN

WASHINGTON CITY

SANDWICHED among her medical duties, Dr. Mary found time to set up a central information center for female relatives hungry for news of fathers, sons, husbands, and brothers. By January, 1862, her Women's Relief Association was posting names and current status of incoming casualties. While not infallible, it enabled many to locate missing kin.

Besides managing furloughs for men needed at home, she researched laws and campaigned for pensions for maimed boys who could neither read nor write. Most of her research was done on behalf of the poor and naive who were too dazed and confused by a system they could not comprehend.

Nothing phased her. She went to bat for bewildered prisoners who broke rules they never knew existed. When she needed answers, she read documents and regulations incessantly, searching for loopholes to aid the uninformed.

"That little lady missed her calling," said one harried government official who encountered her relentless determination. "She would've made a damned fine lawyer."

By this time, Dr. Mary's finances were in a perilous state. Unable to obtain a military commission that would have paid about $130, monthly, or a civilian contract for $100 a month, she was faced with difficult choices.

"I could apply as an army nurse," she mused, "but it only pays $12 a month." She grinned. "I doubt I'd last a day being told what to do, anyway. I need a better wage to support my independence and my charities."

The escalation of the war that many northerners thought would never last brought about the enlistment of accredited Assistant Surgeons. Once

Indiana Hospital had been assigned several of these newly commissioned physicians, Mary felt comfortable leaving her old friend, Dr. Green.

Thanks to her badgering, he had spent more time with his family and his health greatly improved.

Sadly he clasped her hand. "I hate to see you go, Dr. Mary, but I can't ask you to stay on, unpaid. Thank God for your generous contributions. The wards are so much better off now. I can only hope someone half as competent will come along."

He wished her well, as he handed her a glowing recommendation that he hoped would gain her the appointment she so desperately sought.

CHAPTER NINETEEN

NEW YORK, NEW YORK

TO ADD TO HER CREDENTIALS, Mary borrowed money from her father for a post-graduate course at the Hygeio-Therapeutic College in New York City. The dean of the school, R. T. Trall, had accepted several women students, and the resident professor of Physiology, Hygiene, and Obstetrics, was a woman named Dr. Huldah Page.

Besides the lectures, the studies required hands-on internship at Belle-vue Hospital. By now, an experienced student and old hand at doctoring, Mary became a mentor to three other females in her class.

While at the college, she contributed articles to the *Sybil*, two of which were titled "Noble Men in the Army" and "Dress Reform."

The latter was inspired by the spectacle of fashionable ladies strolling the streets, sucking in their nipped waistlines and dragging along layers of petticoats, while Mary and her courageous classmates proudly flaunted the practical Reform Dress of tunic and trousers.

Evenings at the boarding house were filled with gossip about their experiences in a society determined to harness women with tight corsets and voluminous underwear that would surely drown them if they fell into the East River.

They lounged around, enjoying refreshments provided by the landlady, Mrs. Pomphrey, a stodgy old crone who scurried around like a little brown mouse, her hirsute upper lip twitching with disapproval of their unortho-dox clothing.

Nor did she approve that they were studying medicine, of all things. "Any sane body knows that doctoring is a man's work. Staying home and raising babies, that's a woman's lot in life."

Evenings found the four friends engaged in good-natured bantering to avoid dwelling on the horrors of their daily tours in the crowded Bellevue wards.

Often, the topic of women's clothing became fodder for their gossip mill.

"Your trousers are quite handsome, Mary," remarked Safronia Tisdale, a pretty, round-faced girl who preferred looser bloomers to Mary's tailored style. "Did any of your gentlemen acquaintances in the capital wish to borrow them?" she asked, tongue-in-cheek.

"Certainly not," Mary chirped. "Most of them are too fat to even consider it."

Knowing snickers preceded Safronia's saucy rejoinder. "Ah, yes, the brutes want their women thin as match sticks, but it's all right for them to grow gigantic bellies and jowls that hang down to their collars." Four heads nodded in agreement.

At twenty-nine Mary, older and more sophisticated than the others, regaled them with stories of her altercations with "the bigoted fools in Washington who hadn't one smidgen of imagination among the lot."

Over tea, they giggled like schoolgirls.

"I have it on absolute authority that crinolines have altered the rules of courtship," Martha Watters sighed, the back of one limp wrist against her forehead in imitation of a distressed ingénue.

"Do tell," the others chorused.

"Oh yes. Really. Things couldn't be worse," she lisped, her eyes twinkling with merriment. "You see, crinolines are so wide, a man can't even hold a lady's hand any more. And forget about trying to kiss her. He's standing much too far away."

Mary laughed as loudly as the others.

"That's nothing," Elizabeth Biggers replied, extending a dainty pinky as she raised her cup in salute. "Listen to this. I heard that women in crinolines have to kneel down or sit on the floor of a carriage, otherwise their skirts shoot straight up in the air to show all their favors to the world?"

"Oh, no," Mary squealed, holding her aching sides at the mental picture of red-faced ladies straining to collapse their hoops while desperately trying to cover their unmentionables.

Once she'd regained control, Mary offered her own tidbit. She leaned in closer to whisper. "I've read in the newspaper that the New York Omnibus Company has raised the fares for ladies wearing hoopskirts."

"What?" cried Safronia.

"It's true. Instead of seven cents they must pay twelve cents for the privilege of riding the cars because they take up more than one seat."

"Discrimination!" hooted the ladies in unison, clapping their hands and collapsing into laughter.

Mrs. Pomphrey rapped loudly then stuck her head around the doorway, wide-eyed as a hooty owl searching for a field mouse. "I expect my ladies to behave themselves in a circumspect manner," she snapped. "Now quiet down, please. You are disturbing the other guests."

After she'd closed the door, Safronia whispered, "Do you think she heard what we said?"

"Who cares?" squealed Martha, crossing her knees quickly.

Another paroxysm of giggles made Mary's stomach ache. "Stop, stop," she pleaded, doubling her chest over her knees.

For the first time since Cynthia's death, she'd found female friends who spoke her language and understood her passion for improved conditions for women. Even better, they appreciated her sense of humor; something she thought had been lost in the milieu of death and destruction in the capitol.

Unfortunately her hard work and Diploma for Doctor of Medicine from the Hygeio-Therapeutic College, issued on March 31, 1862, was all for naught. Dr. Mary had graduated from another non-regular institution.

cᔕᓚ☙

She spent the summer in Oswego, helping her parents with chores, resting up, and generally avoiding arguments with her sisters. While riding through the serene, neighboring woods, she reflected on the contrast between her home and the war-torn battlefields. Far from the stink of death, she could imagine her beloved country at peace once more.

Her local lectures about her Washington experiences earned generous fees that enabled her to repay Alvah for her tuition advance besides building a small nest egg.

Polly Craig

By September, she was on her way back to Washington City, more determined than ever to become an Assistant Surgeon in the Union Army.

CHAPTER TWENTY

WASHINGTON CITY

IN THE FALL of 1862, the tumult in Washington brought the Union's desperate state into stark focus. Still another foe stealthily pursued the presidency.

At 5:30 on the evening of February twentieth, a 'bilious fever' had robbed Lincoln of his beloved son, Willie. Though desolate and disheartened, the President put aside his own grief to console his deeply depressed wife.

Between arguing with his cabinet advisors and poring over maps and books searching for some magic military strategy that might quell the Southern insurrection, the exhausted leader's patience grew uncharacteristically thin.

The next few months would shake the President to his very soul.

The War was costing the Federal government over two million dollars a day, and proceeds from the new Internal Revenue Act that taxed everything were hardly keeping pace. "Greenbacks" were printed and the new national currency came into being.

Devastating reports from his field commanders increased Lincoln's misery. His aching heart was further assaulted by the knowledge that other father's sons were dying in unspeakable ways that he felt powerless to stop.

The romance of saving the country from a despicable band of 'slave beating upstarts' was over. Grim reality quickly brought increasing disenchantment to the brave men who had rushed to the Union's defense.

One Federal officer describing his soldiers just after he had ordered a charge, wrote, "They seemed to be paralyzed, standing with eyes and mouths wide open and did not seem to hear me."

That common reaction was dubbed 'Seeing the elephant,' a phrase dating back to a group of awe-struck farm boys who stood on the grounds of a traveling circus gaping at the leviathan shoulders and ropy trunk of a leathery, prehistoric creature the likes of which they could never imagine in their wildest dreams.

General George 'Little Mac' McClellan, who once boasted to President Lincoln, "I can do it all," was relieved of his duties as commander-in-chief of the Union Army because of his reluctance to commit to battle. While he could organize and whip his regiments into shape, he lacked a spirit defiant enough to deploy them in a timely manner. Instead he set them to digging breastworks, long, muddy, brick red trenches whose excavated dirt created buffers between his Army and the Confederates.

His troops became more and more disgruntled. "Let us fight," they grumbled. "We can't keep hiding in these ditches like holed-up rabbits."

One disgusted volunteer wrote his wife, "If we keep hiding in the ground and never get at the enemy, when will this war ever end?"

The government's constant demand for fresh enlistments to swell the ranks of the Federal Army made recruiting officers too lax in their selection of volunteers. In many cases, the physical exams consisted of a 'walk-by.' Men who limped or failed to stand straight as they marched past the recruiting desks were rejected. All others passed muster.

The regulation stipulating each recruit have a 'stripped naked' physical exam was totally ignored. Consequently many patriotic young women, hiding their gender under thick masculine clothing, snuck into the ranks along with epileptics, syphilitics, and tuberculosis carriers.

Once infected recruits co-mingled in the camps, healthy farm boys with no immunity against populace diseases contracted the city-bred ailments.

Without proper facilities or sanitation standards, camps contaminated with lice, mosquitoes and flies became cesspools of infection. Hospitals were choked with sick patients who took up the bed space denied battle-scarred war casualties.

On the streets of the capital, soldiers and civilians were stopped and interrogated. Fear became a constant specter, as rough, untrained sentries mistreated innocents who had ventured abroad for legitimate reasons.

To prevent non-military persons from sneaking into battle camps, travel to those sites without official passes became impossible. But telling Dr. Mary Walker her destination was forbidden was tantamount to shoveling sand against the tide.

"We'll see about that," she said as she donned her severest tunic and trousers of navy wool, and knotted a bright green scarf at her throat. She braided her dark curls and stuffed them under a jaunty hat that sported a pheasant feather. She reviewed the list of contacts in her head.

CHAPTER TWENTY-ONE

WARRENTON, VIRGINIA

RUMORS WERE RAMPANT that the Union Army's hospital corps stationed near the main battlefields functioned under the most disastrous circumstances. Dr. Mary called in a few favors and was soon sneaking through the lines, hitching rides wherever and however possible.

At the camp outside Warrenton, Virginia, she found conditions even more deplorable than reported. She wrote to Papa: "This structurally unsound building that houses the casualties could collapse from the weight of its own damaged roof. It's a cold, barren place that stinks of rusty blood, creosote, and human excrement.

"Surgeons in charge are beyond exhaustion, stumbling among the wounded, cursing their commanding officers for abandoning them with no supplies or medicines. Male orderlies lacking towels, bandages or food have no way of providing the basic elements of nursing care. Sanitary facilities for bathing the patients are non-existent. Terrible bedsores cover the bodies of boys lying in their own filth. The stench of urine and rotting flesh is overpowering."

She encountered bedridden men on lice-infested pallets sprawled in stoic resignation too weak to cry out. The tattered remnants of their government-issued, mud-colored undershirts and drawers barely covered their chilled, ravaged bodies. Clearly, these worn-out troops, some stricken with the dreaded Typhoid Fever, were never in good health to begin with.

Mary quickly assessed the situation and hurried out to her trunk that had been carelessly dropped from the wagon on which she rode into camp. She selected some pretty cotton nightgowns, tore them into squares and handed them out to the male nurses.

"Wet these compresses and apply them to their foreheads," she advised. "It will bring them a little relief, but your comforting touch will help even more."

Later, when she told this story at a polite soiree, critics were scandalized because she had the uncivilized temerity to mention "pretty underclothes" in polite company. For weeks, she was vilified for social impropriety, instead of being commended for her generosity and resourcefulness.

"It took forever for me to live that one down," she later wrote a friend.

Dr. Mary's ministrations were far too lacking to satisfy her. She commandeered a horse and canvassed the surrounding areas to beg for cooking pots or basins to hold water, but she encountered such misery among the local residents that her heart bled for those innocent victims of plundering marauders—both northern and southern.

They admitted her to their homes apologizing that they could offer her nothing more than a drink of water.

"Please help me," she pleaded. "I have dying patients that need bathing and hot food."

"Forgive us," the poverty-stricken citizens tearfully replied. "We'd like to help, but we have nothing left to give. The armies took everything, our utensils, our tools, even our food. We are living on what we can hunt and scavenge in the area."

A young, blonde girl, little more than a child herself, clutched a swaddled infant against her chest. She wore a flowered cotton dress, tattered but scrupulously clean, and worn out house slippers on her bare feet. Tears rolled down her cheeks as she offered the mewling baby to Mary. She spoke with the thick drawl of the backcountry.

"Can you help us out, at all?" the painfully thin mother cried in desperation. "She's so awful sick. She has a terrible high fever."

"What's your daughter's name?" Mary asked, more to relax the mother than the need to know.

"Melanie," the shivering girl replied. "Melanie Colfax."

"Put her down on the table, Mrs. Colfax," Mary said, unstrapping her knapsack and throwing back the flap. She took out a dull pewter spoon then squeezed the baby's cheeks till the little bird mouth popped open. She leaned over and depressed the tiny tongue with the handle of the spoon in order to peer down the infant's gullet.

The baby gagged, hands and feet flailing at the indignity.

Mary smiled. This Melanie was a spunky little fighter. She'd come out all right.

"Her throat doesn't seem to be infected," Dr. Mary reported, relieved at not finding a telltale gray membrane covering the tonsil area. No scarlet fever, she thought. Thank God. I have nothing to treat it with.

"Sponge her down with cool water every couple of hours, and try to get as much liquid into her as she will take."

Dr. Mary stayed long enough to treat the child along with several other severely ill citizens. She was rewarded with a miniscule supply of stale corn bread that she saved to divide among the sickest soldiers who were subsisting on nothing but hardtack and hickory nuts or acorns boiled into coffee.

On the way back to camp, the stillness of the pathways and the bleakness of the landscape weighed on her. She began to weep uncontrollably. I'm just tired, she thought. No. That's not it, at all. I don't understand this terrible war that is destroying our country. If you are there, God, why are you letting this happen?

But Mary had not relied on Papa's God for years.

With the horrors of the camp haunting her like demons from a nightmare, she devised a daring plan. She bullied another young officer into lending his mount, swung astride its back and followed hasty directions through the woods and across fields picked clean of crops, till she arrived at regional headquarters where she discovered that General George McClellan had been replaced by General Ambrose Burnside.

No matter, she was prepared to harass anyone in authority if it meant saving the desperate men she had pledged to help.

Close to the main camp, she paused at a small stream to freshen up and rearrange her long, dark hair under the narrow brimmed hat. She pulled a few curls forward around her face and pinched some color into her cheeks. She brushed her tunic and trousers with damp fingers, and rearranged the green scarf. "Best I can do," she said and climbed back on her horse.

A startled look from the outlying picket proved there was no mistaking the petite lady's gender. Her bossy, no-nonsense attitude reminded him so much of the granny who raised him that he passed her through without a hitch. After all, what harm could a slip of a woman do to an important general who was surrounded by an army of officers and enlisted men?

Mary tethered the tired mare to a tree near a few sparse clumps of winter grass. She resettled her hat and approached the commander who happened to be standing outside his tent, discussing strategies with his first lieutenant.

His left hand rested on the back of a rickety wooden chair that had been commandeered from some hapless housewife. Five gold buttons on his knee-length blue field coat were undone to accommodate his right hand, which was tucked in against his chest.

Burnside spotted her from the corner of his eye and motioned her to wait her turn. He continued his spirited conversation, gesticulating with his left hand and shaking his head at the lieutenant. Then he gestured toward the bivouac and finally pointed to the south end of camp.

While she waited, Dr. Mary studied the tall man in hip-length boots and high-crowned felt hat. The full brim that shaded half his face did little to hide his bushy, brown cheek whiskers that were sprinkled with silvery strands. His generous, handlebar mustache was full enough to make her old landlady, Althea Bainbridge, shiver with pleasure.

Once the lieutenant was dismissed, Major General Ambrose Burnside turned to Mary and swept off his hat. True to the requirements of charm and chivalry, he bowed low at the waist presenting Mary with the shiny dome of his huge, round, bald head.

She bit the inside of her cheek to keep from giggling. No wonder he has no hair on his head, she thought, it's all on the poor man's face.

"Dr. Walker is it?" he asked. "I heard of your presence in the field. Now that you are here, what can I do for you?"

Mary quickly collected her wits. This was no time for impudence. "Ah, General, it's what I can do for you that is of importance here."

"I can hardly wait," was his dry reply.

He offered her the chair, but she declined with an impatient shake of her head.

"You have men dying at the hospital near Warrenton," she stated in a clear, authoritative voice. "I propose to personally escort them to Washington where they'll receive proper care. They are good, brave lads who deserve a better chance than they've got in that pig sty they're housed in."

The general winced at her description, but refrained from commenting on the conditions.

"They are good boys," he answered, fluffing his right sideburn. "You're right about that."

"Give me a pass on the railroad and enough healthy men to help, and I'll see that they are delivered to Washington safely," she promised.

The general played with his whiskers for a time, pondering the pros and cons. He studied Mary closely, seeing a small compact dynamo who probably wouldn't take no for an answer. The Rebs were close by and vicious to a man. He was damned if he did, and damned if he didn't. The determined look on the little doctor's face convinced him to go along with her.

"All right," he said. "Come inside and I'll write your orders."

His spurs jingled as he stepped into his tent and sat at a makeshift table that served as a crude desk. He leaned over, pulled a sheet of parchment from his knapsack and dipped his quill in the bottle of black ink that stood nearby. He penned the following:

> *"Headquarters Army of the Potomac,*
> *Warrenton, VA-Nov 15/62*
>
> *The General directs that Dr. Mary E. Walker*
> *be authorized to accompany and assist in the*
> *caring for, from Warrenton, Virginia, to*
> *Washington, the sick and wounded soldiers now at*
> *the former post. The Surgeon in Charge there will*
> *afford every facility to Dr. Walker for that purpose.*
> *Dr. Walker is entitled to transportation to*
> *Washington and she shall be furnished with*
> *temporary rations if required.*
>
> *By order of Major Gen'l Burnside"*

Blowing on the paper to dry the ink, he eyed his visitor. A strange one, he thought, especially in that funny get up. Still, there was something very special about her tenacity.

"May I offer you some refreshment before your return journey?" he asked with drawing room politeness, though his larder could produce nothing more than Army fare.

"I have no time for that now," she said, and snatched the authorization from him. She ran to the borrowed horse, threw herself into the saddle and cantered away, leaving the bemused general still fiddling with his whiskers.

Time was of the essence. Rumors were rampant that the Confederates were destroying the railroad tracks to cut off retreat between Warrenton and Washington.

Returning to the hospital at the gallop, she pulled the horse up short and leaped to the ground. She threw the reins to the nearest foot soldier and began firing instructions for preparing and transporting the sick and wounded back to the capital.

Under marching orders, military personnel were already breaking camp, able-bodied troops having been directed south to pursue the enemy.

Two locomotives towing a string of freight cars and one passenger coach were commandeered for the mercy flight back to safer quarters.

Once the rest of the Army had advanced southward, the remaining officers, along with several visiting congressmen, fell over one another in their haste to get away from the morbid camp. They clambered into the first car and ordered the engineer to stoke his fires and get a move on.

The burly, weather-beaten fellow, his clothes wrinkled and soot stained, crossed his arms and shook his head. "I got no orders," he said. "My train don't move without no orders."

The congressmen threatened, flaunting their credentials, and the officers pointed menacing fingers at their gold braid.

Nothing phased the stubborn engine driver. "It's my dang train, and I give the ding dang orders to move her or let her sit."

The brass dispensed a chorus of epithets that would raise a flush on the cheeks of a drunken sailor, but their words fell on deaf ears. No amount of cursing, cajoling or bribing could move the obstinate, old codger.

Meanwhile, Mary was loading her precious cargo onto the freight cars, arranging them as comfortably as possible under such adverse conditions. Cots littered the aisles, broken bodies shifted uncomfortably on the un-padded benches. Not a soul complained. They were leaving the fighting zone, and that was all that mattered.

Once all her charges were safely aboard, Mary hurried forward to find the engineer. He was still standing with his arms resting on his protruding belly, one grubby fist clasped tightly over each elbow. His lips were clenched around the stem of an unlit pipe.

"You can get your train started now," she said, with a satisfied smile.

He uncrossed his arms, took off his hat, and scratched the top of his head. "Who the devil are you?" he said.

Bad enough the high and mighty gents tried to order him around, but this bossy little minx was barking up the wrong magnolia if she thought she could give him permission to start his own danged engine.

Officers and congressmen gathered around to listen, knowing glances passing among them as if to say who's this little twit—in trousers, no less?

"I'm Dr. Walker, and I have patients to transport. Please start your train, now."

The pipe came out of the old man's mouth. "No, ma'am," he said. "I cain't do that." The pipe popped back into his mouth and he bit down hard.

"It's doctor," she said. "And why not, may I ask."

The bystanders were grinning by now. Did this little upstart think she could do what they had been unable to? They watched as the battle of wits progressed.

"I asked you why that is," Mary demanded a second time.

Huffing loudly, the engineer looked from the group of men, to the ar-rogant little woman standing with her hands on her hips like a mama scolding her naughty child.

His patience was dwindling, and he damned well did not appreciate people, male or female, telling him how to run his railroad.

This time he left the pipe in his mouth and mumbled around it. "I don't have no authority," he said and made the mistake of turning his back on the lot of them.

Furious, Mary stepped around in front of him and glared up into his face. "Then I will give you orders," she said crisply. "Start for Washington, at once."

He did a double take, removed the pipe and spit brown juice on the ground at her feet. "You cain't order me to do that," he sneered.

Dr. Mary recognized the contest and resented the insolent audience who stood by waiting to see her fail. "Oh, yes, I have the authority," she exclaimed, waving her letter from General Burnside under his nose. "Now start this train immediately," she ordered.

He looked at the sheet, barely reading it, but General Burnside's signature was all he needed to see. He nodded curtly and started toward his engine.

Mary watched him retreat and tripped ahead a few steps till she was nearly on his heels.

"And, sir," she added with a wicked grin, "May I advise you to run slowly and cautiously because of the imminent danger of damaged track and also to keep from jolting my poor patients any more than necessary."

The doubting Thomases clapped their hats on their heads and hopped aboard, lest the diminutive witch leave them behind if they dallied.

Duly chastened but mad as hell, the engineer sputtered and snorted. "Fire up the boilers," he shouted. Fifteen minutes later, the long train crawled out of the depot.

Mary played conductor, pacing the aisles, tending to the sickest soldiers, offering the only comfort she had—a pat on the shoulder, a sip of water, a kind word.

When the train pulled into Alexandria, the engineer stubbornly refused to proceed further without new orders. The battle lines were drawn.

Once again, Mary stamped her feet, bristling at another needless delay. "I order you to go on to Washington, immediately," she bluffed. "If you dare to refuse me, I will see that your case is reported to my friends in the War Department."

"Ah, well, if you put it that way," he fretted, puffing furiously on his smelly pipe.

The train huffed out of the station, "immediately."

On the second lap of the trip, Dr. Mary lost two of the most severely stricken men. Heartsick, she collected all their pertinent information and later reported it to the War Department for notification of next of kin. She wrote to one family, describing the soldier's valiant death. Twenty years later, this thoughtful gesture helped the soldier's aged father secure a pension. That letter triggered an important suggestion to other relatives who were unable to get information from the Pension Office.

"If all else fails, present any letters that were received from or about your loved ones while they served the Union Army," she advised. "These will constitute proof on their own merits."

After the War, Mary became an expert at helping wounded soldiers to receive government aid. However, her own trials with the Pension Office presented a different story altogether.

CHAPTER TWENTY-TWO

WASHINGTON CITY

THROUGHOUT THE FOLLOWING WEEKS, Dr. Mary made the rounds of the six Union hospitals to check on her Warrenton patients.

The Patent Office, home of the Indiana Hospital, was now vastly over-populated. Wards had spilled down into the archives section of the facility where beds were lined up in the eight-foot aisles, sandwiched between huge glass display cases containing prototypes of inventors' recorded instruments and machinery. Displays included ingenious inventions from the tiniest tool to the largest gadgets, all carefully catalogued and labeled with neatly printed signs.

It was down these crowded halls that President Lincoln passed on an inspection tour. He modified his long-legged stride to accommodate his short wife who clung to his arm for support. Her voluminous, black hoop-skirts whispered against the cots, as she brushed past.

The President tried his best to smile at the patients, but his craggy features seemed frozen, his sad eyes misty beneath heavy brows.

A visitor just ahead of the First Couple handed a leaflet to one of the bedridden men. The emaciated patient looked at it, laughed cynically and threw it to the floor beside his cot.

Mrs. Lincoln tugged her husband's sleeve and nodded toward the offender.

"Why are you behaving this way, young man?" the President gently chided.

"I couldn't help myself, Sir. The pamphlet is on The Sin of Dancing."

"Is that an excuse for rudeness?" asked Mrs. Lincoln, barely suppressing her indignation.

"It's just so much tomfoolery now," said the soldier, throwing back his blanket. "Both my legs bein' shot off and all."

A wet track glistened down the President's chiseled cheek. He squeezed the man's shoulder, took his wife by the elbow, and ushered her forward. There was nothing more to say.

Following her philosophy that a cheery attitude and a kind word were as important for healing as sunlight and fresh air, Dr. Mary approached every ward with a sunny disposition. No matter how exhausted, she found a smile for each patient, leaving him in better spirits than before.

One murky December afternoon, as a combination of sleet and rain rattled the windows of Ward B, Dr. Mary stopped beside the bed of one of her boys, a lad of sixteen with grayish green eyes and full lips. His untrimmed hair lay shaggy against the pillow, and his chin was covered with the soft peach fuzz of a novice shaver.

Mary remembered him for his bravery and his courteous manners. He had lain in his underdrawers, in that drafty mausoleum at Warrenton, suffering quietly amid the pitiful bleatings of his fellow casualties. Not one moan escaped his lips as she dug out shell fragments and debrided the blackened edges of his infected wounds with her scalpel. She cleaned and bandaged the gashes with scraps torn from her own nightgown. She recalled his endearing modesty as he struggled to cover his nakedness with the tattered remnants of his grimy blue uniform.

When she finished the dressings, he'd kissed her hand. "Thank you," he had murmured in a voice heavy with exhaustion. "My Mama will pray for you, and the Good Lord will reward you," he promised.

Now, because of her cheeky audacity with General Burnside, he was here in Washington, better fed and medicated, his recovery assured.

"How are you feeling?" she asked him, as she gently pulled back his cover to examine the ugly scabs on his legs.

"I'm healing up just fine, thanks to you, my dear Doctor."

He clutched her hand and drew it to his lips, a gesture of one far older than his tender years. "It's because of you that I'm not buried in some Godforsaken spot in the hills of Virginia," he cried. Tears filled his eyes. "If you hadn't come along when you did . . ."

"Now, now," she soothed.

He was many years younger, but it had been a long time since a man had been sweet to her. Poignant memories of Edwin Fowler drifted up from that secret place deep in her heart.

A girlish blush bloomed on her cheeks. She withdrew her hand and quickly pulled the light blanket up across his chest.

To still her thumping heart, she stepped to the nearby window and studied the melting droplets tracing snaky rivulets down the foggy pane. Edwin's face appeared in the mist.

Turning back to the boy, her lips curved in a smile. Her eyes crinkled at the corners as she thought of Papa. "When I was little, my father used to say this weather was fit for ducks and geese, and the rest of us had better stay indoors and keep dry." That was better. Papa was a much safer memory than darling Edwin.

"But, Dr. Mary," the boy persisted, "if you hadn't saved me I wouldn't even be able to see that rain now. I wouldn't mind getting soaked to the skin with it, right this minute."

"Over my dead body," she said, laughing at the thought of the boy cavorting half naked in the freezing weather.

To change the subject, Mary pointed to a small leather wallet that lay beside him.

Presuming it held a picture of his sweetheart, she said, "I suppose the sweetest face in the whole world is in that case."

His eyes dropped to it. A mischievous grin lit up his gaunt features. "Yes, it is," he replied. "You open it, and you will see the sweetest face I ever saw."

She picked up the worn leather folder. A flush stained her face scarlet to the roots of her curly, black hair. One hand flew to her cheek. "Oh, my goodness," she exclaimed as she squinted into a tiny round mirror, its surface scratched and mottled. Her own startled expression was staring back at her.

Quickly she snapped the case shut and returned it to its place beside him. "You get some rest now," was all she could think to say before she hurried away.

The young man's laughter followed her down the corridor.

Dr. Mary's rounds were not always so pleasant.

She poked her nose into the daily business of the army wards, and uncovered too many cases of malpractice and neglect. She was not above snooping to get information, and when she harped on the second-rate treatment of her brave boys, many of the doctors in charge of the badly managed facilities declared her a damned nuisance. Word got around Washington that the 'little devil in britches' had appointed herself as watchdog for the invalids.

Her keen eyes missed nothing, from the smallest disservice to the largest error in judgment. Once she discovered some bone of contention, she chewed at it like a tenacious terrier, barking and growling her criticisms to anyone she thought could change the status quo. The most horrific problem was—in her estimation—the exorbitant number of amputations being performed, either because the Ward Surgeons were too lazy to extend extra treatment, or because they were more interested in honing their skills than saving arms and legs.

More often than not the mutilated victims were poor, illiterate men, many of them simple farmers who needed all their limbs if they were to return to productive lives.

Early one morning Dr. Mary lingered unnoticed in an alcove near the surgery, a small, square room with two large windows that took advantage of the outside daylight.

A narrow, wooden block with chunky legs served as an operating table. Its surface, as well as the legs and the floor around them, was covered with gore and bloodstains, some fresh rusty red, others dried black with age.

The operating theater had the odor of a killing shed not far removed from a hog slaughter. Filthy cloths littered the area, and unwashed instruments lay nearby on an upturned wooden barrel. Bits of flesh and clots of blood clung to the tools of amputation: a tenotomy knife to sever tendons; a catling (two-edged scalpel); two bistoury knives; a hand saw; forceps; and several probes. Such was the setting for the terrible drama unfolding there.

Dr. Mary peered cautiously around the doorframe to find a youth of nineteen or twenty pinned to the table by two burly orderlies. The hair rose on the back of her neck as she listened to the poor lad begging, "Please don't cut it off. For God's sake don't cut off my arm."

She stepped back, but the sounds of his struggle with his tormentors reached her clearly. She stuffed a fist in her mouth.

"Come along, now," the doctor ordered, "we have to do this if we are to save your life."

"But it's healing. Can't you see it's healing?" he screeched, bucking and straining against his captors.

"Shove that rag in his mouth and hold him down," the surgeon snarled. "I don't have the time or the patience for these childish histrionics."

Mary bit down on her fist to keep from screaming herself as the young soldier choked and gagged and then mercifully fainted.

Tears engulfed her as the specific warnings of her Medical Jurisprudence Professor at Syracuse restrained her from interfering. One of the cardinal rules he ordained was, "Thou shalt not come between a brother physician and his patient."

But she also recalled another rule, "First do no harm."

When the surgery was over, the unconscious patient was placed on a cot well away from the surgery. It would never do for new victims to see the end results.

Dr. Mary waited until the surgeon had left the building before examining the boy's wound, which was still oozing blood. It looked as if a guillotine had missed his head and taken his arm off. The butcher had severed his left one halfway between his elbow and shoulder.

The lad groaned and slowly came awake.

"What's your name," she asked, avoiding his eyes as she examined him.

"Darsey Johnson," he whispered, his chalky face a mask of agony and regret.

She looked at him then. "How do you do, Darsey Johnson," she replied. "I'm Dr. Mary."

He swallowed hard, gulping back nauseous bile, as he looked toward the place where his arm should have been. "Oh, my God," he moaned as he wagged his head from side to side on the pillow. "How will I ever face my family? The girl I'm to marry? I'm a cripple. I'm half a man."

"Stop that. Stop that, right now," Mary commanded, her tone stern as his sergeant's had been.

He quit, immediately.

Her voice softened. "No, Mr. Johnson, you are more of a man, now. You gave up something precious in a fight for your country. Don't ever think of yourself as anything but a hero. That is how I will always remember you."

He cried a little more, quiet tears oozing from the corners of his eyes.

She packed the bloody stump and wrapped it snugly to stem the blood and protect the exposed muscle endings. When he began to moan in agony and shock, she dosed him with laudanum, took him in her arms, and crooned to him like a child until he drifted off to sleep.

Hours after she went to bed that night, she could not close her eyes. She tossed and turned, hearing the ghastly cries from the operating room reverberating through her aching brain.

It was nearly four A.M., when she fell into the dark pit of a nightmare haunted by the pitiful boy who had been mutilated for no legitimate reason. The sound of the surgeon's saw ripping through his humerus was so real she shrieked herself awake.

Soaked with sweat and choking back rasping sobs that threatened to tear out her throat, she rocked back and forth on her cot in an effort to gain control. Once she had calmed herself, she got out of bed, threw a shawl over her gown, and sat barefoot at the window watching pale rosy streaks forecast the dawn of a lovely day.

But Darsey Johnson's day would never be truly beautiful for him.

Her racing mind sorted through solutions, searching for clever ways to prevent such tragedies in the future.

Absently she rubbed her cold feet. Still in the depths of a brown study, she rose and went to the chest of drawers to find a pair of heavy stockings. She drew them on, relieved at the warmth they afforded.

Pacing her small cubicle, she examined the options. It would never do a bit of good to complain to any surgeon about an incompetent colleague. That was a fact. Physicians stood behind one another, because each knew he might some day need the same courtesy for himself. That was another fact.

Besides, it would not help her get her illusive commission if she were branded with the stigma of a tattler. But there was more than one way to plough the fields, as her Papa was heard to say. There's east to west, and north to south, and corner-to-corner. Make a choice and get on with it.

She wrote of her decision: "I then made up my mind that it was the last case that would ever occur if it was in my power to prevent such cruel loss of limbs . . . Having had a little experience and observation regarding the inability of some ward surgeons to diagnose properly and truthfully, I considered that I had a higher duty than came under the head of medical etiquette."

From then on, she surreptitiously examined every victim she found awaiting imminent amputation. If the arm or leg, hand or foot, had the remotest chance of being saved, she swore the man to secrecy and instructed him on how to avoid the surgery.

"The doctor cannot amputate without your permission. Just stick to your guns. Scream and holler. Do whatever it takes to fight for your rights and refuse the operation."

Dr. Mary took a huge risk. If the Ward Surgeons discovered her treason, she would be barred from military hospitals forever. Her Union Army commission would be a dream gone sour as month-old cream.

No matter. The welfare of patients was her first priority. If she were discovered, so be it. She would find other ways to help the needy soldiers.

Dr. Walker was not the only protester against unnecessary amputations. Brave nurses like Sophronia Bucklin at Gettysburg and Mary Newcomb at Mount City Hospital stood up to chop-happy surgeons and saved the limbs of patients with superficial injuries. Civil War tradition declares that many a soldier returned to his loved ones all in one piece, thanks to the boundless courage of the plucky little surgeon from Oswego.

CHAPTER TWENTY-THREE

FREDERICKSBURG, VIRGINIA

REPORTS FILTERED BACK to the capital after the horrendous battle of Fredericksburg: 1180 dead, 9028 wounded, and over 2000 men missing.

With the Confederates less than thirty miles away from Washington, most terrified civilians hustled to complete their errands by daylight and scurry back to lock themselves into the questionable safety of their homes.

On her evening strolls, Mary felt profound distaste for her surroundings but absolutely no fear of them. She strode the familiar avenues with the air of a regent surveying her realm, staring down any young punks who dared to approach her. That she even dared to venture forth after dark among the marauders in the city is a typical example of her fearlessness and her faith in her own immortality.

An outspoken prohibitionist, she was revolted by the depraved behavior of the sodden drunkards she dodged as they staggered along the sidewalks, clinging to buildings and lamp posts to keep from falling on their faces.

She silently cheered as Military Police raided brothels, gambling houses, and saloons, dragging out besotted, disorderly wretches by the scruffs of their unwashed necks. Mary despised fornicators and adulterers even more than she hated drunks. They would become subjects covered in both her published books written later on.

By mid-December her patience was overloaded. Sick to death of the backbiting and petty politics in the Army Wards and fed up with Washington's chaotic climate, she packed her trunk, outfitted her medicine kit and began the arduous trek over land and river to Fredericksburg, where battle-abused men sorely needed her expert ministrations.

Polly Craig

❧❀☙

As she stood on the slippery shore of the Rappahannock, a biting wind stole her breath, billowing it around her head in a foggy mist. Her feet and hands were numb with cold, but her heavy woolen circular kept her body warm and cozy. A knitted muffler covered her head and ears. Her felt hat with its perky feather was fitted over the scarf and pulled low on her forehead, shading her eyes from the snowy glare.

Even the horrors at Warrenton had not prepared her for the scene she faced as she crossed the river toward the scene of General Burnside's sickening defeat.

Her stomach churned as she walked along the foot of Marye's Hill beside Sunken Road's Stone Wall, the breastwork that had concealed the crafty Confederate troops. It was there they had patiently hunkered down, rifles at the ready, while the Union Army forded the muddy river on their ponderous pontoon bridges.

She imagined the Rebels, safely hidden, as their booming muskets and rifles mowed down Burnside's advancing army. Like shooting fish in a barrel, she grieved.

The noxious miasma of spent gunpowder still hung on the air, deadly testimony of the massacre. Despite the freezing weather, the battlefield was redolent with the stink of rotting entrails and evacuated feces as soldiers' sphincters relaxed at the moment of death.

Fredericksburg, the once graceful little Virginia city, squatted in the twilight, still cringing from the firestorm of 5000 shells raining down on the defenseless town during General Burnside's infamous two hour, pre-battle barrage. It lay embarrassed to silence by the gaping black holes that pockmarked its weathered brick houses. Melting icicles hanging from damaged eaves dripped wet tears, weeping over the charred walls of ancient ancestral homes hideously defaced by fire.

Before the battles began, a confederate order had evacuated the town's six thousand inhabitants.

Afterwards, the enraged Federal Army had raced through abandoned houses, shamelessly looting, plundering, stealing what they wanted and smashing everything they could not use. The stately groves became a wasteland of broken furniture, books, and artifacts. A china-faced dolly lay in the snow, its tiny flower-printed dress soiled and torn. Somewhere a little girl mourned for her kidnapped baby.

Mary was glad that the town's citizens had not been there to witness such devastation.

Burial details shooed away relentless, scavenging crows that flapped and cawed as they attacked the pitiful carrion that were once proud soldiers fighting for their lives.

She turned her attention to the wounded warriors of the Army of the Potomac lying in houses and outbuildings that had been commandeered for hospital use. The dead were beyond her help. The living must be cared for.

One of the first sights to greet her was a scraggly-looking ambulatory soldier, sitting in a doorway on the blackened skeleton of a kitchen stool, sucking on a wrinkled cigarette.

Arms akimbo, she approached him, scowling like an angry fishwife. She stamped her foot on the frozen ground. "Look at you," she growled.

He stood quickly, toppling his seat.

"Snuff that thing out," she ordered. This is a hospital."

She walked right up close and peered into his red-rimmed eyes. "You shouldn't be smoking anyway. It's disastrous for your lungs."

The young man stared her up and down, caught the heat of her anger and pinched off the lighted end. He stuffed the butt into his pocket. Lord knew when he would find another.

"How did you come by tobacco out here, anyway?" Mary asked.

"Why, Ma'am, we traded our coffee and sugar with the Rebs whilst we was waitin' to go into battle." Proud of Yankee ingenuity, he boasted, "We made little boats and floated them back and forth across the river."

"I see," she replied, shaking her head. "Well, don't let me see you light that filthy thing in here again."

"Yes, Ma'am . . . er . . . I mean, no, Ma'am," he stuttered and limped off, rushing to escape her fury.

My God, she mused, the poor fools on both sides trade with their enemies one minute and kill each other the next. How ludicrous. How totally obscene.

Without even checking her references, the frazzled Managing Surgeons in Fredericksburg directed Mary to choose the cases she wished to evacuate then prepare them for transport to Washington, this time by boat.

The horrendous injuries she encountered broke her heart. Young lads in their teens lay twisted and broken, one with a silver dollar size hole in his skull through which she glimpsed his pulsating brain before he quietly expired. Gut-shot farmers, their ropy, gangrenous intestines held in place with dirty towels, drifted into unconsciousness, crying for their mothers.

Here in this foul place, frightened men awaited amputations that, once again, she deemed unnecessary. Exercising great care, she launched her surreptitious campaign. After soliciting their solemn oath of secrecy, she whispered to the victims behind the surgeons' backs, "You are not obliged to submit to surgery. Your body belongs to you. Protest the amputation, and if the surgeons insist, swear like a dock worker and tell them if they force you to have the operation, you will never rest after your recovery until you have searched them out and shot them dead."

That should show those over zealous-quacks we mean business, she told herself.

Her justification for "ignoring etiquette towards her medical and surgical brothers," was threefold. Besides the prevention of unnecessary crippling of the soldiers, families were saved from the loss of their menfolk's full earning capacities, and the government was saved millions of dollars in pensions and disability benefits.

Long after the war was over, she continued to defend her position against wholesale amputation. One of her strongest arguments appeared to be the fact that under such adverse conditions in the field, post-surgical soldiers died anyway of trauma and infection from the very procedures that were meant to save their lives. On the other hand, when wounds were antiseptically treated, patients generally survived with a limp or a stiff arm, so much better than a vacant spot where the usable limb should still be.

Dr. Mary evacuated as many of the desperately injured as the transport boats would carry. On the first day, the weather had warmed unseasonably. Underfoot, the ground thawed, and brick-red mud sucked at the boots of the Federal soldiers slogging through knee-deep muck that later in the month prompted one officer to exaggerate his need for '50 men, 25 feet high, to work in mud 18 feet deep.'

Mary appeared on the dock in her tunic and trousers, her slender waist encircled with a bright green sash signifying surgeon's status–that by right she was not entitled to wear.

She monitored the loading with the skill of a drill sergeant, checking, watching, listening.

To her dismay, the healthy personnel sweating over their burdens, were carrying her precious wounded charges head first down the gangplank. "Hold on, there," she shouted, running forward, her stout boots making clip clop sounds as they pattered down the wooden dock. "Here, you, turn my patients around," she cried. "Can't you see that tilting their heads downward can only give them more pain than they already have? Besides, on a warm day like this you might cause serious congestion in their brains."

There was no escaping her vigilance. Every bearer did an about face. Every stretcher bore its cargo, feet first, down the gangway for the rest of the day.

During the return trip, as the ship lurched on its winding course, one of the patients, a ten-year-old boy whose legs had been completely destroyed as he drummed the troops onto the field, died without revealing his identity. Nobody aboard knew the child's name, either. Mary was beside herself, mourning the fact that some frantic mama would never know what happened to her baby.

Back in Washington she encountered a disconsolate mother searching the Women's Relief Rolls for the name of her little son. Mary gently described the miniature hero, and the distraught mother, recognizing her child, collapsed into the doctor's arms, too devastated to weep.

Later over tea the woman, a recent widow with dishwater complexion and wispy, mouse-brown hair sobbed quietly as she told Mary that Jonathan had been her only child.

"My husband is gone; my son is gone; I have nothing to go home to," she cried. "Let me stay here and work. I can help other mothers' sons, Dr. Walker. There must be something I can do."

Mary questioned administrators as she went about her rounds, and soon found the woman a position in the Washington Insane Asylum caring for pitiful victims who had nowhere else to go. The woman stayed until the end of the war, giving her love to shell-shocked boys who were lost to the world around them.

Although she hated to admit it, Dr. Mary was exhausted and nearly broke, again. She decided it was time to replenish her capital. The little money she had made in New York was spent bribing her way to Fredericksburg after she had personally paid for the drugs, balms, and sedatives to outfit her medical case.

Except for an inadequate place to lay her head and meager army rations to eat, Mary had received no compensation for her diligent work. Her normally slight little body was frailer than ever.

In late January of 1863, Dr. Preston King, a colleague at Fredericksburg, who had witnessed her selfless dedication first hand, advised Mary, "I've written to the Secretary of War on your behalf with a glowing list of your services. I requested that you be refunded the money you paid out of your own pocket for expenses and disbursements for soldiers' relief."

When his request was refused, he could scarcely contain his anger. "Unfortunately," he said, bitterness hardening his voice, "there's no lawful authority making allowance to you, therefore, no reimbursement will be forthcoming. I'm so very sorry, Dr. Mary.

"Nor," he apologized, "will there be a commission for you. There's no precedent for it, and no one in the War Office will take the chance to set one."

One more discouraging rejection was added to her long list.

But quitting was not on Mary's agenda. There had to be a way around the bureaucratic red tape, and, by God, she would find it.

She promised Dr. King that she would return to the front as soon as her resources allowed, and Dr. King was grateful for every word of it.

CHAPTER TWENTY-FOUR

NEW YORK/WASHINGTON/AQUIA CREEK

DURING HER LECTURES, audiences up and down New York State sat mesmerized as Dr. Mary described the disastrous scenes she'd witnessed at Warrenton and Fredericksburg. Her prepared speech was meant to encourage questions from her listeners, yet they sat tongue-tied as she related her grim experiences.

"Death was my enemy," she declared, gritting her teeth. "The casualties at Fredericksburg were slaughtered like cattle. They were sprawled in frozen heaps, while the wounded lay among them, begging for help, praying to heaven, or screaming for God to deliver them from this hell on earth.

"After dark," she continued, "eerie Confederate music drifted across the desecrated fields as the Aurora Borealis, oblivious of the carnage below, lit the night sky with its wondrous colors."

Men and women alike, most with relatives in the Union Army, snuffled into their handkerchiefs as she went on. "I saw bloated corpses relieved of their shirts and jackets and shoes by freezing Confederate soldiers who were reduced to robbing the dead, because they were too poorly outfitted to withstand Virginia's rigorous winter climate."

A few mothers fainted at the tale of the little, legless drummer boy, and others fled the auditorium as she described the pitiful, overcrowded conditions of the Union hospitals.

"I do not tell these harrowing stories to titillate or horrify but to encourage your contributions of money, blankets, and linen for bandages." Her audiences reached deep into their pockets and ransacked their attics for unused extras.

For relief from the harshest details of war, her lectures were softened with anecdotes about Washington City and the nation's first family. Hungry for news of their leader, loyal listeners ate it up.

"Mrs. Lincoln is lively and pleasing in appearance," she said "while the President is cordial and does not unduly feel the dignity of his position. He is roughly handsome when he smiles—which is seldom."

Amazed gasps from the listeners followed as she related, "There were delightful evening dinners served at beautifully appointed tables beneath sparkling gasoliers."

Since their heavier meal was eaten at noon and a lighter supper served after sundown, the common folk wondered how those Washington people slept with all that rich food roiling around in their bellies.

Her intimate knowledge of the city enabled her to describe famous landmarks that the curious country citizens might never get to see. Her descriptions were vivid and her authoritative comments on the temperament of the capital's population raised many a surprised eyebrow.

Clad in her usual costume, she constantly took the opportunity to campaign for dress reform. Women in their steel boned corsets patted their caged waistlines and nodded their agreement, but few changed their minds about their clothes. One needed the steadfast fortitude of a fearless Amazon to buck male public opinion, and that measure of bravery was in short supply.

Despite her busy schedule, Dr. Mary kept up with current events through the newspapers, and she was not shy about refuting facts with which she disagreed.

In March of 1863, she contributed a witty article to *The Sybil.* "Women drag their soggy long skirts and petticoats through the muddy streets of Washington, looking like laundresses lugging double loads of dirty wet wash tied to their middles." One week after it was published, she spoke at a Dress Reform Convention in Rochester, New York, where she was elected sixth vice president.

The last article she sent to the magazine in 1863 described her work as a volunteer and earned the thanks of the Republican Party along with those of hundreds of Federal soldiers.

"The exercising of one's right to vote is guaranteed by the United States Constitution, and, therefore, is the prime responsibility of every adult citizen, male or female."

On the Saturday night previous to the election, she sat up until midnight, helping to write transportation orders for the furloughs of New York soldiers so they could get home in time to vote the Union ticket.

Her fight for women's suffrage would continue long after her war duties ended.

However, she never sent an account to *The Sybil* about her altercation with the police in New York City when an overweight Irish copper clad in a brass-buttoned uniform placed her under arrest. At the trial his explanation of the charges to the black-robed judge brought titters from the gallery.

"Yer Honor," he began in a brogue as thick as potato soup, "I glimpsed this apparition strollin' along Grand Street, big as life."

The giggles from the crowd brought a rap from the judge's gavel, but the officer's chest swelled with his own importance. "I was astonished at the sight of all them long curls hangin' down the back of her coat, because, when I looked down below, I saw the owner was wearin' a pair of trousers."

Mary told the judge, "I always walk around the capital in my trousers."

The judge shushed her. "Go on, Rooney," he ordered. "Well, I says to meself, well, this is a fine kettle of fish, Patrick Rooney. So I arrested the lady for appearin' in public dressed in men's clothing."

A lawyer named Mott who'd heard Mary speak jumped up and asked, "If it please your honor, I pray for leniency. Dr. Walker's benevolence to the poor Union boys fightin' the dastardly slavers deserves that, at least."

The judge let her off with the warning, "Go home and put on a dress, Madam."

It was the same old speech she'd heard in another courtroom.

Matthew Brady, famous war photographer, exhibited his work in a New York gallery. When Mary stood staring at his poignant battlefield portraits of the dead and dying, her heart lurched in her breast.

Passers-by wept with her as tears ran down her cheeks, tears for all the lives and limbs she had been unable to save. Oh God, she thought, what am I doing here, safe in New York, while my brave boys are lying in agony on some freezing ground in Virginia?

She totted up her earnings and assembled her travel gear. With her finances in satisfactory order, it was time for her to get back to her mission.

Her arrival in Washington found the political climate a mixture of blistering contempt by Democrats from the heartland who fought conscription and encouraged desertion from an army that was fighting to 'free the Negroes and enslave whites,' while heated arguments from the Republicans supported the Emancipation Proclamation with equal passion.

Mary's politics were simple and basic—help the injured, heal the sick, and rehabilitate the wounded. She saw need and jumped in with both feet, as her father would say.

In May of 1863, she wangled a ten-day pass to Aquia Creek, a spillover running between the Potomac and Fredericksburg. Casualties were being transported through viscous, rust-colored sludge in covered, two-wheeled horse-drawn vehicles so overcrowded those on the bottom were in danger of suffocating. Victims were jostled so roughly they arrived with fresh bruises and newly broken bones. They came in from Fredericksburg, Culpepper and Manassas to await disposition to other billets.

Dr. Mary bandaged them and empathized with their bitter feelings of loss and betrayal, comforting them all, counseling many, and burying the pitiful gonners who had 'crossed to the other side.'

When her pass expired, she overstayed her welcome until she was ordered back to Washington.

CHAPTER TWENTY-FIVE

WASHINGTON CITY

ON AUGUST 18, 1863, Indian Agent, "Buffalo Bill" Cody was the featured speaker at a meeting of the Union League of America, a patriotic group organized the year before. Its first and most pressing agendas were the encouragement of enlistments and the soliciting of financial support for the war policies of the Republican administration.

Whenever she was in Washington, Dr. Mary attended these meetings and often lectured to the constituents.

The newspaper, *The National Republican,* reported Cody's speech and mentioned Mary's dissertation on her experiences with the Army of the Potomac. She closed her remarks with a poem she had adapted, a parody on a popular ditty of the times, entitled *The Old Arm-Chair.*

Poets may cringe at its literary merit, but her flowery words are sincere testimony to her deep and abiding loyalty of country and flag.

In a rousing, emotional delivery she recited the following:

> *"I love it! I love it! Oh who shall dare*
> *To chide me for loving that flag so fair?*
> *I treasured it long for the patriot's pride*
> *And wept for the heroes who for it died.*
> *'Tis bound by a thousand spells to my heart,*
> *Nothing on earth can e'er us part.*
> *Would you learn the spell?*
> *There is liberty there,*
> *Making that flag the fairest of fair.*

Then chide me not if here I wave
That flag, redeemed by my brothers brave,
For while I live that flag shall be
Waving over you and me.
When I'm buried 'neath the ground.
Wrap that flag my corpse around,
Plant that flag above my grave,
There let it wave! Let it wave!"

Information from the front indicated that the Yankees were having a miserable time of it. August heat and humidity on the Virginia battlefields were felling the weary soldiers as often as Rebel bullets were knocking them to the ground.

A relentless sun beat down on unclimatized northerners who were baking inside their heavy, woolen uniforms. They were short of palatable drinking water, and lugging burdensome gear up hilly terrain raised their temperatures to dangerous highs. The lads dropped by the roadsides, their frazzled minds disoriented from heat and sunstroke.

These horrendous conditions brought matters close to Dr. Mary one hot, muggy night as she tossed and turned on her rooming house cot. She sat bolt upright as a loud knocking battered her door. She drew on a wrapper and hurried to see what caused such a ruckus.

Standing outside on the stoop were two frantic women who, Mary later learned, were a Mrs. Wrenn and her daughter-in-law.

Not a 'how-do-you-do' nor an apology for waking her was offered by either visitor. Instead, both launched their pleas in voices strangled with tears, neither making a bit of sense. Mary glanced around then urged them inside.

"Stop, stop," she said. "One at a time."

"Please, Dr. Walker," cried the older one, a nervous, grandmotherly woman who twisted the strap of her small handbag.

"I beg you, find my son and bring him home to us. He has suffered from sunstroke and is confined to a hospital in Virginia."

"I can't . . ." Mary began.

The woman clutched the front of Mary's loose gown. "Please don't say no. You are our last resort."

The younger one, pretty but disheveled in her grief, interrupted. "Let go of her, Mother Wrenn, you are not helping matters."

With tears pouring from her eyes, the girl explained. "Our little boy is dangerously ill. We could lose him at any moment. He is the apple of his Papa's eye . . ." Her voice trailed off.

"We've tried everything we could," cried the grandmother, taking up the plea, "but we are not allowed to go to the front to search for him." Her shoulders shook with convulsive sobs she seemed powerless to stifle.

To calm them, Mary fetched them water and ushered them into the landlady's parlor.

She made a note of all the particulars they could give her. "Go home and take care of your little boy," she advised. "I'll start for Virginia at first light."

"You will find him," the young one said. "I know you will."

"I shall do my best, but that is all I can promise. Now go home and see to your baby."

As she packed her gear, Mary thought about Secretary Stanton at the War Office, but there was no telling when she could get an audience with the man. Given his anti-female politics, he probably would refuse her permission to travel to the battle area, anyway.

Foregoing the problems of wrestling with bureaucratic red tape, Mary set off at dawn, without a pass. The moment she crossed the Potomac, she was challenged.

"Halt. State your business or turn back," ordered a stocky young soldier, brandishing a long-barreled Springfield rifle.

Mary didn't bother to enlighten the sentry. She squared her shoulders and pointed a finger in his face. She ordered in her most officious voice, "Take me to the officer of the guard. There's no time to repeat my story twice."

"Oh, I don't know, Ma'am," he replied, keeping his weapon at the ready.

"Do it!" she commanded. "Now."

The soldier did an about-face and hustled off with Mary dead on his heels.

Once she reached the lieutenant in charge, she made quick work of her explanation. At first he insisted that civilians without authorization were not allowed beyond that point.

"Those are my strict orders, straight from headquarters," he said. "It's just too dangerous out there. Quite frankly, I cannot fathom how you even got across the bridge."

"I've been to many fronts in my capacity as contract surgeon," Mary lied. "I assure you I know exactly what to expect."

He scanned her trousers and tunic and smiled. "You that Dr. Mary what brung the boys back from Fredericksburg?"

"The very same," Mary replied, allowing a tinge of pride to creep into her voice.

"Well I'll be damned . . ." His cheeks flushed crimson as he stuttered, "Please . . . 'scuse me Ma'am . . . I didn't mean . . ."

Mary smiled and waved her hand signaling forgiveness at his lapse.

"Very well, I'll let you go," he relented, "but you gotta bring your man back this time, too."

"That's just what I intend to do," she promised.

She hitched a train ride at Alexandria, traveling with officers headed for the Headquarters of the Army of the Potomac. One of the gentlemen wrote a description of the cocky little woman who traveled on her own:

"She was attired in a small straw hat with a cockade in front and a pair of blue pantaloons and a long frock coat. Over all she had a linen duster and this, coupled with the fact that she had rips in her boots gave her a trig appearance. She was liberal in her advice to all comers and especially exhorted two newspaper boys to immediately wash their faces, in which remark she was clearly correct."

At the end of the train line, the doctor found herself still five miles north of the camp where Lieutenant Wrenn was last stationed.

It took considerable coaxing before The Christian Association at the depot lent her a horse, and she rode off on her own with skimpy directions and no map to consult.

Shouts and rifle shots echoed on either side of her, but she kept her head low over the horse's neck and urged him on.

When she arrived at her destination, Major Drummond at Headquarters was astounded that she had traveled alone through territory where the rival armies were skirmishing.

"I heard the gun fire," she told him, "but I didn't have time to worry about it. I need to take your Lieutenant Wrenn back to his family immediately. If his little son dies without his father, the man won't be any good to the army, to his family or to himself."

The Major shook his head in wonder, thinking he wouldn't ride through that hostile territory alone if the order came from President Lincoln, himself.

He issued a leave of absence for Wrenn and ordered an ambulance fitted for travel.

But first Mary had to stabilize her patient.

Enlisted men stood gawking, bug-eyed, thinking even their own mamas would not do the things this woman did to a grown man's body.

The tiny doctor rolled the unconscious lieutenant out of his woolen uniform and bathed his naked torso with cool water to lower his temperature. To get a few precious drops of fluid into him, she soaked her fingers and shoved them into his mouth, rubbing his throat to make him swallow.

When she had done all she could to relieve the lieutenant's symptoms, she loaded her patient and climbed in beside him. A safer return route was chosen, and one soldier drove the wagon while Mary pillowed Wrenn's head against the bumps and jolts. A second soldier was sent along to return the borrowed horse to the station.

The trip back was a nightmare for the sick man. Nausea and dizziness from heat exhaustion exacerbated by the rolling motion of the cart left him limp as a rag doll.

After jolting for miles in the army wagon, he was carried to the train where Mary made a comfortable nest of blankets for him in one of the boxcars that rocked and rolled along the uneven tracks. Two small candles commandeered from the Christian Association dimly illuminated the murky interior of the car.

At Alexandria, Wrenn was transferred by ambulance and stretchered onto a boat that carted them to Washington. From the boat the poor man was carried to a streetcar. When the tram reached the soldier's street, Mary convinced the conductor it was his patriotic duty to carry the sick soldier to his front door.

Grumbling that he was too old to be conscripted, the fellow threw the lieutenant's arms about his neck and hoisted him onto his back. Mary grasped the waistband of Wrenn's trousers and hefted some of the weight. They trudged up the walk and banged on the door.

Dr. Mary and the disgruntled conductor were ignored completely as mother and wife screamed their welcome to a man who could barely fathom how he came into their presence.

She treated the soldier and his son for several days until both were out of danger. The lieutenant and his little boy recovered fully, and Wrenn returned to duty.

Back in Washington, Dr. Mary tended to civilian patients for payment to make up for her non-existent income from the military. She wondered if there would ever come a day when her efforts would be recognized and rewarded.

CHAPTER TWENTY-SIX

WASHINGTON CITY/CHICKAMAUGA

MOONLIGHT washed through her boardinghouse window, but Dr. Mary found no relief in the sleep she craved as she lay on her cot—her thoughts of Edwin too near the surface.

Edwin. Why can't I forget you after all these years?

She recalled his soft brown hair and impish smile. His brown eyes haunted her. But even the ghostly longing for him could not distract her for long. She willed herself to think of current events.

Terrible casualty reports were bombarding the grief-stricken capital, with no respite in sight. The Confederates were exacting a horrendous toll on the Federals who were ordered to attack despite the odds against breaching protected breastworks.

Earlier that day, Dr. Mary had again been denied her commission by a contemptuous official who quickly scanned her letters of recommendation and threw them down on his desk. "They are not relevant," he said. "Women are not fit for service in the Union Army Surgeons Corps."

As she lay there, hot tears spilled down her temples, dampening her pillow. Her reasonable mind tried to reject the questions she could never answer. Still they came.

Why was her expertise so desperately needed on the front lines dismissed so casually? Surely she was more experienced in trauma treatment than the young medical students who were being chosen instead of her. How would they know that the farm boys needed special counseling because they were so susceptible to communicable disease? How could they have the patience to comfort them when they were dying of homesickness?

Surely she could save countless lives while the new recruits were cutting their teeth on hideous injuries for which their schooling had not prepared them. On-the-battlefield-training would cost lives. God forbid amputations increase.

I have to stop this wallowing, she thought, swiping at her wet temples. I haven't come this far just to let the prejudices of stupid men defeat me. Somewhere, someone will give me a chance.

But in the meantime, her boys needed her, pay or no pay.

Chickamauga means 'river of death,' a fitting name for one of the bloodiest battles ever fought in the Western Hemisphere. Its carnage was exceeded only by the infamous slaughter at Gettysburg and the three-day massacre for control of a marshy Virginia tract called the Wilderness, fought in the spring of 1864 between General Grant's Army of the Potomac and General Lee's Army of Northern Virginia.

That Rosecrans had believed the lies of Bragg's infiltrating, 'deserter' spies who sneaked behind Union lines to plant misinformation about the retreat of the Confederate Army is beside the point. The devastating results of the defeat at Chickamauga were undeniable.

Sluggish waters of lazy creeks with unfamiliar Indian names ran scarlet with the blood of fallen soldiers fighting under the banner of the Army of the Cumberland. Damaged trees genuflected over stream banks as if the bloody waters could miraculously rejuvenate their twisted limbs.

Thousands of dead mules lined the roadways as exhausted soldiers on half rations shuffled by foraging for food. Coarse horse corn was all they could salvage from the fields around the burned-out farmhouses.

Abandoned to the carnivores that scavenged among them, mutilated bodies perfumed with the sickish, metallic smell of violent death sprawled in the trenches. They lay broken and twisted, their sightless eyes staring into oblivion.

Between skirmishes, spiritually beaten men huddled in scraggly groups, sharing cigarette butts and speaking little. Weakened by diarrhea and scurvy, they sat toe to toe, their backs hunched over, their dirty faces etched with despair.

Some wrapped themselves in tattered blankets and slept on the hard ground with weapons beneath them hidden from thieves.

Before each battle every last one of them tasted fear. They were afraid to go forward for fear they would die. They were afraid to retreat for fear they'd be labeled cowards. They fought mostly because the men to the left and right of them fought, squeezing their sphincters to contain bowels that had turned to liquid the instant the "forward" sounded.

Morale had sunk into the pits. The half-naked troops were cold, vermin infested, filthy and scared. Yet, when it came time to fight, the soldiers hauled themselves up the steep slopes like mountain goats scuttling for the top. The dawning sun glinted off their hoisted bayonets as the exhausted fighters screamed their battle cry, "Huzzah."

Such were the horrific images that greeted Dr. Mary as she entered the Chattanooga battle scene.

By now she had adopted the permanent, unofficial uniform that was meant to set her apart from civilian orderlies. Her Navy blue tunic was cut like that of a Federal officer's, and a wide stripe of gold braid marched down the sides of her matching trousers. Her heavy braid was tucked up beneath a straw hat adorned with a perky ostrich feather. The unauthorized green surgeon's sash still circled her narrow waist.

Secreted in one pocket was a small black identity case containing her vital information lest she be killed or wounded while working on the battlefields.

Her leather physician's kit contained tin bottles of opium for diarrhea, mercury and chalk boluses for constipation, quinine for fevers, a pokeroot solution for "camp-itch." Hidden under mustard plasters was a precious vial of chloroform that she dispensed only when performing the most painful surgeries.

She refused to carry the usual stock of whiskey or brandy for pain, and one day she astounded a surgeon by pouring his supply of alcohol over a patient's wound instead of pouring it down his throat.

"What are you doing?" he cried. "The patient is supposed to drink that to ease his pain."

"I'm sterilizing his wound, sir," she said with a straight face. "It will do more long-term good on the outside, but once he drinks it, the effects will soon be dissipated."

Quietly, she practiced medicine, arranged furloughs for family emergencies and secretly counseled victims against amputations.

She approached every commanding officer she met, pleading her case for a commission. Failing that, she cited her ability to travel the countryside and begged to be used as a spy. Generals Winfield Hancock, Darius Couch, and George Meade refused her to a man. While sorely tempted, they decided it would be impolitic to employ such a visible woman.

Each denial she received stabbed her heart. She was giving every ounce of her energy and expertise to the war effort, yet her gender was the only thing that the obtuse commanders could see. They didn't mind asking her for help when it served their interests, but suitable rewards for it were not to be given.

She had done her best under the most horrific conditions. No matter how often she prayed for relief, treatable men were dying for want of proper equipment and adequate supplies.

Finally, exhausted, her medicines depleted, her morale at its lowest ebb, she accompanied a train full of wounded back to Washington.

Hiding her frustrations behind her inevitable smile, she bustled about among her boys, reassuring them that all would be well once they were admitted to the better hospitals in Washington. She was thankful that the railway cars were now more suitably fitted out to accommodate the wounded.

To accomplish this, Dr. Elisha Harris of the U. S. Sanitary Commission had revised train car interiors into more comfortable accommodations for casualty transport. He had all the passenger seats removed from the cars and replaced by tall racks. Stretchers were then suspended from the racks with heavy India rubber bands. As the slow-moving rail cars puffed and jerked along the tracks, the stretchers swayed like oversized cradles, soothing and lulling the strapped-in patients.

The engine screeched and rattled, hissed and shuddered, permeating the air with a noxious mixture of wood smoke and scalding axle-box grease. The trip seemed endless as Mary stared through the smutty windows at the sparks and black soot belching out of the huge-bellied smoke funnel.

Back at the capital, she once again distributed her sick and maimed boys among Washington's teeming hospitals, renewing military acquaintances and checking on chronic patients as she went.

But on the trip home from Chattanooga, she had hit on a plan altogether different from any she had previously tried.

It was time to plough the field in a different direction.

∽⟋❀⟍∽

Edwin Stanton threw the communication on his desk, slammed his fist down on top of it, and jumped to his feet. His chair went flying, and half of the important papers on his desk scattered to the floor. He stamped up and down the room, smacking the fist of one hand into the palm of the other. Whap. Whap. Whap.

"That damnable woman is at it again," he yelled, though no one was in the room to hear. "When will she learn to take no for an answer?"

Everyone on the floor of the building heard the outburst and smiled. Since Dr. Mary was the only person who twisted the Secretary's dander into such a snit, they knew exactly whom he meant. "That damnable woman" had become an unofficial heroine around the War Office.

Stanton was so incensed at Dr. Mary's audacity, that he took the rest of the day off. The moment they saw the back of his britches, his staff hustled in to get a look at the offending missile. They found it crinkled up from the boss's angry fist:

"Washington D. C. Nov.2nd, 1863

Hon. Mr. Stanton, Sec'ty of War
Will you give me the authority to get a regiment of
men, to be called Walkers U. S. Patriots, subject to
general orders for Vol. Regts.? I would like
authority to get them in any legal states, & the
authority to tell them that I will act as
First Assistant Surgeon.

*Having been so long the friend of soldiers, I feel
confident that I can be successful in getting
reenlistments of men who would not enlist for any
other persons . . . also some from prisons who were
paroled and I suppose there would be no law against
it.*

Dr. Mary Walker"

Though they knew he would refuse her, they laughed heartily at Stanton's expense and silently congratulated the pesky little doctor.

In the interim, Mary took up a new crusade. Throughout her travels, she had run across a considerable number of young women who masqueraded as men to enter the Army, some from extreme patriotism, others to be near husbands and sweethearts. She never gave them away unless their conditions warranted it.

One dauntless soldier named Frances Hook had enlisted several times. Her baggy uniform hid her identity through several battles, until she was disrobed to be treated for wounds sustained from a Confederate shell.

Dr. Mary was so impressed with her fortitude that, during her stay in Washington, she wrote Hook's story and sent it to the papers, stressing the argument that, "Congress should assign women to duty in the army with compensation . . . They perform their duties as well or better, and their stamina is well documented. Patriotism has no sex."

Mary's reputation as a Good Samaritan had gotten around. She was besieged with letters and visits from people crying out for assistance. She did her best to help as many as she could, often using her own funds to pay the way.

A Medal for Dr. Mary

Mrs. Mary Livermore documented a particularly heartrending case.

On one of her frequent visits to Indiana Hospital, Mary stopped to treat Jason Eldred, a young New Hampshire volunteer, survivor of half a dozen long marches and bloody battles. The boy had contracted consumption during his long sojourn in the steamy Southern swamps.

The moment Dr. Mary finished her examination and turned to leave, he began to cry pitifully. Perhaps her soft touch and tender words had triggered the boy's emotions. She did not know. She only knew that she had to help this brave, young soldier.

"Don't cry," she comforted. "Tell me what I can do for you."

"I need to see my mother before I die," he wept. "I haven't seen her for over a year."

Dr. Mary didn't believe in lying to patients. Jason knew his condition, and she knew that lying to him would only undermine his confidence in her.

She approached the Surgeon in charge and pleaded with him to let her take the patient back to New Hampshire.

"You'll never make it to the border with him," the man said, shaking his head in refusal. "The boy will surely die on the way."

"Then let him die trying," Mary snapped. "He deserves that much."

"Very well," the surgeon relented. "But you'd best get a move on if you have any chance of beating the odds at all."

She hurried back to Jason's bedside. "I'm going to take you home, lad. You must hold on for a while longer."

"I will see my mother again," he vowed. "I will see her."

Dr. Mary enlisted the help of a couple of the ambulatory injured and got Jason to the train within the hour. She bought the tickets herself while they supported the fainting patient.

They carried him aboard and laid him in her arms, hopping off just before the engine began chugging toward its destination.

As the train rocked and shuddered its way north, she held him close, patting him now and again to assure him she was still there. It wasn't long before she noticed the other passengers smirking and whispering behind their hands. Their insulting behavior was too much for the fair-minded doctor.

Carefully, she laid the boy down on the bench and stood to face the crowd.

Never shy about standing up for a victim, she looked each one in the eye and spoke with the authority of the righteous. "This young man is Jason Eldred. He has given up his life for his country, and now he is going home to die in his mother's arms."

Satisfied that she had chastised them sufficiently, she sat back down and took him to her breast once more.

The crowd murmured in sympathy. "We didn't know." "How can we help?"

From then on, the passengers did everything in their power to ease the lad's trip.

When they reached his town, the boy was carried to his family, whom Mary had forewarned about his perilous condition. Within the hour, the grateful soldier died, clinging to his weeping mother and sister.

Mary's tears mingled with theirs. The old anger at Cynthia's death ate at her soul, bringing with it the gift of understanding at how deeply the grief of a stricken family could run. When in God's name would all this unholy dying come to an end?

CHAPTER TWENTY-SEVEN

WASHINGTON CITY

MARY THREW BACK the comforter and padded across the room to huddle on the window seat. She watched shadows changing shapes as a gentle wind played hide and seek among the skeletal branches outside. She propped her chin on her hand and succumbed to the disturbing memories of the past few weeks.

Her beloved country was coming apart at the seams, its lifeblood leaking out on thirsty battlefields. Here in the city, things were not much better.

Just a few days before, as she had passed along the east side of the United States Treasury building, she spotted a policeman who stood gaping at a pool of fresh blood soaking into the sidewalk.

Oh, God, she thought, I see blood everywhere I go. Hmph. God? What does He have to do with the monstrous evil that stalks my country?

Instincts heightened by perils she'd encountered in the field triggered a jolting shot of adrenalin. Her hands and feet tingled, and the hair stood up on the back of her neck. She put her hand on the Colt revolver tucked in a side pocket and glanced around to check for danger. Seeing no one skulking about, she released the gun and approached the officer.

"Who's hurt? Can I help? I'm a doctor," she said, taking hold of his sleeve to distract him from his morbid fascination with the bloody spot. Judging from his horrified expression, he never could have coped with the gory sights she had witnessed on the shores of Chickamauga Creek.

"What?" he said, a bewildered look crossing his pale features. He removed his cap and ran trembling fingers through his sparse, sandy hair. He was head and shoulders taller than Mary, but he seemed to shrink before her.

"What happened here?" she repeated, pointing to the stain.

"A lady," he said. "A lady in the family way."

"Yes? Yes?" Mary insisted, urging him on.

"She was walking along and fell down there. She was bleeding . . . a lot of bleeding," he whimpered, folding his trembling hands into fists. "It was just pouring out of her . . ."

Dr. Mary, thinking the worst, grasped his elbow. "Where is she, now? Tell me where she is."

The man's face clouded with confusion. "I don't know. I put her in a carriage and sent her to the station house for instructions."

"What! Why didn't you take her directly to a hospital?" she demanded.

"Ah, the lady, Ma'am?" He spoke with conviction gleaned from experience. "She was alone. There ain't no city hospital that would take her in."

Mary dragged the story out of him, bit by bit.

"The young woman's a soldier's wife. Expecting their first child, she is. She got no letter from him for months, so she came to the city to find him—maybe in one of the hospitals.

"Said she'd check on his condition and then go home. She walked till she was near dead, trying to find a hotel. Nobody'd take her, though she had enough to pay her way."

An uncomfortable look darkened the policeman's features, as he tried to minimize his dereliction. "She seemed an honorable and intelligent woman," he exclaimed, "but, her condition was so evident, no one wanted to be responsible for her."

Mary ignored his discomfort and questioned him further, "Is there no woman's home in the city?"

He sighed with relief. At least the doctor was not blaming him.

"No, Ma'am, there's nothing of the kind. Us police officers stationed at the Baltimore & Ohio Depot try everything to place women like her. We donated more than we could afford to lotsa desperate ladies in serious trouble. We can't bear to see women suffer, you see," he finished lamely.

Feeling more confident, now that he had her ear, he pointed to one of the evergreens in Jackson Square opposite the President's House.

Mary's eyes followed his finger.

"See over there, Ma'am," he told her, "there was another woman, of good social standing, not very young, either. She had plenty of money in her pocket to pay her expenses, but she stayed under that tree the whole night. Not even a blanket to keep her warm."

Mary was stunned. Her frown knitted vertical furrows between her dark eyebrows.

"Why on earth didn't she seek lodging in one of the rooming houses?"

"When I asked her that," he replied, "the poor lady told me she visited every respectable hotel in the city, begging for a room. She didn't have no cases, except for a little handbag. They said they didn't take unescorted women who had no baggage. She had money in her pocket. Even offered to pay her expenses in advance, Ma'am, but it still made no never mind."

Mary jumped, startled out of her reverie by the scratchings of bare branches against her windows. The wind had picked up. She hugged herself for warmth.

She shuddered, remembering her experience with the little drummer boy's mother. The silhouettes of all the exhausted women she'd seen trudging the dangerous streets marched before her eyes.

"I have to find a way to comfort them and shield them from stupid, ungrateful Washingtonians who forget these women are related to courageous men who stand between them and the enemy a few miles away."

Her Women's Relief Association was helping find news of their relatives, but nothing was being done for their own safety and comfort. The situation was unacceptable. The War was killing and maiming their family members, and no one seemed to care enough to show them a speck of gratitude. "Well, we'll see about that," she vowed."I'll find a way to remedy this discrimination."

If she could not minister to the boys directly, right now, at least she could see to it that their womenfolk were helped and protected.

She hopped off the window seat and snatched up her writing case. There were two meetings she had planned to attend where the first speeches on Women's Franchise ever held in Washington were to be delivered. One would take place at the Union League Hall on 9th Street and the second, a couple of days later, at Odd Fellow's Hall on 7th Street. Surely, the committee heads would give her time on their agendas.

She wrote furiously, jotting down facts and figures to support her request for money to fund her new charity.

Without question, both organizations arranged for time at the end of their meetings. Her pleas were so eloquent, that she received pledges of help to establish a special home to relieve the problem.

Before the week was out, she had rented a house on 10th Street for $40 a week, one month's rent due in advance. The home was opposite Ford's Theater, a handy landmark that made it easy for people to find. A matron was hired to run the shelter, and Mary, determined to get it furnished properly, headed for the first place that came to mind.

By now all of Washington was used to seeing this tiny, imperious woman quick-marching through the streets of the capital, head down, lost in thought. Clad in her severely tailored tunic and trousers or her generous, flowing cape, she had become a local attraction. Smiles greeted her wherever she went. Those who did not know of her good works, made fun of her eccentricities, but Mary was too busy to give a hoot.

Word had spread among the ranks that she would spare no energy or expense to help the common soldier. More important, nobody better try to butt heads with this lady.

❧❀☙

Dr. Mary stalked past a startled sentry guarding the outer doors of the raw wooden building, staring directly ahead as if he didn't exist. Boot heels clicking, coattails flying, she two-stepped down a long corridor.

In a tone that warned she would not take no for an answer, she addressed the wary guard standing just outside the office of Brigadier General Edward Canby.

"I must see the General, at once," Dr. Mary advised the sentinel and kept right on walking, straight past him. He made a half-hearted attempt to stop her, but she pushed the inner door open. He followed along behind.

"I'm sorry, General, I tried to stop her . . . ," he whined.

The senior officer waved a dismissive hand. "It's all right, Ames, let her be."

Edward Richard Sprigg Canby, the Assistant Adjutant General at the time, was a clean-shaven, serious man with dark, brown hair short enough to display the over-large ears that framed his broad face. He sported a nose in direct proportion to his ears, but larger than his narrow mouth warranted. Dark, shaggy brows shaded his light hazel eyes.

Rows of brass buttons decorated a uniform that was impeccably pressed. His manner was cordial as he stood to greet Mary.

Earnestly the doctor dispensed with amenities and began at once, knowing better than to try buttering up a busy official with whom she had no appointment.

She extended her hand and got down to business. "General. Good morning, Sir. I am Dr. Mary Walker here to beg a favor."

"I know who you are, Dr. Walker. Everyone in Washington knows who you are."

He held onto her hand, pressing it between both of his. "Let me offer you my official thanks for the evacuation of our casualties from Warrenton."

She withdrew her hand. "That was a labor of love, Sir," she replied, fingering the gold watch at her breast.

"Nevertheless, it was a fine deed and very brave as well," he answered with great sincerity. "Now, Ma'am, what can I do for you?"

"I've come to you on a mission of mercy, General. I need your help for the wives and mothers of our brave boys who are fighting in the trenches."

The general, relieved that she was not there to pester him for entry into the surgeons' corps, smiled down into her snapping blue eyes and motioned for her to take a seat.

He had been apprised of Mary's dealings with his colleagues at the front. The lady could probably get anything she requested short of a commission in the Union Army, which was not his to give, in any case.

She leaned forward in her chair. "It has come to my attention that there's no suitable space available for anxious women and children looking for news of their fathers and brothers and sons," Mary began. "They wander the streets and even sleep in the park.

"No one will help them because they are unescorted. Of course they aren't. Their men are at the front," she snapped. Then, moderating her tone, she explained, "Some of them are infirm or advanced in years; and, forgive me, Sir, some of them are heavy with child."

The general blushed at the intimate reference, but nodded his understanding.

Mary hurried on, slightly embarrassed, herself, at speaking so frankly to a strange gentleman. "Many have sufficient funds, but that doesn't seem to matter. In short, General, there is not one decent place in Washington where an honest, reputable woman can find a night's rest."

General Canby's forehead wrinkled, expressing his consternation. "I didn't know that was the case," he said.

"Don't fault yourself, Sir. I had no idea until recently, either, but that is unimportant, now. I know we can help them. You, especially, can help, Sir."

"I'd consider that a duty, Dr. Walker. Tell me what I must do?"

"I've rented a house to take these women in, but we have no furnishings. We have great need of cots, chests, tables, chairs, as well as blankets, sheets and pillowcases. I'll take anything the Army cannot use. If linens are torn, we'll mend them; dirty ones can be washed; condemned cots that are not fit for soldiers' use can be repaired," She stopped for breath. "I can see to all that, General," she promised. "All I need are the materials to work with."

"You needn't say another word," he declared. "I'll get you everything you've requested." A huge smile chased the sadness from his eyes. A ray of sunshine in a desolate world. Here was something positive he could do for his brave men.

Dr. Mary reported her good fortune to the police, who were overjoyed. They promised to refer all pertinent cases to the home on 10th Street.

Volunteers painted walls, scrubbed, mended and repaired all the donations that flowed in from General Canby's supply depot.

But once she got started, Mary could not leave it at that. Respectable women were not the only ones in the city that needed help. In her midnight strolls, she had seen the others melting into the shadows: sick and abused waifs of the night with no kind word to sustain them.

The newspapers carried notices of smothered newborns found in rubbish heaps and girls with slit wrists, bleeding out their pathetic lives in back alleys.

Who would help these unfortunates?

Who, indeed?

Besides the house on 10th Street, she acquired a small apartment in the city hall basement, secured from a family who was urged to move to another location so their quarters could be used for female indigents and girls 'in trouble,' who might offend the sensibilities of the gentle ladies in the shelter. She also took over two leisure rooms formerly used by local policemen who gladly gave up their space for a good cause.

Once the homes were stocked and habitable, the following advertisement appeared in all the Washington newspapers:

Lodging Rooms for Homeless Women

Dr. Mary Walker has the pleasure to inform those females who are homeless that she has secured respectable rooms where they can remain overnight, free of charge. Let no woman who is nearly out of means perish on our streets, hereafter. She will also hear the cases of prospective mothers who are without homes and means to take care of themselves, and begs leave to inform all such who will endeavor to lead better lives that they need not commit suicides or murder innocents, for they shall be cared for and their misfortunes not be published to the world . . . We shall have a temporary Foundling Hospital for the present supported by voluntary contributions.

M. E. Walker, M.D. 374 Ninth Street.

In one fell swoop, Mary had established a home for unwed mothers and an orphanage for their offspring besides supplying a decent place for transient families of military personnel.

When both locations were operating smoothly, Mary shuttled back and forth, checking on new occupants, making changes where needed.

Next, she worked on the matter of transportation for women who were scouring the city for their loved ones, exhausting themselves and their resources. She approached General Rucker, officer in charge of transportation services for the military. From him, she wangled an ambulance and driver who reported daily to the shelter to ferry the ladies around to the various hospitals.

⸭⊶⊚⊷⸬

Some of the visitors who stayed in Mary's shelter had money to finance their room and board, but many did not. Dr. Mary secured donations to support the rest, but often had to supplement with her own funds.

Before the shelter was established, the only other woman's group ever active in Washington was church sanctioned and called the Dorcas Association after a Christian woman in the New Testament who made clothing for the poor.

Mary placed notices in the newspapers that volunteers were needed to aid soldiers' families. As helpers came forward, an association to solicit funds and support the charity home was formed. Mary served as its president until she had instructed others on how to handle the duties. She became its secretary and remained as medical officer while she saw to the actual management of the two establishments herself.

The Association grew and prospered, and Mary eventually left it in the capable hands of a number of physicians' wives.

She proudly claimed the title of the first and only woman physician in Washington at the time with the exception of Dr. Lydia Sayer of Middletown, New York, who stayed only a short while until she left to marry and become Mrs. Lydia Hasbrook, editor of *The Sybil.*

Dr. Mary's humble little shelter, with its shabby furnishings, cast-off linens and donated funds helped thousands of women and children throughout the war. Afterwards it became the foundation for two organizations: the current day Women's Christian Association and the Women's Hospital and Soldier's Orphan Home.

Some of Mary's clients were rescued directly off the street. One such case was a motherly looking soul with pale sunken cheeks and scraggly, graying hair. She was bent from hard work, wrinkled before her time and barely clothed decently. She stood staring intently at the tempting array of cakes and fruits displayed on a sidewalk stand.

"Do you want something, dear?" Mary asked

The woman smiled wistfully. "Oh, no, I can't afford to get anything," she said in a small, desperate voice that curdled Mary's stomach.

This poor lady is starving, she thought, she can't even feed herself.

"Take whatever you want, and I'll pay the man myself," said Dr. Mary.

Gratefully, the woman selected a couple of small cakes and began nibbling on them, immediately. She chewed slowly as if to make the food last for a long time.

Mary patted her shoulder. "There is more, if you need it," she said, tears sparkling in eyes dark with pity.

Once Edwina Farrington had eaten, she began to tell Mary her troubles. "I'm a widow from Philadelphia. I've been searching for days for my son, Robert, a drummer boy in the Army of the Potomac."

Mary's heart dropped to her boots. Not another dead little drummer boy, she worried. I cannot bear it. Nevertheless, the next day she piled Edwina into the confiscated ambulance, a horse drawn wagon with a makeshift, canvassed roof, and they drove from hospital to hospital inquiring for the child.

They came across an ambulatory soldier who had served with the boy. "Ah, yes, I know of the lad. Robert, is it? He was taken to a deserters' camp just on the other side of the Potomac."

There was no time to waste. The women headed out that very afternoon. They were halted at the Chain Bridge, but, with papers in order, they were allowed to pass.

"Best get back before dark, Miss," the sentry admonished. "We take the planks up at night and nobody crosses either way."

"We'll keep that in mind," Mary replied. "Thank you for the warning."

Once inside the camp, they were bitterly disappointed.

"Oh, no," the commander told them. "That boy isn't here. He took down with a fever, and we transferred him to the deserters' hospital."

"Where's that?" cried the distraught mother. "Is Robert bad off?"

The camp commander shrugged. "I can't keep track of every soul." But his answer was civil enough. "The hospital's located in a large house in the northwestern part of Washington."

Back in the city, Mary shoved her pride in her pocket and took Edwina to meet her old nemesis, Secretary Stanton. She was determined to secure the youngster's discharge.

Fearing Stanton would not see her, Mary had the aide give Mrs. Farrington's name only. However, the sergeant mentioned that there was another lady, also. He whispered, "She's wearing trousers, Sir."

A thundercloud appeared on Stanton's horizon. "Don't tell me that little beggar's here about her damned volunteer regiment? Show them in," he ordered, gritting his teeth.

"I might have known," Stanton bellowed, as Mary trotted into his office on the heels of Edwina. "What are you doing here, Dr. Walker?"

Mary ignored the question. Once she introduced the mother, and explained the situation, she began to plead for the child. "He is underage, Mr. Secretary, and he is the sole support of his widowed mother. Can we get him released, right away?"

Stanton, who couldn't help but admire Mary's unflagging audacity, took pity on both women. The release was signed, and the two hurried off to the hospital.

When Edwina caught sight of Robert, she threw her arms around him. "Son," she screamed as she squeezed his skinny frame tight against her breast.

"Let go, Ma." He tried to wriggle away. "Me bunkmates'll poke fun at me for being a mama's boy. I did fight in the war, after all."

Though pale and sickly from his ordeal, he found the strength to extricate himself. His face was scarlet with embarrassment, as they hooted and whistled and clapped their approval. "Take him home, mother," they shouted. "He done his time in good faith."

"A brave lad, Missus."

"He's a pistol, that one. You can be proud of yer young man."

Mary sent the pair home to Philadelphia, breathing a sigh of relief that at least one story had a happy ending.

CHAPTER TWENTY-EIGHT

WASHINGTON CITY

WHILE SHE WAITED in the city for Stanton's reply to her request for a volunteer regiment, Mary continued to service the military without pay. She also treated private patients for small fees most of which she reinvested in her retreats.

The campaign for donations to the shelters was flagging. Some kind of fundraiser had to be organized to replenish the coffers.

The doctor smiled when the weekly papers recorded accolades for a young zealot, charismatic Anna Elizabeth Dickinson, whose specialty was bashing slave owners at the same time she pleaded for women's rights. My kind of woman, Mary thought, and hurried off to recruit her.

The twenty-two-year-old, often written up as the 'Joan of Arc of the North,' had given a rousing speech before the United States Congress, denouncing the South's tenacious defense of slavery.

After hearing stunning reports that her emotional lectures on abolition brought tears and cheers from standing-room-only audiences, the citizens of the capital were clamoring for a look at her.

Mary caught up with the young speaker and explained her quest.

"Of course, I'll help," Dickinson promised, and a date was set for a speaking engagement. Audiences flocked to the door waving tickets they had paid premium prices to obtain.

When it was over the Association was richer by $1000, the entire proceeds from one lecture given by Miss Dickinson. Mary was ecstatic.

Edwin Stanton read of the benefit and smiled to himself. His admiration for Walker's accomplishments had surely increased, but the Secretary of War could not bring himself to reverse his decision to keep her out of the military.

He would never refuse her skills when donated, but he simply could not sanction a commission for her. No Way. No how. Period.

A week after the fundraiser, his summary dismissal of her request reached Mary at the shelter. Nearly a month had gone by.

She read the letter twice, before crumpling it up and shoving it into her pocket. She walked the streets for hours, stuffing her disappointment down until she could scarcely breathe for the weight of it.

It was one more nail in the coffin of her dying dreams.

She confided in no one, maintaining a steady outward calm, while inside her soul was screaming for vindication.

Crushed with disappointment, she fled to New York for a few weeks, but Stanton's refusal plagued her like an aching tooth, robbing her of sleep, interfering with her pleasures.

Totally fed up at this point, she decided to go to the Commander-in-Chief himself. She hustled back to her quarters in Washington, and, after much revision, penned the final draft and hand delivered this to the President's residence:

"Washington, D. C., Jan. 11, 1864.

*To his Excellency, A. Lincoln, President, U. S. A.
Whereas, the undersigned has rendered much of valuable service to her efforts To promote the cause of the Union, not only in acting as Assistant Surgeon at various times in hospitals and on the field, but in originality and urging several measures that are of great importance to the Government, one of which is the Invalid Corps, she begs to say to His Excellency that she has been denied a commission, solely on the ground of sex, when her services have been attested and appreciated without commission and without compensation, and she fully believes that had a man been as useful to our country as she modestly claims*

to have been, a star would have been taken from the
National Heavens and placed upon his shoulder.
The undersigned asks to be assigned to duty at
Douglas Hospital, in the female ward, as there
cannot possibly be any objection urged on account of
sex, but she would much prefer to have an extra
surgeon's commission with orders to go whenever and
wherever there is a battle that she may render aid in
the field hospitals, where her energy, enthusiasm,
professional abilities and patriotism will be of the
greatest service in inspiring the true soldier never to
yield to traitors, and in attending the wounded brave.
She will not shrink from duties under shot and shells,
believing that her life is of no value in the country's
greatest peril if by its loss the interests of future
generations shall be promoted.

Mary E. Walker, M.D."

The President agonized over his answer to her impassioned request,
wrestling with the facts of her remarkable service as opposed to his obligation to support the decisions of his appointed representatives.

He wrote his reply on the back of Mary's letter:

"The Medical Department of the Army is an
organized system in the hands of men supposed to be
learned in that profession, and I am sure it would
injure the service for me, with strong hand, to thrust
among them anyone, male or female, against their
consent. If they are willing for Dr. Mary Walker to
have charge of a female ward, if there be one, I also
am willing, but I am sure controversy on the subject
will not subserve the public interest.

A. Lincoln, Jan. 1R6, 1864"

A glimmer of hope! "I also am willing," he'd written. That was all she saw. Her heart sang for joy.

It was a beginning, a tiny chink in the unforgiving wall of prejudice, and she would pick away at its edges until she made a hole big enough to step straight through it.

CHAPTER TWENTY-NINE

WASHINGTON CITY

AT THE JANUARY MEETING of the Union League, Mary delivered another speech on women's rights. Once again, she closed with lines from a poem by Arthur Coxe. Its rousing stanza summed up her vision of the distressed times:

> *We are living, we are dwelling*
> *In a grand and awful time,*
> *In an age on ages telling*
> *To be living is sublime.*

Clearly, the 'grand and awful time' reflected what she had seen during her service to a country embroiled in a war that pitted brother against brother. Is it any wonder that her heart and soul were committed to her relentless quest?

About the time that Mary was waxing poetic at the Union League, Assistant Surgeon A. J. Rosa of the Army of the Cumberland expired suddenly, leaving the 52nd Ohio Volunteers without a medical officer.

General George Thomas remembered Mary's courageous service in and around Fredericksburg and Chattanooga. He issued orders for her to report to Col. Dan McCook for the purpose of replacing Rosa.

She was hired as a civilian contract surgeon, but at least she was hired! The satisfaction that her efforts had finally been officially recognized tempered all of her past disappointments. But her ordeal was not over.

Before she could report for duty, regulations dictated that she face a pre-contract examining board in the same way 5,500 other non-commissioned contract surgeons had already done. The purpose of the board was to determine whether or not the applicant was qualified for duties in the field.

Easy as pie, Mary thought, as she hastened to keep her appointment at the War Office. Acting Surgeon General Wood knows I've been doing the work for over two years. He would have authorized my appointment soon after the war began if it hadn't been for that officious ignoramus, Finley.

However, her positive thoughts flew out the window as soon as she opened Wood's door for her interview. Instead of a meeting with her friend, she was appalled to find that Acting Director of the Army of the Cumberland, Dr. George E. Cooper, had replaced her old champion. She had run into the man before, and his disdain for women had been so obvious she had written him off as being harmful to her cause.

Cooper, a runt of a man with a scraggly beard and a supercilious expression constantly painted across his rat-like features, sat like a robber baron licking his chops over his tax-paying subjects. The moment he noticed her tunic and trousers, his nose began to twitch above his suddenly pursed lips.

"Get out of this office," he shouted after reading her orders. "There will be no female surgeons in my Army. First thing you know, you'll get a commission, then I'll hear you're a major and then a general. Not while I'm breathing. Is that understood?"

She pointed to her orders, carefully keeping her voice in a neutral tone. She was not here to pick a fight. "These say differently, Sir. They were sent by Surgeon General Wood to Surgeon General Perin and are signed by Brigadier General Whipple who, I believe, outranks you."

Cooper's face went purple with rage. How dare this arrogant little twit speak up to him. His temper exploded in a spray of spittle. "Surgeon Wood had no business to send me these," he sputtered as he threw the papers to the floor. "The man hasn't a brain in his head. He's a disgrace to the Army, and I will not have the dignity of my profession trampled upon by female invasion into the military department."

Mary kept her cool . . . only just. Red-faced with indignation, she scrambled to retrieve the scattered paperwork. At least his rudeness had allotted her an extra moment to think.

When she had recovered everything she stood before him, shuffling the documents against his desktop to square them up.

"Very well, Sir," she said, an innocent smile skirting the corners of her mouth. "I shall inform General Thomas who originally requested my appointment that you will not honor his orders, and, surely, Colonel McCook who is without a surgeon to care for his brave troops, will be most unhappy with your decision."

Resolutely, she threw her shoulders back and spun on her heel. Let him think that over for a bit.

Cooper's face fell. "This damned woman might be just hateful enough to make trouble for me," he fumed. "Well, we'll see who has the last laugh."

As she turned to go, he stopped her. "Very well, MISS Walker, but you must submit to the usual examination for which I am sure you are completely unqualified."

"It's DOCTOR Walker, and I am ready for any test you may put to me. The sooner, the better."

"Report here tomorrow morning, nine o'clock, and we will see how far you get before you become stymied and run out of here in tears."

Mary left then, using every ounce of her self-control to keep from slamming the door behind her. Tomorrow was another day.

She went straight from Cooper's office to call upon General Thomas and apprise him of the man's churlish behavior.

In September of 1865, while trying to get her pension straightened out, Mary dashed off a letter about this incident to President Andrew Johnson.

Although a year and a half had elapsed since the hearing, her usually disciplined handwriting slashed through with vicious underlines, still betrayed the extent of the explosive emotions she retained for Cooper and company.

The letter also contained an interesting statement that suggested her upcoming appointment might be more than that of a mere contract surgeon:

"I left his (Cooper's) office & called on the noble Gen'l Thomas, & he gave me encouragement that I should have all the opportunities for a double mission that I wished."

Was Dr. Mary to do a little spying on the side?

Considering her fearlessness and patriotism, it seems natural that she might engage in espionage. Certainly, she would be less suspect than any of Allan Pinkerton's secret service men who did not acquit themselves well, in the field. In fact, their faulty information contributed to the downfall of 'Little Mac' McClellan who hesitated too long because of Pinkerton's overestimation of Confederate strength in the Richmond area.

Mary's niece often expressed the belief that her aunt was 'one of Grant's trusted spies.'

Some official evidence appears in a document regarding her pension request that declares her work was of a most confidential nature.

But then, how many spy activities have ever been acknowledged by any civil government?

Mary's letter to Johnson went on to say:

"Knowing my own abilities, & fully believing that his (Cooper's) board would do what was right, I went at the appointed hour."

So much for good faith and self-confidence.

❧◉❧

The members of the board, some in full military dress and some in mufti, bristled as she entered the room clad in her pseudo uniform. Wisely, she had omitted the green sash she wore at the front.

Regardless of the fact that her appointment had been sanctioned by Assistant Surgeon Wood and General George Thomas, the group's prejudices disallowed any change from the norm. To a man, they resented her gender, her unconventional clothing and her unparalleled audacity in thinking she could find a career in a profession they were determined to keep exclusively populated by the superior male.

Cooper's influence was evident in their faces. She had not opened her mouth, yet their hostility bubbled like a pot of noxious stew.

Roberts Bartholow, an army surgeon with the rank of captain, seemed to be the leader of the group, but he let others speak first. He was decked out in handsome Federal Army regalia, pistol and sword, to boot. Surely his full dress was meant to intimidate, but Dr. Mary had dealt with a great

210

many similarly clad officers in the past two years. His military appearance did not frighten her, but his hostile manner worried her. He wore the same unfriendly expression she had seen on Cooper's face the day before.

"Good morning, Miss Walker, take a seat over there," said the middle-most man, Martin Morely, a corpulent, bewhiskered toady with nary a hair on his naked head. Not a "please" to be heard.

She nodded to acknowledge that she'd heard Morely then stepped forward to present Bartholow with her credentials from Syracuse Medical College and Hygeio-Therapeutic College along with several letters of recommendation. She glanced toward the appointed seat but stood her ground.

For one split second her thoughts leaped to a courtroom in New York State, and the antipathetic divorce judge's features superimposed themselves over Morely's.

Her mind jumped back to the present as Bartholow sniffed, ran his knuckles across his nose and barely gave her documents a glance. Curling his lip, he leaned forward and handed the packet back to her without sharing it with the others.

"It's Doctor Walker, and I prefer to stand, thank you," she replied, retrieving her papers and planting her feet at parade rest.

"Yes. Yes." Bartholow groaned. He had been warned of her arrogance by his friend, Cooper. He waved a limp hand toward a colleague who took up the questioning.

"Now, then," said Jed Wilkins, a pale, sickly looking man whose pock-marked face brought to mind shell craters on the battlefield. "Can you tell us about postnatal uterine bleeding?"

What? What the devil does uterine bleeding have to do with battle injuries? Her fingers folded into fists to conceal their trembling. "Sir? I don't understand why you're asking that," she stuttered, a baffled expression clouding her face. She was too tongue-tied to pose the question of relevance.

"You said you were a doctor, did you not? Just answer the question . . . if you can, that is." He sought the approval of the others, smiling as widely as a grinning gargoyle.

"Yes . . . but? . . ." Mary stammered out a textbook description less expertly than a novice medical student could have done.

Other questions in the same vein came too fast, sometimes more than one at a time.

Finally she understood. This examination was a complete farce. Most of what they asked had nothing to do with battle wounds or soldiers' diseases. The board had no intention of passing her.

Dr. Mary Edwards Walker, who had braved enemy fire and spent over two years tending to desperately sick and injured Union Soldiers, was nearly reduced to tears. She clenched her teeth, refusing to cry. She'd never award them that satisfaction.

The rest of the interrogation passed in a blur as she answered their ridiculous queries, struggling to get her voice around a lump in her throat that would choke a small horse.

Before leaving, she pocketed her pride and begged them to give Cooper a favorable recommendation. The men did not even have the decency to wait till she left the room before breaking into laughter.

All the way to her boarding house, she castigated herself for letting them get the better of her. The moment she entered her secluded quarters, she crumpled onto her cot. Hot tears spilled over her cheeks. Wrenching sobs cramped her chest and bruised her throat. She had let Dr. Wood down. She had let General Thomas down. Worst of all, she would not be allowed to serve with Colonel McCook's brave volunteers of the 52nd Ohio.

Bartholow later described the examination to the editor of the *New York Medical Journal.* "First," he complained, "to offer a surgeon's contract to such a medical monstrosity dressed in that hybrid costume was the most absurd action I had ever been called upon to witness."

He branded Mary as a masterful manipulator who tried to get the examiners to take it for granted that she had the knowledge needed for the position.

Further, he wrote, "The board unanimously agreed that she had no more medical knowledge than an ordinary housewife and that she was, of course, entirely unfit for the position of medical officer. And," he finally added to all of that invective, "She had never been, so far as we could learn, within the walls of a medical college or hospital for the purpose of obtaining a medical education."

On March 8th, 1864, the official decision was forwarded to Surgeon General Abner Perin, stating "she displayed such ignorance as to render it doubtful whether she has pursued the study of Medicine." Their conclusion: she might find work as a nurse in a General Hospital." Had Dr. Mary's dream been shot down once again?

CHAPTER THIRTY

CHATTANOOGA, TENNESSEE

D R. MARY had the last laugh on her tormentors.
On March 10, 1864, Surgeon General Perin received a communication to dispatch her to Colonel Daniel McCook in Chattanooga, posthaste.

Feeling obliged to cite the unfavorable report sent out by Cooper's examining board, Perin wrote back the next day to explain the circumstances to Thomas and Wood.

"Hmph," said General Thomas. "Either they interviewed the wrong doctor, or they're still living in the dark ages. Disregard the report, and send her to McCook."

Acting Surgeon General Wood said, "Those jackasses on the board made a serious mistake. Forget the review, and send Dr. Walker to Chattanooga."

On March 11, Assistant Surgeon General Perin forwarded a message to Mary from the Medical Director's Office at the Headquarters Department of the Cumberland:

> *"In compliance with the directions of the General Commanding, you will report without delay to Col. Dan'l. McCook, Commanding 3rd Brigade, 2nd Division, 14th Army Corps now on duty at Gordon Mills."*

Hallelujah! Her orders had come straight from General Thomas. She was to serve directly south of Chattanooga. The 52nd Ohio Volunteers Unit defended the furthest outpost at Lee & Gordon's Mills. It was exactly where she had asked to be sent.

After clicking heels and toes in a spirited victory dance, Mary grew sober and thoughtful. God bless General Thomas, she thought, as she threw her kit together and rushed to Chattanooga.

On March 17th, Colonel McCook received a packet of papers along with the order:

> *"The female doctor not being a Commissioned Officer cannot give a valid receipt for property furnished her. Your Quartermaster should furnish her with a horse, saddle, etc. and if they should be lost, an affidavit of the Quartermaster Sergeant or other non-Commissioned Officer, or enlisted man, stating the manner in which they were lost would be sufficient voucher."*

Dr. Mary was officially with the Union Army in a civilian capacity and unofficially given the rank of lieutenant. As far as the records go, she was the only woman surgeon to serve with the military for many, many years. Even women physicians who offered their services as late as the First World War were refused acceptance.

When Mary arrived at the first camp, everything was in a state of flux. There were no separate accommodations for her. Instead of kicking up a fuss, she threw herself on the mercy of the commander. After all, a lady must have her privacy.

"Please take my tent for the night," said Colonel McCook, a courtly, thirty-three-year-old West Point graduate, and the most colorful of the fifteen 'fighting McCooks.' During the battle at Peach Orchard near

Shiloh, Daniel, a poetic man, was heard to comment on the shower of pink petals that drifted to the ground as bullets smashed the blossom-laden branches. "They are spring's offering to the heroic dead," he said, brushing tears from his eyes.

Handsome as a play actor, he sported a shock of brown hair shot through with red highlights and swept up from his broad forehead. Except for a generous mustache above full lips, his ruddy face was as smooth as an infant's bottom. He towered over Mary, his broad shoulders blocking out the rose and orange sky, all that remained of a setting sun that had disappeared behind the trees in the background.

"I shall bunk with one of my officers," he said as he pulled back his tent flap and ushered her inside.

The word never got around to the Colonel's thirsty cronies who appeared nightly for a well-earned liquid libation after a dusty day of commanding the troops.

The moon had long since risen and Mary was snugly tucked up when the first of the captains appeared for his nightly refreshment.

Thinking the Colonel had retired early Captain Broderick reached into the tent and yanked at the mound beneath the blankets at the foot of the bed. This was no time for a nap. Serious business was afoot.

One minute he was licking his chops over the expected potation, and the next he was fleeing for his life.

"Unhand me, you scoundrel," Mary screamed, shuffling under her pillow for her trusty weapon. "I have a pistol here, and I'll shoot you dead where you stand."

Bodies catapulted through every tent flap in the camp, rifles at the ready. Colonel McCook was seen laughing fit to kill as he pulled up his britches and shouldered his suspenders. "Run, Broderick. Run," he shouted at the captain's disappearing backside. "I hear she's a dead shot."

There was instant and genuine admiration as Daniel McCook watched Dr. Mary, chest heaving in her trailing white nightdress, coal black, curly hair tumbling about her shoulders, aiming a nasty pistol straight at one of his favorite drinking buddies.

"Damn. That is one feisty little woman," he chuckled. "And good looking, to boot."

Two Southern millers who found it prudent to cooperate with the Army of the Cumberland owned Lee & Gordon's Mills, a grinding station located on Chickamauga Creek. The fact that their property was already surrounded greatly influenced their decision.

Sleeping accommodations were soon arranged for Mary in the Gordon Household and she bunked with the miller, his wife and their children in the family kitchen.

The cramped, rustic room contained a trestle table, half a dozen rugged chairs and several bedsteads lined up beneath the windows. Cooking pots flanked the fireplace, and sturdy work clothing of various sizes hung from wooden pegs on the inside walls.

Mary was given a corner to herself near the doorway that led to a spacious hall where the campaign leader made his headquarters. Beyond that, a large bedroom had been appropriated for officers' sleeping quarters.

Mary didn't care that she was relegated to the kitchen. She was rarely there, anyway. Besides, it was a lot better billet than some improvised blanket tent that had recently been vacated by a bloated corpse whose lingering scent provoked her gag reflex.

Colonel McCook was so taken with his petite surgeon that at one time he allowed her the special privilege of reviewing the troops in his absence. She sat astride her handsome, government-issued mare, back straight, chin tucked in, and rode along the ranks pretending not to see the repressed smiles as the men remembered Captain Broderick's hasty retreat from her screaming threats.

In her all-too-brief memoir entitled *Incidents Connected With the Army* she wrote:

> *"While at Gordon's Mills, Georgia, General Dan.*
> *McCook, who had charge of the forces at that*
> *point. . . .*
> *he was at the time but colonel, a grand revue was to*
> *be had a few miles north of that, and as he wanted to*
> *go early in the morning with other of his officers, he*

*instructed me to take off my green sash and put on a
red one and revue the videttes in his absence. I did
so, having the orderly ride by my side; and on his
return he asked me if the guards turned out for me. I
replied that they did. This is the only instance in
war, as far as I am aware, where a
woman made revue."*

Nothing came easy for Dr. Mary even after her appointment. Now that she had official sanction to pursue the daily activities of camp life, there were those who felt she had no place in the army. Officers and soldiers alike were nervous and embarrassed at having a woman laboring daily under such deplorable conditions. They thought of their mothers, wives and sweethearts, and could not imagine such hardships visited upon them.

One of her most outspoken critics, Reverend Nixon B. Stewart, could hardly be considered without prejudice. Like Cooper and his flunkies, he felt that women should be kept in their place; and that place was not in the front lines with good and true men of the 52nd Ohio.

He pontificated, constantly and with great passion. "She wields her new found authority with such vigor that the men seem to hate her. It is inappropriate and scandalous behavior when 'that female' exhibits no shame as she kneels beside strange men, examining their naked body parts with nary a smidgen of embarrassment."

Contrary to the good reverend's assessment, Mary received countless grateful accolades from the 52nd Ohio Volunteers long after the terrible war had ended.

The fact that she rode out into the surrounding countryside to treat civilians irritated Stewart like a burr in his britches. "She doctors our adversaries on our time and with our medicines," he complained to anyone who'd listen.

The good reverend's final assessment declared that, since she was so interested in the southern population, Mary must have been hired as a spy and not for her dubious medical training, at all.

One day his curiosity got the better of him. He posed the question that had been on his mind for weeks. "Why do you persist in traveling through dangerous enemy territory, giving succor to the traitors of this great and noble country?"

Mary's reply was simple and straightforward. Her eyes flashed with indignation as she responded. "Where you see southerners, Mr. Stewart, I see human beings.

"Better send up your prayers and ask the Lord to make Confederate Surgeons equally as compassionate for the unlucky Unionists who fall under their care."

Legend has it that a picture is worth a thousand words.

A photographer published in *Above and Beyond* under the heading 'The Only Woman,' mute evidence to demonstrate Mary's devotion to her duties.

An ambulance wagon waits nearby as two soldiers carry a litter bearing a wounded man. In the foreground Dr. Mary is seen clad in her uniform tunic with its shoulder boards and bright buttons. Her heavy mane is tucked under a fatigue cap. She kneels among the weeds, bandaging the wounded leg of a soldier who leans against the ragged stump of a desecrated tree. Let all the Stewarts and the Coopers, and the Stantons argue that Dr. Mary had no place on the battlefield. The lives and limbs she saved became eloquent evidence against their dogmatic misgivings.

CHAPTER THIRTY-ONE

TENNESSEE

DR. MARY never came to terms with the politics of the war given the friendly overtures of the vedettes on either side as they traded tobacco and newspapers in direct defiance of their orders to stay out of 'enemy' shooting range. She wrote of it:

"In our own war there was a special cruelty in relatives and those under republican form of government, fighting and killing each other. That both sides feel this is evidenced by the friendliness between the soldiers of both factions, which does not exist to such an extent between any parties that stayed at home on either side."

Her belief in the necessary solidarity of the Union prevented her from sympathizing with Confederate doctrines. However, people were her priority—no matter their politics, their color or their gender.

Southern civilians from the surrounding areas became as important as the valiant men she treated on the battlefield. They flooded the camp, begging for food and medical help, and Mary could never refuse them.

"They have no politics. They're just hungry women and children," she told her commanding officers. His benevolence usually won out in the end.

Armed men were supposed to accompany Mary on her trips to outlying farms, but often she rode the trails alone.

It was dangerous going, and two armed officers and two armed orderlies were supposed to travel with her. She carried two pistols in her saddlebags, as well.

After a while, she refused to dawdle until an escort could be assembled. When riding alone, she left her weapons behind.

"Wait for your escort," the colonel ordered as she was about to leave.

"Not today." she replied "If I have an escort, there'll be a confrontation and a fight for our lives. If I'm alone and unarmed, I can talk my way out of any situation."

"You put too much faith in the correctness of your mission, Doctor."

"Trust me. I'll be fine," she replied and sprang into the saddle.

⌒◯❀◯⌒

In the spring of 1864, disenchanted civilians, sick of losing their children to a war they had not sanctioned, took matters into their own hands.

They secreted their pubescent sons in caves and woods to keep from them being conscripted by the Confederate Army. The hope of these naive farmers rested with the sons they'd raised to be God fearing, hard-working heirs who would tend the farms and raise families of their own to continue the cycle. They must be kept safe.

Their sisters carried food to them in little buckets hidden under their dresses so marauding Rebels would not find and press the boys into service.

Mary snuck to their hideouts where she treated cringing, undernourished children for exposure, Tetanus and Typhoid contracted from drinking contaminated swamp water. If discovered, she would've been shot dead on the spot for aiding traitors to the Confederacy.

The loyalties of many simple country people who'd given lip service to the wealthy slave owners without understanding the consequences were turned around by her kind acts.

Dr. Mary put herself in harm's way to treat her patients, sometimes escaping marauding groups of soldiers secreted in requisitioned farmhouses.

One morning, she was called out to extract an infected tooth for the wife of Col. George Washington Gordon, who was a long distance away in the Confederate Army.

A jagged shell hole had opened up the west wall of her home and Mary could see several men in a variety of clothing, lolling about the kitchen, drinking from tin cups, and smoking scraggly cigarettes. She saw their rifles standing against the wall, and read desperation in their hate-filled eyes.

She suspected they were rebel soldiers in mufti who only restrained them-selves because of the presence of the colonel's wife.

Once she was sure the Mrs. Gordon was not going to hemorrhage from the extractions, she packed up and left the house. She strode to the edge of the thicket where her mare was tethered and gave a little whistle to her escorts waiting further in the woods.

She cocked her head back toward the house. "Rebs," was the only word she needed to whisper. All five riders moseyed their horses a hundred paces out of ear shot and hightailed it out of there before any confrontation could take place.

Her errands of mercy took her far into enemy territory where she de-livered scrawny infants to undernourished women who begged her for food and a few bits of cloth to swaddle their babes. She did what she could to sustain them, but it was her innate kindness and lack of concern for her own safety that won their hearts.

Because the southerners expressed such gratitude for her services, there came a time when she lost all fear of 'anything being done to myself.' She traveled more and more alone and unarmed.

⌘

On one of her solitary expeditions, she had ridden about three miles out from headquarters, paying minimum attention to the sounds around her. Her mind was on other things.

The forest was silent except for the irritable chirping of a few nesting birds, interrupted in their noonday siestas. The muffled echo of the mare's hooves beat a plodding tattoo that lulled Mary into a quiet reverie.

She remembered Cynthia and their intimate talks together. How she would love to confide her fears and expectations to her beloved sister. Even now her throat tightened at the thought.

The trail took her past a decrepit barn, its splintery siding faded to chalky gray from years of exposure to sun and rain. Surrounding it on three sides stood a high fence fashioned from closely fitted boards as weathered as the sagging building it shielded.

Polly Craig

Her mare, Thomasina, shied suddenly then skittered sideways beside the broken gate. Suddenly, two scruffy men confronted Mary. Thomasina stomped and snorted, agitated at the interruption of a pleasant trek through the countryside.

"Halt," shouted the younger one, a flunky by the look of him. His filthy clothing was prune wrinkled, his knee length boots covered with caked red mud. He rode slouched forward, his forage cap tilted far back exposing an unruly shock of sandy colored straw that could use a trim to keep it out of his milky blue eyes.

Mary's nose twitched. One of the unwashed rebels, this gawky stranger, she thought.

"Where ya goin'?" asked the older man, a scowl making an inverted crescent of his thin lips. He wore a cadet gray over-blouse that bore faint markings where braid had been ripped away. His baggy trousers were tucked into knee-high boots that had seen better days, and his underfed horse could do with a good grooming.

Both men appeared close to exhaustion. Clearly, they had been on the move for days without respite. But who were they?

The leader removed his slouch hat and steadied his nervous mount. Short, straight hair as ebon as Mary's own, sprang in different directions. It exactly matched his bushy, black beard and mustache.

For a moment, the doctor sat riveted in her saddle, staring into his dangerous black eyes. Take care, she thought, this is a man to be reckoned with.

"Yore with the Union Army," he drawled, noting her navy blue uniform with its gold buttons and the green sash wound twice around her waist, its fringed, eighteen inch drop draping casually over her saddlebags.

She raised her chin a couple of inches and met his gaze without flinching. "I am. I'm Dr. Mary Walker, and who are you?" she asked.

He ignored the question, using his brown felt hat to flick a heavy twig from his horse's tangled mane. He slapped it back on his head and glanced beyond the gate.

Mary's horse continued to fidget.

"Pull your mount into the barn," he ordered.

Mary played for time by patting Thomasina's neck to steady her down. "What for?" she asked.

The aide spoke up, his drawl thick enough to cut with a bayonet. No question where his loyalties lay. "Do as he say, and be quick about it," he warned.

At the sharp tone of its master's voice, his horse danced sideways a dozen paces away from the others.

Mary's mind was flying, but, outwardly, she appeared perfectly calm and unafraid. They're not military, she puzzled. Outlaws, she guessed. She was damned if she'd submit to scoundrels.

"I don't have the time for that," she said, her tone level and confident. "I have a patient to see to."

"You're an Army Surgeon, then?" the older man asked.

"That is correct, but I have a civilian patient waiting for me at the moment. A *Southern* civilian," she said to force his understanding that she was a doctor, not a soldier.

His lips twisted in a wry grin as he mulled this over. Strange duck, he thought, what will those damned Yanks come up with next?

His eyes crawled over her neat uniform, her shabby boots, her well-cared-for mount and then dropped to her saddlebags. "Do you have any revolvers in those bags?" he demanded.

"Certainly not," she replied indignantly, while she silently breathed a sigh of relief that both her weapons were back at camp.

Curious now, the fellow relaxed a bit. "Well, whadya you have in there?"

"Surgical instruments and dental equipment. I am on my way to extract some teeth for a woman who is suffering. I will be happy to show them to you if you like. The instruments. Not the teeth."

His eyes flickered at her insolence.

She transferred the reins from her right hand to the left and stretched to open the bags.

Perhaps he thought she was reaching for a weapon, because he spoke up very quickly, "Stop. Ah don't need to see your instruments."

He wheeled his mount around and approached his sidekick. Out of earshot, they conversed secretly, occasionally glancing in her direction. They traded a few nods and gestures before the leader's horse, prompted by a gentle flap of the reins, pranced back toward Dr. Mary, stopping close enough that its master's boots rubbed against her own.

"You can go," he said, "but Ah'd advise you to be more careful in the future. These are not friendly times."

Not friendly times? Indeed!

With that he jabbed his horse with his star-shaped spurs and galloped away, his cohort hot on his heels.

Mary sat very still acutely aware that her life had just been spared. She felt cool beads of perspiration trickling down inside her shirtwaist. Every hair on her head tingled, and her breath came in short, sharp gasps. She began to shake with dread. "Get a hold on yourself," she gasped in a choked voice. "The danger's over, now."

It was several long minutes before she had the strength to cluck her mare forward.

The visit to her patient was cut shorter than was prudent under the circumstances. Her bedside manner had strangely disappeared. For the first time, Mary suddenly felt a strong urge to be in the company of her own camp mates.

Back at headquarters, she related the incident to General McCook and his staff officers.

"What did the man look like?" McCook asked.

Mary's description was complete down to his lean, hungry expression and fiery black eyes.

McCook exploded. "Good Lord, Doctor, are you sure?"

"Of course I'm sure. We talked for several minutes, and I had plenty of time to observe him."

"Do you realize you are describing *the* most hateful of all the Confederate renegades? It had to be that murdering scoundrel, 'Champ' Ferguson."

Captain Broderick spoke up then. "No. It can't be Ferguson. I don't think he's in this part of the country, right now. Besides, that polecat lives by the 'black flag' code. He has sworn to kill every Yankee that falls into his hands, and I'm told the killing takes a long time."

McCook reacted as if he were seeing a man with two heads. A muscle in his cheek jumped. "Captain," he said between clenched teeth, "Never, and I mean never, try to second guess that murdering son of a sidewinder. He's like a ghost that floats through our lines, and no one sees him. He's there. But nobody sees anything but the mutilated bodies he leaves behind."

Dr. Mary slept little, that night; and, when she did, the two cruel faces she would never forget haunted her dreams.

Years later, when she was working at the General Post Office building in Washington, a watchman named Hall showed her his book of memoirs, a careful compilation of his travels during the War.

Shuffling through it, she came across a picture of the taciturn man she had met in the woods.

"Ah, yes," Hall told her, "that's 'Champ' Ferguson, the wiliest, meanest, most blood-thirsty son of a coyote ever to cross Chickamauga Creek.

"The man was so brutal the sound of his name struck terror into the hearts of Yankee troopers. He took no prisoners; torturing and killing every unfortunate blue coat he could lay hands on. That skunk had the killer instinct born and bred in his black heart. He jumped up and down like a delighted child when he bragged about his escapades. He dyed the forest red with the blood of the poor devils he slaughtered.

"That was the man you met up with, Dr. Mary. You're damned lucky he didn't separate your head from your shoulders, Ma'am."

In June of 1864, General Sherman, standing at the site of another of Ferguson's bloody massacres, equated the outlaw with General Nathan Bedford Forrest of whom he had said, "Forrest is the very devil, and I shall hound him to the death if it costs 10,000 lives and breaks the Treasury. There will never be peace in Tennessee till Forrest is dead."

After Hall's identification of 'Champ' Ferguson, Mary wrote in her memoirs, "I was so faint with the very thought of how narrowly I had escaped death that I could hardly stand up."

CHAPTER THIRTY-TWO

TENNESSEE

CIVILIANS outside the lines gave Dr. Mary a bed and food whenever she ventured too far from camp to be safely back by nightfall. Increasingly, her sympathy lay with the remarkably resourceful women of the territory. The people in those areas were in pitiable condition. Both armies had thundered through, stealing supplies and damaging property. The Confederates pressed every male they found into service, even those who seemed much too young. That left the women 'to root hog or die.'

The McHugh Farm with its fields of rich, brick-colored soil, radiated from a graceless clapboard house with disappearing paint and sagging shutters. The acreage had once afforded a decent living for its owners, but now it lay fallow and unworked for lack of adequate help and usable equipment.

Once successful and comfortable, Clara and Delbert McHugh—who limped badly because of a club foot—had been stripped of nearly everything they owned by merciless marauders who confiscated food and property "for the good of the glorious Confederacy."

The original home, a square, two-story affair with no redeeming front porch to break up the mediocre architecture, had been supplemented by an extra room cabooosed to its back wall. There was no connecting door between it and the main building, so access was gained by exiting through the kitchen and walking halfway around the addition to its entrance.

Despite her Union uniform, Mary was welcomed into their home. "We are honored, Dr. Mary, that you're willing to share our extra room with our daughter."

During the good doctor's first visit that saw her services well used in treating the family and their neighbors, Delbert issued an open invitation.

"Whenever you're in the vicinity, be sure to come stay with us. We don't have much, but we'll gladly share whatever the Lord provides."

The next time her rounds led her close by, Dr. Mary took McHugh at his word.

Mrs. Delbert, even more pale and malnourished than before, was clad in a spotless cotton gown, mended in several places with odd bits of fabric. Her fine, salt-colored hair was tied in a skinny knot atop her well-shaped head. Undoubtedly pretty at one time, her deteriorating health had sapped all the young juices from her stooped body.

Mr. McHugh, her taciturn husband of twenty years, was bitter and old before his time. He grieved for his two sons sacrificed to the Confederacy. Neither would be returning to carry on the family heritage. His fragile hope for the future lay in his sickly, eight-year-old son, Tansy.

In honor of their special guest, Clara McHugh had fussed over preparations of the only victuals they could provide—a small rabbit trapped in the back field plus a few dried vegetables.

The muted yellow glow of an oil lamp flickered over the simple supper of thick rabbit stew served with roasted turnips and unleavened bread. The woodsy aroma of boiled acorn coffee steamed from blue enamel mugs placed beside each plate.

After the heartfelt blessing, Mary, still a strict vegetarian, politely declined the meat dish and, recognizing their impoverished circumstances, ate sparingly of the rest.

She really needed more food than she took, for she had been running on half rations for weeks. However, she had conditioned her body to function on very little. Alvah Walker would be sorely distressed at his daughter's self-imposed, health-threatening deprivation.

Clara and Delbert seemed delighted with Mary's company; but the moment it came time to retire, the situation grew sticky.

The father, clad in a clean but badly frayed work shirt, remained at the end of the table. He puffed on a corncob pipe that swirled malodorous fumes around his head. Courtesy kept the doctor from chastising her host's use of even ersatz tobacco. Besides, she was stuck for the night and certainly did not relish sleeping out in the open where enemy soldiers roamed the nearby woods.

Tansy McHugh, the skinny, tow-headed son curled up in the corner near the fireplace, a folded rag under his head offering minor comfort as he snored softly, exhausted from his chores. The flames hissed and crackled, but the child slept on.

Though her eyelids weighed heavy with fatigue, Mary helped with the washing up. She dried her hands on the rough dish towel and smiled at the daughter, Charlotte, a delicate lass with straw-colored hair, high cheek bones and cornflower eyes, who wore her mended cotton shift with a certain elegance, surprising in one so removed from civilized society.

Had a healthy bloom heightened her complexion instead of the sallow pallor that sapped her color, she would have enjoyed that classic beauty so unique to the southern belle.

"Will you be coming to bed now?" Mary asked the girl, suppressing a yawn. "I cannot keep my eyes open another minute."

Mr. McHugh shifted his buttocks in his creaking chair and cleared his throat with an unhealthy rattle. Mrs. McHugh hemmed and hawed, wringing chapped hands as if to rub away the scaly skin that disfigured them.

Mary's stomach flipped. Her intuition flashed a warning. Something strange was afoot, here, yet she had no idea what it could be.

"Uh," Clara said, flushing with embarrassment, "you must take the extra room, and our daughter will stay in the main house with us, tonight."

Carefully, Mary folded the damp dishtowel into thirds and laid it on the table, all the while gauging the changing expressions on her host's weathered face.

"I really would not be comfortable sleeping on my own with no connecting door to the house," she replied, though she really had no fear. "It would seem prudent to have a second person in the room with me in case of a raid."

She unfolded the towel and laid it across the back of a chair to dry then crouched before Charlotte, searching for an answer.

"Why are so unwilling to spend the night with me the same as last time?"

The girl slumped into a chair and dropped her forehead against arms she had folded across the edge of the table.

"What is it, child?" Mary probed, as she gently shook the girl's shoulder. "Did I do something to offend you?"

"No. No," the daughter cried. "It's . . . it's . . ."

The puzzled doctor persisted. "Come, now, Charlotte, you're a big girl. You must tell me what the trouble is."

The daughter raised her head, and Mary glimpsed tears glistening on cheeks aflame with mortification.

Alarmed, she took hold of the mother's arm. "Surely, Charlotte has said nothing against me? You must know I did her no harm, at all."

Mrs. McHugh looked stricken. How to tell their benefactor that inquisitive neighbors judged their guest to be other than what she claimed to be? Beads of perspiration appeared on her upper lip. Her daughter's reputation was at stake.

"Tell the doctor, Charlotte. Tell her truthfully," Clara urged, her voice cracking with embarrassment.

The girl raised her head and dropped her trembling hands to her lap.

"B-b-because," she stammered, "Mr. Wilkins and Mr. Scroggins s-say you're a man, and my virtue is now in question, and no honorable gentleman will ever c-consider me."

The girl's hands flew to her face as sobs shook her slender body.

Clara placed a comforting arm about her daughter's heaving shoulders and shushed her. The distraught mother's demeanor was protective and apologetic at the same time.

"It's true," she declared, sadly. "All the neighbors are talking about it."

At first, Mary was appalled, then disgusted. She reflected on the mean-spirited cowards who would probably run the other way if they were faced with a legitimate fight.

"Scroggins? He was the fool who poulticed his boil with manure, and bawled like a motherless calf when I had to lance the ugly mess. Drat," she fumed, "I cured that infection that could have cost him his right leg."

To Clara she said, "Wilkins! Didn't I deliver his premature son who decided to be born rear end first?"

Charlotte collected herself when her mother told her to hush. Both mother and daughter nodded their heads. "Yes, Ma'am," the girl squeaked.

Inwardly, Mary cringed. All her efforts on behalf of these impoverished southerners had been tossed aside. Though sickly, half starved and abandoned, those people she'd helped still turned out to be miserable, nit-picking gossips who criticized her instead of appreciating her efforts. Where was the justice in that?

"Now why on earth would people say that I'm a man?" she asked, positive that it must be her uniform.

Charlotte took a long moment before replying. Her red-rimmed eyes darted about, seeking escape. To tell or not to tell? Should she embarrass the generous friend who had treated their illnesses and supplied them with extra medicines?

The stricken girl sucked in her breath, then blurted out the truth. "They say it's because you know too much. No *woman* could be a doctor, and a surgeon and a dentist, the way you are. They say only a man can do all that."

Had it not been so unfair, Mary might have burst out laughing at the whole ridiculous concept.

Instead, she gritted her teeth and paced to keep from screeching. "Because I know too much? Good God Almighty. Deliver me from this constant, damnable, male bigotry!"

Clara gently grasped Mary's hand. "Please, sit down."

Shadows from the oil lamp darted across her distressed features as she struggled to make her guest understand the family's position.

"I am so sorry, Dr. Mary," she sighed. "Our good names are all we have left, and they must be protected at all cost."

"I understand that, but I've done nothing to compromise this child," Mary protested.

"Mr. McHugh and I know that's true; but, still, everybody says you are a man, and I cannot have my daughter sleeping in the same room with you. Don't you see? The appearance of scandal is just as bad as scandal, itself."

Mary jumped up so quickly the chair toppled over backwards. She grabbed Clara's elbow, yanking her to her feet. "Come with me, both of you. We can put an end to this nonsense, right now," she said, seizing the oil lamp.

She hustled them through the back door around to the entrance of the outside room.

"Sit," she ordered, pointing to the quilt covered bed.

She released the heavy knot at the nape of her neck. Her thick tresses fell in an ebony cascade over her shoulders and down her back.

Guiding Mrs. McHugh's hand toward her head, she offered, "You can take hold of it and pull my hair as much as you like, and you will see that it is all mine and long like a woman's."

Clara gathered a mass of curls in one hand and gave a gentle tug, and then another.

"I'm sorry, Dr. Mary, we've heard there's a way of attaching false hair, and we thought . . ."

"Yes, yes," Mary spat. She removed her tunic and rolled up the sleeves of her shirtwaist. "Do these look like the arms of a man?"

Clara eyed Mary's slender forearms and delicate wrists. The irrefutable evidence of the truth struck her full force. "I do beg your pardon," she said, noting the rounded contours of the doctor's heaving bosom. "Please, you must forgive us. You must understand the intolerance that can ruin reputations in our community."

The scene at Coolidge farm in Oswego with its peppering of rotten eggs and rank horse apples loomed in Mary's mind. After all these years, the stink still remained.

She nodded and lay down. "I must get some rest. Please excuse me."

Charlotte crept into bed beside her. The matter was never mentioned again.

But the insult rankled. Mary ached with the realization that a generation of bigoted males might never admit women were equal in talent and intellect.

She fumed. Why can't they just acknowledge that we have clever brains and abilities, too? Why should that pose a threat to them? And when will they realize these assets are not exclusive resources for their damned egos?

CHAPTER THIRTY-THREE

GEORGIA

IN THE FIRST DAYS of 1864, General Ulysses S. Grant still commanded the western armies resting in winter quarters at Nashville. He was already preparing equipment and ordering supplies for the spring offensive.

About the same time that Mary received her civilian commission, Grant was promoted to the rank of Lieutenant General. President Lincoln then appointed him General-In-Chief, which gave him full command of the Federal Armies.

Grant moved east and appointed Brigadier General William Tecumseh Sherman to fill the vacant post in the west.

General 'Little Phil' Sheridan was selected to reorganize three cavalry divisions of the Army of the Potomac.

A brilliant master plan was devised to engage the rebels in their own territory. An all-out offensive would send a wave of blue coats to sweep the whole southern front and annihilate the Confederates, once and for all.

Grant's orders to General 'Chump' Sherman were written succinctly, "You, I propose to move against Johnston's army to break it up and to get into the interior of the enemy's country as far as you can, inflicting every damage against their war resources."

To Brigadier General George Meade, a skillful, patient leader, he gave the task of dogging Robert E. Lee, former Superintendent of West Point, and probably the most brilliant field commander in American history.

"Wherever Lee goes, there you also go," Grant ordered.

Confederate Generals Lee and Johnston naturally had opposing plans.

Though their troops had been 'worn out, killed out and starved out,' their determination to drive the foe from their hallowed soil would wear out, kill out and starve out thousands and thousands more before they'd quit the battle.

The tenacious Southerners refused to give up without a fight to the death.

Unfortunately, the citizens of Tennessee and Georgia sat smack in the path of the two offensive thrusts. Marauders from both sides pillaged and vandalized private homes, stealing food stores with nary a thought of the victims' plight.

Devastated civilians devised clever deceptions.

As both armies pillaged their stores, the farmwomen plotted and planned knowing that whatever they raised would be taken from them. The chickens were so rangy that at one place where they killed the best in honor of Mary's visit, the meat was too tough to chew.

The swine, scrawny from insufficient food, were half the size they should be and incapable of nourishing their young.

Mary learned that all of the cunning in the United States was not Yankee cunning, for the southerners were wily enough to keep from starving to death barely.

When she saw how little food they had in the house, she asked, "How do you manage to live?"

Their confidence in her was so great that they confided, "We put food in barrels, bury them in pits, and every time we want something we dig one up and then plow over the patch to fool them.

"Some of us who have cellars dig a small pit under the floor, and then we nail the floor down so that searchers from either army won't find anything hid there. When raiders come around asking if we got any smoked meat somewhere, we deny having a cellar or having anything hid in the house. Some people even hide their provisions in their beds."

And they did it so cleverly that they were left unmolested.

Mary sincerely pitied these people.

Though her patriotic soul rode with the Union army, her tender heart was torn between her boys and the impoverished civilians. With no regard for politics, she ministered to the needy southerners and helped them cope with their losses.

Fearless to the point of endangering her own life, she rode the countryside, unarmed, toting her medicine kit. Always in defiant disobedience of General Meade's direct order that she refrain from spying, she watched and listened, recording and relaying Confederate activities to headquarters.

⊷⊶❀⊷⊶

Dr. Mary's errands of mercy throughout the Georgia countryside sometimes placed her in delicate situations. Many in the communities around Dalton had benefited from her kindness and expertise. They trusted her and felt comfortable requesting favors of her. This tickled Mary, because her superiors had already warned her against consorting with the 'enemy.'

Well, she decided, there are enemies, and there are friendly enemies. Many of the latter had changed their allegiance after her visits and began appearing at command headquarters to renounce their southern connections. This put a great strain on Union commanders because they felt obliged to feed the refugees and find billets for them.

The Widow Wellencott seemed better off than some of her neighbors, though not by much. The family's clothes were in shameful condition, and most of their farm implements had disappeared. Their horses had been confiscated, but they had managed to save a few hens and a scrawny, useless rooster that was too listless to service his harem.

When Dr. Mary came knocking for a night's lodging her reputation had preceded her.

Agatha Wellencott introduced herself as the lady of the house. Her gray complexion nearly matched her thinning hair, and rotted teeth flawed her warm, welcoming smile.

She appeared to be suffering from malnutrition, and Mary suspected this mother gave up her own food for her sixteen-year-old daughter and her only son, a pale, sickly lad she had hidden in a root cellar to keep him from the clutches of the Confederate's Conscription Board.

The boy only emerged from his dark cave late at night for exercise and nourishment. His confinement had taken a terrible toll on his health and disposition. Still, hiding was better than fighting a war that had already killed his Daddy.

Agatha had also secreted some Confederate specie for necessary extras, but since the central government in Richmond kept issuing more dollars without regard to inflation, the money was hardly worth the paper it was printed on. One gold dollar was worth over $50 Confederate, which would purchase little more than a pound of coffee or two pounds of butter. Not that it mattered. These items were unavailable, anyway.

The Wellencotts gave Dr. Mary a place to sleep and shared the family's meager food supply. After a sparse breakfast of bitter, ersatz coffee and dry corn bread moistened with a dollop of honey, Agatha took Mary aside.

"Will ya lend yore horse and take Cordelia ta the mill ta git some thread," she drawled in that soft patois so typical of the region. "I would deem it a great favor, iffen ya did."

"Thread?" Mary asked, her forehead furrowed with wonder.

"To weave into cloth," Agatha said in answer to her guest's puzzled expression.

"Ah, I see," Mary laughed. "In the North we call that cotton yarn."

"We are in terrible need of a new Sunday-go-ta-meetin' dress for Cordelia. Her clothes are so worn out they're in danger of fallin' right off her. We have ta keep up appearances, ya know."

Mary thought the money might be better spent on healthy food, but she understood the fierce pride that drove the mother to do for her child.

"Where is this mill?" she asked, worrying that Confederate soldiers were probably patrolling the area.

"It's about six miles ta the east, towards Chatsworth," Agatha explained.

Dr. Mary frowned. That was dead center of the enemy lines.

"I'm afraid if I go down there in my Union blues, they will seize my horse and take me prisoner," she apologized.

Cordelia spoke up, "Please, Dr. Mary. Ah cain't git there no other way."

The daughter was the spitting image of her mother, except that her teeth were still intact. Her pinched features and mousy hair had lost the robust look a farm girl should have if she ate good food and drank plenty of milk.

Agatha had a solution. "You're about Cordelia's size. You can put on one of her raggedy, old dresses and a bonnet over yore head. You'll look exactly like one of us, iffen ya don't say nothin'."

Cordelia laughed out loud. "Ah can teach her how ta speak right once we're on our way."

Mary smiled at that. Speaking 'right' depended on what part of the country you were standing in at the moment. The women giggled like excited children as Mary struggled with the shabby outfit.

She didn't dare take off her trousers for fear of catching cold, so she rolled up her pant legs. The ruffled edge of the gown barely hid the cuffs, but the overall effect would hopefully fool any stray rebels hanging about.

Out at the barn, the women went to work on Thomasina–named in honor of General Thomas, the officer who had been responsible for Dr. Mary's commission. To disguise the mare's rich chestnut coat, they smeared rust colored mud on her flanks and legs before she was backed between the shafts and secured to the traces. The proud army mount turned balky at the indignity of being hitched to the Wellencott's rickety hay wagon, but she soon gentled when she got a lick of sweet honey from the palm of her mistress.

Mary received one more malevolent glance from Thomasina as she clucked and snapped the reins. However, the cart moved forward, and the unlikely threesome set off toward Ringgold Mill.

On the trail, Cordelia was good at her word. By trial and error, she instructed her northern friend on the pronunciation of the broad "Ah" instead of "I," and how to soften the endings of the "ing" words.

The woods rang with their laughter, as Mary's harsher Yankee tongue struggled to deal with the soft southern syllables.

The doctor had also noted that the family was less educated in proper grammar, and she silently practiced the double negatives and unusual contractions characteristic of the local farmers.

She thought of Cynthia as they jounced along, chatting and joking like childhood buddies. Their trip through the dappled trails to Ringgold's was uneventful, and the spontaneous freedom brought a moment of joy to both ladies.

Once inside Ringgold Mill, they were waited on by the grizzled, disgruntled owner, a mountainous fellow with thick lips and a head of fiery red hair that ringed his bald pate and scraggled down over his ears and massive shoulders.

Mary spied a small pistol tucked among the folds of a humongous belly that flowed over the top of his wide leather belt like lava from the lip of a volcano. This one had not yet experienced any hunger deprivation.

In a great foghorn voice, he complained, nonstop, about the war, the lack of supplies, the damned abolitionists, the thieving Confederates, and the cowardly Yankees.

Dr. Mary shifted from one foot to the other, barely able to hold her tongue, while Cordelia went about her business, oblivious to the political harangue.

She selected $5.00 worth of gaily-colored yarn and sidled up to the counter, where she removed her shoe, extracted a Yankee greenback and offered it as payment.

The mill owner's shaggy eyebrows shot up. "Where'd ya git this money," he demanded, suspicion darkening his homely visage.

The girl turned ghostly white, afraid she'd be reported to the authorities. "Uh, mah Mama received it sellin' butter 'n eggs ta them damn Yankees."

Mary watched the man's expressions change from question mark, to indecision, to hungry greed. Should he, or shouldn't he?

She empathized with him, sensing the mayhem this dilemma created with his conscience. Union money was worth its weight in gold, but loyal southerners were forbidden to trade with it. Besides, if he were caught, he could pay for his actions with his life. Treason was a serious offense, and little mercy was shown to those who practiced it.

Perspiration beaded his forehead as he wrestled with the problem. He toyed with a lock of greasy hair, twisting it around his stubby forefinger.

He retrieved a nasty rag from the hip pocket of his baggy trousers and honked his spider-veined beak, snuffling and wiping and snuffling, again.

Mary could see the wheels turning, as he played for time. He lusted after that money so badly he could taste it.

His eyes flicked to the doorway then his head swiveled around the mill. Nobody was within earshot. "Ah don't dare take Yankee money. They's a law agin it," he said in a halfhearted whisper.

Speaking just as softly, Mary mimicked Cordelia's southern drawl.

"Suh," she said, "We ain't got no Confed'rat money. We come so far ta buy yore goods, and this here greenback is all we got in the world. Now, iffen ya don't say nothin', we won't say nothin'. Ya kin just hide it somewheres, and we'll git on our way."

Cordelia stifled a giggle before it gave her away. Dr. Mary had learned her lessons well. She was talkin' jest fine.

The man's features lit up like the breaking dawn. Beneath his handlebar mustache, his huge teeth practically glowed, as he shoved the bill into his pocket and handed the package to his customers as if nothing unusual had taken place.

On the trek back, the doctor drove while Cordelia gleefully congratulated herself for successfully passing the greenback and for choosing such pretty thread for the cloth her mother would weave for her new dress.

Mary's attention drifted as her sister's precious face floated before her. Cynthia used to squeal with the same delight when Mama promised to make her a new dress.

Absently, the doctor's foot massaged the brake to help Thomasina navigate the steep hill that led up to the final stretch of lonely road back to the farm.

When the wagon was nearly at the top, the sound of rapidly approaching hoof beats startled her from her reverie. She looked back to see six riders galloping toward them, but the dust was so thick she could not identify their clothing.

The whip, a slim switch cut from a pecan tree, fell out of her hands. Mary was in a quandary. Should she jump down to retrieve it, or should Cordelia do it?

She thought, it's not safe for me to get down. If this dress rides up, they'll see my pants. She tucked her chin down so the calico sun-bonnet hid her face."Go lang," she said to the horse, mimicking Cordelia. The girl clutched Mary's hand, as a stern-looking Confederate soldier reined up alongside to check the two women over. He was handsome but trail weary, his uniform threadbare and his boots in no better condition. Mary understood the signs. He'd probably been on patrol for days without much rest.

Since she was afraid to push forward, it took every ounce of her strength to keep her foot jammed on the brake, preventing the weight of the wagon from dragging poor Thomasina back down the hill.

The officer leaned down to get a better look at her, but Mary, scared to death he'd notice her fresh complexion, so different from the pastier look of the local farm women, ducked her head further down, hoping the calico sunbonnet covered enough.

Mary worried about Thomasina as the man chewed on his lips and pulled at his goatee. He studied the mare for a full minute.

Then she began to fear for her own and Cordelia's safety. Damn, she thought, as the other officers drew up ahead. We're way out here in the middle of nowhere. They can do whatever they want to us, and there's no one to help. To be taken prisoner would be serious enough. To be raped by marauders was unthinkable.

She wished she had her pistols. Then, at least she could give them a fight.

Her head shrunk lower into her shoulders as she pretended to be too shy to speak.

"Who are you?" he demanded, "And where are you headed, way out here?"

Cordelia found her tongue just in time. "We been ta the mill, sir," she blurted out, and held up the thread for his inspection.

"We best be hustlin' home ta be stitchin' up shirts fer our brave boys at the line."

Without a blink of her eye, she could lie like a trooper. She had learned her lessons, well.

The officer looked the goods over and glanced into the empty wagon.

Apparently satisfied, he nodded to his men who surrounded them as Thomasina began to back a little.

Chivalry prevailed. The leader seized Thomasina's bridle to lead her up-hill, and the rest of the men spurred to the rear to tailgate the wagon and keep it from slipping out of control. Once the women had gained the crest of the hill, the officers galloped away as quickly as they'd come.

Suddenly Mary remembered the gold-striped uniform trousers rolled up beneath her shabby camouflage, and her limbs turned to jelly. She shook uncontrollably as the potential consequences struck her like a lightning bolt. There would have been no defense against the evidence she wore on her person. Had the officers seen through her disguise, she surely would have been shot as a spy–and her young friend right along with her.

Cordelia noticed Dr. Mary's horrified expression and put her arm around her companion's trembling shoulders.

"My Lord, I thought we were goners," gasped Mary.

Thinking the doctor meant they'd escaped being ravaged, Cordelia tried to soothe her. "No such a thang," she twanged. "Them's officers, Dr. Mary, they ain't common soldiers. They's a big difference, see."

Mary saw no need to explain. "I'll take your word for it," she said, her voice shaky with aftershock. "Let's get back to the farm before we run into any more of those fellows. We may not be so lucky, next time."

Cordelia reached across and slapped the reins. "Go lang," she chirped to Thomasina, and the obedient mare broke into a trot.

CHAPTER THIRTY-FOUR

GEORGIA/TENNESSEE

THE FRIGID RAINS of March gave way to the perfumed breezes of April.

Spring, the South's most sensuous season, spread its mantle of seduction across the land. Sun-warmed trees sprouted sprigs of yellow green to shame away the few rusty brown leaves that managed to cling to winter's naked branches.

And still brother raged against brother in the unholy war that was destroying the fabric of Dr. Mary's beloved country.

General Grant's new commanders were scrambling to assemble their hosts of troops in preparation for the all-out push to crush their principal adversaries, General Robert E. Lee and General Joe Johnston.

Supplies trickled in, ferried up the Tennessee River on cumbersome steamboats, and ugly scows, and then hauled in rumbling army wagons to Chattanooga depots. General Thomas's troops had nicknamed the operation 'Cracker Line,' after the army's chief staple, hardtack, which came stashed among the other stores. Not nearly enough of anything was getting through, but at least the troops were kept from starving.

Secret conclaves explored strategies to invade the farthest reaches of the Confederate-held territories. Full-blown battles would soon replace the rapid attacks and retreats mounted by both sides.

Union Private Robert G. Carter reflected the concerns of all his bunkmates in a letter to his parents:

"The summer days are almost here, when we shall be wearily plodding over the roads in search of victory or death. Many a poor fellow will find the latter. I dread the approaching campaign. I can see horrors insurmountable through the summer months."

ꝏꙮꙅ

On the 10th of April 1864, Dr. Mary left the command post on an errand of mercy into territory currently controlled by the Confederates.

Her commanding officer would no longer authorize an armed escort, declaring it too dangerous for his men to be out and about in too few numbers.

"The Southerners will not harm me," she promised. "I shall go it alone to see my patients." She packed up her kit and rode across the border into Georgia.

She let her mare set a leisurely pace as she soaked up the burgeoning beauty around her. Except for Thomasina's gentle ploddings, all living sounds were absent. Bright wild flowers, red tipped Photinia bushes, melodious birdsong, and the rich, fertile odor of earth awakening to new life, all contributed to her momentary feeling of peace. She shivered with pleasure as she inhaled the heady aromas of the Dixie countryside.

Spring comes early here, she thought. It would be at least another month before Oswego's fields would waken from their winter slumber. Memories of home brought a familiar stinging to her eyelids.

Nostalgia assailed her, as she pictured Alvie helping Papa around the barn, readying equipment for the planting. Mama would probably be seated by the fire, mending worn summer-weight socks to replace the heavy wools of winter. For one sad moment, Mary wished herself back there.

She settled comfortably into the saddle, rearranging her blue, cloth jacket and matching, knee-length cloak that flowed over Thomasina's strong rump. Licorice tendrils spilled from beneath the jaunty, black felt hat that shaded her remarkable blue eyes. Her knee-high leather boots rested in the stirrups, her small, capable hands held the reins loosely.

The mare stuck to the rude path, needing little guidance as her hooves scuffed up the dense covering of leaves and pine needles on the forest floor, adding their pungent bouquet to the mix.

Dr. Mary traveled with confidence, unarmed, as usual. No premonition of disaster unsettled her. She had ridden alone many times before. Her expression was serene, her body relaxed. She delivered a continuing, soft commentary to Thomasina. The faithful mare flicked her ears in patient understanding. "There must have been serious skirmishing here," she muttered, grimacing as she noted the heavy, conical bullets littering the landscape.

Thomasina snorted and nodded her head.

Mary leaned forward in the saddle and laid her cheek against her horse's healthy mane. She examined the rings etched in the weighty, earth-colored bullets fired from the lever action Spencer rifles. Her shoulders shuddered at the pale smoothness of deadly, virginal-looking missiles from slow loading, fast firing Colt rifles.

Among the dried leaves, she picked out the wicked fragments of the Springfield musket's ugly brown minie balls which she hated worst of all. The devilish missiles created helpless cripples as they ripped through flesh and irreparably shattered the legs and thighs of luckless troops.

Her heart ached. How many boys fought for their lives in this desolate place?

Deep in the thrall of her reverie, she failed to sense the presence of the Rebel picket, waiting, still as a fence post, until she ran smack dab into his clutches.

His shabby uniform was incomplete, and the filthy toes of his left foot poked through his tattered boot. The pale peach fuzz on his undershot chin betrayed his age at no more than fifteen or sixteen; yet he handled his rifle with the confident aplomb of a seasoned fighter.

"Here, you," the boy demanded, "where ya think yore going?"

Good Lord, she thought, that was mighty stupid of me. Why didn't I pay better attention?

Recovering quickly, she offered him a bunch of correspondence tied together with a heavy piece of cord. "I have a packet of letters for citizens behind your lines," she replied. "Would you be kind enough to take them and see them delivered safely?"

A triumphant grin stretched across a mouthful of uneven teeth. Power surged through his chest as he set the stock of his weapon against his shoulder and sighted down its barrel. Lord be praised. He had him a damn Yankee! "Madam," the boy replied, with studied arrogance. "I'll take the letters, and I'll take you, too."

Too surprised to be scared, Mary brazened it out. She decided that authority was something this child might understand. She spoke in the ringing tones that had been successful in handling obstreperous students in her long ago classroom. "You'll do no such thing, young man." She held up her leather field case. "I am a doctor on a medical call."

The skinny teen-ager, so confident despite his nondescript rags and flattened forage cap, was hell bent to impress his superiors. A Yankee prisoner might just get him promoted to corporal. Wouldn't his pappy be proud?

He sneered at the unarmed woman's bravado and seized Thomasina's bridle. The mare tossed her head as she backed away from his rough grasp, but the boy held firm.

The first prickle of fear slithered up Mary's spine. This cheeky lad was not going to give in. "Stop. Stop, this instant," she demanded in her most imperious tone. Still chuckling, he turned away, dragging the balky mare along behind.

Her quick wits had delivered her from the vicious insanity of 'Champ' Ferguson who had promised violent death to every damn Yankee that strayed into his beloved Dixie. She had survived a second time by posing as a simple farm girl to hoodwink a passel of Confederate officers outside Dalton, Georgia.

Then there was the third time, which drove her crazy whenever she thought of it.

While riding Colonel McCook's stallion to deliver medical supplies beyond the lines, she had stumbled into a cadre of enemy soldiers who had never learned the meaning of respect.

The dastardly ruffians had laughed at her, stole the handsome horse and the supplies, then shipped her back to her own headquarters, seated on the bony back of a disreputable-looking mule. The indignity of it still rankled.

But this fourth encounter appeared to be the last straw. Dr. Mary's incredible luck had finally run out.

Confederate Major J. W. Ratchford wrote in his private memoirs of her capture:

"While our army was fighting Rosecrans in Georgia, we took a prisoner who proved pretty much of a white elephant on our hands. She was indignant and protested against being taken prisoner. Her indignation was still in evidence when she was brought into camp Gen. D.H. Hill, was much amused, replying that she was probably giving him as much inconvenience as he was giving her, for he could neither keep her nor turn her loose. He sent her to General Bragg. Her appearance excited a good deal of curiosity in our camp, as she was the first American woman to wear publicly bloomers, yet her patent leather boots and plumed hat gave her a very dainty appearance. She was not pretty, but she was far from ugly."

General Hill sent her to General Johnston who was promptly in a dither at the unorthodox interruption of an important strategy meeting. Had she been an ordinary prisoner, he would never have known of her existence.

"Just what am I supposed to do about it?" he fussed. "That wily bastard, Sherman, is on the move and I have an army to gear up, here."

Johnston dealt with the situation swiftly by banishing her from his jurisdiction. "I'm much too busy to be bothered with this..? this..? whatever. Just send it off to Richmond and let them worry about it."

❦

Dr. Mary was confined to a holding pen until an escort could be arranged to accompany her to the capital.

Her trek to Richmond on horseback involved a tedious journey across the rough terrain of the Carolinas and on up through Virginia. She developed painful saddle sores, and every bone in her body ached from the gut-wrenching pace over hills and through woodlands. Her cheek bled profusely when a sharp branch snapped back and smacked her.

The military escorts–seedy Confederate soldiers enjoying the sport of ridiculing her strange clothing and unusual accent–did their utmost to humiliate her. But their jibes and insults only strengthened her resolution to show no weakness.

On the third day on the trail, a young private, Ezra Philbert, a scarecrow in raggedy gray uniform, grabbed his throat making ugly, guttural sounds. "I'm sick," he croaked, hoping her medical bag contained a pint of whiskey. "Get me some of yore magic medicine."

Dr. Mary's eyes, dark as a stormy ocean, narrowed to slits. He was out to make a fool of her." There's nothing wrong with you that a few days hard work wouldn't cure," she shot back and wheeled her horse away from him.

A lewd expression crossed his whiskered face. "Well, now, woman. You haven't even looked me over," he menaced, glancing around to check if his buddies were impressed.

Some of the men were uncomfortable with his disrespectful manners. Their mamas had taught them better. Yet, every eye was gauging his performance, hoping to see their tiny prisoner cowed with fear.

Not on your life, you Rebel devils. Dr. Mary considered herself ten feet tall and dangerous as a pit bull.

Abhorring his bullying tactics, she decided to rub his face in his mistake. She drew herself up in her stirrups and looked down her nose with the manner of a cattle dealer appraising a substandard bull that had no business cluttering up the auction block.

Her eyes turned hard as agates, her lips clenched tight. Every soldier within earshot held his breath. A trembling leaf could have roared in the silence.

Finally, she addressed Ezra like a tyrannical schoolmarm about to take a willow switch to an incorrigible miscreant. "First of all, you will not address me as 'woman,' and secondly, you will call me 'Doctor' or use the term 'Ma'am'if you ever find it necessary to speak to me again."

His companions giggled nervously like naughty boys caught teasing a stupid, little girl.

Now, Ezra's pride was on the line.

He pulled his horse up close to hers and roughly yanked her bridle.

"Prisoners don't talk to me like that," he said, his threatening tone promising retaliation.

Mary's firm hand kept Thomasina from bolting. She stared him down, her small chin thrust forward, her back straight as an arrow. She'd better handle this little woodworm right now or he'd make her life miserable for the rest of the journey.

She ignored the others, but shot Ezra a withering scowl, shriveling his ego with her utter contempt. "And enlisted men do not speak to officers at all, unless they are addressed, first." she spat, "What will you do, beat me up or murder me in front of all these witnesses?"

She waited a moment for his reaction, pleased with herself as she caught the glimmer of uncertainty in his eyes. One little threat ought to finish him off. "Perhaps your commanding officer would be interested in your blatant maltreatment of a captured surgeon who has risked her life to treat Southern civilians."

Impressed with her haughty manner, the men decided they'd better tangle no further with her.

"She's gotcha there, Philbert," one snickered. "Best leave it lay."

Everyone left her in peace after that, giving her privacy whenever the need arose.

Somehow, the troops managed to secure liquor in their occasional forays into the countryside. "Join us in a drink," they invited as they offered her a pull on a jug of homegrown corn whiskey.

"No thank you," she deferred, quite politely.

She later reported of the incident:

"I ultimately gained from those who were there that respect which all drunken people invariably showed total abstainers."

Food, however, was a problem of a different kind. She became so starved because of the inadequate rations that when the entourage reached Richmond her heart soared at the shouts of "Fresh Fish."

"Where can I get a bit of that," she asked, her tongue fairly salivating for something besides dry hardtack and stale water.

"Say, what?" asked the corporal beside her.

"Fresh fish," she answered.

He exhaled a rip-roaring snort and nearly fell from his saddle, laughing.

"Hear that boys? The doctor wants fresh fish?"

Finally, he swiped the spittle from his chin and, still chortling, gave her the bad news. "Madam, *you* are the 'fresh fish'."

"That's the most insulting thing I ever heard," she muttered.

Grandstanding to bystanders, the young showoff grabbed the reins and cruelly yanked at Mary's horse. Thomasina, balking at the rough hands dragging her bridle, resisted every step until the corporal smacked her sharply on the rump.

Mary cried out. "There's no need to hurt her, just release your hold and we'll go wherever you wish."

The entourage moved forward to the Provost Marshal's office where a Captain Semmes, spit-smart in his fresh uniform, stepped outside to hear the details of Mary's capture.

The reporting corporal's every other sentence was interrupted by a countering tirade from his furious prisoner.

"You have no right to detain me," Mary insisted. "I am a surgeon, not a soldier, and I do not appreciate your disrespectful treatment one whit. You will be severely punished for your crime against an innocent doctor."

Semmes was unmoved. He personally escorted the group across the compound to the gate of the squat, ugly building facing his office. His prisoner was still sounding off as she was pulled from her saddle and shoved toward the guard.

"Lock her up and keep a close eye on her," he ordered the surprised private who had never seen the captain put himself out in such a manner. "This here's a damn Yankee spy captured in the act."

The wooden door of the holding cell was slammed behind her. The heavy bolt screeched as it was rammed into place. Slightly bewildered, she backed up against the wood panels, her heart thumping with the debilitating combination of anger and fear.

Dr. Mary's cherished freedom was now a whisper in the wind.

Worse still, spies were shot, were they not?

CHAPTER THIRTY-FIVE

RICHMOND, VIRGINIA

THREE YEARS to the day Virginia swore allegiance to the South, Dr. Mary was unceremoniously dumped in the Confederacy's capital.

She found the gracious city suffering the privations of a desperate war.

In the beginning, Richmond's homes rang with gaiety as Confederate officers strutted in spanking new uniforms of cadet gray, striped with gold chevrons and belted with handsome polished buckles. They captivated the hearts of the local belles at festive teas and gala balls. These refined swashbucklers swore in their broad southern patois to dispatch the murdering Yankee buffoons and be home in time for the spring cotillions.

Now, two years later, every elegant household had been stripped of its silver, brass, steel, copper and lead altruistically 'donated' for the noble war effort.

Graceful manners still prevailed as Richmond ladies went about their business, speaking in soft, mellow drawls that carefully camouflaged their inflexible endurance.

They trod the streets in threadbare gowns and shabby boots, ignoring the looming prisons festering like carbuncles blighting their fair city. They averted their eyes and covered their noses with frayed lace hankies to ward off the stench when their errands took them too close to the prisoners' quarters. It was unladylike to acknowledge unpleasantness.

The long overland ride from Tennessee to Richmond, together with the insufficient trail diet, had sapped Mary's strength. She arrived in the capital filthy and exhausted, but she sat her saddle with the bearing of a general reviewing the troops.

Once they got her there, they had no clue what to do with her, nor could they classify her role. She couldn't be a doctor, could she? There was no such thing as a woman doctor. Could she be a Federal spy? Was that reasonable when she made no bones about her service to the Union Army?

Was she a soldier, gussied up in a pseudo uniform? No telling what those mannerless Yankee bumpkins might conjure up.

Captain B. J. Semmes expressed his distaste and disrespect in an accompanying letter:

> *"This morning, we were all amused and disgusted too at the sight of a THING that nothing but the debased and depraved Yankee nation could produce—'a female doctor'brought in by pickets this morning. She was dressed in the full uniform of a Federal Surgeon, looks hat & all, & wore a cloak(she is) fair, but not good looking and of course had tongue enough for a regiment of men. I was in hopes the General (Joe Johnston) would have her dressed in a homespun frock and bonnet and sent back to Yankee lines, or put in a lunatic asylum."*

The first encounter with the Richmond man appointed to administer her case brought Mary to tears, but not for the reasons her interrogator envisioned.

Brigadier General William M. Gardner wanted this troublesome woman exchanged immediately. There were no accommodations suitable for female prisoners in Richmond or anywhere else in the Confederacy, and he could not, in good conscience, put her in with the men.

The forty-year-old Georgian had a broad, square face, heavy-lidded eyes and a generous mouth that had long forgotten how to smile. His coarse brown hair, parted on the right, hung straight to his ear lobes. He was clean-shaven and carried himself with the rigid bearing of his strict West Point training.

Numerous surgeries to avoid amputation after his leg had been severely macerated by a Federal minie ball during a charge at Bull Run left Gardner with a severe limp. Perhaps that was the shot that killed his sense of humor.

He was a reasonable man whose disposition had mellowed considerably since he came to terms with his brush with death. He handled authority well, and his underlings respected him as well as the position. His troops obeyed orders without question.

But petite Mary Walker posed a huge challenge to him. Her caustic reputation had preceded her, and he vowed to nip her protests in the bud.

When she stood mute before him, worn out and unwashed, his heart softened.

"My dear young lady," he began gently, hoping to ward off a tirade, "you understand, you could have avoided all this hullabaloo if only you had dressed in a more feminine garb?"

Mary, sick of the same old song, said nothing. She closed her eyes and sighed, the patient sigh old Job must have used when he answered his critics:

"Behold my eye has seen all this,
My ear has heard and understood it."

The general motioned to the straight chair before his desk. She sank gratefully onto the seat and folded her hands in her lap.

He spoke quietly, without rancor or sarcasm. "You appear to be of good birth and refinement, and you seem to have a superior intellect," he began. "Do you not understand the foolishness of your behavior? The battlefield is no place for a woman."

His fatherly demeanor surprised and unnerved her. She could handle ridicule and disrespect, but kindness from a captor was totally unexpected. She needed her anger for strength. Pride in her appearance had always given her confidence. How could she be confident when she looked like a gutter rat?

Suddenly courage deserted her. Tears welled dangerously close. She was so very tired. Her body was chafed and aching, and her legs had turned to rubber after dangling endless hours from Thomasina's saddle.

Her first horrifying impression of Richmond's infamous military prison had made her suspect that there wasn't an ounce of pity in all the Confederate military.

She clenched her fists and bit her lip as his soft voice belied that thinking. Here was a man of compassion who was expressing genuine concern for her welfare.

General Gardner's kindness had reached a place deep inside–a place she had suppressed since her dealings with her old friend, Dr. Green. She steeled herself. She could not afford to enjoy his compassion, but the tears came anyway.

Gardner later bragged in a letter:

"I must have impressed her with the indignities that she had invited for her composure finally gave way and she got to crying–just as an ordinary woman might have done."

But he also described her as "the most personable and gentlemanly looking woman I ever saw."

For all of his tireless efforts, Gardner was unable to arrange a timely exchange, and Dr. Mary became another victim of Castle Thunder's cruel environment.

✦

Two of the many prisons in Richmond were directly across from one another—Libby and Castle Thunder where Mary was incarcerated. She was assigned to the second because her exact crime was never defined. Besides, it boasted a number of compartments to separate the inmates.

This facility was used to detain "the murderer, the robber, the deserter, the pickpocket, the skulker, the spy, the reconstructionist, the disloyal and the 'semi-Yankees' who reportedly helped the Negroes escape to the north." A number were accused of treason against the Confederate States of America.

Military prisons in both the North and the South were festering cesspools, where more than 30,000 Federals, and 26,000 Confederates died in captivity. Armies could hardly waste their skimpy food supplies on the enemy when they lacked enough for their own people.

A few months before Mary's imprisonment, Castle Thunder's commander, Captain George W. Alexander, was called before the Confederate House of Representatives to answer charges of 'harshness, inhumanity, tyranny and dishonesty.'

Alexander was exonerated, but not before he declared the prisoners to be 'wharf rats' who deserved nothing better.

Three hundred prisoners and fifty untreated hospital patients were detained within the battered walls during Mary's stay.

When she entered the three-story, rectangular building, a converted tobacco warehouse, Dr. Mary's nostrils flared. The sharp tobacco redolence that permeated the woodwork was barely noticeable above the other stinks that threatened to overpower her.

Closely set, unglazed windows ate up most of the wall space inviting dampness and insects. Common troughs where prisoners washed and drank contained fetid water covered with slime. Sanitation was non-existent, and the little food distributed was unfit to eat.

Bitter bile regurgitated into her esophagus. She choked it back to keep from puking, as

her passage down the long corridor to her cell allowed a preview of the evils to come.

She passed pitiful, long-term prisoners so wasted and debilitated that all their muscle and fat had shriveled away, leaving bones visible beneath the transparent, parchment skin stretched over them. Spongy, swollen gums, devoid of teeth, protruded beyond blistered lips rampant with canker sores. Vermin-infested heads showed ugly bald spots where clumps of hair had fallen out.

Men too weak to greet her were slowly dying of vicious diarrhea, malnutrition and the hopeless certainty that they would never see their loved ones again.

The battlefield had been ugly, but this egregious waste of human life angered her beyond reason. The place was a killing factory.

Many of the sickest were paroled into the arms of the Angel of Death, while others committed suicide by shuffling beyond the specified limits of the exercise yard, knowing a rifle ball would end their agony.

The Richmond newspapers celebrated Dr. Mary's capture, not because of her notoriety, but because it had been a long time since they could entertain their readers with anything as titillating as this 'strange, unsexed apparition.'

Local gossips pored over the special events pages gleefully devouring spicy details about 'the strong-minded female surgeon.'

Traditional belles in their tacky hoop skirts laughed behind their fans at the descriptions of her attire that seemed more suitable to a camp follower than a respectable lady.

One reporter wrote:

> *"Dr. (Miss) Walker is about thirty, good looking*
> *but strong-minded and no doubt a disciple of*
> *miscegenation."*

Where the idea that she favored marriages between whites and coloreds originated was anyone's guess.

Prison officials showed Mary the newspaper articles with the hope that their sarcasm would stifle her sassy tongue. Little did her tormentors know that she'd heard it all before.

When she read the phrase "she was handsomely attired in male apparel," her short fuse ignited, and she was off. She penned a letter that was typical of her dedication to dress reform. She wrote:

"Sir: Will you please correct a statement made in this morning's *Dispatch* in regard to my being 'dressed in male attire,' as such is not the case. I am attired in what is usually called the 'Bloomer' or 'Reform Dress,' which is similar to all ladies' dress with the exception of its being more physiological than long dresses."

Though hungry, frightened, weary and discouraged, her indomitable spirit prevailed. Dr. Mary would continue to defend dress reform until the day she died.

CHAPTER THIRTY-SIX

RICHMOND, VIRGINIA

EARLY IN THE WAR, prisoners were being repatriated, man for man; but when General Grant took full command of the Union forces, he abolished the system on the premise that every released Rebel became a potential killer of Federal soldiers.

It was argued that the reverse could be true, but the general had an answer for the dissenters who screamed for the release of fathers and sons dying in droves–killed by the murderous conditions in every prison camp.

"That may be true," he said, "but the South does not have fresh replacements for its regiments. The North, on the other hand, has no problem recruiting fresh troops."

Grant had set aside his pity for the unfortunate captives, stating, "They will have to stay where they are. That they probably will not survive their confinement is regrettable but unavoidable."

His decision did not bode well for the Union Army's only female surgeon.

Mary paced her small cell, feeling lonely and useless. She had no privacy as there were no doors on the individual cubicles. Damp night air seeped through the window openings, chilling her bones.

She felt naked without her surgical kit, which had been practically glued to her side since her first days at Warrenton. It was as if her right arm had been amputated at the elbow.

At least, if she had her instruments, she could treat her fellow prisoners' putrid, pus-filled sores before fatal gangrene set in.

"I beg you, please bring me my medical bag," she cried, but her pleas fell on deaf ears. The guards had no authority to return them, even if they were so inclined. After considerable haggling, she finally obtained an audience with the Provost Marshal.

Early one soggy April morning, she was escorted to his office. The dew count was so high, droplets appeared on her shoulders, and her hair frizzed into ringlets.

She'd lived with the hope that her release, along with the return of her medical kit and her faithful Thomasina, would only be a matter of time. Her argument was a good one. No reasonable man could refuse.

Disheveled and hungry, she began to doubt her chances as she followed the guard. The sergeant's nervousness corroborated her fears as they approached headquarters. She suspected she was in hot water before she even pleaded her case.

She was ushered into the presence of Brigadier General John Henry Winder, and his stern countenance confirmed her worst fears.

His eyes nearly bugged out of his head as he caught sight of her untidy uniform. In all his sixty-four years he had never seen a woman clad in anything but a graceful gown.

His thin lips puckered with distaste. A steely glitter emanated from hazel eyes that raked her body from head to toe as if they could not credit their first impression.

Two deep folds creased the space between his sparse gray brows, and his clean-shaven dewlaps bulged against the stand-up collar of his regulation uniform. The distance between the end of his large nose and his thin upper lip was too short for even a modest mustache. Iron gray hair, curled up on the ends, left most of his large, flat ears exposed. His chunky torso covered the middle third of his wide desk, and Mary thought he might be tall if he decided to stand on his feet.

He did not offer her a seat, but left her planted upright before his desk. His animosity was palpable, giving her the impression that he would just as soon wring her neck as deal with her.

"Sir," she began, hoping flattery would curry his favor, "do I have the honor of addressing the general in charge of this post?"

"I am Provost Marshal and prison commandant," he replied, puffing with pride.

"Then surely you are in a position to grant my simple requests," she fawned, hating to kowtow to this proud, boorish man. Anyone who overlooked such dreadful conditions in his jurisdiction surely had little compassion.

"What is it you want?" he inquired, his tone implying she had no better chance of getting her wish than a pig had of getting into heaven.

"First, I would like to inquire for my mare," she said, her tone reasonable and respectful. "Is she receiving proper care and food while I am detained?"

"You needn't worry about her," he sneered. "She has been confiscated and turned over to a Confederate officer. I'm sure he will take very good care of her."

Mary's eyes stung. Poor Thomasina—a proud Union mount in the clutches of a southerner. How she would miss her old friend, but she could not quibble over the fortunes of war, right now.

She squared her shoulders and swallowed her sadness. I'm here to demand my freedom, general."

The man was speechless, in danger of swallowing his teeth.

She raised her hand to stem any protest. "Hear me out, please," she implored, hurrying on. "No incriminating evidence was found on my person; therefore, I do not understand my imprisonment. Along with my military duties of caring for wounded soldiers, I have been treating Southern civilians who were abandoned by your own physicians. That is why I was out alone and unarmed at the time of my capture."

"You had no business being in Confederate Territory dressed as a Union Officer. You took your chances, and you got yourself caught."

She ignored his tirade, as if he hadn't spoken words that rang true. She was certain that there was no way the Rebels could know she had passed along vital information garnered in her travels through the rural south. Her activities had been closely guarded by the few who knew of her efforts.

She forged ahead unafraid. "I also came for the purpose of retrieving the medical belongings that were taken away when I arrived," she said. "Do you have sufficient authority to grant my request?"

Winder bristled at what he considered a slur against his power. He was in full charge, and he took his position very seriously.

"Yes, I have full authority," he barked, "and no, sir, you have no rights, here. As a matter of fact, I am not obliged to even grant you an interview."

Mary was not quite sure she heard correctly. Did he just call me sir, she wondered.

She ignored it. Her imagination must be working overtime.

"Don't you understand," she insisted, "there are patients who are in desperate need of treatment? Some could lose their limbs if their wounds are allowed to fester any longer."

Winder, polished to the nines, his flaming superiority complex much in evidence, turned up the corner of his lip. The expression gave him the appearance of a hungry cur growling to protect his food. "That is of no concern to you. The prisoners are my sole responsibility."

She knew a sharp retort would alienate him further, but she could not contain her aggravation. Prisoners needed her help. "But you are not taking responsibility," she said as mildly as her anger allowed. "There are no doctors in attendance, and I must insist that you give me the chance to help them."

The man was astounded. "You insist? How dare you walk in here and demand anything from me. You are a prisoner of war with no rights, whatsoever."

"I have a responsibility as a surgeon to help the afflicted, regardless of prejudice. I treated your southern citizens without questioning their political affiliations. Now, my fellow countrymen deserve the same courtesy."

Winder pulled a cigar from his breast pocket and chomped off the end. He flicked the scrap out with the tip of his tongue. The soggy remnant hit the desk and lay there like a squatting roach.

Mary bit the inside of her cheek to stifle her disgust for his nasty habit. Not a good idea to give a lecture on the evils of tobacco just now.

He exploded at her suggestion. "I believe you are a spy, sir, and I shall keep you here till it is ascertained. You cannot go, sir."

Damnation, he did call her sir! This was no time to equivocate. She would explain so even this idiot could understand. "It is not 'sir,' she roared." I am Dr. Mary Edwards Walker. That's Mary—M A R Y."

"Well, Mary," he snapped back, "I might be more sympathetic toward your cause if you dressed like other ladies."

Her eyes rolled heavenward. Same old tune, she thought, just a different jester. But it was the last straw. She would not compromise her pride even if it meant immediate freedom.

"Understand me, sir," she thundered. "Men have no more right to dictate how women dress, than women have the right to dictate the same to men. Women who drag along yards of fabric use up half their energy lugging that load around. They are not only weakened by the weight, but they are always in other people's way."

The veins in Winder's forehead pulsed dangerously. "Sergeant," he yelled. "Take this, this prisoner back to quarters, immediately. Pass the word that she is never to be brought to this office again. Is that understood, sergeant?"

The man saluted his superior officer then prodded Mary with his rifle.

"No need for that," she insisted as she shoved the barrel away from her.

Stepping out smartly, she quick-marched back to her filthy cell on the third floor where she sank down on the cot to mull over her predicament.

Her cheeks flamed as she recalled the commandant's rudeness. Sir indeed!

So much for the southern officer's chivalry she had heard about from her little friend, Cordelia.

⚜

Smarting from Winder's disdainful treatment, Dr. Mary grumbled to herself long after she returned to her cell. I'll show that pompous ass, she thought, defiantly. Somehow I'll show him.

Days afterward, she watched a parcel of Union soldiers assigned to Libby Prison marching down Carey Street past Castle Thunder. The bedraggled troopers were astounded when they caught sight of a figure at a third floor window saluting them. One man reported that a 'non-descript shape made us a salutation.' The men returned the salute and later discovered that it was their own Dr. Mary.

Though two other Union surgeons were also being detained, medical treatment of prisoners by unauthorized persons was strictly forbidden.

Secretly, she began administering aid to fellow prisoners, debriding infected wounds, even extracting teeth with whatever means she could come by: a sharpened spoon handle, improvised tools fashioned from bucket bails and a pen knife that had been smuggled in on the person of a political prisoner.

One man, a Virginian, was arrested for "a crime against the Confederate States," though what that crime was, he was never told. Roughly manhandled and beaten about his head, he lay semi-comatose for several days, alternately hallucinating and moaning incoherently. His conditioned worsened with frightening speed.

One of the Virginian's cellmates came for Dr. Mary in the middle of the night while their elderly guard slumped at his post, snoring away. The farmer shook her awake, hissing to shush her before she could scream.

"Who are you," she demanded, alarmed at being accosted in the dark by a strange man.

"Shh, you'll wake the guard," he whispered placing his fingers gently over her lips.

"My name is Luther, doctor. Private Luther Ellerby. We need your help a few doors down from here."

It was not the first time she had been summoned in the wee hours. Relying on her instincts, she took the man's word on faith alone. Furtively, she followed him down the hall, slithering through the shadows, hugging the walls till the two of them melted through an open doorway to reach the patient's cot.

A sickly, sputtering candle cast grotesque shadows on the walls of the six-foot square room. Several inmates slept on, oblivious of the drama unfolding nearby.

By the time Mary was called in to help, the muscle in the Virginian's shoulder had become fully involved with a massive, life-threatening infection. He drifted in and out of consciousness, and his body was scalding hot from a sky-high temperature. His elegant, pleated, cotton shirt was unspeakably dirty where it stuck to the wound that stank of putrefaction.

"What happened to him?" she asked.

"He was slashed by a bayonet, and the cut was never tended to."

"What's his name, do you know?"

"Alonzo Devereau. He said he was born right here in Richmond."

"Good Lord, now they're throwing their own people into prison," was her bitter reply. "This man should be in a hospital."

"They don't have no room, and they ain't no doctors there, anyway."

Mary's expression was grim. Damn those ignorant fools.

The man might be handsome, but it was hard to tell. His left eye and both ears were badly swollen and, in the eerie light, looked black with bruising. His lower lip was fat with a blood-filled contusion. A shock of dark, curly hair was matted to his scalp above a half-healed cut on his aristocratic forehead. Obviously he had taken a severe beating.

She reached into her pocket and extracted her little penknife, slid it open and held it over the flame to heat it thoroughly.

"Can you hear me, Mr. Devereau," she whispered close to his thickened left ear.

"Uh," the man groaned.

One of the other inmates turned over in his cot and called out a word she could not distinguish. She jumped with surprise. She waited till all was quiet then leaned toward Alonzo, once more.

"I need to cut the sleeve from your shirt, sir."

All Devereau could manage was a nod.

She went to work, then, ignoring everything but her patient. Gently, she separated the fabric from his flesh and ripped the shoulder seam. A stink erupted from the wound that made Luther gag.

"Quiet," Mary barked. "Just hold your breath for a minute. You'll get used to it."

Luther doubted that with all his heart.

Quickly the doctor lanced the huge pustule that blossomed from the seat of the infection. Viscous yellow gunk squirted up coating the surrounding redness with thick, greasy pus.

"That should make him feel better already," she promised as she scraped away the mess. "See if you can get some water for me," she told Luther. He scurried away, happy to escape the disgusting odor, even though he would be punished if discovered outside his assigned quarters.

He returned a short time later with his grubby hat full of water scooped from the common trough.

Mary's nose wrinkled with distaste, but she had no other choice. She bathed the wound with the stale water, hoping that its foulness would not exacerbate the infection. She tore apart the lower portion of the gentleman's sleeve and placed the cleanest side of the compress against his bloody shoulder. She made Luther turn his back while she ripped a strip from the bottom of her shirtwaist to fasten it down.

Alonzo, exhausted, fell into a restless sleep. Mary laid her hand against his forehead. His temperature had lowered a bit. His flesh was no longer burning hot.

She turned to Luther and asked, "How is it you care so much about a southern gentleman?"

"Why, Ma'am," the soldier answered, "he believes in our country, same as we do."

Nothing more need be said. She understood, completely.

"Make him drink some water," she ordered. "Watch him carefully. If he worsens, come and fetch me. Otherwise, I will be here to treat him again, tomorrow night."

"Yes, ma'am," promised the Yankee patriot.

Her work finished, she crept back to her own digs and lay down on her cot. "God be with him," she whispered, "I've done everything I can."

By the grace of the Almighty and Dr. Mary, Alonzo Devereau struggled slowly back to health. On her final visit to him, he caught her wrist as grateful tears welled in his eyes. He pressed a tightly creased fan into her hand.

"Take this Dr. Mary," he offered, "along with my undying gratitude. It belonged to my wife and it is all I have of value."

Mary tried in vain to return it. "I cannot accept it, Mr. Devereau. It's your only souvenir of your beloved. Besides, I only did what I was trained to do."

"Not so," he insisted. "You saved my life at the risk of your own. Rebecca would want you to have it. Please take it."

Mary accepted the gift and shoved it up her sleeve away from the guard's prying eyes. She left Devereau's cell just as dawn was brightening the eastern sky, insinuating its watery light into the dark corners of Castle Thunder.

Once in her room, she turned her back to the open doorway, and slid the fan from its hiding place. She flicked her wrist to snap it open the way she had seen the fashionable ladies in Washington do it a hundred light years before.

The right side of it was decorated with delicate blossoms intricately entwined with fragile twigs and branches.

When she turned it over, she gasped in surprise. There, bold as life, lay an accurate replica of the stars and stripes of the American flag, hand painted in glorious colors.

Her heart leaped with joy, as she clasped the flag to her breast. A treasure, beyond priceless! Tears spilled down her cheeks. Alonzo Devereau would never know how much his generosity had touched and uplifted her.

Thereafter, Mary became even more daring. With no regard for consequences, she waved her precious flag at captured Yankees marching by her window. The abuses they received for proudly saluting it were a small price to pay for a glimpse of their most important symbol of home.

No effort was made to confiscate the fan. Perhaps Southerners admired undying loyalty equally as well as their Northern brothers did.

After the war, repatriated soldiers who lived through that terrible time wrote of the comfort they gained from glimpsing Old Glory just before the dark tomb of Libby Prison swallowed them up.

⁂

Most nights, Mary slept badly, if she slept at all. Demons, parading in the forms of horribly maimed casualties, bedeviled her dreams.

The faces of dead and dying soldiers lying on bloody battlefields floated through them, nightly. The moment she drifted into restless sleep, the sightless eyes and broken bodies of fifteen and sixteen-year-old patients haunted her. She woke, drenched with sweat, crying tears that could never wash away the terrible sights she'd witnessed at Warrenton, and Chickamauga.

But, awake, Castle Thunder's living devils created as much havoc with her psyche as did her troubled dreams.

Cruel, half drunk guards thought it great sport to fire their weapons into the prisoners' cells, missing, by inches, inmates who cowed in terror. She was manhandled and threatened with bodily harm in ways no woman should have to endure.

She became a night creature, removing her trousers and tunic only when absolutely necessary, waiting till the darkest hours to use the latrines or wash her body in the fetid water of the common troughs. The constant dampness invaded her joints till they screamed with pain.

As the weeks crept by, Dr. Mary's morale eroded. She was steadily losing weight, as she gave most of her maggot-filled rice and moldy bread to the rats skittering around the dark corners of her cell.

Her pleas to her father's God did little to comfort her. She had relied so long on her belief in Spiritualism that the prayers died aborning.

She believed in Papa's Methodist God, all right, but she had depended too long on her own strengths and abilities to place herself completely in His care. She knew God was there to support her, but she must do the work herself.

She cried privately whenever she thought of home and her dear parents. Long hours of inactivity allowed Cynthia and Edwin to invade her thoughts, bringing more tears.

When she summoned enough grit to put aside her grief, she wrote a cheery letter to her parents, blatantly lying to protect them from the ugly truth:

"I hope you are not grieving about me because I am a prisoner of war. I am living in a three-story brick castle with plenty to eat and a clean bed to sleep in. I am well, the officers are gentlemanly and kind, and it will not be long before I am exchanged."

Inevitably, her health began to fail. Her boundless energy diminished, her skin and hair grew lifeless from lack of proper nourishment. She constantly fought with herself to bear up.

Convinced that albumen was the only thing that could keep her alive, she persuaded a commissary clerk she had treated for painful carbuncle to smuggle in fresh eggs for her. He boiled them and secreted them in the inside pockets of his disintegrating frock coat. General Winder did not take kindly to Southerners who aided the damned Yankee invaders.

Later, when she spoke of this in her lectures, she credited that young man with saving her life.

Months passed. Her weight dropped and her once rounded body took on skeletal proportions. Dr. Mary was wasting away, but her fertile mind refused to succumb. She would get herself out of this mess or die for the trying.

CHAPTER THIRTY-SEVEN

RICHMOND, VIRGINIA

A S MARY REREAD outdated Richmond newspapers wheedled from one of her more permissive guards, it became clear that Southerners favored a Democrat to win the Union Presidential election in November. The man they considered to be the lesser of two evils, 'Little Mac' McClellan, had the looks and background that stemmed from an old and distinguished family. Besides, he was methodical and patient, always erring on the side of caution.

If the South were to go down in flames, its citizens would prefer to be governed by a man of patience and good breeding, rather than that damned backwoods radical who'd denounced slavery and led the country into the war in the first place.

As the scuttlebutt heated up, Mary's fertile brain began to cook. Though her loyalties lay with Lincoln, she could pretend to be a 'copperhead' who craved an end to fighting and a return to the old status quo. It could be her ticket back to civilization.

She begged some paper and pencil from the same guard then spent hours crafting a document to pass off as her campaign platform to get McClellan elected. When it was finished, she sent word to General Gardner that she had important information that he should see, immediately.

If anyone could help her, surely it would be the kindly officer whose gentle manner had coaxed her reluctant tears.

The moment she entered his office she noted the grim pain lines biting into the corners of his mouth. His leg was giving him fits in the humid summer weather.

He remarked on her pale appearance. "You don't look well, at all, Miss Mary. Are you ill?" he asked, though he had no way to treat her if she were.

She thanked him for his concern, downplaying her deteriorating health. "I'm doing as well as one can expect, under the circumstances," she replied, "but you don't look so chipper, yourself, general."

He sighed. If he wasn't careful, this little chit would take over. His lips parted, more a tired grimace than the warm smile he had displayed on her former visit.

He pointed to his damaged leg. "A twinge or two to remind me of a stray Yankee mini ball," he explained.

How absurd. They sounded like two casual friends at a chance meeting, instead of jailer and captive.

To change the tenor of the meeting, he gestured towards the paper she clutched to her breast.

Hiding her triumph, she handed it over.

His narrow eyebrows climbed up his broad forehead as he gave the page a cursory glance. Very interesting. He hid his curiosity. "Very well, I'll review the document more carefully at the earliest opportunity.

"You understand, Dr. Walker, you have been officially reported to the Confederate Congress as a spy."

"That is absurd," she exclaimed. "I was only delivering personal letters on my way to treat a patient."

"That may be," he admitted, "but appearances indicate otherwise."

Her lips formed a droll, little grin as she remembered Cordelia's need for a Sunday-go-to-meeting dress. "Ah, yes, you Southerners set great store by appearances, do you not?"

He laughed at that. At least she kept her sense of humor, despite her precarious predicament. A lesser woman might have fainted at the word 'spy.'

Once again, she asked for the return of her medical kit. "If you will do me this courtesy, I promise to treat your people as well as my own."

"You know that is out of the question, Miss Mary. I cannot, in good conscience, put potentially lethal instruments into your hands, no matter how much you promise to use them for the welfare of others."

"I'm a surgeon. I do not take lives, I do my best to save them—Northern or Southern."

He stood firm, but there was a note of gentle apology in his voice. "The answer still must be no."

"Then, perhaps you can grant me a different favor," she said, showing her dimples.

"Yes?" he asked, regretting it the moment the word was out.

She's a manipulator, this one, he thought. Puts me in mind of a girl I damn near married a few decades ago.

Mary softened her words with a compliment. "I do not believe my poor, uncivilized Northern gullet can swallow one more mouthful of your delicious corn bread," she said. "Do you think you might serve us wheat, instead?"

What she did not say was that she could not get one more bit of that coarse, gritty, yellow sawdust down her throat without puking it back up.

He stroked his beardless chin to cover a threatening grin. What a presumptuous little minx.

Mary had delivered the request more or less as a lark. She hadn't a hope in the world of getting her wish. However, she was flabbergasted when, a couple of days later, the Northern prisoners received unleavened wheat bread for their main staple, while Southern traitors still got their ration of grainy pone.

Emboldened by her success with the bread, she figured nothing ventured, nothing gained. "We really need fresh vegetables, especially cabbage," she begged. "It would be better for the prisoners because it contains more iron than anything else."

Luckily, the farms nearby were producing enough of the vegetable to feed the inmates at Castle Thunder. Cabbage was subsequently served, three times a week.

Back in Washington, after her release, her tongue-in-cheek, open letter to *The Republican* described the bread and cabbage episodes. In the same article she wrote, *"Thank you, President Jefferson Davis, for my entertainment at the Hotel de Castle Thunder."*

⁓⊙✦⊙⁓

The Cartel between the warring factions, signed in July of 1862, arranged for all captured prisoners to be released, man for man, i.e. a general for a general, and so forth.

However, the agreement ceased to work the moment escaped slaves serving in the Union Army were captured by the Confederates. The stubborn Southerners treated these prisoners as runaways who should be returned to their rightful owners, but the Federalists insisted they be regarded as normal prisoners of war.

Between that and the stern edict by General Grant, the exchange program was dealt a deathblow. Prisoners remained where they were.

In August, General Grant's attitude became mitigated by admonitions from congressmen besieged by the unrelenting demands of their constituents. 1864 was a critical election year. He ordered a conference for the sole purpose of deciding what to do with the thousands of detainees held on both sides.

Commissioners from North and South gathered to discuss the issue. The dickering went on endlessly—each faction intent on gaining the advantage.

When the smoke cleared, four hundred twenty wounded, nurses, officers, and enlisted men from several Confederate camps were scheduled for exchange with their Northern counterparts.

Based on her bogus political treatise, General Gardner and General Winder had already discussed the possibility that Dr. Mary might be among the first released when the new terms were decided. "She's rambunctious enough to campaign for the Democrats," Winder said, "but will the people listen to her?"

Gardner smiled. "She could bend the ear of an archangel, John."

Winder laughed out loud. "She is a bit of a spitfire, isn't she? And that outfit is not to be believed."

"Did you see Captain Semmes's note? When they picked her up I swear he said that she has mouth enough for a regiment."

"Then I pity old Abe Lincoln, when she gets on his tail."

"It's settled then? Walker goes out with the first group."

"Yes. Yes. It'll be a blessed relief to get rid of her," Winder admitted. "She'll give those Yankee politicians a run for their money. It'd be a hoot to see her electioneering, anyway."

Finally, on a sultry August 9th, Castle Thunder delivered up its most controversial inmate, 'the notorious Miss Dr. Mary E. Walker, Surgeoness of the 52nd Ohio Regulars.' She—along with Drs. Culbertson and Hembleton from Chambersburg, Pennsylvania, and Captain Sam Stearns–was to be transferred out of the prison to board a steamer sailing from Richmond to Hampton Roads, then onward to Fort Monroe.

Mary's fingers shook with excitement as she braided her hair and tucked it up under her plumed hat. She brushed her shabby uniform trousers carefully, and, despite the sweltering heat, buttoned her threadbare tunic close beneath her chin.

Her green surgeon's sash circled her fragile waist, the fringes bedraggled and tangled. No matter. "I came into this place a Union Surgeon, and by God I'll at least resemble one when I leave."

She paced, hardly daring to breathe for fear the plans would change. Nervously, she spat on a piece of newspaper and rubbed at her scuffed boots. It would take a lot more than spit to repair the wear and tear of the past few months.

She straightened her cot for the umpteenth time. Her heart fluttered up to her throat as she peered out the window.

Waiting waiting waiting.

At last, the moment of exchange was at hand. A tall, attractive Confederate major presented himself in her doorway, respectfully removed his cap, and held it to his chest.

Oh, ho, she thought, he's a foot taller and a major, to boot—a bit on the skinny side, but I'll consider this an even swap.

His voice was as deep as the mighty Mississippi and equally as liquid. His old world manners bespoke a careful Southern upbringing, a credit to his aristocratic mother.

"I am Dr. Lightfoot of Tennessee, at your service, Ma'am," he said, folding his long frame in a bow low enough to show her the top of his carefully combed head. Every steel gray hair had remained in place.

"I am Dr. Walker of New York," she replied with a twinkle, extending her hand.

He took it, bowing till his lips nearly touched her fingers.

When his hand came away, he held the tiny knife she'd used to lance numerous infection sites, boils, and carbuncles.

"Why, thank you, Ma'am," he exclaimed, realizing what she'd given him. "I shall treasure the gift of a brave surgeon for the rest of my days."

She nodded graciously and stepped past him into the hallway.

Forever afterward, petite Dr. Mary bragged that she had been swapped for a 'handsome, six-foot Confederate surgeon, a major from the state of Tennessee.'

The moment before she walked out of her miserable prison a repatriated woman, she summoned every last ounce of strength she owned. Adrenalin pumping till her legs and arms stung with the rush, she sprang through the door, swept off her plumed chapeau, and whipped it across to her left shoulder as she bowed at the waist.

Then raising the hat above her head, she cried, "Huzzah!"–the dreaded Yankee battle cry her brave boys of the 52nd Ohio screamed as they stormed Confederate trenches.

"Huzzah!" the waiting escorts shouted back, clapping, and stomping, and raising their arms in salute.

The dreadful rigors of the past months fell away.

She turned to grace her captors with a dazzling smile that lit up the square. Dr. Mary could afford to be generous.

SHE WAS FREE!

⌒⊙⊛⊙⌒

All the Union prisoners were placed aboard the steamer *New York*, which chugged down the James River, its funnel spewing acrid smoke that trailed along behind like a sooty fog. The ship traveled under a flag-of-truce shouldering her cumbersome way to Fort Monroe, the stone and brick fortification that, a couple of years before, had witnessed a crucial battle between two heavily armed, iron-clad warships, the newest innovations in naval warfare.

Members of the garrison stationed in this important Union bastion watched in horrified admiration as the *USS Monitor* fired its deadly fusillades to protect the Federal blockade at Hampton Roads from the deadly guns of the *CSS Virginia*.

Surely this historic fort was a fitting place to repatriate the brave prisoners of war.

Mary stood on the deck, damp river air cooling her flushed face. Her heart leapt to her throat, and great tears spilled down her cheeks as she caught sight of the star spangled banner, its glorious red, white, and blue colors flapping skyward in the stiff coastal breeze. Tattered and battle weary, it stretched full-out above the massive guns guarding the tip of the Virginia Peninsula where the James River dumped its frigid waters into Chesapeake Bay.

She strode to the bow of the ship, assumed full attention, and smartly saluted her beloved flag. The others behind her followed suit.

Lines from a poem rang in her head:

> *"'Tis bound by a thousand spells to my heart,*
> *nothing on earth can e'er us part."*

Her brain was reeling with the pride of it. New plans were already formulating. By all she held sacred, she would do her part to see that the Union prevailed. She was prepared to give up her very life for the cause.

CHAPTER THIRTY-EIGHT

WASHINGTON/LOUISVILLE, KENTUCKY

BACK IN WASHINGTON, Dr. Mary, liberated from her abysmal prison diet, devoured fresh vegetables, eggs, sweet milk and whole grain breads. Gradually, she regained her strength, and with it her feisty spirit. She forced the dehumanizing ugliness of her four-month stay at Castle Thunder to the back of her mind, rarely dwelling on it. There was no energy for that.

It was time to reenter the civilized world. She replaced her shredded prison uniform with a couple of well-tailored ensembles and a spanking new green surgeon's sash, splurging on calf-high boots of soft black leather, several changes of linen underwear, pleated shirtwaists, and sturdy stockings.

She gained weight, slept in a proper bed with clean linens and languished in the bath, relishing the luxury of clean, hot water, imported castile soap and fresh-smelling towels.

Soaking in the steamy water, she permitted her mind to wander through poignant memories. She cried often and laughed a little.

She wrote cheerful letters to Oswego, but declined to visit. No time for that now.

During the weeks following her release, she read everything available to catch up on the war from the Yankee point of view.

Richmond's newspapers had dispensed sugarcoated propaganda while she cooled her heels in prison, fuming because she was not out there in the thick of it.

She swelled with pride as she discovered facts about Sherman's 'Operation Crusher,' his bold campaign to defeat General Joe Johnston's Army of Tennessee. She gobbled up accounts of his regiments as they battled their way across 425 miles of hostile Georgia territory and chortled with glee at the reports that her own favorite, General Thomas–the Rock of Chickamauga–and his Army of the Cumberland were acquitting themselves admirably.

Old ambitions propelled her forward.

She longed to visit her army cronies, especially General McCook, not yet aware that he had been killed in action at Kennesaw Mountain in July. She also needed to retrieve her trunk full of belongings, and say a final farewell to the brigade.

❦

On September 2nd, 1864, when word reached Washington that Sherman had entered Atlanta, Lincoln and his cabinet members were ecstatic. The wily general's masterful military maneuvering left him in control of the Confederate's second largest manufacturing center. An important supply depot had been destroyed.

Sherman, declaring the city a military installation subject to summary retribution, ordered civilians piled into every available wagon and rail car. The terrible spectacle of women clinging to their children and their few pitiful possessions left him outwardly unmoved. Their plight could not deter him from his ultimate decision—destroy, destroy, destroy.

On his orders, Federal engineers set about finishing the annihilation the Rebels had started by blowing up their own factory. Soon, greasy torches lit up the pewter sky, a grisly graveside pyre for more than 8,000 Confederate casualties.

Craggy 'Uncle Billy,' who had wept openly over the body of his friend, Major General James B. McPherson, shot in the back by skirmishers, had put aside his raggedy old suit and surveyed Atlanta's destruction in full dress uniform, sitting grim faced and stony astride his handsome steed.

Confederate General John Hood protested the wanton destruction, "Stop, he begged, "in the name of God and humanity."

Sherman, determined to eliminate the last vestiges of Confederate pride and capacity for retaliation, sent back the message, "You might as well appeal against the thunderstorm."

Flames crackled between exploding ammunition depots and abandoned train sheds, igniting shops, mills and private homes. Libraries, banks and offices were licked up by the ferocious inferno. The eye-watering, funereal smoke was redolent with the stink of singed animal carcasses mingled with the throat-searing fumes of burning wood, scorched metal and expended explosives.

When the holocaust ended, Atlanta, proud gate city to the south, lay in smoldering black ruins. The only things remaining intact besides the ghostly telegraph poles and lonely brick chimneys searching the skies for redemption were a billiard parlor and a hard liquor bar.

While Northerners celebrated by nominating General Sherman their national hero, Southern morale deteriorated to its lowest ebb. The death of the Confederacy was near. It was merely a matter of time.

Mary recalled the devastation she had encountered after the battle of Fredericksburg, and her heart ached for the innocents of Atlanta. Their homes and possessions were gone; their lives forever altered for the worst.

If there is a God in heaven, why can't this damnable destruction ever be ended?

Even as Sherman cut a bloody swath through Georgia, Dr. Mary's self-indulgent euphoria began to pall. It was time to get back to business.

First, she applied to the Medical Director's office of the Army of the Cumberland, requesting back pay for her services as a civilian Contract Surgeon with the 52nd Ohio.

Secondly, she would seek a new posting as a full-fledged Contract Surgeon with suitable army rank.

Her old friend, General Thomas, received a request from the Acting Surgeon General, Colonel E. D. Townsend that asked, "Is anything due the woman, and, if so, what amount of Secret Service was performed?"

The general took time out from his horrendous schedule to write personally on her behalf. His hand-written answer is one of the few documented references to Mary's espionage activities. It reads in part:

"Headquarters of the Cumberland
Before Atlanta, August 20, 1864

Mary Walker came to Chattanooga last winter with
a letter from Asst. Surg. General Wood. As I now
remember she desired to be sent to the fifty-second
Ohio as acting Assisting Surgeon, so that she might
get through the lines and get information of the
enemy. I consented to let her go and she was soon
afterwards captured.

(Signed) Geo. H. Thomas
Maj. Gen'l, U.S.A. Comd'g."

When questioned about her rate of pay, Thomas fired off a brief communiqué above the same signature:

"I would recommend that she be paid as Contract
Surgeon from the 11th of March to the present time
at the rate of $80.00 per month. She was captured
April 16, 1864."

Shortly thereafter, the good doctor received the grand sum of $432.36, 'in payment for services rendered from March 11, 1864 to August 12, 1864.'

⁂

Speculation around the capital that Dr. Mary would travel and lecture about her wartime experiences had, indeed, been a plan she entertained but only after the War's end.

Some unexplained but relentless anxiety still plagued her. The coveted army commission dangled in her subconscious like the proverbial carrot on a stick. She was determined to finish what she started.

Also, she fully intended to support her President's re-election, positive that Lincoln was the only candidate compassionate enough to reunite the country during the post-war crisis.

In late October, she threw herself into electioneering in her home state of New York even as she resumed her own campaign to get an official commission.

On September 14th, feeling unready to resume battle duty, she addressed a rambling epistle to General Sherman in which she explained in detail her service to the Union since the 'Commencement of the Rebellion.' She asked that she be given a commission with the rank of Major and that she be assigned to supervise some two hundred or more female prisoners and refugees confined at Louisville, Kentucky.

She implored in her letter:

> "I beg to inform the Gen'l that if there should be a hesitancy, on the ground that no woman had ever received such a Commission, I have but to remind you that there has not been a woman who has served the Government in such a variety of ways of importance to the great Cause which has elicited patriotism that knows no sex. I only ask that simple justice be done me as a 'Military Necessity.'
>
> Most Respectfully,
> Mary E Walker MD"

On September 16th, Dr. Mary stopped over in Louisville, Kentucky, on her way to meet up with the Army of the Cumberland. She would petition Sherman personally for the commission she felt she had already earned.

Once again, a colleague's death manipulated her plans. One of the surgeons at Louisiana's Refugee's Barracks exited to his final reward, and Dr. Mary was ordered into the breech.

She was immediately put to work at her current pay rate, and stayed on as a fill-in surgeon until October, receiving her usual $80 per month.

When her replacement arrived at the Refugee Barracks she hot-footed it to General Thomas.

Little did she know that the wheels of progress had been grinding along at bureaucratic pace. General Sherman had notified Surgeon Joseph B. Brown who sent word to Assistant Surgeon General R. C. Wood who forwarded the information to General Thomas who had started the ball rolling in the first place.

Finally, her formal contract as Acting Assistant Surgeon became a reality. She was given the rank of Major along with her Commission to commence duty on October 15, 1864. Her pay would be $100 per month, and, per her request, she was assigned to the Female Military Prison at Louisville.

Hallelujah! At long last she was an official officer in the Union Army.

Her petition for a quick visit home before she undertook the running of the prison was signed, "Dr. Mary E. Walker, Surgeon-in-Charge and Temporary Commandant."

The Captain and Post-Adjutant allowed the furlough, and she rushed off to share her jubilation and show off her new uniform to the Walker clan.

CHAPTER THIRTY-NINE

OSWEGO, NEW YORK

ON OCTOBER 24, 1864, a Republican demonstration turned bois-terous at Oswego's Doolittle Hall. As principal speaker, Dr. Mary seized her chance to speak out against the horrors of war while lobbying for the re-election of President Lincoln.

Still exulting over her commission, she strutted before the group in her official, gold-buttoned uniform with its stiff shoulder boards and gold striped trousers, her green surgeon's sash glistening in the gaslight.

Her detailed experiences on the battlefield elicited their pity, and they wept as she described the indignities she endured as a prisoner of war.

"Desperate wives and mothers in Richmond are rioting against high prices," she said. "Politics aside, Southern families are starving and sick to death of war. They pray for the Democrats to oust the Republicans because they think they'll fare better with a new regime."

The campaign had turned ugly when McClellan called Lincoln, "the orig-inal gorilla." Republicans, in turn, called the vengeful general a copperhead who made peace with the enemy and war upon his own government.

"Even now," she advised the fascinated listeners, "there are secret fac-tions in several Confederate states. The Heroes of America, for instance, have organized to promote dissatisfaction and aid the sympathetic South-ern Unionists seeking defection to the Federal side."

Then, eyes atwinkle, she gave the fascinated New Yorkers a blow-by-blow description of her devious deception to obtain early release from Cas-tle Thunder by masquerading as a staunch Democrat.

She quoted from the thirty pages of her fictional electioneering speech in which she promised her captors that the Southern candidate, "Little

Mac" McClellan, would have a landslide victory over that "ape" in the White house."

"Well, here is what I really think of that speech," she cried dramatically, as she held up symbolic pages and tore them to pieces, fluttering the remnants down on the audience.

The hall erupted with cheers and applause. Wonderment and admiration were expressed in the shouts that followed. And Mary lapped it up.

"You always were a slippery little fox, Mary Walker," yelled one grizzled farmer who had known her from the time she was a mischievous child.

"That's giving the old Rebs what for," hollered another neighbor.

"Three cheers for the Major," shouted a young soldier whose empty left sleeve hung at his side. He raised his good right arm to lead the accolade, "Hip, hip hooray!"

The guest of honor stood breathlessly still, blushing furiously, but smiling so widely her face ached with the pleasure of it.

When the ruckus subsided, Mary finished her speech with a final tribute to her President:

> *"I do believe that if the worst Copperhead could but*
> *see the President after a 'Cabinet Meeting,' just*
> *catch one glimpse at his careworn face, and feel that*
> *his great heart was constantly throbbing for the best*
> *interests of the most envied of countries in the World,*
> *they would forgive everything they censure him for,*
> *and put their shoulders to the wheel of the mammoth*
> *Republican car, instead of blocking the same."*

Vesta Walker, heavier and grayer than Mary remembered, had arranged a farewell dinner after church on Sunday to see her daughter off to her new duties at the Female Prison.

Alvah, as gray as his wife, but far thinner, had passed the word around that all the Walker siblings were to attend along with their own families.

Indeed, he looked forward to having his whole brood under one roof, a pleasure he had not witnessed since Cynthia's sad funeral fifteen years earlier.

Around one o'clock, they arrived in groups, handsome, well dressed, substantial citizens, proud of their accomplishments, but there was an underlying tension among the sisters that accelerated as the afternoon progressed.

Mama's table was laden with steaming platters and bowls of bounty grown on the Walker Farm. Crusty fruit pies waited on the sideboard to provide a sweet finale to the sumptuous meal. Mama had not lost her touch at the kitchen stove.

Papa said the grace from his place at the head of the table, and the food was passed from hand to hand.

"I thought your speech at Doolittle Hall was excellent, Mary," Alvie said around a mouthful of fluffy mashed potatoes. "Talk afterwards indicates a lot of the men got an eye-opener, I'll tell you that."

Though Mama maintained a similar view, she cast a hurried scowl in her son's direction. There were others at the table who were not so admiring of her daughter's accomplishments.

An expectant hush fell over the group. Utensils scraped against plates. Not a sound was uttered for all of two minutes.

Vesta, Jr. was the first to voice her disapproval. She slammed down her fork and dabbed at her lips with her linen napkin. "Well, I for one am embarrassed that she stood up on that stage at all." She wrinkled her nose as if she smelled something rotten. "It was so unladylike."

"Shush, now, let's have a peaceful meal," Alvah said, holding a forkful of rutabaga halfway between plate and mouth.

Vesta, Jr., sounding exactly like a disobedient child, issued a sharp retort. "I will not shush. I do not enjoy hearing my sister spout politics, nor do I care to hear her expert opinions on the ugliness of war. Best to leave those details in the field with the soldiers where they belong."

Vesta, Jr.'s husband, Willet Worden, tugged at his wife's sleeve and frowned at her. She pulled her arm free and shot him a dirty look that stopped him cold.

Papa opened his mouth to protest, but Mama put her hand over his to signal silence.

In her elegantly quiet manner, she implored her children, "Please, let's enjoy our meal without discussing unpleasant matters."

Aurora Borealis snorted, "What else could we expect?"

Lyman Coates, Aurora's spouse, knew what was coming next. Lord knows, he'd heard it often enough. He leaned sideways and whispered, "Now, Rora."

She ignored him completely. "Oh, Mother, I knew you'd take Mary's side. You always have, ever since we were little."

Mama remained calm. "This has nothing to do with sides. I want this dinner to be pleasant. Now let's hear no more about it."

Vesta, Jr. was furious at her condescending tone. "You can't treat us like children, Mother. We have a right to say what we please."

Mama bristled. "You are guests in my home. I insist you behave like it."

During the exchange, Mary sat with head bowed waiting for the axe to fall. Her sisters had never understood her motives before. Why should this afternoon be any different?

Smarting from the reprimand, Vesta, Jr. snapped back, "What do you expect us to do? Should we look the other way when she walks around town in that ridiculous costume and professes to know everything there is to know about the War?"

Papa, mindful of his wife's restraining fingers, interrupted gently. "Mary is wearing the Federal uniform. Let's be respectful."

Aurora huffed in disgust then contributed her two cents' worth. "The Farm Club talks about her at every meeting. Half the time, we don't get through the agenda."

Lyman threw up his hands. His wife was off and running.

"It's Mary this and Mary that. And their comments are not the least bit flattering when they hear that she spends weeks in the field with all those men around her." She stopped to breathe.

Mary clattered her fork down on her plate.

"Oh, for God's sake, Rora. Why must everything be reduced to the sexes? Those men are my patients. There are nurses in the field, also. Do you think they are scarlet women because they comfort men who are dying?"

Aurora's little girl, christened with the unwieldy name of Vestaluna after her two aunties, hid her face in her napkin.

Vesta, Jr. rushed to Aurora's aid, her haughty voice invading the conversation. "We are only reiterating what is being bandied about among the local citizens. There are reputations at stake here, Mary, and you have a duty to protect our family's honor."

Papa had heard enough. "Stop this, at once. Your mother has issued a request, and I expect you to be respectful of it."

"Well, of course you would, Father," was Aurora's petulant reply. "Anything for your precious Mary."

Alvie made a half-hearted attempt to interrupt his sisters, but his pretty wife, Sarah, shook her head at him. Don't get into it, her look implored.

Papa shouted, "That's enough."

Aurora stood up, her chest heaving. A painful grimace distorted her features as she shouted back. "No, sir, it is not enough. Don't think for one minute that you can slight all of us for her. We are your daughters, too."

She sucked in her breath. Now that she'd started she would say her piece, whether her parents liked it or not. "Tell me this, Father, why can't she settle down and raise a normal family like the rest of us?"

That's what it comes down to, thought Mary. I don't conform, and it's killing them.

Twelve-year-old Byron, Vesta's only son, gasped aloud. His eyes bugged out of his head. It was unthinkable that a daughter could address her father in such disrespectful tones.

Luna and Wickham Griswold sat mute, toying with their food and studiously avoiding any contribution to the argument. Unspoken orders commanded their children to absolute silence.

"When she starts living like a respectable woman, that's when I will respect her," Aurora shrieked.

Mary lost what was left of her temper. She sprang up and threw down her napkin. Her voice was level and controlled, but there was no mistaking her anger.

"You, Rora, are a spiteful, vindictive woman with neither regard nor understanding of anything beyond your own narrow little circle."

Every eye turned in her direction, and a collective gasp rose from the group. The hint of a smile flickered in Lyman Coates' eyes. Aurora Borealis had met her match.

"Please, stop," Mama cried. "I can't bear this bickering when I have no idea how long it will be before we see Mary again."

Aurora banged her fist down hard. "See, I told you. It's always about her, isn't it?"

Mary walked to the foot of the table, put a hand on her mother's shoulder, and faced her family. "It's time you all woke up to some very unpleasant truths," she began, struggling to check feelings she'd suppressed for years.

"You'd better believe I am an expert on war, Rora, and I hate it more than I hate the devil himself. I have been to the battle fronts and seen his evil devastation first hand."

"Oh, here we go." Aurora mimicked her sister. "Now we'll have to listen to her sad, sad story."

Mary wanted to slap Aurora's jeering puss. She bit the inside of her cheek to keep from screaming. Suddenly she was very tired, but she could not quit.

"Well hear me now, sister dear. I have seen streams running red with blood, and, by the way, Union blood and Confederate blood are exactly the same color. Did you know that, Rora?"

Angry tears sparkled in her blue eyes, but she swallowed hard and rushed on. "I have seen amputated arms and legs thrown in piles to wait until some kind soul buries them. Sometimes, that soul was me. I have watched a child younger than Byron, a drummer boy with both legs shot off, cork up his feelings and die bravely so his fellow soldiers wouldn't hear a whimper out of him."

Mama started to get out of her chair, but Mary's hand pressed her back.

A sob caught in the young doctor's throat as she relived the carnage. "Brave young men, scared witless, slogged through snow and mud to their certain deaths for the honor of their country, and I even knew some of their names."

Now her tears were running freely down her face. "Do you know what a bullet the size of an acorn can do to a leg? It smashes and rips and tears, till the limb is so shattered it has to be cut off."

Luna clapped her hands over her ears and huddled against her husband's shoulder.

Aurora's face went whiter than her mother's.

Vesta, Jr. clasped her son's hand to her breast.

"Don't," she begged, nodding toward her child. "He does not have to hear this."

Mary refused to be stilled. "Oh, but he does need to hear it. I see him playing at war with his friends, and they laugh as they pretend to kill one another."

She looked hard at her nephew. "Well, killing is not a laughing matter, Byron. It's ugly and brutal and final. Men in the field do not get up and laugh when they are felled by bullets or bayonets. They bleed, and they scream, and they cry for their mothers. And, finally, their bodies lie in the mud and stink until the burial detail arrives. That is what war is about."

She pressed her face against her mother's hair. "I'm sorry to spoil your dinner, Mama, but I could not keep quiet any longer."

She ran from the room and stumbled towards the barn. Vesta's old mare, Tildie, rested in her stall, head down, snoozing.

Mary flung open the barrier, threw a halter on the horse and sprang onto her bare back. She ducked her head as they burst through the barn door. She dug her heels into Tildie's flanks and leaned forward over her neck.

With tears streaming down her face, she sobbed, "Git up, girl."

Tildie, older, but still strong of heart, took off like the wind.

❧⚬✿⚬☙

Later, Alvie and Sarah came home to find Mary sitting on their cottage doorstep hugging herself against the chilly evening breeze. He carried a fragrant apple pie covered with one of Vesta's clean dishtowels. The pie's mouthwatering cinnamon aroma spiced the air around him.

When he caught sight of his sister's stricken expression, he set the pie on the porch, plopped himself down and placed a protective arm around her.

A fresh paroxysm of weeping shook Mary's narrow shoulders. "I never meant to make everybody angry," she wept. "Why does everything have to be so difficult?"

Sarah sat on Mary's other side sandwiching her close between them. "It's the price you pay for being different, dear," was her wry assessment.

Mary snuffled, swiping angrily at the unwanted tears. "Is being different all that terrible, Sarah?"

The lovely young wife smiled. "Not to me and certainly not to Alvie. But then we are not your run-of-the-mill couple either."

Alvie laughed out loud at that. Nothing more need be said.

"Come on, I'll walk you back to the barn," he offered, squeezing her shoulder roughly. "Mama was really worried about you."

"Has everyone gone?" Mary asked.

"Yep. Hightailed it out of the house after Papa gave them what for. Never even waited for dessert." He pointed to the pie. "Their loss, our gain," he chuckled.

"Seriously," he continued, "it was hot and heavy for a few minutes, there, but you know Papa. And poor Mama was smack in the middle, trying to calm everybody down. Anyway, get this. Sister Luna never said a word the whole time. Her family left with the rest, and they had to go all the way back to Copeland."

He added a bit of satirical humor to cheer her up. "But she got the other pie, though," he offered, his charming grin warming the remark.

An anguished smile crossed Mary's lips as she stood and strode toward Tildie. "Dear Lord, what have I done, now?" she said, more to herself than to the others.

Alvie rose quickly, catching up with her, determined to comfort her just as she had comforted him, years before when the townspeople had snickered at his artistic efforts and called him 'queer.'

"Not to worry, Mary. Things never change around here. They'll be just the same the next time you come home. The girls will be disagreeable, and Papa will raise the roof. It will be the same old argument, all over again."

Sarah followed them to the rail fence where the patient mare stood munching on a small clump of grass. She hugged her sister-in-law, tightly.

"Just come back to us safe and sound, Mary," she said. "The rest will heal itself."

"And if it doesn't, Sarah. What then?"

Sarah laughed, trying her own brand of humor. "Then, you come live with us, and we'll be three bad apples, together."

A heavy sigh escaped Mary's lips. Her triumphant homecoming had fallen far short of satisfying. "I hope you're right, Sarah," she replied. "I truly hope you're right."

CHAPTER FORTY

LOUISVILLE, KENTUCKY

STEAMING with humiliation, the stocky, pint-sized keeper of the Louisville Military Prison stomped up and down his office, slapping his heavy thigh with the communiqué from headquarters clutched in his right hand.

Army Surgeon E. O. Brown, his pockmarked face crimson with rage, bore a scowl that could stop a bullet in mid-air. "I will not have it," he fumed. "I will not surrender my post to a woman."

Lieutenant Stephenson, lean, gangly and clean-shaven as a newborn babe, shrank against the doorjamb, observing his irate boss with wary vigilance. Major Brown's short fuse was a constant danger to a young lieutenant's career, and the cowering Stephenson had no wish to take the brunt of it.

"But the order comes directly from General Sherman," was the aide's timid response.

"I don't give a fig if it comes from the President, himself, no scrawny female dressed up as a man is going to take over my prison."

Against his better judgment, the cautious lieutenant pointed out an obvious fact. "But, sir, she will only be in charge of the females."

"I'm in charge of the females. Do you not understand that?" the surgeon bellowed. "Anyway, Sherman is down in Georgia sweeping up the crackers."

"Assistant Surgeon General Wood has requested we give her every consideration, sir."

"Bully for him. She didn't take his job away, and he doesn't have to look at her every single day. A woman in uniform! It's a damned abomination, if you ask me."

"I understand she is quite winsome, sir. At least that is what some of the Cumberland gents say."

"That remains to be seen. Remember, lieutenant, she's to receive no aid and comfort from our side of the prison." His lips curled in disgust. "We'll see how long she stays around without our help."

Lieutenant Stephenson, mulling over the rumors he had heard about the infamous Dr. Walker, was slow to answer.

"Is that understood, lieutenant?" Brown snapped.

Stephenson looked up with a start, hastened to reply. "Completely understood, sir,"

He got the message that the new boss of the female prison should receive no support from him. In other words, it would be in his best interest to make her life as miserable as possible.

The papers documenting Dr. Mary's appointment were crumpled to shreds when Brown tossed them to his junior officer.

"File these with the other trash," he ordered, shaking his fist. "Now get out and leave me be."

Stephenson scuttled away like a rabbit fleeing a mountain lion, but once outside the closed door, he straightened the tattered orders as best he could and hid them in the back of a file drawer. Destroying official papers was a punishable offense, and, sure as shootin' he'd be blamed if Brown were caught ignoring Command Post policy.

How he'd handle Dr. Mary Walker's appointment was another question altogether. He was damned if he did thwart her and damned if he didn't. Sometimes the life of a commandant's aide was not so pleasant, after all. Safer than the battlefield–but only just.

What neither man knew was that Lieutenant Colonel J. H. Hammond, Post Commandant, had written a letter to Assistant Surgeon General Wood in which he abhorred the lax conditions in the female prison. His orders were perfectly clear:

> "Brown has allowed the place to become no better
> than a brothel, and I want it cleaned up. Dr.
> Walker must be given complete control of her own
> building and Brown must be kept from any further

interference. Pray, let Miss Walker straighten it out, and tell Dr. Brown to stick to his own building and patients. I will consider that a distinct improvement."

A.S.G. Wood returned the commandant's letter along with his own note that read, "An order has been issued placing Dr. Mary E. Walker in charge."

A wall of angry women shuffled their feet as they faced Dr. Mary.

Undaunted, she stood before the group in full-dress uniform, boots polished, ebon curls tamed into a braided bun at the nape of her neck. On either side of her were two young orderlies, Charles Griswald and Cary Conklin. Years later they would testify at Mary's pension hearings that Lieutenant Stephenson continually harassed her throughout her tour at the prison. Both men were barely out of their teens, but Dr. Mary's previous interview with them indicated they were strong, willing to help and totally loyal.

To gain the milling prisoners' attention, she rapped her knuckles on the small table that stood between her and the group.

During her first inspection, she'd found the facility unbelievably squalid, littered with rubbish, and ripe with the stench of human excrement and stale body odors; but what absolutely flabbergasted her was the filthy appearance of the women and children. Grubby faces, greasy hair, filthy extremities. No wonder the place stank like a sty.

Her face was grim. How could any woman allow her own flesh and blood, much less herself, to wallow in such deplorable conditions? It was beyond imagination.

Well, her orders were to clean up the place physically and morally. And, by God, that's what she intended to do.

This was the time to show the prisoners who was boss, and the only way to accomplish that was to set down some strict rules.

In keeping with her philosophy that cheerfulness wins, she greeted everyone with a smile and a pleasant good morning. There was no reply from the glowering group.

"The Post Commandant has placed me in control of the female section of this prison," she began.

Her remarks were instantly met with derision and catcalls. Griswald made to step forward, but one glance from Dr. Mary kept him in his place. She would handle this her own way.

"Good gawd," growled one slovenly woman, "y'all see what them damn Yankees done sent to take Dr. Brown's place?"

"What is that?" came a quick response from a woman whose squinted eyes raked Mary from head to toe.

"Looks like one a them pretty boys done up with a wig," giggled another out of the side of her mouth.

Conklin bristled, but he had gotten the message to hold his position.

"That's enough," roared Dr. Mary. "There will be certain rules that must be followed, and there will be consequences if they are broken."

"In a pig's arse," shot back a woman whose lips were scabrous with ugly sores. "We answer to Dr. Brown."

Mary ignored the remarks. She did not raise her voice again, but the steely edge to her words conveyed the impression that she would carry out her threat without skipping a beat.

Her eyes turned icy as she stared at each of the outspoken ones in turn. Every woman there felt the cold anger that bubbled just beneath her calm surface. The grumbling subsided to a few mutterings. Griswald and Conklin relaxed.

"The first order of the day is to clean up the trash littering the floors," Mary ordered.

"We ain't here to clean floors," spat a grizzled old harpy.

Another spoke up. "What? What do you think we are, servants?"

"I know who you are. You are prisoners of the United States Army, and I am their appointed representative. You will do as I say," Mary snapped back.

Conklin suppressed a smile as Griswald turned and surreptitiously winked in his direction.

"Secondly," she continued, "you will clean yourselves up and your children, as well. The stink in this place would flatten the Confederate Army if it ever could get within smelling distance."

That stopped them for the moment. Every woman there was sadly aware that the bluecoats were defeating her loyal Southern man.

""Third," Dr. Mary counted, "you will refrain from singing Rebel songs, and I will not tolerate disloyal talk. This terrible war has not changed the fact that you are still citizens of our grand country."

"The Confederate States are our country," yelled one irate woman who'd been arrested as a spy.

Mary turned a cold eye in her direction. "The Confederate States will cease to exist once General Lee surrenders to the North."

There were half-hearted jeers, but the prisoners knew the score. The Federal Army was way ahead of the game.

"Last of all, there will be no fighting or profanity among you. No prisoner will be allowed to abuse another, for any reason. If there is an altercation, both sides will be punished, so I suggest that you learn to turn the other cheek. That's all, for now."

There was more foot shuffling, but comments were kept to a minimum. Dr. Brown would have something to say about this crazy woman, and then the shoe would be on the other foot.

The new administrator motioned for her orderlies to usher the prisoners out of the room, then spun on her heel and walked away. Once inside her own quarters, she sank onto her cot and clutched her chest. Her heart was beating so fast she feared everyone in the complex would hear it.

Well, I'm glad that's over with, she sighed. Now all I have to do is follow through on it.

Mary woke to a strange sound in the wee hours of the morning. She lay rigidly attentive, blinking sleepily, while willing her ears to identify the unfamiliar racket. It took a moment to realize she was listening to the squalling of an infant, practically newborn, by the sound. There were other noises, as well. Raucous laughter drifted up from the kitchen area. Close by, bedsprings squeaked rhythmically.

"What?" she muttered. "What, now?"

She lay totally still, giving herself the chance to come fully awake while her ears tuned in to the commotion. Finally, unable to stand it any longer, she sprang up from her bed, pulled boots onto her bare feet, and shrugged into a heavy house robe. Her black hair was a tumble of curls around her face, the massive length of it hanging in a heavy queue down her back.

She thrust her hand into the pocket of her robe and felt the small revolver nestling there. She was ready to meet any emergency.

The rusted hinges grated as she opened the door into the corridor. First things first. She followed the rickety bed sounds that were suddenly augmented by low moans.

Three doors down the hallway, the glimmer of a candle showed under a closed door. Mary stepped quietly up to the portal, turned the knob and pushed it open. This one did not squeak.

There, on the single cot, exercising an energetic mating ritual, lay one of the male cooks and– judging from the flailing buttocks–one of the more athletic prisoners. Though she had expected it, the scene had the air of a ridiculous pantomime.

"Halt," was the only word she could think of, but it was loud enough to get the couple's attention.

The cook jumped up, covered his privates with one hand, and grabbed his britches with the other. He was out of the room, lickety split.

Without a trace of embarrassment, the female lay back on the bed displaying her wares in the flickering candlelight.

"Cover yourself," Mary spat. "You are disgusting."

The arrogant woman remained as she was, except that she placed both hands behind her head, relaxing from her chores. "Well, now, could it be the Major was wishing for a tumble, herself?" the woman asked with a sly twinkle. "Slippery Sarah can service you, too. Won't cost you a penny."

Dr. Mary ignored her insolence. Instead she pointedly stared at the woman's sagging breasts and scraggly pubic thatch. "The cook must have been desperate to bed a hag as old and ugly as you," she said as she started out the door. "I'll deal with you in the morning."

Sarah's eyes narrowed. You bitch, she thought. Then she grinned. There would be plenty of time to get even for that remark.

Dr. Mary took shallow breaths between pinching her nostrils against the smell of sex and unwashed bodies. She hurried to the stairs as the infant's cries rose to frustrated screams. Where in God's name was the mother?

At the top of the steps, the noise was deafening. At least the child had healthy lungs.

Mary rushed into the small, unlit room and ran to the baby's crib. "There, there," she crooned as she leaned over to pick up the little one. A fetid odor like rotting food stopped her cold.

The infant continued to scream as Mary groped around for a candle and matches. Just then, an inmate known as Hally came through the doorway with a sputtering light. Both women gasped at the contents of the crib. The child, obviously afflicted with a foul, watery diarrhea, had kicked until the green mess ran down its legs and splashed every corner of its rumpled bed. Tiny fingers and toes were sticky with filth.

Dr. Mary felt the bile rise in her throat. This infant would die if these symptoms persisted.

Hally turned away, altogether, swallowing hard against her gag reflex.

"Whose baby is this?" Mary demanded. "And why is it lying in its own excrement?"

"He belongs to Hester Riddle. She leaves him here every night while she goes down to the kitchen to play around with the cooks. The way things are going, she'll have another one in her belly before too many moons go by."

"Go to the kitchen and fetch her, at once. If she refuses to come, call up the stairs, and I'll come for her, myself."

"Yes Ma'am," said Hally, happy to be escaping the pitiful scene.

"Leave the candle," she said as an afterthought. "I'll need it to see by."

The less than adequate light was set beside the child's crib before its owner scurried out the door.

"And bring back a bucket of water and some soap, if you can find it," the doctor called after her.

While she waited, Mary checked around the room. There was little extra there in the way of clothing for the infant. Something would have to be done about that.

She spied a white linen petticoat hanging on a wall peg. This'll do, she thought, and began tearing the garment into swaddling clothes.

Hester, once pretty, now showing the effects of poor food and loose living, caught Mary halfway though the task. "What the hell do you think you're doing with my best petticoat," she demanded. "That was a present from the major, hisself."

The major? Mary's eyebrows shot up. She filed that remark for future reference.

Bent on finishing her task and getting back to her own humble digs, Hally attempted to slip past Hester with the bucket of water that she plunked down several feet from the crib.

Dr. Mary, icily calm, continued to rip the cloth. "I'm making some napkins to cover your little boy."

Hester took a step toward Mary, a malevolent leer on her face. "You been asking for it ever since you came here. You and your high-and-mighty uniform. Well, this is the last straw. Now put that down."

Mary, amazed at Hester's defiance, calmly tore another strip from the petticoat.

A low growl of rage gurgled in Hester's throat, her every muscle tingling to attack.

Hally, caught in the middle between the two women, stepped sideways toward the wall.

"Stop, there, Hester," Mary said with the quiet confidence of one used to dealing with unruly subordinates. Her right hand slipped into her pocket.

"You gonna make me?" snarled Hester, still moving forward.

Hally inched closer to the wall. Just let me out of here, she thought.

Mary pulled out her pistol. "Yes, I am," she replied in the same tone of voice. "Now get over there and see to your baby. He's very sick. If he dies, I'll have you thrown in chains for mistreating him."

"I've done nothing wrong. I was only gone a short time," Hester insisted.

"His condition indicates otherwise. Now, hear me. If I ever catch you leaving him alone, again, I will take him away from you and deal with you very harshly."

Hester took another threatening step toward Mary. "You wouldn't dare," she snarled.

Hally's sharp intake of breath alerted the insolent mother.

Hester saw the glint of the gun barrel and the wind went out of her sails. She slouched over to the crib and glanced at her baby, distaste clearly evident in her expression.

Dr. Mary stood by until every speck of excreta had been sponged away. She left the mother nursing her child, making a mental note to check him for dehydration in the morning.

Not another word passed between the two women, but Mary knew she'd made a dangerous enemy.

⋞◈⋟

Word got around that the new prison doctor carried a pistol.

There was no truth to the rumor. Actually, Mary, afraid she might be ambushed and disarmed, kept her weapon locked in her trunk, but she strolled around with her hand in her pocket to perpetuate the illusion that she was prepared for whatever came. The bluff seemed to work. The troublemakers gave her a wide berth.

Hally Polloch became a helpful ally, especially where the children's welfare was concerned. Childless herself, she had a warm spot for the orphans thrust upon unwilling relatives.

One precious little girl, Bitsy Slaton, had lost her father to the war, and her mother, confined only as a refugee, had died in the prison around the first of October, 1864. The shy four-year-old, along with two siblings, was left in the questionable care of the father's twenty-year-old sister who had been detained for political reasons.

Mary had been keeping an eye on the aunt, Ada Slaton, and twice had made her scrub her seditious graffiti from the corridor walls.

Though they were attractive enough, Ada could barely stand the sight of her nieces. She refused to mother them and punished them severely for the smallest infractions.

After supper one night, Mary caught her trying to hang Bitsy with a rope suspended from the rafters. "My God, woman, what are you doing?" she cried, snatching the weeping urchin from the aunt's clutches.

"I was only gonna scare her a little," Ada said. "She ain't behavin' and I ain't got time to see to her. I got other things to do."

"Oh, yes, I'm aware of your other things," declared Mary. She ordered Ada to the kitchen to scrub the pots after every meal. "Do anything to harm those children again, and you'll be scrubbing chamber pots for the rest of the war. Is that clear?"

Her threat was met with an ugly glower and a flounce of hips, but Ada beat a strategic retreat toward the kitchen.

At the morning meal of thin gruel and chicory coffee, Mary once again demanded the group's attention.

"I'm making every woman in this facility responsible for every small child here. The little ones have done nothing wrong. They're here out of necessity, and, out of that necessity, comes the need to nurture them as best we can.

"I've seen barn cats give better care to their kittens than these babes receive. More than that, I have seen the slave women you consider inferior shield their children from harm with their own bodies."

She emphasized every word of the next pronouncement. "Now hear this. I expect our children to be cared for decently and treated with tenderness. Be aware that anything less will incur my very great displeasure."

Mumbles and whisperings went from table to table. What would this harpy come up with next?

What Dr. Mary knew, but didn't say, was that some slave women loved their children so much that, rather that turn them over to a life of mistreatment with cruel masters, they smothered them in their sleep.

What monumental courage that dreadful deed must have taken, Mary mused, and what a pity her female prisoners were not endowed with such love and courage.

CHAPTER FORTY-ONE

LOUISVILLE, KENTUCKY

"SHE'S GONE too far this time," raged the ousted commander of the Female Prison while his lieutenant stood mute before him. "She's refused to let me into the women's quarters and she's fired the four men I hired as cooks and replaced them with females."

He rapped the knuckles of one hand against the palm of the other.

"And, now, she's had the harlots' tents removed to interfere with the recreation of my guards."

Dr. E. O. Brown, as with all incompetent bosses, placed the blame on his subordinate's shoulders. "How could you let these things happen, Stephenson? You are in command of the guards at her post." He pointed an accusing finger at his aide. "This is all your fault for not keeping abreast of things."

Stephenson flexed his fist, suppressing the urge to sink it into his boss's flapping jowls.

"I did my best, sir, but she gets an idea in her head and there's no stoppin' her. And she is my superior in rank. Besides, she's absolutely impossible to reckon with. She ordered me out of the building. Said I had no business there and not to come back again."

"She's a runt of a woman, you half-wit. How can you let her get the better of you?"

"I'm not sure, sir. I only know when I kicked the door down yesterday to get into the storage rooms, she appeared out of nowhere. One minute, all the women were there, eggin' me on, but soon as she arrived, big as billy-be-damned, they shut right up and scooted back to their quarters. I swear, sir. One look from her . . ." He shook his head, still not believing what had happened. "They just disappeared. They scuttled off like Satan hisself was on their tails."

"Well, try something else, you nincompoop. I won't lose to some insignificant little twit with no brains to her name. Now get out."

After hustling his skinny frame to the other side of the door, Lieutenant Stephenson fell against it, weak with anxiety. Sweat poured off his forehead and streamed into his eyes. I'm never gonna get through this alive, he thought. Either the major will kill me, or Dr. Walker will, for sure.

⸙

Dr. Brown demonstrated his anger in a letter to Assistant Surgeon General Wood:

> *"I have the honor to state that I regard Dr. M. E. Walker as incompetent to prescribe for the sick in the Female Prison, and would further state that her tyrannical conduct has been intolerable not only to the inmates of the Prison, but to myself."*

While his boss's letter to A. S. G. Wood was being delivered, Lieutenant Stephenson continued to undermine Mary, as ordered. He convinced several irate female prisoners to form a committee and send a scathing denouncement of their common enemy to Colonel Fairleigh, Military Commander of the 26th Kentucky Volunteers. He helped the less educated unfortunates to formulate the wording:

> *"We the inmates of the Female Military Prison do hereby ask and request of you that you will remove Dr. Walker as none of the inmates will receive her Medicine, and that you will give us another Surgeon, if not let us remain without any Surgeon. Most of the Prisoners are in favor of Dr. Brown if*

you can let him return as we have had
him once and all like him."

Colonel Fairleigh forwarded the prisoners' complaints to A. S. G. Wood who refused to "disregard the official request of Major General Sherman." Dr. Mary would stay put.

Secretly, Wood was congratulating the little major for cleaning up a disgraceful mess. Post Commander Hammond issued permission to banish the tents of 'those disreputable camp followers' ensconced on the outskirts of the prison camp. When Wood heard she had sent them packing, he quietly celebrated with a double shot of good old Kentucky bourbon.

While all these shenanigans were taking place, Mary set about relieving the overcrowded conditions of the women's facility. She wheedled transportation from Lieutenant Colonel Hammond to send a bunch of young Indiana girls home to the custody of various relatives. Among them were fifteen-year-old Adelaide Simpson from Madison; seventeen-year-old Nellie Johnson from Albany; and Annie Scuttles, seventeen, of Carrolton. She gave her word that the youngsters would do no harm to the Union and would surely fare better in their own environments far away from the erudite influences of the 'fast' women in the prison. Naturally, those left behind grew even more hostile, resenting their detainment all the more. Mad as hornets, they grumbled about no longer being allowed to consort with their "gentlemen friends."

ᘓᗜᗢᘖ

In January of 1865, Mary's ally, Lieutenant Colonel Hammond was replaced as Post Commandant by a narrow-minded administrator named Coyle who was spoiling for a fight the moment he got a look at the Surgeon-in-Charge of the females.

Obsidian eyes behind heavy lids hid a brooding, unforgiving soul. The stubborn know-it-all made no effort to research the intricacies of handling a population of angry, uncooperative women. Instead, he decided that he and Dr. Walker could not co-exist in the same environment, and he was damned if he would be the one to leave.

Although the new Lieutenant Colonel had no conception of the logistics of running the Female Prison, he proceeded to find fault with Mary's methods, and, worse still, undermine her authority.

In short order, she became fed up with his interference. Alone in her room, she gave vent to her frustrations, fussing and fuming over the facts. Here was a man who had no inkling of the horrendous hurdles and crapulous behavior she had already overcome, nor did he know anything about the day-to-day disciplining of a passel of immoral, disobedient, lazy female prisoners. All he seemed to care about were the complaints of the inmates, Rebel sympathizers at that. Mary wondered, more than once, which side he was on.

When he criticized her for actions she considered consistent with her official responsibilities, she was determined to set the record straight.

She dashed off a scathing three-page letter that castigated him in a way that only Dr. Mary could:

> *"You have done me a gross injustice in speaking of me as you do, when I appealed to you to sustain me in the right. I thought you a man of sufficient discretion and judgment to comprehend things as they exist,-and then I thought you had sufficient moral courage to pursue a course consistent with an enlightened conscience . . ."*

She went on to explain the circumstances surrounding the neglect and abuse of children, the near hanging of an innocent little girl, the slovenly, immoral behavior, and the downright disobedience of her charges.

The letter goes on to say:

> *"I had one woman handcuffed about two hours for calling the Guard to his face 'D.S.B.' and threatening to 'kill two other prisoners' and daring me to come up stairs . . ."*

With no illusions about where she stood with the inmates or with some of the other officers. She continued:

*"I am an eyesore to them, and they want new cooks
again and a man doctor. . . .Give them their filth,
unrestrained disloyalty and immorality and it will be
satisfactory times for them . . . They glory in a
Lieut. that chops open doors and allows them to
surround him in the operation."*

Of Lieutenant Stephenson, she advised in the same missile:

*"The food question is only a pretense and if Lieut.
Stephenson had three grains of common sense he
would see it. They complained every meal when there
were four men cooks and I gave no direction
whatever. He would not have dared make such an
outright idiot of himself if Col. Fairleigh had been
here. Col. Fairleigh has learned my true motives for
all I have done and appreciates the trying position I
hold, and all my greatest superior officers have
confidence in my having done well under all
circumstances, and that confidence is merited.*

*With due respect
Mary E. Walker U.S.A."*

Lieutenant Colonel Coyle was furious. "How dare this woman call him
to task for doing his job in a right and proper manner?" he ranted. "How
dare she suggest that a faithful young lieutenant in the United States Army
had no common sense? How did she suppose he became a lieutenant, in
the first place?"

Well, he would fix her wagon, all right. He marched right over to visit
his friend C.C. Gray at the Assistant Surgeon General's office.

"This woman is an overbearing, disrespectful shrew," he complained.
"Nobody can do anything right, but her, and furthermore, I cannot stand
to see her parading around in that monstrous outfit she calls her uniform."

"What would you have me do, Coyle? She's a protégé of General Sherman. You want me to override our commander? Word is, when the general suggested she put on a dress like a proper lady, she told him she was an officer in the Union Army and that she wore its uniform." Then she said, "When your other officers put on dresses, General, I will be happy to oblige."

Gray chuckled at the image of the most important General being upstaged by a slip of bitty woman. Privately, he thought she had a point. The sturdy uniform made sense to him, for he had seen too many nurses plowing the edges of muddy battlefields in their layers of dragging material and thought then how ridiculous their costumes were.

Coyle waved his hand as if to swat away a pesky fly. "I don't care what she told the general." He thought for a moment. "Send her a letter on official stationery," he decided. "That might help."

"I'll see what I can do. But no promises, hear?"

Dr. Mary was heartbroken when, instead of the expected support, she received Gray's orders to "confine your work to strictly professional (medical?) affairs, and you will exercise no other authority than that of a physician and inflict no punishments."

Her heartbreak lasted all of ten minutes. General Sherman had given her a task to do. Lieutenant Colonel Hammond had reinforced the orders of Assistant Surgeon General Wood, and she was damned if she would let Coyle, or Gray, or any other ignorant lackey for that matter, deter her from her goals.

It was business as usual for all concerned.

Years later, she would argue that female prisoners were entitled to be supervised, guarded, and doctored by women. "Men," she said, "simply do not treat women inmates properly." Nor, she thought, do they have the compassion needed to deal with the feminine psyche.

Six months after her assignment to the Female Prison, Dr. Mary had had whining women, backbiting colleagues, and nasty tricks up to her eyeballs. For two months she begged for reassignment to the front, but her pleas went unanswered. She threw herself on the mercy of Post Medical Director

Phelps, a fine surgeon and sympathetic friend who had backed her to the hilt.

Lieutenant Stephenson had once hauled Mary and one of her patients into Phelps's office for an infraction of the rules. When Phelps saw the two pint-sized women flanked by menacing guards holding rifles at their backs, he was fit to be tied.

In deference to the ladies, he kept his language printable. "What the devil do you think you're doing?" he demanded.

"The lieutenant caught these here women sneakin' around the grounds, sir," the taller one explained.

Mary snorted. "We were not sneaking, we were walking upright, taking the air."

"The lieutenant says prisoners ain't s'posed to be outside the buildin' without a escort," contributed the second guard.

Phelps who had nothing but admiration for his spunky doctor smiled warmly at her. He turned a scowling countenance toward the two men. "You go back and tell your lieutenant that he has no business interfering with the Medical Department of the Prison, and further, if the Officer in Charge of that department chooses to take her patients to Canada he should not interfere with her business, as she alone is responsible."

The two men ducked and ran, while Dr. Phelps apologized to Mary. "I'm sorry, my dear. It was all a misunderstanding, I am sure."

"Of course it was," said Mary, dimpling, and rolling her eyes.

Dr. Phelps was saddened but not surprised when, a few weeks later, he received Mary's urgent request:

"... it has been an untold task to keep this institution in a good condition MORALLY and I am weary of the task and would much prefer to be where my services can be appreciated and I can do more good DIRECTLY for the cause."

The Medical Director summoned her to his office. "Please sit," he said, indicating the chair in front of his desk.

Soon Mary's throat was choking with tears as Phelps praised her for her diligence. "You are possessed of superior talents, my dear, and you are to be commended for your energetic and persevering spirit that is characteristic of your entire military career. You have rendered more service to your country than many of our efficient officers."

"Then send me to the front, sir. Routines have been established here, someone else can easily take over the reins."

She ignored his pitying expression and hurried on. "I do my best work in the field with the men."

He looked at the frail woman, her intense eyes huge in her pale, gaunt face. In his mind, he quickly ran over the events of the past year: service on the battlefield, incarceration in a death camp, and finally the rigorous duties of her tour at the Female Prison. Clearly, the diminutive doctor was worn out.

"I don't think I should do that, Mary." She started to protest, but he shook his head to stop her. "First of all, I doubt your health would permit another stint at the front."

In her heart, Mary knew her friend was right. Her energy level was at its lowest, and her stomach often rebelled at food she stuffed down to keep her body going.

Phelps smiled and shuffled a few papers around. "Anyway, I need you to straighten out another little problem for me. I need you down at Clarksville, Tennessee. The orphan asylum and refugee home there need your expert organization. Will you do that for me?"

"Put in those terms, I can hardly refuse"

She packed her uniforms and medical supplies and headed for Clarksville.

On March 28, 1865, the *Louisville Daily Journal* reported:

> *"In conformity with the recommendations of the Medical Director of the Department of Kentucky, and her own wishes, Mrs. Mary E. Walker, Acting Assistant Surgeon, U.S.A., is released from duty in the Female Military Prison at Louisville . . . Mrs. Dr. Walker has been in charge*

of the Female Military Prison for upwards of six months and we believe her government of the institution received the approval of all loyal people, being a surgeon of fine ability and one whose experience well fitted her for the position. Her removal will be deplored by many. To whatever field of duty she may be assigned, we doubt not that she will meet with the success which her splendid talents merit."

On a blustery, dreary day, amid the derisive cheers of the worst female offenders, she was driven away in a wagon containing her few belongings. She never looked back.

CHAPTER FORTY-TWO

CLARKSVILLE, TENNESSEE

DR. MARY'S spirits plummeted as she settled into Clarksville, a dismal compound that housed displaced refugees and children deprived of their parents through sickness or battle injuries.

Instead of confronting aggressive female prisoners, she was now faced with pitiful bundles of humanity sitting in corners, sucking thumbs, pulling at their hair, and crying for their parents.

Still, she refused to let disappointment color her decisions. She was ecstatic that President Lincoln had been inaugurated after overwhelmingly defeating General George McClellan. Between Lincoln's leadership and Sherman's march across Georgia a final settlement of the dreadful conflict was assured, sooner rather than later.

Though she preferred tending soldiers in battle, she threw her efforts into reorganizing the Clarksville facility despite opposition from those already assigned to the orphanage.

Her heart ached for her displaced Southern charges. How to make their lonely lot a bit easier to bear?

"Clean up this building," she ordered the aides. "And I want adults constantly within sight of these poor children. The least we can do is comfort them when they're frightened."

Nights were the most difficult. The little ones wailed for their mamas or sat like wide-eyed zombies, staring at walls and chewing their tiny fingernails until the cuticles bled.

Mary patrolled the hallways, stopping to hold a trembling waif or comfort a weeping adolescent, always smiling tenderly to hide her own hopelessness.

"I can't replace what they've lost," she told her aide, "but I'll do what I can for them. I want extensive records kept with all facts available so their families can be found. Maybe after the war relatives will come forward to claim these babes and give them normal lives."

At every opportunity between duties, Mary poured over skimpy reports of Grant's advances toward the Confederate capital. Days after he had affected its capture, stories trickled in.

The Confederate government fled on Sunday, April 2nd, and the retreating Rebels detonated the main arsenal. Richmond went up in flames. Armories exploded, sending fire balls to gobble up homes, businesses, bridges, and ships in the harbor. Newspaper accounts compared the destruction to the devastation of Atlanta.

Refusing to surrender, the exhausted troops fought bravely though all supply lines had been cut off.

Lee's forces camped on the south side of the Appomattox River. To avoid further useless bloodshed General Grant sent a compassionate request for the surrender of the Army of Virginia.

North and South negotiated terms, and on April 9, 1865, Robert E. Lee, elegant in a pristine gray uniform, his engraved sword at his side, appeared at the home of Wilmer McLean who had evacuated his family from Manassas Junction during the battle of Bull Run. In at the beginning, in at the end, the willing host reckoned.

"I have probably to be taken General Grant's prisoner, and I thought I must make my best appearance," General Lee explained to his aide.

The faithful aide turned away unable to summon a reply past the lump in his throat.

Arriving straight from the field, half an hour late for the meeting, the Commander of the Union Army, clad in a dirty private's blouse and mud splattered boots and trousers, apologized for his tardiness. General Ulysses S. Grant wore no sword.

If General Lee was insulted, he hid it well.

A handshake and polite conversation about a previous meeting followed the initial greeting before the two generals were seated at separate tables some distance apart. Generous terms were offered and accepted. Tears of gratitude stung Lee's weary eyes when General Grant ordered 25,000 rations sent to feed the hungry Confederates.

The Great War between the States was over.

Mary was making her rounds in the infirmary when the news reached the orphanage.

She clutched the iron rungs of a child's bedstead to steady her buckling knees before she sank heavily onto the straw mattress. The orderly who delivered the message put out a hand to help, but she waved him away.

Great sobs of relief wrenched up from her very soul as she gave in and wept. The messenger, astonished at the flood of emotion from his stoic commander, turned and fled.

When the paroxysm was over, Mary looked up directly into round, brown eyes that nearly filled the pinched, grave face of a small boy of five or six whom she only knew as Benny. A faded smock, several sizes too large for his emaciated frame, covered him to his knobby knees. His stubby toes peeked through holes in his gray felt carpet slippers.

"Are ya sick?" he asked. "Do ya need a cup a water?"

Mary gathered him close and rocked him back and forth. "No. No, child, I'm fine. Really, I am."

Benny pulled away from her bosom but remained in the circle of her arms. His miniature forehead furrowed as tiny fingers, light as cobwebs, traced the wetness on her cheeks.

"Yer cryin'," he whispered, awed to see the formidable major's tears.

"I'm crying because the war is over," Mary explained.

"Are ya sad about it?"

"Not at all. Sometimes, I cry when I am very happy. Grown up ladies do that, you see."

He did not see at all. He had been miserable since his Pa had disappeared with a gaggle of marching men armed with squirrel rifles and pitchforks, and then Ma had died screaming as the body of her stillborn infant refused to leave her womb.

Each night tears flooded his straw mattress as he muffled his tortured sobs with the scrap of greasy blanket he carried everywhere.

"If there ain't a war," he said thoughtfully, "will my Pa be comin' back?"

Mary took his little face in her hands, searching his eyes, finding a strength in them that no child should have to draw upon.

"We'll have to wait and see," she replied, unsure if the child's father was alive or dead. Not knowing was the worst burden of all.

'Go on, now,' she said, turning him toward the door. "Go find the nurse and tell her to give you a sugar tit.'

He whirled about, his lips grim. "I ain't no baby," he said, insulted at the mere suggestion.

Mary smiled through her tears. "Of course you're not," she said, patting his fragile shoulder. "You're a big, brave boy."

He trudged off, a miniature old soul, dragging the tattered remnant of his faded baby blanket behind him.

Mary raised her eyes heavenward. "If you're up there, Lord," she said softly, "have mercy on this motherless child."

⟡

April 16, 1865, was one of the worst days of Mary Walker's life.

That morning, she received word that, at 7:22 AM, on the previous day, her Commander-in-Chief had succumbed to a fatal wound inflicted by the monomaniacal actor, John Wilkes Booth.

A crimson, numbing rage consumed her as she learned that the dirty coward, fortified with a couple of stiff brandies, sneaked into the Presidential Box at Ford's Theater during the evening performance, took deliberate aim and fired a .44 caliber derringer at point blank range into the back of her revered leader's head.

The lethal missile had torn open the President's skull and lodged behind his right eye. That it took Abraham Lincoln nine agonizing hours to die gave evidence of the great man's strength and tenacity.

Because she thought of Lincoln as immortal, or perhaps because assassination seemed so unthinkable, she could not come to terms with the reality of his death. Even losing her adored sister had not affected her so deeply and completely.

Too shocked for tears, she walked the Clarksville streets, a pale ghost, oblivious to the curious stares of celebrating passers-by.

The world continued to turn on its axis, sun and wind were unchanged, but her compassionate leader lay cold as stone, leaving her beloved country rudderless.

She pounded her thighs as she agonized over America's fate. Who would bring the nation into a conjoined union where North and South coexisted without rancor? Who would bind up the wounds that had split the United States into opposite factions where brother fought brother and father fought son?

For the first time in years, Mary prayed to the God her parents trusted. It was the only thing she could think to do.

CHAPTER FORTY-THREE

CLARKSVILLE, TENNESSEE

D R MARY was out of a job.

Dr, George Cooper, who replaced the Chief Medical Officer of the Army of the Cumberland, never forgave nor forgot that Generals Thomas and Sherman ignored his recommendations to deny Mary a commission and keep her away from the battlefield.

With a memory as long as a Sultan's elephant, the vindictive surgeon waited for his chance to get some payback. The moment he dared, he exercised his spiteful pleasure and relieved Mary of her post at Clarksville.

Her face flamed as she read his terse severance letter:

"Madam: I am informed that your services are not needed at the Refugee home in Clarksville, Tennessee, inasmuch as the Medical Officer in Charge can do all the work required of him. You can present yourself at this office or that of the Asst. Surgeon General as your services are no longer required in this Dept."

The tenor of the document was no surprise. After all, Cooper had been instrumental in humiliating her by instructing the Board of Inquiry to ignore her years of trauma experience. Instead of saluting her extensive service on the battlefield, his debasing report had negated her education and insulted her intelligence.

That she was relieved of duty at the orphanage was not a crowning blow. She was champing at the bit to return to her old duties with the Army. What really stuck in her craw was the vision of Cooper chortling with malicious glee as he wrote the words that robbed her of her post.

Never mind, she thought, I'll push forward with my career, and Dr. Cooper can go hang.

Just as well she did not foresee the many disappointments that lay ahead.

CHAPTER FORTY-FOUR

WASHINGTON CITY

THE POLITICAL CLIMATE in post war Washington was so explosive that a united front was all but impossible.

The new president, in complete agreement with Lincoln's policies, set out to fulfill his slain hero's dream of a soft peace: *"with malice toward none; with charity for all; . . . to bind up the nations wounds; to care for him who shall have borne the battle, and for his widow and orphan."*

Unfortunately Johnson's enemies in Congress had the opposite in mind.

Somehow, the fledgling President must find a way to strike a satisfactory reconciliation between vindictive Republicans and bitter Southern governors. Radicals like Massachusetts Senator Charles Sumner and Pennsylvania's Representative Thaddeus Stevens opted for punitive measures against the defeated Confederates, while rebellious Southern lawmakers remained dead set against bestowing citizenship to the hordes of repatriated Negroes flooding their countrysides.

Mary was caught up in the drama of it all. Time lay heavy on her hands, and she yearned to get back to work. New duties would take her mind off the health issues plaguing her since her release from Castle Thunder.

Her political sympathies were divided. Her brave Union lads deserved every consideration, but she recalled their rapport with the Confederate soldiers while at rest between battles. They traded, they joked back and forth and shared music.

"If youngsters facing death in the field could find a way to communicate, why couldn't adult politicians?" she railed to any who would listen. "Are money and pride so important that the cream of America's youth, both Northern and Southern, can be ignored?"

She thought about the simple innocents she had encountered in her rounds through the Southern countryside. Did they not warrant consideration? And what of the Negroes? Poor, frightened refugees, left to shift for themselves, but determined to remain free.

And what about me, she wondered. Don't I deserve a break? For four difficult years, I've given every ounce of energy I can muster—much of the time without pay. Shouldn't I be rewarded for my work?

Her surgeon's commission would expire in June, but instead of returning to Oswego to languish in her accomplishments, she opted to stay in Washington while her service record was still fresh in the minds of her advocates. She sought a postwar commission that would win her the rank and pay of major. It seemed only fair that it be retroactive to her appointment at the Female Military Prison in Louisville, Kentucky.

Canny as the generals she'd worked with, she aimed her campaign toward an institution that catered to Negroes, with the certainty that she would run into far less opposition if she were asking to care for former slaves instead of white soldiers.

Her application for Medical Inspector for the Bureau of Refugees and Freedmen was accompanied by glowing references from prestigious sponsors like W. H. DeMotte of the Indian Military Agency, D. E. Millard of the Michigan Military Agency, and W. A. Benedict, Connecticut State Agent for the Freedmen's Bureau, who wrote:

"Her appointment could not fail to give satisfaction to those who best know her worth, especially to the officers and soldiers of our noble Army."

President Johnson, impressed by the continuous flow of commendations, took time out of his horrendous schedule to address an executive request to Secretary of War Edwin Stanton:

"It would seem that Dr. Walker has performed service deserving the recognition of the Govt.—which I desire to give-if there is any way in which-or precedent by which this may be done?"

Instead of Stanton, the President's request was routed to the new Surgeon General, Dr. M. B. Ames who knew nothing about Mary.

Somehow, the media got hold of the story and featured it.

Walker's request for extended commission so incensed Dr. George Cooper that he threw a raging tantrum. He considered it his righteous duty to apprise the new surgeon General–a man he'd never met–of that pretentious female's deficiencies. He promptly sent along a copy of the Board of Examiner's evaluation with a note of explanation. The following excerpt conveyed his animosity:

> *"Surgeon General*
>
> . . . .*I put her with the Refugees at Clarksville, Tenn, but I got rid of her as soon as practicable. She is useless, ignorant, trifling, and a consummate boor and I cannot imagine how she even had a contract made with her as Actg. Asst. Surgeon.*
>
> *Your Obd't Servant*
> *Geo. E. Cooper"*

Taking the examining board's interview at face value, Ames took the safe road and answered his President: "Even recognition of her services, other than payment of them desirable, there is no manner in which it could be accomplished consistently with law and regulations."

Throughout August, favorable correspondence bombarded the Executive Mansion. Late in the month, Secretary of War Stanton forwarded a letter to Johnson from Dr. J. Collamer, an Army Surgeon, who wrote that Dr. Walker's request was 'novel in character' but certainly worthy of attention, especially since Army Surgeon E. E. Phelps, General Sherman, General Thomas, and Assistant Surgeon General Wood all agreed that she had served bravely and selflessly in the United States Army. This advisory was followed by a testimonial from F. E. Spinner of the United States Treasury that encouraged Johnson to make her commission retroactive, since it "would be gratifying to me and many others of her friends if she could be commissioned in 1864 when she was Surgeon in Charge at Louisville, Kentucky."

Mary discovered that her old nemesis had reared his ugly head–again. On September 30th she sent a blistering condemnation of the underhanded tactics of Dr. George Cooper-and his Board of Examiners. It arrived on Johnson's desk along with more testimonials of Walker's accomplishments.

The besieged Chief, overwhelmed with the blizzard of correspondence, dropped his face in his hands and cried, "Will someone please do something about this young woman before I lose my sanity?"

The War Department's Bureau of Military Justice stepped into the fray. The adjudication fell into the lap of the stone-faced Judge Advocate General Joseph Holt who had prosecuted, convicted and executed John Wilkes Booth's co-conspirators. The death sentence of Mary Elizabeth Surratt, the lone woman involved, was still a matter for considerable controversy. Neither Johnson nor Holt would accept the blame that a plea for clemency for Surratt had been overlooked.

No matter. Fifty-eight-year-old Attorney Holt had not achieved his position as the highest-ranking lawyer in the United States Army by being insensitive to the vagaries of his Commander-in-Chief. The President was a tough, fair-minded man, a champion of the little people. Holt was determined to give Dr. Mary Walker's case every consideration under the law.

Like all good Judge Advocates General, he gathered up and plowed through the thick files of evidence and wrote a long and authoritative treatise on the case. Dr. Walker's services had been invaluable, but she also assured him that she would not apply for officer's pay. And she promised to resign her commission, once it was granted.

He reported, "Dr. Walker contributed services above and beyond the call of duty as documented by Generals Sherman and Thomas who attested to her fortuitous efficiency while engaged in the 'secret service' of the Army before she was arrested as a spy."

General Thomas testified:

> " . . . while so employed she passed frequently
> beyond our own lines far within those of the enemy
> and at one time gained information that led Gen'l.
> Sherman so to modify his strategic operations as to

save himself from a serious reverse and obtain
success where defeat before seemed to be
inevitable . . . this party has devoted herself with a
patriotic zeal to the relief of our sick and wounded
soldiers . . . to the detriment of her own health, and
has among other hardships endured that of being
held for four months in a southern prison . . ."

Despite all the favorable evidence, Holt wrestled with the appropriateness of honoring a woman with such elevated status.

He agreed with Surgeon General Ames's view of 'lack of precedence,' though a few notable women had held public office. However, he took his objection one step further.

Despite the mountain of testimonials, supporting documents and college credits, Holt declared, "Dr. Walker's sex is an insurmountable obstacle to her receipt of official recognition. What will the country come to if, even in such extreme circumstances, a mere woman is elevated to heroic status?"

Discounting incontrovertible proof of her capabilities, he cited her confrontation with the Board of Examiners and underscored Cooper's ruling. He dashed off a letter containing the words:

" . . . notwithstanding all the evidence as to her merit
and efficiency in public service, Miss Walker has not
succeeded in satisfying the requirements of the
medical department of the army. She was pronounced
unqualified for the position of medical officer."

Embarrassed by this one-sided denouncement, the Judge Advocate General threw in a lump of sugar to sweeten the bitter pill, vacillating on a final decision by cleverly shifting the onus back to Stanton:

"'Because His Excellency has recommended that she is deserving of recognition . . . is there any precedent by which this may be done? The

Secretary of War will please report whether there is any law by which an honorary or complementary brevet might be conferred on Mary E. Walker . . . (it is recommended that she be awarded) such formal and honorable recognition of those services as may not be in conflict with the law."

And then Holt tossed a bureaucratic monkey wrench into the mix to cover his butt.

> *"I admire the lady, but I'm unwilling to defend such an action. Inasmuch as this will become an inconvenient precedent, and the government will again be called upon to testify its appreciation of a case of similar character and merit. This lady's sacrifices, fearless energy under perilous circumstances, endurance of hardship and imprisonment at the hands of the enemy, and especially her active patriotism and eminent loyalty may well be regarded as an isolated case in the history of the rebellion." He did another about face. "To signalize and perpetuate it as such would seem to be desirable." "Although the Army should not gainfully employ her, a denial should not preclude some 'commendatory acknowledgment' of her good deeds rendered in behalf of the Union Army."*

He breathed a sigh of relief as he quickly sealed up the document and shipped it, forthwith, to the War Office.

How long Mary sat in the old wooden rocker clutching the official envelope to her chest, she could not say.

A bottomless dread seized her. "What will I do if they refuse me?' she cried, rocking to comfort herself. "The Army is my life."

It took every ounce of her will to unseal the long envelope and remove the crisp message dated November 2, 1865.

The War Department's terse decision took only a few lines:

"Madam:

Your application for commission in the military service of the United States has been considered by the Secretary of War, and decided adversely. There is no law or precedent, which would authorize it.

Asst. Advt. Gen'l. E. D. Townsend"

The denial hit her like a punch to the solar plexus. "Not even a polite thank you for my years of dedication, my risked life, or my poor health," she cried. Clenched teeth prevented the bile from gushing up from her gut.

Hot tears coursed down her cheeks to drip from her chin. Her bodice was soaked with them, but she couldn't stop weeping. One moment she had control, and then a fresh paroxysm shook her.

"Where is Papa's God now?" she cried. "And where are the generals and the foot soldiers that I risked my life to help?"

Grief consumed her. She abandoned the rocker and crawled into bed, pulling a heavy quilt up to her ears. Who would care if she ever left its protective cover again?

❧✦☙

When President Johnson saw Advocate General Holt's report, his sense of fair play was offended. Townsend's brusque notice to Mary pleased him even less. On November 11, 1865, he did the only thing a grateful sitting President could do under the circumstances.

The National Republican carried an announcement, "President Johnson was pleased to honor Dr. Mary E. Walker with an order inscribed on handsome parchment, which by law was the only compensation possible because she happens to be a woman."

The reporter acknowledged that: "much of the service rendered by her to the Government could not have been accomplished by a man."

His editorial comment declared, "Until Congress can do Miss Walker some degree of pecuniary justice, she must be content with the noble parchment testimonial of the President so justly bestowed and all that he has the power legally to give."

When Dr. Mary read the article, she snorted with contempt. "Because I am a woman?" she fumed. "Damnation!"

Relenting a bit, she smiled. "At least they admit I've done many things no man could do." Of that, she was absolutely, unequivocally in agreement.

The Oswego Historical Society has the original copy of President Johnson's order as issued from the Executive office:

"WHEREAS, It appears from official reports that Dr. Mary E. Walker, a graduate of medicine, has rendered valuable services to the Government, and her efforts have been earnest and untiring in a variety of ways, and that she was assigned to duty and served as an Assistant Surgeon in charge of female prisoners at Louisville, Kentucky, upon the recommendations of Major Generals Sherman and Thomas and faithfully served as a Contract Surgeon in the service of the United States, and has devoted herself with patriotic zeal to the sick and wounded soldiers, both in the field and hospital, to the detriment of her own health, and has also endured hardships as a prisoner-of-war in a Southern prison, while acting as a Contract Surgeon; and, WHEREAS By reason of her not being a commissioned officer in the military service, a brevet or honorary rank, cannot, under existing laws, be conferred upon her, and, WHEREAS, In the opinion of the President an

honorable recognition of her services and sufferings should be made, "It is ordered that a testimonial thereof shall hereby be made and given to said Mary E. Walker, and that the usual Medal of Honor for meritorious service be given her.

Given under my hand, in the city of Washington, D.C. this 11th day of November, A.D. 1865.

*Andrew Johnson, President
By the President,
Edwin M. Stanton, Secretary of War."*

On November 13th, John Potts received a hastily written note that instructed him to have 'engraved by tomorrow' a medal of honor for Dr. Mary E. Walker.

On January 24, 1866, with the entire Congress looking on, Mary entered clad in her usual outfit of dark tunic and trousers. She stepped up to the podium to receive the cherished Medal of Honor for Meritorious Service from the President, himself.

She smiled up at him, dazzling blue eyes twinkling with triumph.

Towering above the diminutive heroine, Johnson smiled back and gently placed the ribboned Medal about her neck. Resounding cheers filled the rotunda.

She clasped the hand of her Commander-in-Chief between her own, holding on tightly for a long moment. Then she turned to the audience. Her cheeks flushing pink with pleasure, she grasped the thin round Medal and bowed low before Senators and Representatives, gracefully accepting what she considered her due.

Ironically, the receipt Dr. Mary wrote out for the medal reads:

*"Washington D.C.
Jan. 24, 1866*

Polly Craig

Received of Bvt. Maj. E. D. Townsend, Assistant
Adjutant General, USA, The 'Medal of Honor'
awarded me by the President of the United States.

Mary E. Walker, M. D."

Beneath her signature is a flourish of curlicues as if she were saying, "There, Mr. Assistant Advocate General E. D. Townsend, take that and that and that!"

The Medal was, and still is, the highest honor the United States bestows. To date, of the 1.8 million women veterans, Dr. Mary Edwards Walker is its only woman recipient. The proud patriot wore her Medal every day for the rest of her life, sometimes on a ribbon about her neck, sometimes pinned to her breast.

She also wore a shield-shaped badge of gold that was presented to her by fellow soldiers. The engraving reads: "Mary E. Walker, M.D., Extra Assistant Surgeon, Army of the Potomac, War of 1861."For a few shining hours, Mary rejoiced. Her hard work and sacrifices had finally been recognized and appreciated. After the festivities ended, she escaped to her room where she carefully examined her precious prize.

On the front, the moon-shaped disc portrayed a bald eagle, his wings spread wide as if in flight, and inscribed around the outer edge were the words: UNITED STATES OF AMERICA CONGRESSIONAL MEDAL OF HONOR.

All bitterness and disappointment fell away in one triumphant moment as she turned the Medal over and read the inscription on the reverse side: THE CONGRESS TO DR. MARY E. WALKER, A-A. SURGEON, U.S.A., NOVEMBER 11, 1865.

Tears of joy splashed over her lashes as a euphoric feeling of peace filled her heart.

But evil forces lurked in the background. A vindictive scoundrel's belated actions were about to drag her back to reality and plunge her to the depths of hell.

BOOK THREE
1866–1880

There is a certain blend of courage.
integrity, character and principle
which has no satisfactory dictionary
name but has been called different
things in different countries. Our
American name for it is "guts."

LOUIS ADAMIC
"A Study In Courage"

CHAPTER FORTY-FIVE

NEW YORK

WHILE MARY scurried around Washington, petitioning for her commission, Albert Miller was manipulating the Oneida County court system. But he needed his ex-wife's presence to succeed.

Under the pretext of reconciliation, he wrote to various friends for her whereabouts. He even had the audacity to write to a Walker sibling.

Severely critical of her sister's divorce, Aurora Borealis carped, "Mary should reconcile and settle down to raise a family like any normal woman worth her salt."

Her husband, Lyman Coates, wasn't having it. "Miller is a bounder and doesn't deserve any courtesies, much less information that might hurt Mary."

Rora shivered as a thundercloud creased Lyman's forehead, but she had the good sense to keep her mouth shut while he read Miller's letter with a sneer:

> *"Can you tell me where Mary is? I have not heard from her or of her in a long time. I think she will yet see that haste does not always lead to the right & regret our separation. I wish also to know if she is in need of any of the comforts or niceties of life. I would willingly assist her at any time, should she need it. After years of trial and sorrow might she be*

*more apt to see the light. I would be pleased to hear
from any of her family at any time.*

*Respectfully yours.
A. E. Miller, M.D."*

Incensed at Miller's audacity, Lyman clapped on his hat, hitched up the buggy and raced the letter to his father-in-law's home.

Alvah Walker's face darkened with rage as he read the short missile. He had barely finished before he exploded with a stream of invective generally foreign to that good man's tongue. "Why that . . . that . . . no good skulker. That skunk in the grass. That rotten piker . . . that . . . that filthy libertine . . ."

His face turned an unhealthy purple as he sputtered with frustration, finally running out of breath.

Afraid for the old man's health, Lyman patted his shoulder as if he were a temper-tossed child. "Sir, sir," he cajoled. "Please calm yourself. That vulture isn't worth it."

"How dare he?" Alvah yelled, still shaking with rage. "How dare he be so cavalier when he used my girl so badly?"

Vesta, busy in the kitchen making tea for her guest, heard Alvah's shouts and came running. "Darling," she cried. "What is it?"

She looked from Lyman to Alvah and then back again. Her first thought was for her youngest daughter, so far away and often in danger. Tentacles of fear clutched at her heart. Terror stole the breath from her. "What's happened?" she whispered, remembering the desperate months she had prayed for her daughter's safe release from Castle Thunder. "Tell me. Has something happened to Mary?"

Lyman spoke up quickly. "No, no, nothing like that, Mama Walker."

Vesta's relief was so intense, her legs turned to rubber and she was forced to sit abruptly. She swallowed hard and found her voice. "What is it, Lyman? Is it Aurora?"

"No, ma'am. She's fine. Everybody's fine."

Vesta's head swiveled from husband to son-in-law. "What, then?"

Lyman slid the note from Alvah's trembling fingers and handed it to her.

She huddled in the chair as the words burned into her heart. "Surely this man can't be serious after what he put our daughter through," she cried. "He deserted her. He cheated on her, made a fool of her. How can he even think we'd tell him where she is?"

She resisted the temptation to rip the letter to shreds. Instead, uttering a derisive little snort, she tossed it onto a nearby table. Her expression hardened.

"He has no intention of helping her," she thundered to men who were startled at her vehemence. "He has an ulterior motive, you can bet on it."

"Well he'll get no help from me or my family," Lyman vowed. "He'd better watch his step if he comes nosing around my front yard."

Alvah had collected himself, somewhat. "If he shows his face in these parts, Lyman, come and get me at once. I know how to deal with a mountebank like him, and I won't need any help doing it either. I should have taken a buggy whip to him when I had the chance."

For her husband's sake, Vesta forced herself to calm down. To break the angry mood, she said, "Come into the kitchen and have some tea. Cussing the man out will do no good. He can't hear you, and I can't bear to listen to any more of it."

Alvah grumbled, but he followed his wife toward the tantalizing odor of fresh baked cinnamon rolls and applesauce stewing on the stove.

Lyman retrieved the letter and stuffed it in his inside pocket. He had already fought with Aurora Borealis over it, and he would rather not rake it over any more, today. Besides, his mouth was watering for some of Vesta's sweet buns and herb tea.

Because Mary's 1861 divorce decree was won on grounds of adultery, it forbade her philandering husband's remarriage until his ex-wife's death. Miller had few choices. He could either have Mary killed, kill her himself, or more practically, seek his own divorce. Thus he petitioned the court in a different county for a reopening and reversed adjudication of Mary's decree.

Miller freely admitted that he left Dr. Walker of his own accord, taking his books and lecture illustrations after he sold some of their furniture for 'expenses.' However, he swore that he only did so because he had evidence that was so compelling he was forced to believe she had committed the unpardonable sin of cuckolding him.

To accuse Mary Walker of such heinous activity was, in her mind, akin to blasphemy. That the courts even entertained the thought of it was anathema.

However, many judges still believed in Blackstone's Common Law, an old English statute that decreed that husband and wife are one—THE HUSBAND. Under that law, wives had no legal rights. They could own nothing; could be seized and beaten if they tried to escape the union; had no rights over their children; and, even though they could not vote, single or widowed women must pay taxes.

Miller's attorneys, Johnson and Boardman, brought Mary's old decree before the State Supreme Court of New York, and, on November 24, 1865, the first divorce was set aside, and a judgment by default was found against Mary Miller and for Albert Miller.

Mary was devastated by what she considered a 'judicial outrage.' The law she had so revered dealt her a blow from which she would never fully recover.

But Mary was a fighter. For the next four years, between lecture tours in America and on the Continent, she explored every legal avenue available to a 'lowly woman.'

She petitioned the New York Legislature for relief. Assembly Bill No. 623 was introduced. It declared that any action taken by Mary Miller against Albert E. Miller must discount all the time she was absent from the venue while acting as a United States Army Surgeon caring for sick and wounded soldiers. Quickly enacted, it dismissed the statute of limitations in the Miller case.

That ACT allowed Mary to give testimony when seeking relief from Miller's divorce that had been granted while she was in absentia.

Mary's concern was for all women. Whenever she was in the area, she haunted the halls of the New York legislature in Albany where she bugged state legislators to introduce a bill giving women equal rights in divorce actions.

Albert Miller, on the strength of his 1865 decree, married again in 1867. Because his new bride came from affluent New England stock, he was financially comfortable. Delphine Freeman, a licensed physician, had built up a successful career in Needham, Massachusetts, specializing in the ailments of women and children.

In Delphine, Miller finally figured he had married the mate he'd hoped for in his first wife. The new Mrs. Miller was a competent moneymaker who seemed proud to take his name. More important, she supported his unsuccessful runs for town offices and countenanced the frequent lecture tours that kept him away from his own medical practice.

Typical of his narcissism, Miller thought Mary's reopening of his Decree of Divorcement was in retaliation for his happiness with this new wife. The man was dense as a post where Mary Walker was concerned.

The wheels of justice turned an inch at a time, but Mary was as tenacious with her legal recourse as she had been in pursuing her Army career. While she lectured in the United States and Europe, her attorney, B. F. Chapman, kept her apprised of the progress in her case.

⌒⌒✿⌒⌒

And then a bonanza landed in Mary's lap.

Nelson Whittlesey, a former colleague of Miller's, contacted her. "I have first-hand knowledge of Albert Miller's adulteries and fornications," he said. "I and another gentleman named Whidon are more than willing to testify against the doctor."

"Why would you be willing to do that for me?" she asked.

"Miller is a cruel beast. He let my poor wife die in unrelenting pain because he didn't believe in 'over-medicating' his patients. My wife was under the spell of that bounder's smooth bedside manner," Whittlesey choked. "I couldn't get her to see another physician.

"When Miller first started treating my wife," Whittlesey struggled on, "he ignored her symptoms until it was too late for anyone to help her. At the last of it, my wife screamed in agony, begging for relief, and this so-called doctor turned his back on her saying he had no patience with drugged crazed women."

Tears rolled down Mary's cheeks as Whittlesey fought back his own.

He patted his eyes with a handkerchief. "Dr. Walker, I will do everything I can to help you fight this blackguard. He is a liar and a cheat and a fornicator, a despicable cad completely without scruples. I roomed with him on the lecture circuit. I know, first hand, of his scurrilous behavior, and I will happily tell anyone who asks."

In a straightforward deposition, citing dates and places, he related Miller's peccadilloes. The first incident was graphic in nature and described Miller's pride in his sexual prowess.

"I bunked with Miller at the Petersham Hotel in Petersham, Massachusetts. A Miss White from the neighboring town of Templeton was waiting in our room when we returned from the lecture hall." Red faced with embarrassment, Whittlesey pressed ahead.

"Miss White and Dr. Miller adjourned to White's room where he spent the night with her. When Miller returned in the morning, disheveled and dissipated, the arrogant braggart boasted that he 'had connection with her three times.'

The document described further:

1. *Sexual congress with seventeen-year-old Nelly Plott of Fitts William, N. H. whom Miller later put through Mount Holyoke School. He was arrested for the seduction and impregnation of nineteen-year-old Maria Hardy of Marlborough, N.H. The matter was quietly handled when Miller brokered a deal through B. F. Whidon of Lancaster for the tidy settlement of $600.00. (The child lived and flourished.)*

2. *Miller also seduced an underage girl from South Paris who swore the child she carried was fathered by Dr. Albert E. Miller, the Lecturer.*

3. *Miller also seduced an underage girl from South Paris who swore the child she carried was fathered*

by Dr. Albert E. Miller, the Lecturer Then,
Whittlesey's notarized affidavit described Miller's
clandestine affair with Delphine Freeman: "During
the last of Feb., the first of March, 1865, while at
Hyannis, Massachusetts, Miss Delphine Freeman
visited Dr. Miller and stayed at The White House
where he was boarding. She was there several days.
She also visited him in Nantucket . . . Mystic,
Conn. and . . . Boston . . ."

The final paragraph made a damning statement considering Delphine had married Miller with the understanding that his divorce was legal:

"After I married Miller," she remarked . . ." Dr. Mary Walker came too late. Dr. Miller had gotten the first divorce set aside. His own divorce was then secured in Dr. Mary Walker's absence, & could not have been obtained, had she been present to make her defense."

❧◉☙

Mary's vindication came on January 2nd, 1869:

At a Special term of the Supreme Court held at the Courthouse in the city of Utica, on the second Tuesday of January, 1869, Hon. Wm. J. Bacon. Justice, declared Mary divorced and free to marry if she chose. Miller was forbidden remarriage.

In the end, Miller outfoxed himself. Because he had been intimate with a great many very young women, at least two of whom produced offspring, wily Dr. Miller transferred all of their real estate holdings into his wife's name to keep them safe from forfeiture in case of legal suits. When Delphine died suddenly, a will was found that bequeathed all the property to her own relatives. How she managed such poetic justice in so precarious a political time for women remains a mystery. Why she did surely hinged upon Miller's conduct throughout their marriage.

In 1913, Miller died in Orleans on Cape Cod and was buried in Needham, Massachusetts.

It is doubtful that Mary Walker mourned his passing.

CHAPTER FORTY-SIX

WASHINGTON/NEW YORK

MARY HURRIED to the women's side of the Senate gallery anxious to hear the heated discussions over the seating of Southern representatives who strongly opposed newly enacted rights for emancipated Negroes.

The balcony bulged with restless bodies, squirming in anticipation of a lively debate. Her eyes sparkled as she pressed through the milling crowd.

Her hand-stitched navy coat was fitted to the waist then widened to feminine folds that flowed gracefully to her knees. Straight, tailored trousers stopped just above her custom cobbled, leather boots, and a frothy blue jabot peeked from beneath her vee-necked collar. Perched atop her dark curls sat a felt hat sporting a jaunty iridescent ostrich plume.

She frowned at the disheveled appearance of the official doorkeeper, a middle-aged codger with skin the color of age-grayed bed linen. Though his duds looked slept in, he'd taken the trouble to paste six or seven remaining hairs across his shiny scalp.

When she tried to pass, he grabbed her shoulder and turned her away. "Here, you, you can't go in this door," he growled. "This is the Ladies' Gallery."

Heads swiveled at the sound of his gravelly voice. A few women tittered as they recognized Mary, a familiar oddity around the capital.

Surprised and indignant, Mary shoved his mottled hand away and scowled up at him. "I am a lady, and I shall go in. It's my legal right," she noised off, not caring who heard the remarks.

A collective gasp issued from the throats of the bystanders. Women simply did not thwart authority, especially government authority.

"If you are a lady, how come you're wearing them pantaloons?" he spat.

"I'd like to know that, myself," whispered a middle-aged matron who had strapped herself into constricting corsets to minimize the adipose waistline straining a small cartload of stiff lavender taffeta. Fashion was everything.

"I am in the capital of the United States of America," Mary advised with an attitude that suggested the man must be stupid. "I have a right to wear what I please."

"Now she's in for it," the taffeta entrenched woman said in a voice loud enough for the guard to hear.

The old man puffed himself up, barely holding his temper. "That may be true," he said, "but I have no way of knowing you are a lady, and I cannot let you into this gallery."

Several male visitors waiting to pass through to the gentlemen's side gasped in disbelief. Despite her garb, the person before them was clearly an attractive female.

Mary could hear the angry complaints of Jim Crow Democrats defending their promise to keep the south 'pure,' while the opposing Radical Republicans screamed for Negro suffrage.

She peered through the archway to see the horde of angry citizens, flailing their arms and shouting to be heard as they reacted to arguments from both sides of the question for equal representation.

The ugly tenor of the Congressional meeting didn't surprise her. That it was taking place in the People's House distressed her mightily.

Dangerous race riots had erupted throughout Alabama, Tennessee, and Louisiana. Northern papers were filled with stories of the destruction of dilapidated schools commandeered to educate illiterate Negroes. These fledgling learning places had been recently established by the budget constrained Freedmen's Bureau, but the pitiful facilities were being searched out and burned to the ground. Sadly, the white-sheeted arsonists, their identities concealed beneath ugly hoods, were not particularly careful to insure that the rickety buildings were unoccupied.

Mary had witnessed both sides of the coin, making her more determined to get into the middle of the fray.

The gaggle of citizens waiting to enter the gallery began to jostle and push and mutter, but Mary stood her ground. Encouraged by the crowd's impatience, she advanced a few steps toward the door before the guard planted himself squarely in front of her. What a foolish little man, she decided.

Dangerous Southern guerrillas didn't scare her off. Certainly this unarmed lackey was wasting his time.

"You will step aside, sir," she commanded in battlefield cadence. "I do not have time to argue with you. Can't you see that all these other people are waiting to get in?"

Grumbling under his breath, the confused guard, unused to having his orders questioned, hesitated longer than Mary's patience could endure.

She leaned in close enough to smell his heavy tobacco breath. "Now!" she ordered, her face inches from his.

The crowd snickered as he jumped a foot.

Unnerved, he smoothed his few pomaded hairs, and glowered at the shoving crowd before he grudgingly turned away.

"Go on, then," he snarled, determined to have the last word.

Mary smiled her sweetest and swept past him like a whirlwind. Finding a vacant place among the hoop-skirted grand dames in the overflowing balcony was a problem. She pounced on the first seat she spied, fuming that she was unable to get closer to the protective railing to better view the battle below. She could barely keep her seat when the arguments were contrary to what she knew.

☙❀❧

Mary continued her long fight with Congress for a pension to compensate for her physical debilitation as well as her failing eyesight. "My body has suffered," she argued, "through rain and mud and hunger on the battlefield. Conditions were even worse during the four months of deprivation at Castle Thunder.

"My petitions to this governing body are either ignored or ridiculed. Scores of women nurses served bravely and tirelessly just as I had. It seems only logical and fair that we be rewarded with the same pensions and benefits allocated to male veterans." Drawing herself up to her full five feet, she threatened, "You allow my bills to die in committee, so my only option is to go to the press."

But she soon alienated editors by espousing her radical views. "Women who served on the battlefields side by side with the men deserve the same considerations," she insisted. "One of those is the right to vote."

One editor sneered, "That will happen over my dead body,"

Years later, Mary finally succeeded in winning a pension. The unfairness of the amount, substantially lower than that received by nurses and soldiers' survivors, rankled. "I gave up five years of my life," she told one senator. "I endured horrendous conditions, donated countless months of volunteer time, and expended most of my own resources, including money received for pawning my possessions. One of them was the gold watch my father gave me for my eighteenth birthday. I paid for medical supplies and drugs to treat my boys."

During her own battle, Mary helped dozens of soldiers, nurses and surviving relatives to successfully secure deserved pensions, but her own fight for fair restitution was never truly won.

⌀⌀✤⌀⌀

Troubled by both the ongoing legal manipulations of her divorce action and Congressional refusal to approve her pension, Mary abandoned Washington for New York City for a visit with old friends.

One balmy June day, while enjoying her daily constitutional, a queue of adults and children began laughing and pointing, shouting cruel insults behind her proud, straight back. At least they're not throwing horse apples like the Coolidges, she thought, as she hastened her footsteps to escape.

Beat Officer Johnson arrested her for disorderly conduct and promptly brought her before Justice Mansfield at the Essex Market Police Court. The charge was 'appearing on the street in men's clothing.'

Mary was mad enough to chew nails as she delivered her familiar spiel. "This is a free republic. I should be able to wear what I please, when I please."

Unimpressed, Justice Mansfield rapped his gavel and ruled, "$300 bail,"

"What?" Mary cried, "I don't have $300 to my name, sir."

"That's a shame, Madam," he retorted. Ignoring her further protests, he scowled at the bailiff. "Lock her up," he said and shuffled his papers to check on the next case.

The bailiff shoved her none too gently into a filthy jail cell rank with body odors and stale urine. Deaf to her protests, he slammed the barred door closed after her. A horrible stench summoned unwelcome memories of Castle Thunder.

She promptly sent for a sympathetic friend to bail her out.

Too afraid of contamination to sit on the dirty cots, she paced the small space, thrusting a fist in her mouth to keep from screaming. No way would she give the surly guard the satisfaction of seeing her break down.

A reporter for *The times* commented of the incident:

> *"Think of it: that in the year 1866, a lady who had
> distinguished herself as a medical practitioner, in
> care of sick and wounded soldiers in the Federal
> Army in the Civil War just ended, was arrested in
> the city of New York because some senseless men
> and boys were ridiculing her Bloomer style of dress."*

Unwilling to let the incident go, Mary took her complaint against Johnson for arrest without legal cause to the Board of Police Commissioners of New York City. The President of the Board allowed Mary to testify in her defense.

Commissioner Acton, smartly dressed in the latest style brown broadcloth frock coat, creamy high collared shirt, and paisley cravat, appeared the quintessential advocate. His kindly hazel eyes twinkled, and his rosy chipmunk cheeks along with the snow-white curls above his ears lent a distinctly cherubic look to his demeanor. Mary trusted him, immediately.

She treated the rotund, bespectacled magistrate to an enlightening dissertation on the benefits of wearing a costume like hers. "The deplorable hazards to women's health and personal safety from constricting corsets and heavy petticoats and overskirts are well documented, sir.

"I wish it understood that I wear this style of dress from the purest and noblest principles, and I believe that if there is anything woman receives from Heaven, it is the right to live in comfort. Women cannot do it with the present style of dress. The government does not have the right to deny any woman a high and noble life, nor should she be compelled by a couple of policemen to put on a cumbersome dress and live as they think she should."

Defense Counsel Spencer was a tall, lean dandy with a small mustache and a condescending demeanor that, to Mary's chagrin, brought Albert Miller to mind.

"Yes, yes, your Honor. Pray tell, what does all this have to do with this woman's arrest?"

"Let us hear her argument, Mr. Spencer, and then decide the facts," replied Commissioner Acton.

Mary's face registered surprise. Oh, my word, she thought, a man in authority willing to listen. She smiled widely as she launched into the subject close to her heart. Like a seasoned debater, she stated her views, calmly and succinctly.

"It has been my belief as a medical practitioner that the wearing of tightly corseted, voluminous dresses has unnecessarily contributed to the physical ills women are daily forced to endure."

The court regulars were enjoying the tableau, but the defense attorney gradually turned apoplectic as he noted the commissioner's rapt attention to his opponent's remarks. "Your Honor," he whined, "I see no value . . ."

Acton waggled his fingers to silence him before he could submit his objection.

"Pray continue, Madam," he suggested, obviously admiring Mary's articulate explanation. "Perhaps the doctor has a point."

He was beginning to lose patience with fashion-conscious Mrs. Acton who lately seemed peevish over what she called her constant stomach complaints.

"Now, doctor, tell me about the incident," he said.

"There was a throng of people bustling in front of a millinery shop. It seems everyone was there to watch a balloon ascension. The shopkeeper was afraid the crowd might keep business away from her establishment, so she sent for a policeman to break up the gathering."

Mary frowned at Officer Johnson then smoothed her brow as she turned back to the bench.

She gestured contemptuously. "Instead of dispersing the mob, this officer took *me* to the police station. I was so incensed at the time that when the desk sergeant asked me if I could read or write, I told him I did not know one letter of the alphabet."

Alarmed, Acton looked up from his note taking. "Is that true?" he asked.

Mary flashed a brilliant smile. Is he mad, she wondered. I'm a doctor, for goodness sakes. Before the defense seized the moment to complain about her uncooperative behavior, Mary confessed, "I apologize, sir, for my flippancy. Of course I am literate.

"When I left the station, the sergeant asked me if I wanted an escort. At that point, I advised him that when I wanted the protection of a policeman, I would ask for an intelligent one."

The Commissioner concealed a grin as he rapped the laughing spectators to silence.

Then it was Mr. Spencer's turn to give the court his perception of the case. He launched his pompous tirade, citing popular custom as if it were law. "It is a mistake to suppose that a woman can dress as she pleases. The wearing of men's clothing by women is an offense. A woman dressed in this manner will always attract a crowd and cause public excitement, and she should be arrested."

Fortunately for Mary, Acton was disposed to adhere to legalities rather than timeworn customs. "You don't pretend to say, sir, that there is any law against this lady's dressing as she is now?"

Spencer, furious that his words could be questioned, was careful not to rile Acton further. "With courtesy to her, I do say that. And I also say that if she, or any other lady dressed like her appears in public it is a misdemeanor by law."

Witnesses for the defense did not further either defendant's cause. When questioned by Attorney Spencer, Johnson's partner allowed, "The crowd seemed orderly in my mind."

The sergeant from the station testified, "Although no charges were brought against her, she was impudent when questioned."

Mary's expression betrayed no remorse. "My rights were violated, and, under the circumstances, I did not feel bound by the rules of common courtesy."

"Hold on, there," the Commissioner interrupted. "Help me to understand, sir. If there were no charges brought against Dr. Walker, why was she detained and questioned?"

A smattering of applause erupted. Acton rapped for silence.

"Uh . . . er . . . ah," the sergeant waffled.

"I see," said Acton getting the drift immediately.

Spencer aired his own prejudice during his summation.

"I have a great dread of strong-minded women," he concluded. "They disrupt the harmony of the status quo and are endangering society as a whole. She is a menace on the streets, and Mr. Pickett was right in exercising his duty."

Commissioner Acton's ruling summed up the case. "As I understand it, the lady was taken to the station to protect her from the crowd. No complaint was made against her. I consider, Madam, you have as much right to wear that clothing as I have to wear mine, and he has no more right to arrest you for it than he has me."

Mary's heart leapt in her breast. This brilliant man understood!

"Even so," Acton continued, "if you were creating a disturbance, and, if there was a mob gathered there, he would be justified in removing you. He was fearful you would be insulted."

"But," Mary asked, "Why didn't he let me go my way?"

"Because he knew the mob would follow you and hoot after you."

"There was a streetcar I could have stepped into."

Commissioner Acton suppressed another smile. This is one tough little lady, he decided. She deserves her due. "You are smarter than most ladies in the city of New York," he observed. "I would have no hesitation in letting you go your own way, but the officer thought you were a weak woman needing protection."

Mary suppressed a triumphant smile.

Over his wire-framed glasses, Acton glanced at Pickett, then at Johnson. "Let her go," he ordered. "She can take care of herself. And never arrest her again."

Female spectators broke into applause, stamping their feet and shouting, "Good for you, Dr. Walker" and "Congratulations."

Hope swelled in their weary hearts. Tears stung their eyes.

Many hoop-skirted ladies received threatening looks from their male companions; but, for the moment at least, one courageous feminist had defied tradition by thwarting the suffocating rules that demoted all women to second-class citizenship. Most of them hadn't the courage to alter their costumes or walk unescorted on the streets, but, this day, the right to do these things was at least recognized.

To Mary's unbridled delight, *The New York Tribune* stood up for her, big time:

> *"We must record our protest against the arrest of any lady who desires to walk our streets in unfashionable dress . . . The lady . . . was the victim of noisy urchins and male starers, but if the peace was disturbed thereby, the rabble should have been held to keep it, not she.*
>
> *. . . It was not a man's dress and no disguise was attempted. It was, as we understand it, simply a substitute of pantalettes for the trailing skirt and was the fashion Dr. Walker adopted when she attended the sick and acted the part of a humane physician and brave and noble woman during the war."*

Her vindication by the Board of Police Commissioners and *The New York Tribune* was not quite enough to lift Mary's spirits. She was unwell, depressed, and close to broke. It was time to effect a radical change in her life.

CHAPTER FORTY-SEVEN

OSWEGO, NEW YORK

MARY had last been home before President Lincoln's re-election, and she was saddened by how much her mother had aged.

Her intermittent lecturing after the war, plus a short term as a journalist for *The Washington Post* had, for the most part, kept her in the capital. Brief trips to deal with the New York court system as well as her congressional petitionings allowed no time for visiting, and the months sped by with alarming swiftness.

Vesta had shrunk more than an inch in height. The hair that framed her seamed face was snowy white. Arthritis had twisted the knuckle joints of her callused hands, and she favored a painful hip as she hobbled from room to room in the familiar old farmhouse. Her kitchen was as spotless as usual, but Mary suspected it took every ounce of her mother's strength to keep up with the chores.

Alvah, too, seemed plagued with complaints. His spine had curved a bit, and his gait suggested aggravated knee joints, surprising in a man so painfully thin. All that kneeling and stooping as he grafted and cross-pollinated to create new and better berry bushes had taken its toll. He no longer farmed his acres, yet he could not give up his experiments.

When Mary questioned each parent privately about the health of the other, the reply from both was essentially the same. "We're getting on, child. The years add up."

"But what about you, Mary?" queried Alvah when she questioned him. "You'd best let me have a look at you."

"I'm fine, Papa," she replied. "Just a bit tired, is all."

"A bit too thin, too, if you ask me," he complained, adding, "I don't care for those dark circles under your eyes, either."

⊷⊶✸⊷⊶

Sleepless, Mary crept down to the kitchen for a cup of herb tea. The elder Walkers had retired, and the house was silent except for the creaks and groans of its aging joists shuddering under constant buffeting from the relentless Canadian winds that rolled across Lake Ontario.

While she waited for the kettle to boil, she fingered her mother's worn utensils that dated back to Vesta's wedding day. She remembered struggling to keep sane all those lonely nights at Castle Thunder, passing the time by endlessly recounting familiar objects like so many inelegant beads in a grotesque rosary. She was absolutely amazed at how accurately she had re-called every knick and scuff that marred the handles. Here was the wooden spoon her little brother, Alvie, had cut his teeth on, and there was the dented sifter that Mama used to refine the coarse wheat flour for her tender pie crusts.

Alvah quietly watched his daughter from the doorway, his heart aching with worry for the physical and emotional changes in his favorite child's life. Her back was toward him. The tangled curls of her long black hair cascaded down the shoulders of her heavy cotton nightdress like an inky waterfall.

He longed to take her in his arms and comfort her as he had when she was a child, but he'd sensed a chasm between them. Earlier, when he asked about the War she shook her head, saying it was too terrible to describe.

"I can't take you where I've been, Papa," she'd said, "Your worst imag-inings could never conjure up the horrors I've seen. To make matters worse, that black-hearted villain, Miller, has turned up to reopen old wounds."

Alvah sensed something inside his daughter was broken, and he didn't know how to fix it. He shuffled his feet lightly as a warning to keep from startling her. She held the steaming kettle in her hand as she turned toward the sound.

"Papa," she cried, "I thought you were asleep. Did I wake you up rat-tling around down here?"

"No, child, I don't sleep as well as I used to in the good old days. Guess I don't work hard enough anymore," was his plaintive observation.

Mary's heart warmed at his gentle expression. "I'm thirty-three years old, Papa. Will you never stop thinking of me as your child?" she asked, smiling broadly.

"I'm afraid not, Mary. It's a disease of parenthood." He didn't add that she would find that out herself when she birthed her own babes, for he knew without her saying that it would never happen. A cheating philanderer had seen to that.

"What's bothering you, darling?" Alvah asked. "Can I help?"

Mary avoided his question. She rinsed Vesta's heavy flowered teapot with half of the scalding water, then emptied it into the sink. Next, she sprinkled a clump of herb tea into the pot and filled it with the rest of the boiling water.

Alvah took two plain white cups and saucers down from the shelf. "Are you hungry?" he asked. "You didn't eat much supper."

"No, Papa. My stomach's still not back to normal. I just thought the tea would help me sleep. Is Mama awake?"

"Your mother was sleeping peacefully when I left the room. She seems to be very tired, lately."

"You know her arthritis will do that, Papa."

He pushed a forelock of iron gray hair off his forehead. "I know that. Unfortunately, I know that too well, but you can't change the subject again. Something is weighing on your mind, daughter."

Mary lifted the flowered lid and peered into the pot, determined the tea had steeped enough, and poured out two cups. The fragrant steam rose between them as she pushed the honey jar toward her father. "Oh, Papa, it's not any one thing. You know what Albert has been up to in the courts, and the prison experience is still in my nightmares.

"Since I've been refused another commission, I've been trying to get a pension from Congress. All I get is a run around the mulberry bush. Everything seems so useless, somehow."

"It's not like you to give up, Mary. You have to keep fighting for what's right."

Mary sipped her tea, thoughtfully, and then placed the cup back in its saucer. The clink of the china emphasized her thoughts. "It seems as if I've been fighting for one thing or another for my whole life, Papa. I'm just sick and tired of it all."

She offered him more tea, but he shook his head. She topped off her own cup.

"What are you planning to do now, Mary?" His fondest hope rose for a brief moment. "Will you come back here and practice, maybe?"

"I'm thinking of going to Europe, Papa. England, that is. There's a colleague of mine from the *Post* who's been looking into a position for me as a ship's surgeon so I wouldn't have to pay the fare."

Alvah's spirits sank, but he betrayed nothing. Good Lord, England was the other side of the world. "How will you live, once you get there?" he worried.

Mary flicked her wrist, a dismissive gesture. "Dear Papa, you know I always have a little hidden away for emergencies." A rueful chuckle escaped her. "I can earn fees for lecturing, and there are always kind people who'll accommodate a visiting oddity like me."

He took her hand in his own and squeezed it. "Don't demean yourself, child."

She squeezed back. "Oh, Papa, we both know I'm a touch more peculiar than the ordinary woman. You're partly to blame for it, you know."

"Well, just don't let your mother hear that kind of talk. She'd skin us both," he said as he picked up his cup and rose to set it on the sideboard. "I'll be getting back to bed, I think, before your Mama wakes up and finds me gone."

He stooped and kissed his daughter on the top of her head. "Goodnight, darling. Get some rest, now, you hear."

"Yes, Papa," Mary answered. She carried her own cup along with the teapot over to the soapstone sink to rinse them both.

Alvah paused in the doorway then turned back toward her. "Your mother and I have money put by, Mary. You are welcome to it, if you need it."

"I know that, Papa. I hope it won't ever come to that, but I am determined to get away from everything."

"Just remember you must never be in need while I am around to help."

She ran across the room and threw her arms around him. "Oh, Papa," was all she could say as he held her close.

She winced at his painful tread up the stairs then sat for a long time at the table thinking of her future and wondering what lay in store for her across the broad Atlantic. A frisson of expectation slid up her spine. A new adventure would help ease the rage she felt every time she thought of the cavalier attitudes of Miller and the United States Congress.

Some day, she would be given her due.

CHAPTER FORTY-EIGHT

GLASGOW/MANCHESTER, ENGLAND

D R. MARY was puking–again. Her bilious complexion, a sickly shade of pea soup green, reflected the color of the sea pitching the bow of the Anchor Line's steamship *Caledonia* as it lumbered across the Atlantic on its tedious journey from New York City to Glasgow, Scotland.

Unable to get an official working berth, Mary borrowed the money for her steerage from her father. She departed for the United Kingdom in August of 1866 in the company of attractive friends: tall, slender Dr. Susannah Dodds and her pleasantly rotund husband whom everyone, including his wife, called Mr. Dodds.

The endless smoking of restless and bored male passengers had compounded Mary's hideous bouts of seasickness. Their constant puffing filled the lounges and passageways with mordant clouds of acrid smoke that irritated her sinuses and burned her lungs. At every turn, she encountered disgusting, chewed butts flopped like ugly brown turds atop sand-filled safety buckets. Each time she came upon one of the loathsome receptacles, her gorge rumbled up from the pit of her belly depositing slimy, sour bile in her throat. There seemed no respite, day or night, from the insensitive buffoons who stunk up the environment with their disgusting, malodorous cigars while they swilled brandy from silver pocket flasks and poked fun at fellow travelers.

Her stomach roiled with the intermittent heave and toss of the briny; and, more than once, she keeled over in a dead faint. Neither Dr. Dodds nor the ship's surgeon could suggest anything that brought her relief.

She kept her stomach filled. She kept it empty. She sipped hot mint tea or spicy beef broth. Nothing helped. One whiff of pungent cigar smoke and waves of nausea swept over her like an evil scourge that sucked out her innards.

To escape the suffocating atmosphere inside the ship, Mary braved the misty chill outside, often standing on the deck with the wind buffeting her face to clear her lungs and blow away the stench from her clothing. She gulped cleansing breaths of salty air, clutching her cloak about her to ward off the damp.

The impossible situation gave her plenty of fodder for fourteen disparaging pages about the evils of tobacco she later included in her first published book titled *Hit*.

She hated the nasty product with such a passion that she often wished every plant in the world destruction by a blight that left the fields fallow long after her own demise.

A favorite couplet she quoted rolled off her tongue at the drop of a hat.

> *"Tobacco is an Indian weed*
> *and from the Devil did proceed."*

She wrote a friend:

> *"I have been sick enough to feel as disagreeable as*
> *possible, for never in my life have I felt such a*
> *hatred of the vile and filthy 'goatweed' tobacco as*
> *since I left New York . . . The language of all*
> *nations combined would never express my downright*
> *and unqualified hatred of it . . ."*

When the journey ended, Mary Walker was one of the first to flee the ship.

On an overcast, blustery day the *Caledonia* steamed into the harbor at

Glasgow, coming to a halt at a sturdy loading pier. A viscous Scottish mist swirled around hundreds of bobbing heads as the ship disgorged passengers, buzzing down the gangway like a swarm of worker bees abandoning a breached hive.

Mary led the crowd into the busy alleyway between two warehouses trailed by a steward lugging her battered trunk. The Dodds were not far behind.

Before traveling to the northern reaches, she established headquarters in the city at the home of G. W. Muir, a kind editor, who unselfishly shared his home and family.

Mary returned the favor by treating the illnesses of his wife and daughters. She assuaged their fear that the smallest girl was afflicted with tuberculosis, a disease she'd encountered many times in her practice. She diagnosed the child as anemic and ordered a change in diet.

The Muir children treated her like a well-loved aunt, showing her around the countryside. Later on, one of them adopted the trousers and tunic that she'd so admired on their feisty, avant-garde guest.

Mrs. Muir handled Mary's mail and appointment schedule while the busy doctor journeyed through Ireland and Scotland visiting hospitals and speaking to organized groups.

Mary's spirits soared as the enthusiastic reception to her lectures on women's rights, suffrage and reform dress far outshone the negative media attention she'd received back in the states.

Dr. Forsythe of the Royal Infirmary of Glasgow magically opened doors for Mary and her traveling companion, Susannah Dodds. Hospitals welcomed them, and courteous local physicians consulted and happily discussed a variety of illnesses with their two female counterparts.

⌒❀⌒

Mary stood among the participants of The Tenth Congress of The Association For The Promotion Of Social Science, a humanitarian organization that met annually in Manchester, England.

The moment she read of the meeting, she canceled all plans in Scotland, bade farewell to the Dodds and the Muirs and rushed to the site of the conference. The agenda was right up her alley.

She hurried from seminar to seminar, barely taking time to eat or rest. Speaking up with her usual candor, she offered her opinions to all who would listen. Finally, she had the attention of the committee. Although they were a little non-plussed by her clothing, she was invited to speak.

Her treatment of the subject of infanticide raised the eyebrows of the medical community and brought severe criticism from reporters who questioned her motives. One writer even suggested that she was in favor of illegitimacy.

Nothing could have been further from the truth. In fact, she advocated abstinence from the sexual act for unmarried women to circumvent the need for abortion or the murder of helpless infants.

Let the chips fall where they may, she thought as she flung down the gauntlet.

"These unwed mothers were left to their own devices," she lambasted. "They were abandoned by the despicable curs who took advantage of them. These men cheated on their wives then left the disastrous results of their seductions to be dealt with by poor, disenchanted creatures whose only recourse seemed to be suicide or the destruction of the babes they carried in their wombs."

There was stunned silence in the hall. Not a cough. Not a sneeze. Not a shuffled foot.

But Dr. Mary lost her patience as she noted the self-righteous expressions on some of the upturned faces. "I deplore the ostracism of overly virtuous sisters who refuse to aid these misused and abused women," she scolded. "Indeed, the seducer should be treated with as much or more scorn as his misguided victim."

Well, now. Here was another view, entirely. Bottoms squirmed on chairs and husbands cleared throats and averted their eyes as wives stared at them with suspicion on their angry faces.

At the close of the session, participants hurried away. Were they ashamed? Angry? Persuaded? None stopped to speak with her.

The press described her ideas as impractical and unworkable. After all, what good Christian woman should stoop to aid guilty little sluts? And who could blame a decent man for seeking relief and comfort outside his own bedroom if an unsympathetic or uncooperative wife refused his needs?

During the segment designated "The Repression of Crime," Dr. Mary fared a little better.

Her logical arguments commanded reasonable attention, and the press handled them with less emotion and more profundity.

During the few weeks she had been abroad, Mary was appalled to read several detailed descriptions of executions that had been carried out in London. She referred to the victims by name as she offered her own observations.

"It is not right for any government to take that which it is powerless to give back. Capital punishment is barbarous and unchristian. Criminals should be prosecuted to the extent that their crimes warrant, but to kill a man is reducing the government to the murderer's level."

When she was not speaking of these matters, Mary was busy seeking converts to her dress reform campaign.

Fifteen years earlier, Amelia Bloomer had visited England to gather support for her pantaloon costume, receiving nothing but ridicule for her trouble. She returned to America disgruntled and disgusted with the Brits.

Perhaps times had changed, or perhaps Mary's approach to the subject had softened up the hard noses. She certainly presented a far handsomer example in her tailored outfits, womanly hairstyle, and feminine accessories.

In the seminar's session called "Destruction of Life by Overwork," she was quoted as saying, "No wonder fashion conscious women suffer from fatigue and lethargy. Their voluminous skirts and petticoats force them to act as horse and cart carrying around a load of dry goods. Their corsets pinch their breath away and crush their internal organs out of shape so they are forever exhausted and ill."

When the meeting turned to the subject of suffrage, Mary snatched off her stylish hat and got down to business. Her ideas were greeted with catcalls and boos by 'gentlemen' who had no interest in seeing their inferior wives, daughters and mistresses elevated to voting status, let alone given equal rights.

Following that embarrassing treatment, Mary was approached by a group of prominent, frustrated women who apologized for the boorish behavior of the men and invited her to their next meeting.

"What can we do to secure the vote?" they asked, all speaking at once.

"Give me some time to research the subject," Mary said, "and I promise to have more information when I see you again."

The next week a crowd of women gathered at a small private dining room in a quiet teahouse.

Once the group was called to order, Mary displayed a copy of English law that required voters be at least twenty-one years old. All must submit a fee of ten pounds and then register their names next to the candidates on the ballots. Nowhere in the document was any gender requirement noted.

"Go ahead and vote," she advised. "Proceed as if it is your right."

The room erupted with the sound of laughter and happy voices. Word circulated quickly. In the 1867 elections ten thousand women went to the polls and cast their ballots. Parliament had no choice but to succumb to such an overwhelming popular demand.

Mary later related the tale to an audience in New York then gleefully reported, "In 1868, the right to vote on all questions, except members of Parliament, was granted to women."

The general consensus of the news media was that Dr. Mary Walker had made a fairly positive impression on both the men and the women of the British Empire. Her views were logical and straightforward. Although the Brits were curious about her life style, they could not help but admire her spunk.

The British press tended to be more liberal, reporting her innovative ideas on important issues rather than poking fun at her costumes.

One columnist stated that her clothing was "as near an approach to male costume as it is possible for a woman to wear without the least suspicion of vulgarity or indecency."

While the writer did not think it was the wardrobe that would be chosen by the women of England or the United States, for that matter, he expressed his admiration for Mary.

> " . . . It is hardly possible to conceive that the
> gentle face of the wearer can be that of one who has
> earned a mark of distinction by painful labor among
> the saddest scenes of war, or who can endure the yet
> more painful curiosity of the crowd who surrounded
> and questioned her here."

However, when a French reporter, showing off to his colleagues insulted her outfit, Mary quickly put him in his place. "At least ten thousand women in the United States now wear this costume," she insisted, "and if the modistes of Paris do not soon adopt it, their lead in the fashion world will end."

Were there ten thousand women wearing her costume? One wonders who did the counting.

With her health better than it had been for months and her boundless enthusiasm reinforced by the positive reception she'd received in Manchester, Mary was ready to take on England's ancient capital city.

CHAPTER FORTY-NINE

LONDON, ENGLAND

D R. MARY'S arrival in London fostered a strange feeling of déjà vu.
Like Manchester, the bustling city hunkered down on both sides of
a river–this time the mighty Thames with its arched London Bridge, wattle
and daub huts and forbidding stone castles like the eleventh-century
fortress called the Tower of London.

England's capital city smelled old. The unwashed street population
reeked of sweat, halitosis and flatus. Because of improper sewage and
garbage disposal, pollution was London's most horrendous problem. A
fetid putrescence of decomposing detritus punctuated by the acrid pong
of horse droppings, urine and decaying wood permeated the atmosphere.

It's even worse than Washington during the war, Mary thought, as she
traversed a narrow alley, holding a dainty linen handkerchief to her nose.

But the unpleasant ambiance didn't deter her from taking in the
sights. The opulence of Westminster Abby with its marble columns,
stained glass windows, and arches rising to the vaulted ceilings filled her
with awe. She had never encountered such magnificence as the lofty
dome of Saint Paul's Cathedral or Christopher Wren's soaring steeple
atop Saint Mary-Le-Bow. Her mouth fell open at the intricate carvings
and wonderful paintings in every public building. The four hundred
tons of shining glass that made up the Crystal Palace quite simply bog-
gled her mind.

In between her pleasure forays, she frequented private offices to pick
the brains of local physicians and visited Middlesex teaching hospital where
students, though stunned by her costume, treated her with utmost respect.
She was, after all, a practicing physician, American or not.

Word circulated about the 'interesting' little American doctor, and Mary was soon accorded professional courtesies by such renowned medical practitioners as London's eminent coroner, Dr. Edwin Lankester; Dr. Forbes Winslow, prominent psychiatrist of the times; and the senior surgeon of Saint Bartholomew's Hospital, Dr. Holmes Coote.

These men and their colleagues extended professional courtesies as well as social invitations. She charmed the gentlemen with her wit and intelligence, and her exhilarating tales of adventure momentarily distracted the world-weary doctors.

Dr. Mary was scrupulously careful not to cross the line when asked for a consultation. The last thing she needed was a complaint that she was practicing medicine on foreign soil without proper licensing.

Soon, Mary's name became so well known that select groups of empathetic women invited Mary to speak about dress reform. Her feminist ideas were received with cautious enthusiasm, but she was always applauded for her pioneering spirit when she insisted that women's suffrage was inevitable.

"There will come a time," she foretold, "when women will take their places beside men in the world and will never again be forced to walk two steps behind." The gathering roared its appreciation, but their enthusiasm withered as she told them that it was no longer acceptable for women to be forced to be either domestic servants or prostitutes. Ladies of the night were not mentioned in London's polite society.

Most puzzling of all was the variety of descriptions rendered by so-called veteran reporters. Perhaps most of them expected an Amazonian virago with a booming voice and chin hair, and so were totally surprised by such a diminutive, ladylike person with her peaches and cream complexion, cobalt eyes, dainty hands and tiny feet.

Not surprisingly, journalists wrote that Dr. Mary Walker was small, elegant and well built, but at least one declared her tall and slender. Since tall was never an adjective used to describe Mary Walker, one wondered at the writer's own perception of height.

P. F. Andre, a London columnist, dubbed Mary "one of the greatest women of her generation."

The disparity of the reports only served to reiterate the prejudices of the writers.

Crusty, grizzled Charles Dickens, furious over his fight against United States copyright laws and upset with violent attacks on him by the American press, was grudging in his critique. His long separation from his wife and his disappointment in his sons did not help his miserable disposition.

He wrote, "The learned lady was very strong in florid American oratory . . . there was much to deplore and something withal to admire in the performance."

The ticket agent, the larcenous Mr. Nimmo, hovering in the wings, observed the crowd's reaction. Not in the least sympathetic to Mary's agenda of equal rights, he was a little surprised by the extended applause. But he recognized a good thing when it battered his eardrums.

Two days later, he sent Mary a most persuasive note defending his financial settlement after the lecture. He wrote, "I shall be most happy to take over the management of your career and relieve you of tiresome business affairs. I'll gladly obtain an early commitment for a second lecture arena if you will kindly advise me of your schedule."

The man had cheated her out of the receipts from the first lecture. Did he think she was an idiot? She laughed aloud and tossed the communication into the nearest trash bin.

However, it occurred to her that Mr. Nimmo was a shrewd businessman. If he thinks my talks are a drawing card here in London, she mused, I can darn well do it on my own. Now I know how to publicize upcoming lectures and charge reasonable fees for them.

❧✿❧

It was inevitable that the published accounts of her successful tour reached the queen's ears, and Mary was commanded to an audience with Her Royal Highness, Victoria Regina.

"You must wear a long skirt, my dear, or you will not be shown into Her Majesty's presence," admonished a close friend.

"If I'm wanted at the palace, I'll go as myself and not some trussed up dolly who bows and bobs to public whim," she replied.

True to form, Mary ignored his advice and did as she pleased. She designed and ordered a tailor to create a suitable reform dress costume. She loved the outfit so much she commissioned a portrait showing her clad in black silk trousers, and a full-skirted, knee-length tunic in matching fabric. Lapels and trousers were exquisitely trimmed in black velvet. Queen or no queen, Mary Walker had no intention of backing down on a crusade that had lasted most of her lifetime.

At Windsor Castle, Mary was shown to an opulent drawing room with domed ceilings, elaborate frescoes and glittering crystal chandeliers that reflected the glow of their tall tapers. The odor of burning beeswax mingled with the various scents emanating from the queen's milling subjects.

She rejoiced on spying discreet 'no smoking' signs placed on graceful tables decorated with priceless chinoiserie and delicate bisque figurines. Her escort smiled and whispered, "Her Royal Highness abhors cigars and forbids their use in her presence."

Had the palace atmosphere been less stilted, Mary might have clapped her hands and laughed aloud.

Still she smiled as her respect for the queen reached new heights. She whispered back, "Too bad the regent's little signs are not required on the steamship *Caledonia* where all those damnable smokers permeate the public rooms with their choking stink."

Enthusiastic guests sporting their most festive trappings genteelly circled the salon. Jewels sparkled on shell pink earlobes and powdered bosoms, complementing colorful silk gowns whose beribboned skirts billowed about their owners' perspiring bodies. The room whispered with the swish and rustle of brocade, moiré and satin as fashionable ladies moved to and fro, mindful of their temperamental regent and careful not to upset her.

Across the length of the room, Mary caught her first glimpse of England's reigning sovereign. For the moment, the queen sat oblivious of her surroundings. Perhaps she was remembering a Viennese waltz with her beloved Prince Albert, dead these five lonely years.

Clad in a plain, coal black brocade gown trimmed with rows of pleated ruching, Victoria Regina sat rigid as a stick, her tight corsets squeezing her plump waist like a vise. A black mantilla-style headdress and long veil covered thick, dark hair that was parted in the middle and skinned back into a bun. The black netting that framed a round face as pale as parchment, ended in a huge bow tied beneath Victoria's pudgy chin. Wrist-length black gloves covered her chubby, restless hands, and flat black leather shoes poked beneath her skirt. A plain white linen handkerchief was the only spot of brightness about the royal person.

Still in deep mourning over the loss of her precious consort, her 'Dear One,' Victoria, sober and regal, received the masses with a mere nod or blink. Her heavy-lidded eyes mirrored the sadness that sickened her soul. Grief lines etched deep furrows on either side of her grim lips.

Dr. Mary instantly believed all the stories she'd heard about the poor widow's melancholia.

An audible gasp rose from the assembled conservatives already in attendance the moment the guests caught sight of the strangely clad visitor. Conscious of their rude stares, Mary hesitated an instant at the arched doorway then squared her shoulders, and marched proudly between the rows of guests who parted to make an aisle for her. She felt their eyes boring into her spine but kept her eyes glued to the queen, refusing to look right or left.

She heard the chancellor announce in stentorian tones, "Dr. Mary Walker from the colonies."

She bit her tongue to stifle a giggle. The man was about a century behind the times. Colonies, indeed!

When she finally stood before the queen, Mary hid her concern at the lady's obvious depression. Bowing from the waist, she smiled her prettiest and said, "Good afternoon, your majesty."

Again, the crowd gasped. But what could one expect from an ignorant American who had no manners? Everyone knew one did not speak to the queen unless she spoke first.

The ghost of a smile softened Victoria's grim visage. Her voice was soft and kind as she leaned forward in her chair.

"Good afternoon, Dr. Walker," she whispered for Mary's ears alone. "May I say your costume looks the ultimate in comfort?"

"Thank you, Madam," replied Mary, bowing again. "I hope your majesty is in good health."

"As well as can be expected," the queen sighed, and her eyes moved on to the next visitor.

Those closest to the royal seat were flabbergasted. While they had not heard the short conversation, the word soon circulated that the crude little American doctor had coaxed a smile out of their grieving monarch.

Surely, Her Royal Highness must disapprove of such atrocious garments, they sneered, especially here at formal court. Unanimously, they decided that the queen was undoubtedly laughing at that ridiculous outfit. Their derision fizzled when Victoria presented Mary with a handsome gold watch and chain to express her admiration of the doctor's accomplishments.

For Mary, the experience was the highlight of her tour. "The Queen admired my trousers! And I received a gold watch, besides," she bragged.

CHAPTER-FIFTY

LONDON/PARIS

IN THE MIDST of her success, Mary enjoyed visits to good restaurants and historical buildings. She admired Notre Dame Cathedral with its flying buttresses and soaring ceilings. She marveled at the artistry of Napoleon's towering Arc de Triomphe and the majesty of the bridge called Pont Neuf. But nothing in all her travels through the northern and southern lands of her own country had prepared her for the stunning masterpiece that was Sainte Anne de Beaupr's chapel. She wept at the sheer majesty of its vaulted ceilings supported by slender columns that separated stained glass walls. The sheer majesty of it left her breathless.

A few days later, she stood in the Civil Chamber of the infamous Great Hall, awe-struck for totally different reasons. The building's shadowy corridors seemed haunted by the ghosts of the 2600 French victims who had listened for the dreaded rumble of the creaking wooden tumbrels coming to collect them for the fateful journey that ended beneath the insatiable blade of the bloody guillotine.

Mary's mind reeled at the savagery evil men committed against one another. Wars and revolutions, pogroms and genocide. Where was Papa's God when death was wreaking its havoc with the innocents?

To commemorate the Fourth of July three hundred guests, dressed to the nines, began arriving, including handsome Dr. Walker in her black silk finery–britches and all. Eyes shining, ebon curls prettily arranged around her rosy, wholesome face, she exhibited the picture of health. Her five-star bronze Medal hung from a crimson ribbon about her neck, and a wide, tri-colored stars and stripes sash girdled her flattering tunic.

The British press was genuinely irritated when Mary's wardrobe was treated with much favorable publicity at the event. The French couldn't understand why the Brits made such 'une grande clameur' over her bloomer costume. They considered her short dresses flattering and fetching, declaring 'le pantalon' did not in the least detract from the wearer's overall femininity.

Politically, the meeting was a disaster, but the gathering showed no favoritism. Both President Johnson and the Emperor of France were slighted when toasts were raised.

As the champagne flowed and the dull speeches droned on, eyelids fluttered, heads nodded and a few discreet snores could be heard here and there.

Before the master of ceremonies could stop her, Mary took matters into her own hands. She sprang from her seat, strode to the dais and raised her glass of rust-tinged water.

"To our brave soldiers and sailors. Huzzah!" she cried. Then she lifted the edge of her sash to her lips, reverently kissed the colors, and quickly hustled back to her seat.

That jolted the sleepyheads awake. Some of the guests couldn't decide whether to laugh or cheer, but others appeared shocked at her temerity. "How dare Dr. Walker upset the delicate balance?" they gossiped, "especially while Maximillian's troops occupied Mexico by order of Napoleon III. She is a guest in France and protocol forbids patriotic utterances at a mixed gathering of French and American citizens."

Aware, or not, Dr. Mary never missed an opportunity to honor the military's sacrifices she observed during her time with the Army. Her toast came as naturally to her as breathing.

Near the end of her Paris visit, Mary, milling about with thousands of other tourists, began exploring the displays at the great Exposition. She discovered the United States exhibit containing portraits of prominent Americans. Among them, of course, was President Johnson's.

Nearby, his eyes seeming to bore into her soul, was a handsome portrait of General Robert E. Lee decked out in his dove gray Confederate uniform, shiny gold buttons, stars and all.

Mary screamed. The horrors of war were far too fresh in her mind to tolerate a flattering picture of the scoundrel who had been responsible for the slaughter of so many of her boys buried on southern hillsides.

Arms akimbo, she squared up in front of the offending picture. "How dare they?" she boomed, "How dare they place this villain among such honorable men?" She reached up and tore the pasteboard mounting away from the wall.

Surprised visitors stopped to stare at the crazy woman—clad in trousers no less—who dared mishandle a sanctioned painting.

Just entering the area was Commissioner-General Beckwith, head of the American Exhibition. He could hardly trust his eyesight. "What on earth?" he muttered as he quickly closed the distance between Mary and himself.

"Stop," he ordered and snatched her hand away. "You have no right to destroy this man's picture. He is an American, and, as such, is entitled to have his place here."

The small crowd edged closer. The scene was beginning to get interesting.

"You cannot be serious," Mary snapped back. "This man is not an American. He is a rebel and a traitor who fought against his own government."

Heads bobbed and tongues clucked as twenty people eyeballed first the feisty lady and then the Commissioner-General.

"Be that as it may," was Beckwith's sharp retort, "our present government authorized this display, and you cannot take it upon yourself to destroy it."

A couple of men applauded. Mary glowered at them.

Amid the mumbling of the onlookers, Beckwith grasped her arm and dragged her away, ignoring the tears of frustration she brushed from her flaming cheeks.

A few indignant souls fired off parting shots at Beckwith's rough treatment, but most of the rubbernecks quietly drifted on, looking for the next happening.

Aside from the Robert E. Lee episode, Mary thoroughly enjoyed her sojourn in France, and the French people, it seemed, enjoyed her equally.

At a famous London auditorium, Mary shared the podium with a Mrs. Law whose topic was the women's franchise question that had just been hotly debated in the House of Commons. The American physician introduced the popular British speaker, and when the woman's speech was over, Mary invited questions or opposing arguments from the floor. Not one gentleman rose to complain or object.

Before closing the meeting, Mary offered her own opinion, "There are too many injustices done to women because of antiquated British laws governing marriage. It's time to allow us our due. We are not chattel. We are human beings deserving of rights."

Perhaps her divorce problems that were unfolding across the Atlantic prompted some of her remarks, but she kept that information to herself.

The National Temperance League of London was one of the last British organizations to enjoy Dr. Mary's company. Billed as a "Farewell Lecture to the Ladies of London," her dissertation dealt with the evils of modern day dress.

Her return voyage to America was no less difficult than her trip abroad. When it was over, she could barely wait for the tugs to wrestle the huge liner up to the dock.

Joyfully, she sucked in great gulps of clean air as she trudged down the swaying gangway and stepped onto blessedly firm planks beneath her feet.

For the time being, it was wonderful just to be home.

CHAPTER FIFTY-ONE

OSWEGO, NEW YORK

MARY WALKER'S self-satisfied mood diminished as the first few weeks of her return to Oswego flew by. In the year that she had been abroad, the United States had made little progress in the battle for human rights.

She deplored the turmoil plaguing her beloved America as she devoured news from all over the country—candid reports that had been non-existent in an indifferent Europe.

Politicians battled over states' rights as the president's appointed generals established martial law and replaced civil governors in the reconstruction belt. Military men inflicted their laws on private citizens without the expertise to improve the civilian's lot.

She fretted over her southern friends after learning that unscrupulous carpetbaggers and scalawags were plundering the south, seizing properties and pirating assets.

Clandestine stories circulated about the evil cowards in the Ku Klux Klan, the Knights of the White Camellia and the White Leagues of Mississippi and Louisiana who, under cover of darkness, burned, pillaged and murdered helpless victims for the slightest provocation. If, in the eyes of the anonymous vigilantes, a black-skinned man transgressed, he was tortured, mutilated and hanged. White so-called 'nigger lovers' were treated with equal brutality. Avaricious bigots in positions of power turned a blind eye. Worse yet, they profited from the purging.

In the west, American Indians battled the United States cavalry and infantry to preserve their homelands as oxen-drawn Conestogas and horse-driven spring wagons carted homesteaders and miners into their ancestral territories to change the landscape forever.

Hunters murdered buffalo, pronghorn antelope and the mighty elk by the thousands to assuage their lust for hides or for the sheer thrill of the slaughter. Carcasses were left to feed the wolves and vultures. The Plains Indians who depended on the beasts for their food and clothing suffered untold hardship.

Men treated American women like second class citizens, underpaid, under appreciated and deprived of the basic rights that Mary maintained were promised to them by the Constitution.

Constant tales of their mistreatment and deprivation propelled Mary into a debilitating blue funk that lingered for weeks, leaving her morose and despondent.

To exacerbate matters, her messy second divorce action from Miller was still slogging through the courts, and Congress continued to ignore her pension petitions.

The final blow, one that nearly killed her spirit, came when several New York newspapers published a London story about her questionable war credentials. They also printed the adultery charges brought by Miller.

Dr. Roberts Bartholow, the Army surgeon who had conducted the infamous Board of Inquiry, labeled her a medical monstrosity.

Straight-faced, Bartholow swore, "The Board treated the woman with the utmost delicacy and consideration." Furthermore, (even though Mary had offered as evidence her diplomas from Syracuse Medical School and the Hygeio-Therapeutic College,) Bartholow insisted the examiners had no knowledge that she had ever entered a school of medicine, much less graduated from one. He was quoted verbatim: "She was hired to serve as a nurse. It appeared subsequently that this was a design. She was intended as a spy and went forward to be captured. It was supposed that her profession would procure her greater liberties and wider opportunities for observation. The medical staff of the army was made a blind for the execution of this profound piece of strategy by the War Office."

Mary's response: "After all these years that vindictive report continues to haunt me."

Mary's brother, Alvie, and his wife, Sarah, fought tirelessly to defend her. True to form, the sisters dismissed Alvie like a pesky fly and Sarah was ignored altogether.

A Medal for Dr. Mary

⁂

When the fall elections rolled around, Mary's fighting spirit rose like a Phoenix from the ashes. Practicing what she had preached to her audiences in Great Britain, she donned her best outfit and thrust six-inch hatpins through her finest feathered hat. She threw on the old woolen cloak that had warmed her on the battlefield, sprang into the saddle and headed for the voting booth at the town hall.

Most Oswegans were well acquainted with their colorful resident, although they hadn't seen much of her the past few years. Still, there wasn't another female in the area who dared show up in public wearing trousers and riding her horse astride. 'Just not genteel,' they whispered.

Mary eyed the crowd and slid down from her saddle. Her dash to town had polished her cheeks as red as fall apples, and wisps of dark hair curled about her temples.

She clutched her felt hat against the wintry northwest winds, frigid with moisture, as they whipped across the pewter-colored waters of Lake Ontario and roared through the town's main street. She nodded to those closest but quick marched to her destination.

"Looks like Alvah's girl's got a bee up her bum, don't it?" said one man out of the corner of his mouth.

"Wonder what she's up to this time?" questioned a bewhiskered gent who had once encountered Mary's wrath while he was manhandling his wife outside the general store.

Curious individuals, two or three at a time, drifted after Mary up the steps into the Town Office vestibule.

She paused a moment to get her bearings. The dimly lit foyer smelled of oiled flooring and natural gas flame. The eyes of the ancient portraits on the walls seemed to follow her as she passed each one.

Alphonse Scroggins, a scrawny Ichabod Crane type, stepped in front of the ballot box clutching a sheaf of papers to his chest. "Help ya?" he asked.

His yearly election volunteer status puffed the local cobbler up like a strutting rooster—a man of importance.

The old codger's chin whiskers were snowier than his salt and pepper hair, and his wrinkled neck looked too fragile to hold up his oversized head.

The gentleman's suit was not nearly as elegant as Mary's and his shoes were worn thin at the toes as if he spent a great deal of time on his knees, which, in fact, he did. He was forever crawling around his shop looking for the mate to a shoe he was repairing.

Though she had known Alphonse Scroggins all her life, Mary identified herself to him, anyway. Her tone was perfectly reasonable as she held up a previously prepared ballot.

"My name is Dr. Mary Edwards Walker, and, if you'll step aside, I'd like to cast my vote, please."

Aghast, Scroggins quickly covered the slit in the ballot box with a callused hand marred by a purple thumbnail bruise from a careless whack of his tack hammer.

"Where in creation did you get that ballot," he demanded. "Looks legitimate, but it can't be."

"It's a legal ballot. Now stand aside."

His waxy complexion turned paler than one of Vesta's bleached bed sheets. The poor man had never faced such a predicament in all his born days. "Is this some kind of joke?" he squeaked.

A chubby dandy near the door began to snicker but cut it short as Mary fired a drop-dead glance in his direction.

"This is not a laughing matter, sir. I have as much right to vote as you do, and I have come to exercise that right as a property owner and a tax-payer."

"Are you a male citizen?" asked Scroggins.

"Certainly not."

"Well, then you can't vote."

"But the Constitution grants me the right to cast my vote as a citizen born in this country."

He insinuated his skeletal frame between Mary and the ballot box before mumbling under his breath to a fellow inspector hovering nearby. Quietly Scroggins dispatched his colleague to fetch the list of rules. The funny little man, shorter than Mary and wiry as a whippet, disappeared through a nearby office door, and Mary heard the cover of a roll-top desk swivel up with a bang.

When the aide returned he was carrying a sheet of paper that he offered to his co-worker. Scroggins took his time adjusting the wire frames of his little rectangular glasses over his ears then he snatched up the paper, flexed it importantly and cleared his throat.

"Ahem. Nobody except a male citizen above twenty-one years of age, should be allowed to vote," he quoted. "It says so right there," he added, tapping a paragraph in the text.

Mary edged around behind him and tried to insert the ballot Alvie had pilfered for her when he'd cast his own vote earlier. But Scroggins was too quick for her. His hand snaked over the slot in the box and the expression on his face promised he was prepared to stand his ground if it took all day.

"Very well, sir," she conceded. "But, I warn you, there will come a time when women will vote, and the likes of you will not stop us."

Rude jibes followed her out into the windy street where she vaulted into her saddle and snapped the reins, grateful for the chill that helped cool her burning cheeks.

"Some day it will be different," she said as the mare lengthened her stride. "Some day we'll show them all."

Once home, she wept with her head in Mama's lap. "Why is everything so hard?" she cried.

Mary's melancholia seemed behind her as she resumed her speaking tour, but the ugly publicity that followed her from London had changed something inside her. The disheartening experience at the voting booth didn't help.

Alvah tried to comfort her, but she rested her head against his shoulder and admitted, "My belief in my fellow man is tarnished, Papa. I find I'm more wary, more suspicious. I can't take people at face value, anymore. I look for hidden agendas or ulterior motives."

Alvah hugged her close. "You've been through a lot, my girl. You will heal."

"I'm not above a strategic machination here or there, mind you," she said with a grin. "But I promise I'll to always be honest."

She regaled audiences with her run-in with Scroggins. "Maybe if I perjured myself, insisted I'm a man, I might have gotten away with voting, but, I couldn't do that, even to accomplish my goal."

She chuckled at the thought. "But that's pure speculation. I could never in a million years admit to being a man even if no one was aware of my gender."

She always added, "But, my dear ladies, the Constitution already gives women the right to vote. Men are just too pig-headed to accept it."

She cited her source: "We the People of the United States means ALL the people, not just men who had attained the age of twenty one."

She pointed to women in her audience. "You are a person. I am a person. The country cannot function without us. Furthermore," she expounded, "the fourteenth amendment, ratified in 1865, guarantees citizenship rights to everyone, born or naturalized in the United States, and no state shall deprive a person of life, liberty, or property."

She pounded her palm with her fist. "It does not say deprive a MAN, it does not say deprive a MALE, it says it shall not deprive A PERSON!"

Women listeners clapped and cheered while husbands, brothers, and fathers sat on their hands, tightlipped and resentful. Since men held the power and controlled the purse strings, Mary knew it was an uphill battle, but one she could never abandon.

❧❀☙

She decided to ignore the derogatory news stories and get on with her life, embarking on an extensive tour through New York and New England.

She lectured on health issues, women's suffrage, dress reform, alcohol and tobacco. Her audiences ranged from silk clad socialites to simple farmwomen in their cotton and gingham. Everywhere she spoke women came away feeling better about themselves. She gave them hope that one day their rights would be recognized. Mere prayers were not accomplishing their goals.

Wives, both affluent and poor, came to her after her speeches and confessed the indignities they experienced from abusive and/or alcoholic husbands. Some of them wept over the loss of their children to vindictive mates, some railed against the seizure of their property by greedy spouses. Many of them felt they were treated no better than cattle.

The more Mary heard, the more their horror stories dredged up her battle with Albert Miller. Her anger grew like a festering boil that cried out to be lanced.

It was time to return to Washington to challenge the solons elected by men of the United States. "I'll make them understand that times are changing and they must establish new laws for the protection of women's rights. Congress controls the power to change the status quo, Papa, so Congress is where I'll start."

"Be careful, child," he replied. "You are treading on traditions, and men are not happy when women confront them."

She smiled. "Oh, Papa, it's a long time since I've been a child. I fought a war if you recall."

Alvah pulled her close. "You'll always be my child, girl. It's a father privilege."

CHAPTER FIFTY-TWO

WASHINGTON AND POINTS SOUTH

JANUARY, 1869. Dr. Mary Edwards Walker was one of the prominent speakers at the first National Suffragists Convention in Washington.

She wore her usual tunic and trousers, but only one other woman in the group had followed suit. While Mary was busy tending the wounded, Lucy Stone, Susan B. Anthony and Elizabeth Cady Stanton made the decision to abandon the Reform Dress.

"Gaining the suffrage is more important than aggravating unsympathetic women and influential men by flaunting bloomers over conventional clothing," Stanton said.

On the first day of the convention, Mary's mouth twisted in disgust as she stared at the members' swaying skirts sweeping the oiled wooden floor of the auditorium, angry at what hypocrites they'd all become. They abandoned their principles and surrendered to current fashion, willingly enduring the harm and discomfort forced upon their abused bodies.

Before Mary took the podium, Stanton and Barton, both in voluminous, black, bombazine gowns—buttoned to the neck and falling to their boot tops—gave stirring addresses about a woman's right to have a say in making the laws that affected her everyday life. Their costumes belied their resolution.

When it was Mary's turn, she gathered her thoughts, took a deep breath, and began to speak. Unfortunately, the disappointments of past months weighed heavily on her. Instead of her usual rousing denunciation of a world dominated by men, she launched into a long and mournful diatribe about her own troubles.

If she thought her difficult experiences would serve to emphasize the cause, she'd guessed wrong. The audience sighed and coughed with embarrassment as she rambled on about her divorce and the mistreatment she'd received at the hands of judges and lawyers.

Finally, Lucretia Mott, who chaired the meeting, banged her gavel several times and ordered, "Sit down, Dr. Walker."

Red-faced and upset, Mary countered, beating her chest. "I will not sit until I've had my say. I've suffered the injustices men's laws inflict upon women." Her harangue continued until she was satisfied her point had been made.

Journalists had a field day at her expense, denigrating her remarks and ridiculing her costume.

On the second day of the Convention, a resolution was introduced for discussion. Essentially, it purported that the mission of the Women's Rights Movement was to improve family relations by passing laws that protected wives and mothers from the unfairness they faced in a male-dominated society.

"Madam," Mary called out to Mrs. Mott from her seat near the dais. "May I speak to the subject?"

An audible groan rose behind her as the audience dreaded a repeat of the previous day's performance.

Mary was nobody's fool. She acknowledged her faux pas of the day before, but vowed one mistake would not deter her. With a wry smile, she held up her hands, palms outward. "Don't worry," she promised, "You've heard all I have to say about the indignities heaped upon me. Instead, I wish to discuss how we change the laws that will never be satisfactory to us until we have an opportunity to vote on them.

"Until we educate those busy women who tend to exist in their own small circles, they will be unaware of how their sheer numbers could duly influence the ballot." She cited the success of English women at the polls.

At every meeting she attended, her chorus was the same. Many were disturbed by her confrontational attitude. She was a loose cannon and much too controversial to be endorsed by the movement. Even her friend, future attorney Belva Lockwood, rapped the gavel to shut her up several times.

After one meeting, Mary declared that many men were noble in spirit but too ignorant to recognize the plight of their female counterparts. "They speak of giving Negroes the vote, but I tell you now that it is totally unfair to give Negroes, Indians or any other minorities the vote before that privilege is bestowed upon women."

⌒⍩◉⍩⌒

Animosity toward Mary grew, but she had her own fans in the audience. In Cincinnati, for example, when the doctor had not been included on the agenda, an attractive young woman with golden hair and piercing violet eyes rose to protest.

"I wish to ask madam chairman why Dr. Mary Walker was not included on the speakers' list," she said. Gesturing toward the rear where Mary was seated, she raised her voice. "There is a lady who has entertained vast and polite audiences in England before many of today's speakers opened their mouths on the subject of Women's Rights."

A clamor went up from the floor, some voices moaning opposition, many supporting the girl's remarks.

"Let Dr. Walker speak," shouted one plump dumpling seated close to the podium.

"I'd like to hear what she has to say," ordered an opulently attired dowager who pointed her lorgnette like a weapon poised to strike down dissenters.

A round of applause settled the decision. Mary approached the dais. Once there, she pointed out the lateness of the hour.

To the chagrin of the program chairman who had a full day planned for the morrow, Mary swallowed her pique at being ignored and promised, "I shall be happy to address the group first thing in the morning."

A scattering of applause sealed the bargain, though there was no pleasure among the powers that ran the meeting.

Once the hall had emptied, the president called a hasty confab to hash over the pros and cons of allowing Mary to speak. Not wishing to alienate any of the supporting members, it was voted that she be inserted into the agenda, first thing, to get it over with early.

The next morning, the chairman called Mary to the platform with the introduction, "Mrs. Dr. Walker."

Mary walked up close to the speaker. "Not Mrs.," she said pointedly, "simply Dr. Walker, if you please."

∽◈◈◈∾

Mary faced a culture she never anticipated as she toured the South. Her work during the war threw her together with farmers and illiterate backwoods inhabitants who gratefully accepted her help, but city folk wore another face. They shunned her for 'consorting with the colored.' No self-respecting southern lady would be caught dead in the company of a woman who would stoop so low.

The Feliciana Patriot dubbed her a "specimen of depravity who wastes her good education." The article warned, "Get rid of your masculine attire or be arrested in every community where you appear in disguise."

In the north her lectures on health, justice and women's suffrage were highly successful as she delivered her messages to discouraged sisters in spirit.

In New Orleans, she received permission to speak in Mechanics Institute, which housed both the House and Senate chambers of the State Legislature.

Her audiences were a mixture of males and females—both colored and white. The fact that Negroes were assigned seats in a separate section upset her.

One newspaper reported, "We had a visit yesterday from Dr. Mary Walker and found her quite intelligent and very liberal and progressive in her ideas."

Another editorialized that she was "full of her subject, earnest in her opinion, warm in her sympathies, practical and sensible in her views and thoroughly posted in every branch of her subject."

Legislators and prominent intellectuals were surprised to hear Dr. Mary advocate immigration as well as the relocation of the United States capital to somewhere on the Mississippi.

With this last, she seemed only to be buttering up her southern listeners for comfort points. She never wanted the heart of the government moved out of Washington, a city she dearly loved.

A Medal for Dr. Mary

Between her lecture engagements, Mary made her home in the capital where she practiced medicine on a limited basis.

By treating the poor and indigent for little or no money, she infuriated her colleagues. Their criticism bothered her not a whit. A patient was never turned away from her door for lack of funds, and she never spoke of her charitable works. It remained for others to discover them.

A federal act passed in 1868 allowed all practitioners registered before that date to be licensed without a board examination. Either Mary was out of town at the time, or she still fretted about that first Board of Examiners. In any event, she never took the test but continued to treat patients, anyway. Her name appears in several Washington Directories with the notation 'Physician and Surgeon,' but her frequent travels prohibited a formal practice.

Her chief source of income was the fees from her lectures. She relied on friends to house her when her funds were short, and she was not above begging for transportation to and from her engagements.

CHAPTER FIFTY-THREE

LOUISIANA/TEXAS

IN NEW ORLEANS, Louisiana, a poignant case was being heard by the lower courts.

A grief-stricken young mother, shaking with fear, sat in the docket being viciously cross-examined by a vindictive state's attorney. The accusation against her: Infanticide.

A stranger approached Dr. Mary who was on a lecture junket in the area. He related the tragic circumstances and begged her to help the girl. Mary inquired around the courthouse and discovered that the defendant was without family or friends.

Although she considered infanticide a heinous crime and had preached against it many times, Mary rushed to the courthouse to support the desperate young woman. She listened to the sobbing girl's story and believed her blameless of the erroneous charges, offering the attending attorney a few cogent facts to shore up his shaky defense. Surprised and pleased with the unexpected help, he argued brilliantly for the young mother.

Once the jury had retired to deliberate, Mary submitted her comments to the local newspaper. In part, they read:

"A woman has been tried today, not by a woman judge, not by a woman attorney, not by a woman jury, but all the officials in the case were men in a republican country. What about people being tried by their peers? The defendant will be acquitted because there is no evidence to convict her, but the principle is the same."

Asked why she helped a girl she'd never met, the doctor replied, "I know her. I know all the sad young women who are desperate and afraid because they have been abandoned by the men who caused their suffering

387

but are held blameless while the victims of their selfishness are left to suffer alone."

The grieving girl fainted dead away when she was finally acquitted of the charges. Dr. Mary was the first at her side.

CHAPTER FIFTY-FOUR

NEW YORK/WASHINGTON

DURING her strenuous travels from town hall auditoriums to school campuses to church meeting houses throughout fifteen states, Mary was determined to put the time to good use.

She pored over her beloved Constitution then set about ascribing meaning to every single phrase it contained. Her aim was to publish a paragraph-by-paragraph analysis to prove that women were legally and morally equal to their counterparts.

She became expert at citing sections of the document that—in her opinion—absolutely guaranteed women's suffrage.

The final product of her months of study was a major scholarly work entitled *The Crowning Constitutional Argument.*

Throughout the remainder of her life, whenever she discussed the vote, she quoted from it and referred to that revolutionary document as her crowning achievement.

She argued, "The country's Constitution is the most important piece of literature in the Library of Congress and should be followed to the letter."

That mandate, drawn up in September of 1787 declares:

> *"We the People of the United States, in Order to form a more perfect Union, establish Justice, promote the general Welfare, and secure the Blessings of Liberty to ourselves and our Posterity, do ordain and establish the Constitution for the United States of America."*

She preached, "The forefathers did not begin this extraordinary work with 'We, the free-holders' or 'We, the men.' Instead, they simply ordained 'We, the People.'"

"That phrase," she maintained, "was written to include every citizen born in this magnificent country.

"Besides," she pointed out, "the post war 14th Amendment ordered suffrage be given to all United States Citizens, including former slaves. The 15th Amendment specified that the vote not be denied because of race, religion, or previous servitude."

She castigated arrogant men who kept wives and daughters strictly under their thumbs even after the Emancipation Amendment had declared them free.

She argued, "It shouldn't be necessary to go through the arduous process of adding a formal women's suffrage amendment to the Constitution since women's rights have already been guaranteed under the ruling document.

"All we really need," she insisted, "is a Declaratory Act that confirms the existence of those rights already stated."

In 1871, before she took the final manuscript to the printers, she shared its contents with the Supreme Court's Chief Justice Chase who told her, "Your argument is true, and no jurist has seen the Constitution in its true light regarding women. It took a woman's brain to see that it opened the door through which all women could walk and vote."

Under the approval of the Chief Justice as well as that of Senator Charles Summer, she had one thousand "Arguments" reprinted and distributed to every Senator and Representative of the 42nd Congress then sitting.

She told all who would listen, "I had that Argument introduced and published in the Congressional Record.for the purpose of instructing those senators and members regarding the same if such high authorities as Senator Summer and Chief Justice Chase had not seen the Constitution in its true light, even those that considered themselves constitutional lawyers needed to have line upon line and precept upon precept regarding the status of women citizens."

Copies of her chronicle were delivered to Governors in all states to ensure their understanding of the rights of their female constituents.

Because she was sure that most of the lawmakers had never even read the United States Constitution they had sworn to uphold, Mary saw to it that a copy of that binding charter was handed out to every incumbent legislator as well as every member of the Supreme Court.

Whenever possible, she passed reprints of her "Argument" around at Suffrage Conventions, an act that aggravated the leaders, even though most of them privately agreed with her premise.

"She's too uppity," fretted one. "She makes enemies of the gentlemen we're trying to persuade."

Another complained, "Her bombastic attitude and constant badgering of public officials will do our cause more harm than good."

Nods and murmurs of agreement followed a vehement speech of a third suffragist who sharply criticized, "Besides, she's still prancing around in her bloomers that we all agreed to give up long ago. I, for one, do not appreciate the kind of demeaning publicity she attracts."

It was the same old tune sung in the same whining voice.

Mary ignored it all. Her mission was to educate the American People about the rights and freedom of choice promised to EVERY United States citizen.

No mewling complaints about such unimportant matters as bloomers could deter her.

CHAPTER FIFTY-FIVE

NEW YORK/WASHINGTON

THE CROWNING CONSTITUTIONAL ARGUMENT was not the only manuscript Mary Walker struggled over while plodding riverboats, pounding horses' hooves, or puffing steam engines conquered the countless miles between lectures.

That same year, Dr. Mary copyrighted her controversial book, *Hit*, that contains one hundred and seventy-seven pages of advice and information divided into chapters discussing the eight subjects dearest to her heart.

In part, her Preface contains the disclaimer: "I make no pretensions that I have said EVERYTHING that may be said on the interesting subject of Marriage or that what I have said is entirely new, or purely original."

Hit's list of titled chapters and their contents are a revelation of the forward thinking brilliance of a woman born way ahead of her time. Indeed, her views are as pertinent today as they were over one hundred and twenty-five years ago.

For her critics who have suggested she was either asexual or interested only in women, the first chapter should dispel all doubts.

"I believe wholeheartedly in marriage, fidelity, and the comradeship between men and women." Because she had learned from her parents' example, she tempered those beliefs with the firm conviction that women were entitled to the same rights and privileges as their faithful husbands. "Freedom of choice is paramount, and nothing less should be tolerated."

An underlying theme glorifies her respect for the partnership that was shared by her mother and father. Perhaps, too, she quietly yearned for the same passionate feelings she still felt for her first and only love, Edwin Fowler.

"The time is not distant when women will be equal with men in all social and political relations of life. A woman's name is as dear to her as a man's is to him, and custom ought, and will prevail, where each will keep their own names when they marry."

On Dress Reform her writing repeated views she had espoused all her life. "It is a fact that all the vital organs of women are so compressed by stays and corsets that health is impaired and life is shortened. The time will come when every woman will dress in the Reform Style for the advantages are too evident to be much longer overlooked."

She ruthlessly vilified Tobacco and second hand smoke, besides decrying the dreadful addiction of alcoholism.

Her views on Women's Franchise and women's legal rights were reinforced by the speeches and writings of such voluble Suffragists as Elizabeth Cady Stanton, Susan B. Anthony, Lucy Stone, and Belva Lockwood:

"You would spend the last dime you have; you would spill your last drop of blood before you would see your sons causelessly disenfranchised! And yet you lie quietly and unconcernedly down and die without one thought about your disenfranchised daughters."

Memories of her own experiences with chauvinistic judges and unsympathetic laws lent an eerie, reminiscent quality to her chapter titled Divorce: "there are those who have as correct ideas of noble marriage as 'the cattle on a thousand hills'.

"To be deprived of a divorce is like being shut up in a prison because someone attempted to kill you. The wicked one takes his ease and you take the slanders without the power to defend yourself. It is just as honorable to get out of matrimonial trouble legally as to be freed from any other wrong."

On the inequities of the work place, her denunciation regarding LABOR admonished that daughters be given a practical knowledge of some business whereby they can support themselves.

Concerning the delicate subject of Religion, Mary wrote: "In every human heart some religious emotions are to be found. As there is something good in all Religious beliefs, there should be a quiet toleration towards all who represent the various forms or ceremonies that are connected with worship. Any Religion that gives the wife a servile position is beneath the great plans of Deity and must ultimately be considered one of the tokens of barbarism that Christ tried to exterminate by teaching."

The publication set tongues wagging and spawned knockdown, dragged-out arguments in pubs, drawing rooms and humble kitchens throughout the country. Liberal women cheered Mary for the courage it took to put her views on the line, while conservative matrons of the old school hissed and sighed about the inappropriateness of her candid, unladylike lecturing.

Men, of course, were incensed beyond reason. Their domains were threatened and there was little they could do about it except sputter and fume and puff their tobacco in retaliation. Walls of smoking clubs reverberated with their vows to maintain the status quo.

The editor of the Hygeio-Therapeutic College medical news publication, Dr. Holbrook, sent around a letter of congratulation for her efforts that said in part:

> *"I am glad that you are publishing your book. From what I have read of the manuscript, I think it is unique, full of interest and thought. I hope you sell a million copies."*

Mary heard it all and grinned wickedly. Let the old biddies talk, she thought. At least my little book has set people thinking and discussing the issues.

CHAPTER FIFTY-SIX

WASHINGTON CITY

THE SEMIANNUAL Meeting of the American Woman's Suffrage Association convened in New York City in May of 1871.

Since Dr. Mary's book had been published and she was a New York daughter, she was treated more cordially by the local group than she had been at the national conventions.

Inspired by the memory of British women storming Parliament for the vote, she addressed the appreciative crowd. Her delivery would have generated the envy of a stumping politician. "The fact of women attempting to vote in Washington had done more for woman suffrage than all the conventions ever held," Mary explained.

Rousing cheers erupted following her stirring declaration that the cause for suffrage must again be taken to the doorstep of lawmakers in Washington. She waited for the tumult to die away.

Campaigning for serious supporters who were willing to accompany her to the capital, she explained, "Congress is the house of the people, and the people have a right to address its members. There is nothing like the bristling presence of insistent women to force men to pay attention." She paused for dramatic effect.

Targeting the eyes of the most enthusiastic supporters, she raised both arms like a preacher embracing his flock. "We must present a united front and put our government representatives on notice that we will not take 'no' for an answer. Our physical presence will lend credence to our determination."

"Yes, yes," enthusiastic listeners agreed. "Yes, indeed."

Mary's smile broadened as she sensed the crowd's overwhelming support. "We want a Declaratory Act by legislators, which attests that women already have the right to vote," she shouted over their accolades. "The act must be passed by the Congress of the United States. It's the only way to circumvent an immense amount of labor in the fight for the right to vote"

Most of the women came away from the meeting inspired and hopeful. Some were already conjuring up ways to leave their families and accompany her.

❧◈❧

The semiannual convention of the National Suffrage Association that convened at Lincoln Hall in Washington on January 9, 1872, presented a less sympathetic face, however.

All of the big guns were there. One of the most notable was the fifty-two-year-old spinster, Susan B. Anthony, her fearsome figure cinched in stiff bombazine. Glacial and austere, her square jaw firmed in nomological righteousness, she peered through her rimless glasses at the gathering and willed them to agree. "A 19th Amendment to the Constitution is the only legal way to rectify the abysmal practice of denying women the right to cast their ballots on issues that profoundly affect them," she preached.

Second to speak was Mrs. Elizabeth Cady Stanton, Anthony's close confidante, but the exact opposite of her long-time friend. Curly, white hair framed her plump cheeks, and her ruffled gown accented rather than camouflaged her ample body. An air of charm enveloped her like a delightful aura.

Tireless in her efforts, her dancing eyes and outgoing smile belied the strain of keeping up with her duties as the mother of seven children, her studies as a Greek scholar, and her reading of the law with her father, a sitting Judge.

Belva Lockwood, temperance leader and pacifist who would later become the first woman to argue a case before the United States Supreme Court, was only two years older than Walker. Like Mary, she was blessed with clear, piercing blue eyes that could either warm the heart of a friend or kindle fear in the breast of a dishonest culprit. On more than one occasion she had provided a comfortable bed and nourishing meals when the homeless doctor turned up on her Washington doorstep. A warm friendship had developed between the two women who had so much in common.

Lucretia Coffin Mott, straight-laced Nantucket native and oldest of the group, contributed her pure Quaker values to the discussions. She and Elizabeth Cady Stanton had led the Bloomer Girls' first formal Women's Rights Convention held in 1848 at Stanton's home in Seneca Falls, New York. It was this meeting that convinced sixteen-year-old Mary Walker that only a united effort could better the plight of women.

Also present was a true veteran of the movement, Mrs. Mary Livermore, a dyed-in-the-wool New England Brahmin, proper to the core. A teacher and writer for the religious publication, *The New Covenant*, she was the only female reporter to attend the Chicago Presidential Convention at which the Republicans nominated a gaunt but triumphant Abraham Lincoln.

During the War, Mary Livermore ruthlessly exposed the horrors suffered by wounded soldiers confined in government hospitals. Her tales of insufficient supplies, deplorable sanitary conditions, and the dearth of proper treatment inspired the wrath of horrified families.

Her book, *My Story of the War,* published in 1888, is considered one of the most informative Civil War documents describing the dedication of underpaid nurses while exposing the shocking details of thievery and neglect riddling the nation's institutions.

It was Mary Livermore who had quieted the surly crowd at an Ohio meeting a year earlier after Dr. Mary's followers had called for her to speak.

At the beginning of the national meeting, thirty-nine-year-old Mary had wisely chosen a place at the rear of the hall behind all those prestigious suffragists.

Her midnight-black hair was coifed in thick curls framing a face that remained youthful despite her declining health and constant tribulations.

She wore her usual tailored trousers, size three leather boots and a form-fitting frock coat of handsome black broadcloth—a suitable background for her Medal of Honor.

Though she had taken an inconspicuous seat, she scarcely contained her anticipation as she waited for the opportune moment to interject her two-cents-worth.

That evening, she made the first overtures. "I have always been a working woman, and close friend to the working man. I support the Constitution as it stands, and I am against dissension or revolt. But, I tell you now, the time is fast approaching when working conditions will be bettered."

"Hear, hear," were the murmurs of agreement rumbling through the room as she paused for maximum effect.

"A year hence, women will vote," she predicted, and the murmurs became enthusiastic cheers.

The next morning, following Belva Lockwood's speech, Mary carried a pretty basket of fresh flowers up to the dais. With a little flourish of appreciation, she presented the bouquet to her friend.

As Belva walked away from the podium, Mary turned to address the crowd.

Miss Anthony cut the doctor's remarks short with the admonition that another speaker was scheduled at this time. Mary's supporters groaned their disappointment, while her adversaries, recalling her discomforting account of her divorce before the first National Convention in 1869, applauded their leader's initiative.

The second speaker droned on and on. The crowd grew restless, whispering, wagging heads, and wriggling in their seats. Mary Walker was far more interesting than this simpering twit.

Susan Anthony began shushing the audience. The harder she tried, the ruder they became.

"Let the doctor speak," shouted one, and others around the hall took up the cry.

Miss Anthony was furious. Red-faced, she shouted, "Mary Walker is not listed on the program, today."

"We'd like to hear what she has to say, anyway," the group insisted.

Old Susan stood her ground. "We pay for the hall; we have a right to say who will speak. Walker is not on the agenda."

To her credit, Mary harbored no ill feelings. In fact, she helped take up the collection at the end of the session that adjourned without giving her the chance to speak again.

Three days later the entire delegation waited outside the office of General Benjamin Franklin Butler, notable Republican congressman from Massachusetts. Dr. Mary was front and center, as usual.

Sleepy eyed and balding, Butler, a criminal attorney and powerful legislator, had played a significant role in the impeachment proceedings against Andrew Johnson. He seemed a good choice to present Congress with the delegation's petition for immediate Woman's Suffrage that included 35,000 signatures.

Evidently Butler was the right man for the job. His persuasive powers convinced the Judiciary Committee of the Senate to grant a hearing.

That same Committee, later in the year, turned a deaf ear when the dedicated lobbyist, Sarah Spencer, begged for recognition of the women's right to vote.

She had spoken eloquently, reminding the voting block that the Republican Party had emancipated four million human beings and established universal suffrage. "But," she complained"where are the ten million women citizens of this Republic? When will you make your high sounding declaration true?"

She was dismissed without courtesy of discussion.

Most of the supporting members of the current National Convention flocked to the chamber doors demanding admittance to the gallery.

"You ain't allowed in," said the burly doorman positioning his ample physique between the crowd and the entry door.

"Who says we are not to be admitted," demanded a defiant Mary Walker, her snapping eyes the color of stormy Lake Ontario.

"Senator Trumbull, his self," sneered the guardian of the inner sanctum.

Dr. Mary stamped her foot. "We'll see about that," she exploded.

Turning to her fellow suffragists, the Union Army Major's battlefield demeanor quickly surfaced. She had dealt with stubborn generals in her time and no lowly guard was going to tell her what she could or could not do.

"Stay where you are, my friends," she ordered. "Do not budge an inch. Women are getting to be a power in this land, and representing as we do millions of women, Senator Trumbull and his Committee won't dare to exclude us."

The determined suffragists milled closer together. Thick, rustling frocks and bobbing, beribboned chapeaux clogged up the space, precluding any safe passage through the hot, stuffy hallway. Ringed stains dampened armpits and foreheads turned greasy with sweat, but not one woman relinquished her spot.

"Here, you can't stay here," whined the overtaxed guard. "Get out, I tell you. Get out."

Dr. Mary planted her feet wide apart, grabbed the doorknob to the Committee room, and held on as if her life depended on maintaining her position.

Arriving members of the Judiciary Committee became more and more disgruntled as the sheer mass of petticoats prevented their progress through the melee.

"Call the Sergeant-at-arms," demanded one irate senator whose electric-blue cravat had been knocked askew by the wide-brimmed hat of a huffing dowager.

Once arrived, the beleaguered young sergeant tried his best. He pushed and sputtered and elbowed, but he barely made a dent in the crowd that quickly surrounded him.

"Get the Capitol Police force over here and clear these females out right now," ordered a stern-faced, bewhiskered senator as he yanked a taffeta skirt from between his pant legs.

"That should put the fear of God into them," he whispered to the sweating sergeant.

"Yes, sir." The harassed non-com nodded then jostled his way through the tangle of swarming women to the outside entrance, tugging his whistle from his breast pocket as he went.

Capitol Police rapidly converged on the building, but came to a screeching halt as the unprecedented mob swelled. Uncertain where to begin, the surprised gendarmes scratched their heads and stood about waiting for orders on how to proceed. The manual had not prepared them for this horde of shoving, squirming, stubborn women who seemed more than a match for the elite protectors of the realm.

The Chairman of the Judiciary Committee finally threw up his hands in disgust. Wearily he told the guard to let them in. Then he hustled out of the path of the chattering gaggle that streamed past him through the portals of the hallowed chambers. "What in God's good name is this country coming to?" he complained to no one in particular.

The hearing was spirited, but the discussion was slyly tabled. That action amounted to the kiss of death for the petition, but the senators had been put on notice that the suffragists were a group to be reckoned with in the future.

CHAPTER FIFTY-SEVEN

WASHINGTON CITY

FOR YEARS after the war, Dr. Mary fought the United States Congress tooth and nail. Immediately following her separation from the Army, she had requested payment for services rendered on the battlefield and in the hospitals, finally receiving far less than her male counterparts were paid for the same duties. The inequity became further fodder for her speeches championing a woman's right to equal pay for equal circumstance.

Secondly, she demanded fair repayment of her own private funds expended while tending to her military patients, but meager documentation of monies spent for travel and supplies provided the reluctant solons the escape they needed to avoid reimbursing her.

Third, and to Mary's mind the most hurtful as the years passed, was the Representatives' constant refusals to provide a fair pension for her health problems incurred when she endured the deprivations thrust upon her by the Rebels during her incarceration at the deadly Castle Thunder facility.

The uphill campaign was nothing new to the persistent doctor. She knew her vexatious harangues and petitions for equal rights and women's suffrage exacerbated the lawmakers' negative reactions. No matter, she would never give up her feminist crusade for personal gain. It simply was not an option.

"They have no concept of the horrors I've endured," she insisted. "Why can't they separate the two issues and deal with me in a fair and impartial manner?"

Voluminous hand-written correspondence plus reproductions of House Bills dealing with her demands for proper compensation are carefully preserved on Microfilm in the National Archives of the United States. There are letters from the Adjutant General E. D. Townsend corroborating Dr. Mary's service in the Union Army and alluding to her spy activities.

The Microfilm affirms that Medical Director Phelps, Mary's champion at the Female Prison in Louisville, attested to her eye problems. That information is also seconded by Brigadier General Joseph K. Barnes who had been instrumental in ferreting out the nefarious practices of opportunistic surgeons who took advantage of a war-torn country's desperate circumstances to line their own pockets.

Notarized affidavits from several Oculists practicing either in Washington or Oswego supported her claim that four months of deprivation had irreparably damaged the Major's eyesight, thus precluding the handling of many of her duties. If she could not see properly, she was hamstrung in her profession.

Dr. J. Edward Cheney swore, "Based upon his ophthalmoscopic examination, she (Mary) is suffering from amaurosis (partial blindness) or atrophy of the optic nerve."

Dr. B. C. Barrone wrote, "Vision is so imperfect—no lenses improve the power of vision. Nothing but prolonged rest can assure her of retaining that which she already possessed."

At the beginning of the New Year, 1874, after sifting through all the pertinent evidence, the House followed the recommendation of Army Surgeon Phelps and awarded Dr. Mary the grand pension of $8.50 per month.

It was a start.

⋖⦿⦾⦿⦾⋗

Mary needed to make enough money to open an office to practice on a limited basis.

Her political activities attracted the attention of United States Treasurer, Spinner.

Spinner forwarded a recommendation to the Chief Clerk of the Appointment Office who, after the usual formalities of induction, swore Mary into a clerk's position on July 14, 1873.

The Chief Clerk, Mr. Vanderbilt, was a bookish man with nondescript features and a prominent Adam's apple that bobbed rhythmically when he swallowed. Vanderbilt entrusted Mary to the care of a female employee who was instructed to explain the duties and rules of the office.

The painfully plain office assistant, Miss Azamora Tinsley, wore a deep-brown corseted gown buttoned to a strangle hold beneath her double chin, further secured by a cameo brooch displaying the prominent proboscis and ringleted bangs of a Roman nobleman.

Well! Azamora took one look at slender Mary's form-fitting costume and blew a gasket. Huffing and blinking her squinty eyes, she snarled behind Mary's back, "Never in all my born days will I ever work with a creature so improperly attired. How dare this woman prance around in her pantaloons and shake her curls in front of our proper, modest, gentlemanly Mr. Vanderbilt?"

The scandalized clerk's repugnance spread like wild fire. Soon the whole office force was up in arms. "We are ladies, and will not work with an apparition that is an affront to every decent employee on the floor."

The complaint was booted up the ladder to Secretary Richardson who advised Dr. Mary that she must conform to the dress code, or else.

"Bull feathers," the outraged doctor shouted. "I shall dress as I please." Then she added, "I have appeared before the Congress of the United States dressed as I am, I have been sworn into service, and here I shall stay."

Mr. Vanderbilt, puffed up by the ladies' sudden concerns for his welfare, didn't have the guts to fire the new employee. Instead, he issued orders, "Let her come in to work, but avoid her like the plague. She'll soon weary of that and leave of her own accord."

Mr. Vanderbilt did not gage Major Mary very well. From that moment until she resigned, the stubborn doctor reported to the office, on time, every day, clad in her customary costume. The colors might change, but the style definitely did not.

Each workday mirrored the one before. No one spoke to her. Titters and rude stares followed her wherever she went. Fair enough. "I've been laughed at before. I've outlasted colonels and generals and ignorant Confederate lackeys. What can a gaggle of petty, closed-minded women do to me that hasn't been done before?"

But the hardest to bear was the inactivity.

Still she stuck it out, ignoring the slights and physical discomforts with a stoic obstinacy that would make a barnyard mule look like a compliant lamb.

After twenty-one months of her silent tormentors' insulting indifference she'd had enough. Along with her resignation was her request for payment for services rendered.

"No way," said Assistant Secretary of the Treasury, Henry French. "Her appointment was not ratified by Secretary Spinner, therefore, she is not entitled to compensation."

Again, Mary went to the mat. She had been appointed, she had sworn an oath, she had appeared ready, willing and able to perform her duties, and while hanging around to be noticed, she had lost several opportunities for other positions.

Behold the machinations of the federal bureaucracy. The matter was shunted from office to office until months later it finally reached the desk of the Solicitor of the Treasury.

His documented opinion pointed out, "The applicant has been badly treated. It is my finding that Miss Mary Walker has fulfilled all the prerequisites her position required. It was no fault of hers that duties were not assigned to her." In December of 1877, the Solicitor recommended that she receive the equivalent of one year's salary.

In March of 1881, the Second Session of the 45th Congress reviewed the resulting bill, agreed with the treasury's Solicitor's recommendation and awarded Mary $900.

⌘⊙⊙⌘

Armed with evidence from several Oculists, Mary again petitioned Congress for a lump-sum payment for her disability. She badgered Senators and Representatives, waylaying them outside the Capitol, stopping them in the street, bending any ear she could commandeer to hear her sad tale. Each reluctant listener denied his authority in the matter and referred her to another lawmaker who surely would be able to help her.

She became such a nuisance that powerful men took to hiding when they saw her coming. Tenacious as a bulldog, she simply changed her tactics, hiding behind building corners and sneaking up on the unsuspecting from behind.

There is a fragment of a note in the archives that sums up the disgruntled feelings of the day. Written in a bold hand, without formal salutation, and unsigned, it is dated May 31, 1876:

> *"My Dear Sir:*
>
> *In the name of humanity! Why saddle Dr. Walker on me?*
> *Send to Mr. Miller; you know I have not to do with the services, expenditures & sufferings of this lady."*

Numerous bills were drawn up, and, after due consideration, a favorable decision was reached. Dr. Walker's service and imprisonment were true.

"The claimant acted in the capacity of a female physician. The committee concurs with the committee of the last House in recommending the payment to the claimant the sum of $2,000 for the services rendered by her during the late war. But the allowance in this case is exceptional and is not to be considered as a precedent."

Collective derrieres were covered, but the money stayed in the public coffers, anyway. Mary never received a penny.

❦

The good doctor's agonies were not over. Frustrating eye problems continued to plague her. Reading ability was limited and night vision was extremely poor.

Her promised pension had stopped coming in June of '75, creating an ongoing fight to regain what was rightfully hers. Her application for reinstatement was hampered by the problem created when the Pension Office had forwarded all documents pertaining to her case to the House Committee on Military Affairs in 1874.

Lieutenant General J. A. Bentley wrote to Military Affairs,

> *"The file was returned to Pensions in 1876, but a written synopsis and all of the evidence of (the Walker) case were lost or mislaid. Upon the return of the remaining papers reference should be made that all papers missing from the pension claim were those adverse to the right of the applicant to a pension. I will thank you to furnish me with any additional information you may be able to give in the matter of Employment of Doctor Walker, especially as to her Military Status at the time she was captured. The claim of pension is now on appeal to the Honorable Secretary of the Interior."*

Sickened and discouraged by such cavalier treatment, Mary realized she was right back to square one.

Ongoing confrontations with Susan B. Anthony and Elizabeth Cady Stanton became more heated as the chasm between their differing recommendations for solving the suffrage question grew wider. Even Mary's friend, Belva Lockwood, treated her coldly when she attempted to address the annual national meeting in Washington.

At a pre-convention meeting in New York, Lillie Devereaux Blake, exquisitely gowned in ecru lace and pale green yardage, spoke bluntly when Mary showed up to address the group. "You are not wanted here," Blake insisted. "Your presence is a disruption to an otherwise civilized gathering."

Mary drew herself up tall and pointed her cane about the room. Her nose twitched as if she smelled a rat that had died in the rafters. "If by civilized gathering you are referring to this so-called liberal meeting," she replied, "all I can say is that you do not practice what you preach."

Twirling her cane, she spun about and stalked back to her seat. When the meeting adjourned, she attempted to mingle with some of the members. She was roundly snubbed as small groups closed ranks when she drew near. Leaders at the meetings who persisted in swishing along in their cumbersome skirts and petticoats criticized Mary's clothes, conveniently forgetting that they had once sported bloomers of their own.

Swallowing the choking lump in her throat, she parked her beaver hat atop her proud head and left the building. Outside, the tears came, but she angrily brushed them away.

The newspapers had a field day siding with "the graceful, genteel Mrs. Lillie Devereaux Blake," but grudgingly acknowledging that "awkward, red-faced Dr. Walker" had stood her ground like a good soldier.

Her name was again emblazoned in the headlines when she didn't attend the formal New York Convention that followed. Where was the obstreperous doctor, reporters wondered. And always, the reporters covering the events gleefully described her costumes and demeanor in derogatory detail.

"Damn their miserable hides," Mary fumed. "If their columns paid less attention to the pants I wear and more to the ideas I present, maybe the movement would gain some momentum."

Still, she refused to give up her trousers.

CHAPTER FIFTY-EIGHT

WASHINGTON AND POINTS NORTH

1877 was a pivotal year in Dr. Mary's life.
She sandwiched in the polishing of the manuscript for her second book, *Unmasked*, between running a medical practice and haunting Congress for an increase in her pension.

She abandoned her knee length, full-skirted frock coat to adopt a shorter, straighter jacket fashioned after the current gentleman's style.

Needing money to pay her tailor, she sold her glorious black mane to a wigmaker who paid premium prices for long, healthy hair. The disappearance of her shorn locks further scandalized the members of the suffrage brigade who wore their waist-length tresses in pug buns or braids as weighty as building bricks snugged up against their aching necks.

Healing the sick, writing a book, fulfilling speaking engagements on short notice as well as billeting in strange rooming houses had made caring for her abundant curls an increasingly tiresome chore. She knew a short haircut would rattle the establishment, and she did it with glee.

"They're prattling and gossiping about me, anyway, so why not give them a good story while I'm about it?" she told her friend, Belva.

The press snapped at the changes as enthusiastically as ravenous trout snatched at tantalizing lures. "Aha! The truth is finally out. She wants to be a man," they wrote.

Mary laughed till the tears rolled down her cheeks at that one. Cows might fly and hogs produce milk before she ever wished to become a pig-headed, selfish, chauvinistic, vote-denying male. And that was God's honest truth.

Her family suffered a good deal more than she did over the nasty comments that rolled off Mary like water off a duck. "Let them sputter," she said. "As soon as women discover how convenient short curls are, they will be shearing their own locks."

And they did. Her controversial hairstyle was the forerunner of the boyish bob.

꩜

Mary grew more strident and disgruntled as months turned into years and her arguments in Congress were shot down, one after another. Her health was suffering, her eyesight worsening, and the government still failed to compensate her. She was turning into a bitter old woman with little zest for life. In April 1878, she was exhausted and depressed despite the fact her second book was being published.

She wound up in a hospital in Providence, Rhode Island. Newspapers reported her condition as critical, even life threatening. One Washington editor printed the following:

> *"It is very probable that this notable woman is rapidly drawing near her end, and, unless all the medical predictions prove false, she will, in a few days, be where unkind sayings and thoughtless pen thrusts will have no power to give her harm."*

Could the publishers have been feeling guilty for their unkind coverage of her in the past? Their empathy was short lived.

Mary surprised everyone by recovering enough to travel.

She went back home to Papa Walker who dosed her, fattened her up, then accompanied her on a speaking tour around the state of New York where appreciative audiences seemed to buoy her spirits. It was to be the last quality time she spent with her father.

Back in Washington in the spring of 1879, Mary applauded as Belva Ann Bennett Lockwood made history by being admitted to the bar of the Supreme Court with permission to practice before the Court of Claims.

She had graduated from National University Law School only six years before.

Dr. Mary rejoiced as she credited her forty-nine-year-old contemporary with one significant step forward in the long march toward women's equality.

CHAPTER FIFTY-NINE

PHILADELPHIA, PENNSYLVANIA

Mary's second book, published in 1878 by William H. Boyd, 717 Sansom Street, Philadelphia, bore the title page:

UNMASKED
Or
THE SCIENCE OF IMMORALITY

Infinitely more controversial than the first, its blunt discussions of taboo topics created wide criticism among those who would defend the male population's wounded sen"sibilities.

Mary fired back, "It's all right to know about sexual misconduct, but it's quite another matter for a female author to put it down in black and white."

The book, though aimed at educating men for the betterment of relations within marriage, merely succeeded in ruffling feathers. Critics deplored, "Her candid descriptions of sexual proclivities and her liberal use of unladylike and unmentionable words such as penis, vagina, hymen, scrotum, orgasm, incest, venereal disease are scandalous.

"The indelicate diagrams of the female reproductive organs, together with annotated descriptions are beyond disgusting."

"Heavens," readers complained, "these graphic drawings are certainly not suitable for consumption by a non-medical readership."

While Mary wrote little of love, sexual relations and passion were discussed freely. This oversight, intentional or otherwise, was a glaring omission for the romantics.

Even more alarming to the male readers was the author's admonition that sexual relations should be for procreation only.

Gentlemen in their clubs opined, "Good grief, would the woman take all the fun out of life?"

The final paragraph in *Unmasked* reads:

> *"If through the evolution of our thoughts, as contained in this little volume, the women of the future, on both sides of the great waters, shall have better conditions, we shall feel our earth life has been one of noble effort, that no amount of contumely (that is, rude language) from the degraded can rob of pure satisfaction."*

Unlike its well-defined, more scholarly predecessor, *Hit*, Mary's second and final literary offering is a study in contradictions.

And Mary's own life was a contradiction as it began to unravel in the face of every bitter disappointment she encountered in the courts, in the Congress and in the suffrage movement.

CHAPTER SIXTY

OSWEGO, NEW YORK AND WASHINGTON

AN APRIL 9, 1880, EVENT turned Mary's world upside down. Her political life was in shambles, but her personal life was devastated.

Her precious Papa succumbed to pneumonia, struck down on his eighty-second birthday.

Mary shuffled through the motions at the public viewing like a specter in a nightmare, barely recognizing the multitude of mourners who paraded past his simple wooden coffin in the parlor of the house he'd built.

Speechless with grief, she'd lost her anchor. Her sturdy Gibraltar had slipped into the sea of eternity. Never again could she rely on her Papa's strength and support. His memory would live, but it could not comfort her. His essence remained, but it could not advise her, admonish her, warn her, or offer much-needed approval.

Rudderless, her mind tossed about struggling to recall every nugget of wisdom he ever offered.

In private, with no prying gossips to witness, her sisters were harshly critical. "Must you keep up this useless fight with congress?" Aurora sneered.

Luna added her two cents. "You're not satisfied with the public disapproval of the Suffragettes. No, you have to wear those ridiculous clothes that make you look like a, like a Lord only knows what. You're an embarrassment to this family, Mary, and I for one am sick of it."

Vesta, Jr. nodded in agreement.

Alvie spoke up for her. "Leave her be, sisters. Papa would not like this talk before he's cold in his grave."

Sarah, Alvie's wife, quietly cheered the defense of her sister-in-law but dared not defend her openly.

Vesta, paralyzed with grief, remained oblivious to the barbed remarks of her daughters.

❧❦❧

After the funeral, Mary stayed in Oswego to comfort her mother, but it was Vesta who became the strong one, swallowing her sadness to support her daughter.

Mary slept in her old room, waking to keep vigil at the kitchen table, listening for heavy footsteps that would never tread the stairs again. On the third night, she woke from a deep sleep, weeping and choking, grating sobs wrenched from her gut. Panic stricken, she cried out, "Papa," for she couldn't recall his beloved features. She was a child again, sailing in the dark, searching for safe harbor.

She concentrated with all her might. She could sense the smell of him—soap and saddle oil and earth. She could hear his voice, firm, consoling, advising. She could even taste his favorite apple pie, the extra cinnamon sharp on her tongue.

But her dear Papa had no face.

At dawn, she rose from her sweaty sheets, threw on old clothes and trotted bareback on the decrepit Tildie, clopping through dew-dampened fields swirling with mist.

Alvie's household was just beginning to stir as she slid from the mare's soaked back and rapped for entry. The smell of frying bacon greeted her as Sarah flung the door wide to admit her.

"What is it, Mary?" she asked with alarm as she caught sight of anguished features and unkempt curls.

The plodding hoof beats had alerted Alvie who was just pulling on his trousers in anticipation of a hearty breakfast. He rushed to the two women, stopping short before reaching out accommodating arms to his distraught sister. "Is it Mama?" he cried in alarm.

Unable to answer, Mary fell into his arms, weeping as if her life had shattered. Alvie clutched her to his chest as Sarah ran to embrace them both.

"Not Mama," Mary managed to gasp, but she could not regain enough control to explain her panic. Mistaking her tears for a delayed reaction to their father's passing, Alvie comforted her. "It will get better with time," he soothed. "It's the shock. We had so little warning, that's all."

Sarah's eyes stung with tears. In all her years in the Walker family, she had never seen her husband's iron-willed sister so discomposed. Quite the opposite, Mary usually displayed a rigid, outward calm.

Discreetly, the brother signaled his wife to leave them alone for a bit.

"I'll go finish in the kitchen," Sarah offered. "We'll all feel better with a bit of breakfast in us." She turned and hurried from the room.

When she'd gone, Alvie patted Mary tenderly. "You must think that Papa's in a good place, dear. Our father truly believed that. And so do I."

"Is he, Alvie?" Mary asked, delving into the morass of her own shaky faith for some kernel of reassurance.

"Of course," he soothed, "Papa believed that everyone would enjoy the hereafter for which his earth-life had fitted him. If that's so, he is in a wonderful place indeed, Mary, for our Papa was a very good man."

He took her by the elbow and guided her toward the kitchen. "Sarah's waiting," he said, taking it for granted she would eat with them.

When did Alvie stop being a vegetarian, she wondered, as the fragrant aroma of bacon wafted up from the heavy iron skillet pushed to the back of the wood-burning stove.

She sat obediently but picked at her food, eschewing the meat portion yet, contrary to character, offering no comment on its deleterious effect to the human constitution.

On April 11th, the *Oswego Palladium* printed Alvie's tribute to his father. The final paragraph summed up the old man's life:

> *"And last, though by no means least, he was determined to maintain his individuality and he never allowed another to do his thinking no popularity or unpopularity could deter him from expressing that thought, regardless of consequences."*

The tribute could have been written about Dr. Mary herself, but she might have argued that such unladylike attributes as individuality and determination seldom brought happiness or freedom into her own life.

To the amusement and amazement of the citizens of Washington, Dr. Mary's costume became even more outlandish. She appeared in her old neighborhood wearing a boiled shirt with stiff wing collar and a jaunty bow tie beneath clothing tailored in the masculine fashion of the day. Instead of her perky, feather-trimmed chapeau, a formal opera hat perched atop her bobbed curls.

The Suffragettes were mad as hornets. Stinging criticism was hurled as tempers approached the boiling point. Mary Walker's shenanigans stoked a firestorm of protest, and she was pronounced a disgrace to the movement. What else was new?

But the feminists were not the only ones up in arms.

The *Oswego Palladium* reported an incident at the local polls when Mary returned to vote on local issues.

She approached a pert young fellow with an executed ballot. He refused her access to the holding box and commented on her male attire.

"I do not wear men's clothes," she huffed, "I wear my own clothes."

"If YOU'RE going to vote," the startled youth complained, "they might as well dress up all the women folk in men's clothes and bring them down to vote."

Derisive snickers followed, as he chased her from the building, still mumbling to herself that the time would come.

Nearly six years to the day after Alvah Walker went to his reward, his beloved wife, Vesta, followed. To say that the life had gone out of her at her husband's death would belittle her accomplishments in those six years. She had continued with her good works, but the spring was gone from her step, and only her mouth smiled at the world.

Once again, Alvie paid tribute to a parent. This time, his remarks were delivered at the service held in the Bunker Hill schoolhouse, his parents' long ago legacy to the town of Oswego.

Parts of his eulogy were noted in the *Palladium*. He spoke of Vesta's disbelief in the premise of eternal hell, reporting what she told him many times:

> *"She disbelieved that once popular but now obsolete dogma having never lost sight that there was at least one thing that even an infinite God could not do that is, He could not create another being capable of thwarting His own will. He could not make a weight so ponderous that He could not lift it Himself. Mother had not the slightest fear of death, nor of her future condition(she often said) she knew as much about future life as any of them, and that is nothing at all."*

Mary's own philosophy came very close to that of her mother's. She was pleased and proud of her brother's eulogy, and she didn't give a damn that the Christian citizens of Oswego found his remarks in direct contradiction to their orthodox beliefs.

BOOK FOUR
1881-1919

"The world is not so much in need of new thoughts as when thought grows old and worn with usage it should, like current coin, be called in, and, from the mint of genius, be reissued fresh and new."

Dreamthorp

CHAPTER SIXTY-ONE

WASHINGTON/OSWEGO, NEW YORK

AS THE 1880s decade counted its days, Mary survived the winters in Washington by lecturing and practicing limited medicine. She either rented a room or stayed with friends.

Partisan quarreling with a Congress controlled by the Democrats kept the political pot boiling in the capital. Still rankling over the fact that Rutherford B. Hayes won office by electoral rather than popular vote, she was relieved at his defeat. "Good," she said, "his archaic views on women's rights are stifling our feminist movement."

She celebrated the 1880 election of Republican James Garfield, former Union General and veteran of the battle of Chickamauga. "A general who was born in a log cabin, served as a college professor, and then rose to the Presidency can't be all bad," she said.

Garfield was a seasoned politician and an expert on fiscal matters after having served as Chairman of the House Appropriations Committee. Besides, the softhearted man was settled with a lovely wife and five children. Congenial, athletically fit, and handsome. with his blonde hair, heavy mustache, and luxuriant beard, he looked the part of a savvy statesman.

Mary's relief was short lived, however.

On July 2nd, 1881, Garfield, bound for his twenty-fifth reunion at Williams College, hurried through the railway station to catch his train. Charles Guiteau, a lawyer with a history of mental illness, sprang from the crowd and pumped two revolver shots into the President as he strode by.

One of the assassin's bullets grazed the President's arm, but the other one lodged so deeply into his spine that the surgeons could never find it. It lay there wreaking its havoc, preventing the President from rising from his bed.

"I am a Stalwart and Arthur is President," screamed the assassin. The Stalwarts were avid supporters of a third term for Ulysses S. Grant, and, despite the fact that Chester Arthur was not so well known, Guiteau preferred the Vice President be installed as leader of the country.

Mary Walker would never have agreed with Guiteau. During Grant's terms of office, she shouted her criticism of the President. "The man consumes alcohol to the point of intoxication and has to be carted home from parties by his friends. Worse sin of all, this one time war hero continually refuses to recognize both the Constitutional and the God given rights that belong to American women."

Arrested shortly afterward, Guiteau confessed his real reason for the vicious attack. "I rightly shot the man because he refused to appoint me as the United States Consul to Paris."

Although Guiteau behaved like a madman at his trial, the jury found the half-crazed glory seeker sane enough to understand his crime and sentenced him to be hanged. The mandate was carried out in 1882, but his victim never knew it.

Garfield lay wasting away for eighty days, accomplishing nothing, while the country languished in limbo, holding its collective breath.

Vice President Arthur, fair-minded Vermont native, felt it wrong to usurp the man's office while he was still conscious and able to function mentally. In any case, Arthur was still fighting his own demons. His wife had died a year and a half before, and he was struggling to raise his two children, Chester and Ellen.

Finally the country's vigil was over. Garfield slipped away on September 19, 1881, and the attractive widower, Chester A. Arthur, was sworn into the highest office of the land.

Chester hiked up his bootstraps and took over in good faith. Tall, ruddy, and handsome with his light wavy hair and luxurious sideburns, the man, called 'Gentleman Boss' by his aides, indulged in his love for fine clothes and fashionable surroundings.

Declaring the White House a "badly kept barracks," he proceeded to renovate the austere rooms. His youngest sister, Mary Arthur McElroy, was brought in to act as hostess for the lavish parties that followed.

Mary Walker was heard to say of him, "President Arthur was a grand exchange for Garfield, as much as an assassination was to be deplored."

The eighties rolled on. The new President refused to honor the spoils system and urged the congress to remove civil service positions from the clutches of the politicians. To that end, in 1883, the intent of the Pendleton Act was to improve government efficiency and eliminate employment abuses. A three person, bi-partisan commission was formed to advise the President of those offices that needed to be filled by civil service examinees.

President Arthur opened the Brooklyn Bridge; John D. Rockefeller created his moneymaker, Standard Oil Trust; and Robert Ford dispatched Jesse James with a well-placed bullet. All the while, Chester was secretly battling a terminal kidney disease that precluded his running for re-election. Mary wept when a cerebral hemorrhage claimed his life at the end of 1886. He was fifty-seven years old.

Meanwhile, the twenty-second president, Grover Cleveland, had taken over as the first Democrat to sit in the White House since James Buchanan served in 1856.

Good-humored 'Uncle Jumbo' had never been a soldier. Instead, as was the custom at the time, he had paid a substitute to stand in his stead in the Union Army so he could stay home to support his widowed mother and fatherless siblings.

He continued Arthur's crusade for civil service reform, but kept a tight lid on handing out government funds to pensioners.

He disagreed with the congress when they displayed too much generosity to Civil War veterans who had served in the Union Army, vetoing several bills concerning Dr. Mary's claims. She grew even more bitter. "Cleveland never served in any capacity," she complained. "He squashed the Dependent Pension Bill that provided compensation for ex-soldiers who served at least three months and had become incapable of earning a living.

"It's quite clear that he hadn't the slightest notion of the problems and tribulations of deserving veterans."

Mary's fights for women's legal rights and the right to vote remained stalled in the quagmire of male tradition. She walked abroad in a constant state of quiet fury and suppressed frustration, haranguing to all who'd listen, "Will selfish men forever wear blinders and never admit that their wives and daughters, sisters and lovers are their equals under the sovereign laws of the Constitution of our beloved United States?"

CHAPTER SIXTY-TWO

POINTS WEST

DURING THE 1880s and '90s, Dime Museums and Medicine Shows were popular sources of entertainment for country bumpkins who sadly were cheated out of their hard earned cash by slick pitch doctors, silver-tongued pushers like charismatic 'Doc' Healy and 'Texas Charlie' Bigelow, a pretty fellow with shoulder length curls and a velvet voice.

Dr. N. T. Oliver, John A. Hamilton and numerous snake oil salesmen shamelessly plied their sneaky trades. Buffalo Bill Cody entertained with horse, lariat and pistol.

Mary reluctantly entered this mélange booked by agents Kohn & Middleton at $1.50 per week. Desperate for funds, she compromised her ideals, overlooking the bilking of the public by medical charlatans, but not for a moment did she consider selling the owners' mendicants herself.

She dressed in men's clothes because they were less expensive than the specially tailored outfits she previously commissioned. The *Oswego Times* described her costume:

> "Her dress was plain black-the coat a frock cut,
> extending just to the knees, her vest strait laced, and
> her pants large and bagging. Her shirt was fresh
> from the laundry, the smoothly ironed bosom
> embellished with a modest little stud, her neck was
> encircled by a collar that stood high enough and
> straight enough to satisfy a clergyman, and whose
> points were as evenly turned as though they had been

manipulated by a fashionable youth of the day. Her necktie was dark blue, tied to a nicety, and her head crowned with a jaunty brown straw hat."

She was hired to speak of her Civil War experiences and her time as prisoner of the Confederates, but her views concerning suffrage and equal rights for women were always skillfully inserted into the lecture.

She transported her audiences to grim battle scenes, exploiting their prurient interests with lurid details about crime and punishment. They shivered at hearing about soldiers who succumbed to the evils of drink hanged by their hands to tree limbs with their own bayonets tied in their mouths as gags.

"You cannot imagine the rigors of the battlefield, the heat, the un-relenting dust, the creeping chiggers that crawl through clothing and bite worse than fleas," she preached. "Horses bolt at jagged lightening flashes. Crashing thunder brings rain pelting down so hard that bodies emerge from their shallow graves. Soldiers shinny up tree trunks to escape the ever-present mud.

"Winter-frozen corpses were stood on their feet to make it appear there were more troops in the field than actually were, and sometimes those corpses served as shields against enemy fire."

Children gasped as she described the punishment for cowards, "These skulking varmints' heads were shaved and their hips were branded with an ugly C."

Men shuddered at her report, "Deserters were marched between rows of soldiers with fixed bayonets and made to kneel in the dirt to pray before they sat on their coffins, blindfolds in place, to wait for death."

Not a whisper was heard as she explained, "The sergeant called for silence just before he gave his command." She shouted dramatically, "Ready, Aim, Fire."

The crowd could practically hear the volley and smell the gunpowder before the pitiful bodies thumped into their wooden boxes.

Women wept openly as she described prisoners in the camps. "They were shrunken dwarfs with barely enough skin to cover their teeth, livid sores all over their emaciated bodies, too weak to brush away the flies that crawled over their mutilated extremities."

The audience got its money's worth, all right, but the toll on Mary was devastating. No matter how often she relived experiences best forgotten, she was unprepared for the exhaustion that followed. Yet she never failed to express her admiration for her soldier boys. "Courageous men marched to their doom through the blood of their fallen comrades, sobbing for breath as they clambered up the hillsides through air choked with gunfire, screaming 'Huzzah' and praying the racket would frighten the devil out of the rebels waiting up top."

But it was not all bad.

Her love for the limelight was satisfied by the awed reverence of crowds who hung on her every word, plying her with questions about her spy activities and shuddering over the horrendous deprivations endured during her stay at Castle Thunder.

52nd Ohio or Army of the Potomac veterans whistled and shouted their agreement.

Besides, she had found a platform for her vehement dissertations on Dress Reform and her constant denouncements of tobacco and alcohol. She never discovered the irony of that last, since she hadn't a clue that the ingredients of the patent medicines sold by the gallon after one of her speeches contained the very brew she abhorred.

But the reporters were never as kind to her as the crowds. An article in a New York newspaper announced:

> "Dr. Mary Walker will be at Wonderland all next week. There was a time when this remarkable woman stood upon the same platform with Presidents and the world's greatest women. There is something grotesque in her appearance on a stage built for freaks."

Now in her late fifties, Mary's once glorious hair was cropped short, salted with white, and thinning on top. Her flawless complexion had turned sallow, and deep lines etched the space between her eyes and pinched the corners of her mouth. Yet she marched around like a haughty major and spoke in the strident tones of a drill sergeant haranguing recruits.

No longer agile and lovely, the fading beauty garnered solace from positive little happenings that fed her starving ego.

Soldiers she had treated came forward to brag about her wonderful sacrifices and thank her for giving them back their lives. Some wept with gratitude as they proudly described her fight to save their arms and legs from the butchers' saws.

On the home front, her sisters refused to talk about her except to say, "Her sideshow appearances are shameful and embarrassing. She owes it to us to protect our positions as pillars of our communities."

Lucretia Mott had exited the planet, but Susan B. Anthony and Elizabeth Cady Stanton still criticized the little troublemaker, ignoring her views on Suffrage and the Constitution.

Mary complained to all who would listen.

> *"Congress continues to refuse my requests for reparations and reimbursements. They ignore my petitions to increase my pension to at least $12.00 a month—the same amount other contract surgeons, war widows, and nurses are receiving. I know that's the figure because I've helped many of them file successful claims while mine are still being rejected."*

Broke, unable to maintain a steady practice, and suffering from her war-related afflictions, she cashed in the only way she could. She parted with precious antiques, among them her maternal granddaddy's chair that had been in the family for over two hundred years. She leased out the Bunker Hill farm to C. F. Parker, then, cranky as a broody hen, she fought with him about rent, animals, land use, and even visitors.

As her spirit began to lag, Dr. Mary's dynamic personality was inexorably slipping into a paler version of her former self. She frowned at the image in her mirror. "Where have all the years gone?" she mourned. "How did I become this bitter old woman in such a short span? Where do I go from here?"

CHAPTER SIXTY-THREE

WASHINGTON/OSWEGO, NEW YORK

EVEN WHILE supplementing her $8.50 monthly pension with lecture fees and money realized from the Dime museums, Mary managed to spend time in Washington. The city was flourishing, and she reveled in the confrontations she encountered on the streets and in the Congress. She continued to lobby, badgering Congress over pensions as well as women's suffrage. Although that governing body tended to be lenient about private pensions, President Grover Cleveland vetoed one bill after another. Petitions introduced on Mary's behalf were dead in committee.

To those who remembered her war service she was considered an eccentric icon. Those who did not know of her or who ignored her sacrifices poked fun at her male attire, her stubbornness and her downright contrariness.

She cried privately over cartoons depicting her as a graceless buffoon, yet she plodded on, sporting her masculine attire and short hair. Articles praising her illustrious career often ended in snippy comments about her alien costume or abrasive manner as she strove to improve women's rights.

She was referred to as that doctor from Oswego that wears pants and constantly bothers men who smoke in her presence.

Still, nearly broke and morally dispirited, she refused to abandon her heated campaigns against tobacco and alcohol.

As for her pension problems, she fared no better under the Harrison administration, which was consumed with its anti-trust laws, and the tariffs levied on coffee, tea, sugar and molasses. The country, disenchanted with the higher prices caused by the McKinley Tariff Act, deserted the Republicans in 1890 and created a Democratic landslide.

The Democrats were even less willing to increase Mary's pension. Her quest for more money was foiled again.

⁓⊙◉☉⁓

In 1890 Mary declared herself a Democratic candidate for the open seat in Congress. The Republicans chortled with glee, just waiting for this unorthodox creature to win the primary against her conformist opponent. Her political aspirations went nowhere. Bids for support as the Oswego delegate to Washington were thwarted, as well.

She became more domesticated, running the farm with the help of Laura Decker who had been with the family for some time.

The wheels were turning once more in the major's old gray head. Her flirtation with politics had ended in disappointment. Her periodic treks to Washington to fight with the solons were not enough to keep her agile mind interested in the world.

She must find another way to be of service or she would surely die of boredom.

CHAPTER SIXTY-FOUR

WASHINGTON/EUROPE/MASSACHUSETTS

DR. MARY continued to be as much an oddity in Washington as she was in her own hometown. Whenever she visited the capital, she strolled the streets in her male attire, recognized by residents and visitors alike.

In winter, she wore a heavy black Prince Albert coat with shoulder cape attached, and her gold-headed umbrella was ever at the ready to fend off attackers as well as Washington's notorious downpours. She covered her head and ears with a black scarf knotted beneath her chin, protection against the chill winds that buffeted unlucky pedestrians. The scarf was usually topped by her black opera hat.

She practiced some medicine and dentistry, but because of her failing eyesight, performing surgery was out of the question.

With every visit to the capital, came a trip to Congress to plead for an increase in her own pension and relief for many deserving solders' widows and orphans who asked her to intercede for them. While she succeeded in settling most of their claims, her own quest would continue for years. Only once did she accept payment for services rendered.

There is an anecdote about a Good Samaritan act that Mary performed in the Ladies' Room near the Congressional chambers. The compassionate doctor was seen with her coat off, her shirtsleeves rolled up, trying to control a hemorrhage suffered by a poorly dressed black woman. When everything was under control, the doctor simply walked away without waiting for thanks.

Her *Crowning Constitutional Argument* was reprinted several times, and with every publication, Mary fought the same old divisive battle with the National Suffrage Association. At least some members, Mrs. Sallie Clay

Polly Craig

Bennett and her miniscule following, were beginning to agree with Mary's assertion that the Constitution had already given women the franchise.

Susan B. Anthony, however, continued to insist, "There is no doubt that the spirit of the Constitution guarantees full equality of rights and protection of citizens of the United States in the exercise of these rights; but the powers that be have decided against us; and, until we can get a broader Supreme Court, which will not be until after the women of every State in the Union are enfranchised, we never will get the needed liberal interpretation of that Document."

In other words, Anthony's followers recognized they were faced with a catch twenty-two, while Walker, stubborn as a billy goat and twice as cantankerous, continued to butt her head against the stone wall erected by the men of Congress.

❦

1898 was a year of battles for Dr. Mary. She won some and lost some.

In July, the Second Session of the 55th Congress finally increased her pension to $20.00 per month.

Her battle with the National Women's Suffrage Association gained little ground. Her $1.00 membership fee was returned to her with no explanation. Mary thought, aha, they are too afraid of my *Crowning Constitutional Argument*, which is gaining more and more notice.

Following one of Susan B. Anthony's impassioned speeches, she recalled Anthony's galling remarks that "Mary Walker was a failure and a power seeker who lived to be noticed."

At that point, the doctor was heard to say, "Sue Anthony doesn't want suffrage for women at all, for when they get it, her occupation, like Othello's will be gone. You needn't look so astonished for I know all about Sue Anthony. I have seen through her with a lighted candle. The love of power is the keynote of her character."

When some brave soul tried to shush her for fear Mrs. Anthony might hear, Dr. Mary retorted, "Let her hear. She knows every word I say is true. If they had conducted their campaign with any sense; if they hadn't spent so much time trying to suppress me; if they had done as I wanted them to

438

do, women would have been voting for the last fifteen years."

"What are your grounds for your argument?" asked a man in the crowd. "Would you give us your views of the suffrage question? I confess I never understood it."

The reporter who had asked the question documented the story as follows:

> "And then Dr. Walker, like Saul of Tarsus before King Agrippa, stretched forth her hand and spoke for herself. As she stood there with her diminutive form drawn up to its full height, her eyes flashing and her face lit up with enthusiasm, and gave a reason for the faith within her, making the best argument for woman suffrage that I have ever heard, I did an awful thing. I forgot about the hand that rocks the cradle ruling the world, forgot that it was most improper for a woman to dress in men's clothing, forgot everything but Dr. Walker's eloquence. At the conclusion of the speech, I went and shook hands with her and patted her on the back."

Some months later, *The Washington Post* published an editorial titled *The Persecution of Dr. Mary Walker*. In part, it said:

> "Dr. Mary Walker is a speaker, a student, a publicist, a faithful worker in the vineyard of material and moral advancement. Why has she been muzzled so callously and so persistently? We have received an impression of an unkind and intolerant conspiracy against one of the most gifted and willing teachers of the age."

Such vindications, though few and far between, were bittersweet.

SIXTY-FIVE

EUROPE

MARY'S BROTHER, Alvie, was not the only Walker who departed the universe in the 1890s. While Mary was on her second and final visit to Europe, maiden aunt, Vashti Walker, died at eighty-seven. Aunt Mary Walker, for whom she was named, was nearly that age when she made her exit. A long-lived family—the Walker clan.

Dr. Mary, now sixty-three, strolled beneath the linden trees with Otto Von Bismarck, comparing the similarities between the civil wars that had ravaged their countries in the 1860s and the short memories of the ruling bureaucrats.

Bismarck became a national hero when he defeated Austria and forced its exclusion from Germany. But late in the century, political atmospheres were changeable as the wind. His comprehensive scheme of social security to protect the masses against sickness and old age was well ahead of its time, and he was forced to resign in 1890. In commiseration, Mary shared her own humiliating experiences with the archaic views of American Congressmen.

On the heels of that visit, she met with the colorful Archduchess Maria Cristina, widow of Spain's King Alfonso X11, who reigned until her son, Alfonso X111, reached his majority in 1902.

Dr. Mary criticized Europe's latest fad, a whalebone cage that fashionable ladies attached to their derrieres, adding even more weight to their already cumbersome crinolines, corsets and skirts.

Clad in her low-cut emerald gown with its huge puffed sleeves, the Archduchess, descendent of Austrian royalty, sat on her collapsible bustle smiling politely as Mary lectured her on the merits of her reform dress.

The return voyage on the liner, *Germanic*, under the pseudonym, M. J. Smith was a nightmare. The seas were so turbulent that she kept to her cabin sick and miserable the whole way. Most of the passengers were also green with nausea and frightened out of their wits.

"We are forty-eight hours late," the captain apologized. "I've just navigated through the worst storm of my career. But I never feared for our safety. I had faith in my good sea boat that rode the high seas well."

It was the last time Mary would set foot on an ocean-going vessel.

Republican William McKinley won the 1896 election handily after running a ruthlessly aggressive campaign against Democrat, William Jennings Bryan.

The presidential race and party platform orchestrated by a left-over Cleveland capitalist, Mark Hanna, centered on currently popular issues that included maintaining the gold standard, federal arbitration of labor disputes, larger pensions for Union veterans and American control of the Hawaiian Islands.

Mary was all for the larger pensions, especially since McKinley had finally approved her own increase.

However, she protested vehemently against the usurping of Hawaiian territories. "How dare they?" she yelped as she balled up the article and threw it against the wall. "Washington has gone too far!"

Lydia Kamakaeha, born in Honolulu in 1838, was declared heir presumptive to the Hawaiian throne in 1877. She openly opposed the Reciprocity Treaty of 1887 her older brother, David, had signed. It granted factions on the mainland unrestrained, commercial concessions and—worse—it ceded Pearl Harbor to the United States. In her eyes he had given away too much.

Upon his death in 1891, Lydia succeeded her brother. She became Lilioukalani and ascended to the throne as queen of all her domains.

Sanford B. Dole, a lawyer and astute politician, jockeyed for power in the Islands. He established the Provisional Republic of Hawaii and sent annexation papers to the United States Senate.

When Dole declared Queen Lil deposed and announced his provisional government, pending enactment of annexation, President Grover Cleveland withdrew the treaty from the Senate and demanded the Queen's reinstatement. Dr. Mary applauded, "It's about time someone stood up for a woman's rights."

Once President Cleveland was gone, however, Queen Lil sat in the middle of the Pacific with no champion to save her. In an unprecedented action the federal government disregarded the civil rights of peaceful Hawaiians who were minding their own business, harming no one.

This time around, the Queen's protests to Congress fell on the deaf ears of men who saw control and lucrative advantages in annexation. Early in 1895, the queen was placed under house arrest in her Royal Palace, and many of her supporters were sent off to prison.

In 1898, when her own and the queen's verbal protests went unheard, Mary penned a pamphlet titled *Isonomy*, denouncing the imperialistic actions of the United States. She argued vehemently "Congress has no right to dethrone Hawaii's reigning monarch and confiscate her ancestral lands."

Supporters of the take-over debated the opposition, declaring, "Those opposing the Florida and Louisiana acquisitions used the same weak arguments, but look how those states had enriched the Union."

Dr. Mary quickly fired back, "Those two negotiations were handled properly and peacefully. Besides, they were part of the contiguous American continent. Texas, also, was annexed when the majority of its citizens petitioned for entry into the Union. And," she insisted, "no ruling monarchs were deposed, nor were private lands confiscated without compensation, in any of those ventures."

"Annexation (of Hawaii)," she wrote, "means departing from republican justice to a small sister nation with which we were at peace."

Like one obsessed, she prowled the halls of Congress arguing her case with Senators, Justices, and lobbyists. "Twenty-one thousand Hawaiians have sent their names on a petition against the proposed merger. They have a right to be defended," she insisted.

A recognized expert on its contents, Dr. Mary fell back on her beloved Constitution to prove her point.

*"That Document does not give the government the
right to meddle with, or interfere in, the affairs of a
foreign nation with which we are at peace. Here it
is proposed that the government itself shall violate
the Constitution. What respect can the people have
for the Constitution when the Government itself
goes deliberately about its violation?
The Bill of Rights guarantees the right to petition
the government for redress of grievances. Queen
Lilioukalani is losing her throne and her estates. Let
her case be heard."*

Eloquent as a country lawyer, Dr. Mary implored the chairmen of the
Senate and House Committee on Foreign affairs to organize a hearing.
"The Constitution mandates we must give the queen a chance to speak for
her people."

Her pleas were ignored.

She appeared in Equity Court with her petition, waiting patiently for
a pause in the proceedings before approaching Justice Coxe with her written statement decrying the takeover.

Judge Coxe claimed he had no jurisdiction, and sent her away. At the
same time she spoke out for the queen's people who were declared incompetent, uncivilized, and illiterate.

"Not so," she argued. "Hawaiians are more literate than many on the
mainland."

Dr. Mary challenged the 55th Congress. "Give the legitimate monarch
a fair audience to plead her case before the United States Senate. Just because the Hawaiians' customs differ from those of the continental United
States is no reason to seize property rights, depose a perfectly competent
queen, and usurp her governmental powers."

In the end, Queen Lil signed a formal abdication in exchange for the
freedom of her jailed supporters, but she continued to fight for ownership
of inherited lands that had been in her family for generations.

The rest, of course, is history.

CHAPTER SIXTY-SIX

WASHINGTON CITY

AT THE SAME TIME that Dr. Mary lobbied for Queen Liliuokalani, she grew increasingly concerned about the rumblings of Congressmen over the Cuban situation that President McKinley inherited from Grover Cleveland.

The small Island country had become a powder keg. Matters were escalating ever since General Valeriano Weyler, Spain's military governor of the island–along with his chosen militia–continued to wreak havoc on the tiny municipality.

An admirer of General Sherman's tactics during the final months of the Civil War, 'Butcher' Weyler and his death squads tore up the railroads, looting plantations and burning everything in sight. Executed, tortured or starved, his prisoners died in droves.

Outraged citizens demanded U. S. intervention.

McKinley was unhappy about dirtying his hands over the affair. Besides, he hated war with a passion and wished to avoid it at all costs.

A Union Army volunteer at age eighteen, he fought bravely at Antietam, during what historians have designated the bloodiest single day of the Civil War.

"I have seen the dead piled up," said the President, "and I do not want to see that again."

As the specter of a confrontation loomed larger every week, McKinley was between a rock and a hard place. American capital was heavily invested in Cuban railroads, mines and sugar and tobacco plantations. Extensive trade programs had been in place for years. The close proximity of Cuban lands made Florida's shores vulnerable, and southerners who feared invasion wanted protection.

Americans chose to support the 'Butcher's' opposition–Gomez's Guerrillas who were fighting for their lives. American warrior, 'Dynamite Johnny' O'Brien, risked his life to smuggle donated explosives into their hidden rendezvous points along the Cuban coast.

The press dubbed McKinley cowardly, weak, and ignorant because he still tried to negotiate new terms with the Spaniards.

Dr. Mary, on the other hand, prayed he would maintain his original hands-off policy. Shaking her gray head, she preached separatism to anyone who would listen. "I'm not unsympathetic, but I can't bear to think of young Americans being maimed and killed–again."

Then the battleship *Maine* was destroyed in Havana Harbor. Smoking upper decks and shattered masts reared up from the muddy waters like grotesque tombstones that mourned the two hundred and sixty U.S. citizens dead from the blast. Later, during the debriefing, ninety bewildered survivors could never agree on the cause of the explosions.

The President, deciding he had no choice, sent an ultimatum, threatening drastic action if the Spanish government did not cease its harsh treatment of American neighbors. It must abandon its 'reconcentrado policy,' (the imprisonment of Cuban citizens under conditions as horrifying as those at Andersonville).

He demanded that an Armistice be arranged between Spain and the Cuban insurrectionists. Spain agreed to negotiate with them, but said nothing about the prison camps.

McKinley, his political eye on a second term, ignored the concession and ceased communications with the offenders. He asked Congress for permission to use force in Cuba. Representatives and Senators alike knew their constituents were for the war, and the vote fell heavily in McKinley's favor. They passed the Teller Amendment, which promised that the U. S. would withdraw once Cuba had attained its independence.

Dr. Mary approached Secretary of the Navy, John D. Long, denouncing U. S. actions, protesting that the Spaniards had already capitulated and war was unnecessary.

Too late. The army had been increased to 62,000 men with a call for 200,000 more volunteers. They marched to recruiting offices to the strains of John Philip Sousa's "Stars and Stripes Forever" and "There'll Be a Hot Time in the Old Town Tonight."

Gung ho from the outset, Assistant Secretary of the Navy Theodore Roosevelt had his forces well equipped and prepared to go at a moment's notice.

Mary felt the earth churn under her feet. "My country doesn't need another war," she exclaimed. "Like President McKinley, I've seen the dead piled up, but I'm too old to offer my services to save the young men who will be sacrificed."

When she protested even louder to Congress she was laughed out of the gallery. "Who the devil is this grotesque little creature with the outrageous costume and gold-rimmed glasses?" snorted one senator. "Who cares about her Medal of Honor? The country is ready for a fight, and fight they will."

Mary's was a voice crying in the wilderness.

While Carrie Nation went about smashing saloons, Major General Shafter and Lieutenant Colonel 'Teddy' Roosevelt and his ragtag band of Rough Riders were doing a great deal of smashing themselves. Overnight, they became the heroes of bloody battles fought on foreign soil.

While Americans favored the fight over Cuba, they became nervous when Admiral George Dewey rushed his ships into action in the Pacific and sank the proud Spanish fleet.

Mark Twain, so embittered by that aggression, declared, "Americans should scrap the red stripes on the flag and replace them with black ones, and replace the stars with skull and crossbones to represent those murderous attacks."

Dr. Mary shrieked when she read of such an abomination, but she understood Twain's malignant feelings more than most. "Such egregious military tactics are forbidden by the basic principles of our sacred nation," she insisted. "Nowhere does the Constitution allow such naked violence against another country except in defense of America's own shores."

The Armistice between Spain and The United States was finally signed in Paris, and, on January 1st, 1899, Spain transferred the administration of Cuba to the United States.

The Philippines, thousands of miles from the continental United States, were purchased for the staggering sum of $20,000,000. Mary accused the government of imperialism, "First Hawaii, then Puerto Rico, Santiago, Cuba, the Philippines. I beg you, sirs, where will it end?"

Filipino patriot, Emilio Aguinaldo, organized a revolt against U. S. control of his country, but American soldiers employed the cruelest tactics to subdue the insurrectionists.

Dr. Mary was so furious with the administration's aggressive policies that she campaigned relentlessly for William Jennings Bryan and Adlai Stevenson (the 1st) when they challenged McKinley's re-election to a second term. Bryan–the 'Great Commoner'–ran on a platform that vigorously denounced Republican imperialism.

Mary's sharp criticism of McKinley's running mate, Theodore Roosevelt, incensed romantic hero worshipers who still bragged about the escapades of Teddy and his Rough Riders. Even in her hometown, crowds ridiculed and heckled whenever she spoke up for Bryan.

She wept with frustration when the vote went to the Republicans, once again.

⤜◈⤛

The lionhearted warrior seemed to be winding down. She made fewer appearances so the lack of money became a huge problem. Fortunately, her properties were not mortgaged and her needs were simple.

Dr. Mary's valiant heart refused to quit however simple her life may have been. She never gave up the good fight.

In January of 1900, she persuaded the State Legislature in Albany to hear her arguments on the Maher bill that would abolish capital punishment in New York.

Speaking before the Assembly Code Committee, she argued, "Electrocution is a barbarous act and the State is committing judicial murder." Since it did not seem she would win her argument, she capitulated.

Perhaps with George Abbot's execution in mind, she condemned 'judicial murder' in cases other than those with a smoking gun.

"If the death penalty cannot be abolished, at least let us give life imprisonment to those convicted on circumstantial evidence instead of (delivering) such a final sentence, for another might have done the deadly deed."

A Medal for Dr. Mary

In poor health, Mary was forced to rest in the city, an interruption that delayed her return to Oswego. Fresh out of her sick bed, she found herself on the same side of the State House aisle with one of her most ardent opponents in the Suffrage movement. But this particular episode was not about the woman's vote.

Lillie Devereaux Blake had come to Albany to protest a bill before the Code Committee that would limit the length of a lady's hatpin to three inches. It seemed any further length of the pin would then constitute a dangerous weapon.

Mary Walker had no use for a hatpin. Her opera hats and feathered fedoras needed no such help to sit firmly atop her short bob. However, no mere man was going to tell any woman how long or short her hatpin should be. That was an infringement on civil liberty, and the United States Constitution frowned on that sort of action.

CHAPTER SIXTY-SEVEN

BUFFALO, NEW YORK

SEPTEMBER 6, 1901, THE PAN AMERICAN EXPOSITION, BUFFALO, NY: A banner event! President McKinley is scheduled to put in a personal appearance.

On the day before his formal reception, the president spoke to a room crowded with smiling constituents who genuinely liked the kindly man they had elected to a second term—even though some had reservations about his foreign policies.

McKinley's speech was eloquent. "Isolation is no longer possible or desirable," he said. "Reciprocity treaties are in harmony with the spirit of the times, measures of retaliation are not."

Applause and accolades from the appreciative crowd led the President to believe he was on the right track.

However, there was one person present who did not applaud the President—one unnoticed, insignificant little man who skulked about in the background, struggling to control his hatred while he plotted the foulest of crimes.

A young, unemployed laborer, Leon Czolgosz (pronounced chol-gosh), mentally deranged, self-proclaimed anarchist born in Detroit, Michigan, bristled at McKinley's remarks, seething inside.

On this day of celebration, the president's broad face lit up with pleasure as he shook hands with the continuous line of well wishers.

Czolcosz bided his time, his nerves tightly reined. Finally he stepped sideways, facing his target.

The President looked puzzled as he raised his right hand, but the visitor offered his left.

McKinley saw the white handkerchief, and the furrow between his brows deepened.

The muffled shot startled him. In that instant, he felt a sharp tap at the third button of his vest. The bullet had deflected.

The President stood still as stone, too surprised to move.

Czolgosz squeezed the trigger again. The lethal bullet caught his victim dead center. McKinley felt the punch to his stomach, reluctant in that instant to admit what he knew to be true. He had held too many gut-shot comrades on the bloody fields of Antietam.

His knees buckled, but he stood firm. Sturdy hands rushed up to support him.

"I done my duty," shouted the assassin as men grappled him to the floor in a mélange of flailing arms and legs.

The President was helped to the chair behind him. Aghast, the witnesses stared disbelieving as a burgeoning, crimson blossom stained the chalk white of his handsome waistcoat.

Out of loving concern for his precious partner of thirty years, he grasped his secretary's sleeve and gasped, "My wife—be careful how you tell her!"

Friends cautioned him to save his strength. He shook his head. "Don't let them harm the man," he ordered just before he fainted.

The President was carried to a nearby residence where doctors immediately tended to his frightful wound. He did well, at first, but an insidious gangrene ate at his peritoneum. The infection became too gross to overcome.

The end was near. Ida Saxton McKinley clutched her husband's hand, pleading with God to spare her soul mate, her rock and her fortress. The family doctor, their Methodist minister, and a few intimate friends wept in the background.

The President stirred. Ida leaned forward to hear his words.

"Good-bye, good-bye, all," he whispered. "It is God's way. His will be done."

On September 14th, 1901, William McKinley, age fifty-eight, the twenty-fifth Commander-in-Chief of the United States of America, had the dubious distinction of being the third president to be assassinated in Mary Walker's lifetime.

Meanwhile, the vacationing Vice President was on the descending lap of a climbing expedition when a messenger located his party and informed him of the attempted assassination. By the time Teddy came down off the mountain to take a train to the sick room, the President was dead.

Theodore Roosevelt, Colonel of the Rough Riders, and former Governor of the State of New York, was sworn into office on the same day and in the same house in which McKinley surrendered his ghost. At forty-three, Roosevelt was the youngest man to reach that pinnacle.

Leon Czolgosz was arrested and tried in record time. When asked why he had done such a terrible thing, he replied, "All rulers are enemies of the workers. I wanted to kill a ruler."

Outrage spread throughout the country. Justice must be swift. Punishment must be commensurate with the bestiality of the crime.

On September 26, 1901, Czolgosz was sentenced to be executed, and the judge did not call for mercy upon his soul. On October 29, 1901, just forty-five days after his infamous act, the prisoner was dragged to the execution chamber and strapped into the electric chair. No hood covered his features as the wet sponge and lethal cap settled over his head. When the switch was thrown, the killer's mouth contorted into an ugly rictus of pain, and his body convulsed several times before it was stilled forever.

Czolgosz was twenty-eight years old.

September 18, 1901. Huge headlines in Oswego's *Palladium* read:

DOCTOR WALKER'S NARROW ESCAPE

Mary's controversial views nearly cost her dearly.

Several carpenters milled about inside the train station, spouting their opinions about the sensational topic of the day—the assassination.

Mary's ears were burning as she purchased a ticket. She and stationmaster Goble listened to the strident voices of the irate laborers who brandished their lunch buckets, glad-mouthing the speed with which Czolgosz would go to trial. Each speaker had a passionate opinion of proper punishment for the beast who had murdered their President.

Handing her change, Goble said, "They're making short work of Czolgosz, aren't they, Doctor?"

Mary tucked the coins into her purse before answering.

Later, Goble swore under oath he remembered Mary's reply verbatim: "Yes, and it's a shame. It was no worse for Czolgosz to kill President McKinley, than it is for the State of New York to kill Czolgosz. President McKinley has murdered thousands of innocent Filipinos and placed their noble president in captivity."

Later, in the same deposition in the ensuing investigation, Goble recalled replying that she ought to be ashamed of herself, and that, if she were a man, he would go out there and punch her face.

Then he leveled what was considered the most damning evidence against Mary. He swore that she answered, "No you wouldn't punch my face. I don't believe in assassinations as a rule, but in this case it was justifiable."

A burly, shabbily dressed worker plunked his dented bucket on the counter and trumpeted his method of proper punishment. "I'd like to see Czolgosz cut up in inch pieces, and I'd like to take the first cut." His buddies cheered in agreement.

The obscene cruelty of that remark was too much for Mary.

Still with her back turned to the audience, she directed her remarks to the clerk but offered them in a voice loud enough for all to hear. "The State of New York in electrocuting Czolgosz is just as great a murderer as was the assassin in killing the President."

Worse still, she added, "President McKinley, in killing the Filipinos is a murderer, himself."

Shouts of rage rose up among the workers.

The unkempt bully, a threatening fist raised high, stomped toward her. The prissy clerk's eyes grew large as he looked past her shoulder and saw the giant coming. The clerk moved sideways, away from his ticket window.

Mary could not see the man behind her, but she heard his boots clumping on the floorboards.

Built like a tree, thick limbed and tall, he loomed head and shoulders above Mary's frail little body. "Whadya mean by such talk?" he demanded.

Very close now, Mary felt his body heat, his voice growled deep as a foghorn, but she stood fast. She couldn't keep her mouth shut even when it seemed more circumspect to do so. Her opinions were important and she had a right to express them, whether here among a bunch of ornery men or before the Congress of the United States. "The first amendment to the Constitution guarantees every citizen freedom of speech," she said.

She clenched her jaw and turned, eyes blazing, to stare up at the outspoken fellow who would do the carving job on Czolgosz.

Startled at realizing he addressed a woman, the bully lowered his threatening fist and gingerly stepped backward. He sputtered a moment before retrieving his wits. Better not let his anger get the better of him. No use going to jail for it.

"If you wasn't a woman," he threatened, "I'd knock you down. What right you got ta go 'round the country and make such statements?"

Inhaling sharply, he paused, squinting down at her. "Yer crazy and oughtta be locked up and taken care of. Better still, the people oughtta lynch you."

She eyed him with great distaste, stepped around him, and strode from the station, choosing not to dignify his statements with an answer.

The man followed her outside and announced to the crowd of workmen milling about, "Boys, this woman says the dead President was a murderer."

There were loud, angry threats, and one man shouted, "Yer in the same class as Carrie Nation and Emma Goldman, and all of ya oughtta be put out a the way so you can't make no more trouble."

One man, wiser and more restrained, spoke up. "Let her go, boys, she's crazy and not responsible."

Unafraid, head high, Mary walked to the train and daintily climbed the steps without a backward glance.

Back in Oswego, she turned livid when she read the *Palladium*'s account of the incident. The article contained erroneous information, misquotes, and unfair judgments.

She hand-delivered a reply refuting the column's allegations, demanding that an honorable amending be posted, quoting the proper facts.

> *"Sirs:*
> *A lie that has part truth is the worst statement to*
> *meet. What I did say, I am ready to say, anywhere.*
> *I do not believe in any murder by assassination, or*
> *hanging, or electrocution, in this country or in the*
> *Philippines. The taking of life is murder. Another*
> *false statement was about my 'hurried leaving the*
> *depot. 'I am not such a base coward as to be afraid*

to express my sentiments when they are the best of
human life."

Mary suggested that a group of anarchists might be behind a plot to slay the President. Her letter continued:

"If judicial murder is struck from the Codes and life
imprisonment substituted, the assassin in Buffalo
might sometime tell who was back of him. It is to be
hoped that the Governor will do his duty and not
allow the facts behind the assassination to be lost,
and worse men than the assassin go free."

The *Oswego Times* reported the station incident, skewing the facts and comparing Mary to Senator Wellington and Carrie Nation.

It also reported that she accused Roosevelt of putting Czolgosz up to his heinous act.

"Well! First it's the axe-wielding prohibitionist,
Carrie Nation, then it's the Russian born anarchist,
Emma Goldman, and now it's that malefactor,
Wellington. I would not be caught dead in the
company of any one of them," she sputtered.

On September 21st, the *Oswego Times* received a visit from its most colorful subscriber. After an explosive interview with Mary, the paper published the irate doctor's version of the incident. In her statement to the press, she insisted, "the basest slander had been done, regarding her saying that Roosevelt put up the job of assassination of McKinley."

The article went on to say,

"Dr. Walker considers it, also, a slander to be
compared with men and women who do not believe
in law and order, especially since she has been before

the New York Congressional Committees and also before the State Legislative Committees to change the objectionable laws."

Once Czolgosz's death penalty was officially rendered, Mary began circulating a petition to implore Governor Odell to commute his sentence to imprisonment for life.

There were very few sympathizers.

⚜

The Military Archives in Washington, DC, contain various documents pertaining to the 'acts of treason' perpetrated by Dr. Mary Walker in the matter of the McKinley assassination. To those who knew her dedication to the Constitution and to her country, the charges were ludicrous.

Yes, she was outspoken. Yes, she was abrasive. But there was never a more loyal citizen than that small bundle of fire who fought for her flag and for her 'boys' and for their widows and orphans long after her country forgot their sacrifices.

On September 26th, with an eye toward formally charging Mary, a letter was forwarded to Oswego's Police Chief from the Commissioner of the Bureau of Pensions a division of the Department of the Interior. It read:

"Sir:

Information has been filed in this Bureau to the effect that Dr. Mary Walker, a pensioner of the United States, has been guilty of scandalous conduct in vilifying President McKinley since his assassination, in expressing her satisfaction with the murder. An account of her conduct has been published in a newspaper, and it is stated that an assistant ticket agent named Goble of Oswego was with others present at the time and reproved her. I should be pleased to receive such evidence as you can secure showing the

*circumstances in the case (under oath, if possible),
accompanied by sufficient data to enable the Bureau to
identify Mrs. Walker's claim for pension."*

Special Examiner T. E. McLaughlin secured depositions from Smith Goble and carpenters William Eugene Morse and George W. Paine along with Conductor Frank E. Meade. Each gave a slightly different version.

He interviewed two others, Irwin and Coy, but they claimed they had paid no attention because it was such a common thing for the crowds to 'jolly the doctor.' The sport got old after a while.

Dr. Mary was again attracting the country's attention because of her firm stand against the death penalty for Czolgosz. One reporter asserted, "The only thing that saved her from a beating, was a bystander's admonition that she was a bit addled."

Some articles were kind to her because of her past service to the country, which may have helped her situation.

A special examiner from the Pension Office would keep his investigation on file at the Bureau in case Congress called for it. When enemies urged Commissioner Evans to punish her, he was quoted as saying, "I have no authority to revoke the woman's pension, but Congress could do so if it found just cause."

Threats of financial repercussions never phased Dr. Mary. Her passionate fight against death went all the way back to her childhood. Nothing could force her to turn away.

She had grappled with death in sick rooms, on fields and riverbanks, and in the prisoner of war camp. There had been enough death to last her two lifetimes. During the war, death surely chortled with glee as the generals ordered all those mothers' sons into battle to baptize a few acres of enemy territory with their blood and tears.

She had seen enough to know that death did not discriminate. It treated north and south, rich and poor, young and old alike. To Mary, *life* was sacred, no matter the circumstances. That the legal system would deliver another victim into the hands of her old enemy by electrocution was, by her standards, akin to barbarism.

Many of her influential friends, some unsympathetic to her cause, were outraged at the very idea that an inveterate patriot like Mary Edwards Walker could even contemplate an act of treason, much less commit one. They stepped forward and exerted every effort, called in favors, applied political pressure. The matter was reluctantly relegated to the Congressional archives for future reference.

Even if she had lost her pension, or worse, even if she had been tried, convicted and imprisoned, it would have made little difference. She believed what she believed and would have given up everything–including her life–to defend her right to have her say.

CHAPTER SIXTY-EIGHT

OSWEGO, NEW YORK/WASHINGTON

MARY'S DISAGREEMENT with the Suffragettes grew more vehement with every meeting.

In the fall of 1901, the New York State Association held its convention in Oswego, and Mary, at the request of several newer members, attempted to speak. However, Susan B. Anthony and the Reverend Anna Shaw asserted their leadership privileges and denied her access to the assembly. Mary's membership fee was returned for the second time, and she was physically removed from the conference room.

Once again, the old controversy between the woman's constitutional right to vote and the necessity for an amendment was being debated, but, this time, there were many younger people who found merit in Dr. Mary's *Crowning Constitutional Argument* and expressed the desire to hear her speak to the premise.

Mrs. Anthony denied any discussion she could not control. "That arrogant woman must not interfere with my meeting, no matter how many clamor to hear her useless tirade."

Mary was undeterred. To thwart Mrs. Anthony, she had a batch of handbills printed to define her position and distributed them to attendees from the doorsteps of the building.

In a face-to-face encounter with the Reverend Shaw she advised, "The Suffrage Association is wasting the members' hard-earned dollars in a futile effort to get Congress to amend the Constitution. Oh, the solons will listen to our arguments, all right, nod their heads and then table the resolutions as soon as we swish our backsides out of those hallowed halls."

It took Anthony's death in 1906 to end the feud between them.

Privately, at least, at a dinner given by the first Political Equality Club of Oswego, Susan B. had a good word to say about her archrival. Jane B. Taylor whose mother and sister were founders of the club was all ears as the conversation turned to Dr. Mary Walker. Most of the guests spoke harshly about her demeanor, her clothing, and her obstinate disposition.

Mrs. Anthony, however, quietly reminded the guests, "Dr. Mary Walker rendered such courageous service as a nurse in the Civil War that there was not a soldier but had a feeling of affection and reverence for her and would not tolerate a word of criticism or slander against her."

All derogatory gabble ceased, at least for one evening.

In 1911, Mary argued her case before the state legislature over the objections of Anna Shaw and her constituents who walked out of the hearing room as soon as she began to speak.

But Mary had many ardent supporters, among them her close friend, Mrs. Nellie van Slingerland, who was the managing editor of *The Joan of Arc Magazine*, the Official Organ of the Joan of Arc Woman Suffrage League.

That magazine staunchly supported Mary's *Crowning Constitutional Argument* and opposed any bill of amendment brought forward in the Senate.

Nellie was also the Secretary-treasurer of the Betterment League. Among other principles it opposed the death penalty, supported woman's suffrage and favored an anti-marriage law for mental defectives and criminals—all subjects dear to Mary's heart.

Mary's health was failing. She was uncomfortable both winter and summer. The brilliance of sun on snow was agony to her damaged eyes, which she had to rest frequently. She had a low tolerance for icy cold, and extreme heat bothered her worse still.

Yet, she continued to hassle Congress. In the matter of widows' and orphans' pensions, congressmen were courteous to her, but, the moment she commenced her lobby for woman's suffrage, she was greeted with stony stares and cold shoulders.

Her advocacy for simpler women's clothing continued until the end of her life. In 1911, couture designers introduced the hobble skirt. It came closer to Mary's own ideas of fashion than anything, to date. It was far lighter and more comfortable than the billowy costumes that fashion espoused for years.

The Tribune's style editor reported that "Dr. Walker who qualified as an expert in bifurcal garments for women approved the harem skirt."

A direct quote from Mary tickled the readers. "It is the most hopeful sign of eventual adoption of sensible attire by women I have noted yet I welcome any attempt to get rid of the disease-producing corsets and skirts. At the same time, the harem skirt is not as good as regular trousers it won't be long before men and women dress alike. I've worn trousers since I was a girl, and I'd rather die than go back to skirts."

◅◦❀◦▻

At the ripe old age of 80, Mary made an astounding announcement at the conclusion of a hearing before New York State's Assembly Judiciary Committee. Her bill to provide women's suffrage was being heard for the umpteenth time. "Wyoming and Utah territories granted women the vote as early as 1869 and 1870," she argued. "Shouldn't the proud state of New York be as progressive and forward thinking as the virgin west?"

Then she flabbergasted her audience when she announced, "As an expert on the United States Constitution, I, Dr. Mary Edwards Walker, announce my candidacy for Democratic Senator from the state of New York."

While the *New York Tribune* declared her one of the world's most unique women, the description failed to get her name sent to the Democratic caucus for consideration.

Age never deterred Mary. In February of 1912, she appeared before the House Judiciary Committee to advocate yet another bill on voting rights. She insisted, "As in England years ago, if American women flock to the polls in droves demanding their constitutional rights, men would have no choice but to allow them in."

Looking old and thin, she collapsed on a train to Albany as she made her way to lecture for the benefit of the Betterment League. Her subject:

"The Education of Mothers and Children."

She wound up in the Presbyterian Hospital where she called her old friend, Nellie van Slingerland, to be her press contact. "Tell the newspapers that my home on Bunker Hill is to be turned into a haven for women and tuberculosis patients."

The press quoted Nellie as saying, "She is one of the kindest and most self-sacrificing women ever born. She can't expect any benefit from suffrage at her age, as she is a very old woman. She has simply worn herself out working for others and for the principle of woman's rights, as she sees it."

A nurse at the hospital was mortified when Dr. Mary refused a night-dress and demanded, "Take that away and bring me a suit of pajamas or wrap me in a sheet."

The hospital cook shook her head at the menu of bananas and gruel she insisted upon.

A few days later, she threw up her hands in disgust. "Get me out of here, Nellie. Take me to your apartment where I won't have to put up with a lot of coddling and pampering by a bunch of female nurses. I'll get better a lot quicker away from all their tsk tsking about sickness and such. Besides, the smell of death is all around me."

The Mirror, thinking the little Major was on her way out, published an article with a much kinder theme mostly discussing her clothing, but lauding her courageous battles.

When Mary read the article, she harrumphed, "God help us. This thing reads like an obituary. Well, I am not dead yet." As for the text, she snorted, "They still don't get it through their thick heads, do they? Clothing has to do with health not with a woman's constitutional right to be treated the same as men."

While she lay abed, friends, fearing for her life, sent word to her relatives, but none came to visit her. Though others were shocked, Mary said, "I'm not surprised. They've long considered me an embarrassment. They'll be glad to see the end of me."

She issued a press release. "Reporters should put their efforts into more pithy material and save their obituaries until my corpse is cold."

As if to demonstrate her immortality, she recovered and, after a long rest, took herself to Chicago to work for the suffrage movement.

A Medal for Dr. Mary

⊱✦⊰

In 1913, a special celebration organized by the State Historical Society was held in Oswego. The town was in a festive mood as they feted young Franklin Delano Roosevelt then Assistant Secretary of the Navy.

Mary appeared in her plug hat, and black frock coat, its right breast adorned with her Medal of Honor and various other badges. The handle of her trusty umbrella encircled her left wrist like a shepherd's crook, leaving her right hand free to greet her public.

Congressman Mott formally introduced Mary to Roosevelt who smiled warmly at his new acquaintance. His smile faded a bit when the doctor voiced undisguised displeasure with the principles, or lack of same, of Franklin's cousin, Theodore.

However, the famous Roosevelt grin erupted into a spontaneous chuckle when she allowed, "You seem a reasonable enough fellow, especially since you're a Democrat."

⊱✦⊰

By the spring of 1914, Mary had her second wind. She presented a series of well-attended lectures in Washington, these under the auspices of her re-organized Universal Peace Society. Throughout that year and the following one, she traveled about, speaking her mind, indoctrinating some while alienating others. Same old Mary, friends said, shaking their heads.

In December of 1915, she attended some of the meetings of the 47th Annual Suffrage Convention.

"I am the oldest suffragist in the cause," she admitted before complaining that she had been thwarted numerous times from offering her *Crowning Constitutional Argument*, which would have persuaded many members to follow in her footsteps.

CHAPTER SIXTY-NINE

OSWEGO, NEW YORK/WASHINGTON

JANUARY 5, 1916. Dr. Mary, now eighty-four, delivered a proclamation on the steps of Congress. Despite her shabby clothes and wrinkled visage, she stood stalwart and proud as ever. Though hoarse from a cold, her voice carried across the frigid air with its usual authority: "The United States Constitution is the citadel of our liberties and supports a magnificent superstructure. Its solid grounds of justice, polity and general utility apply to all citizens. I proclaim that the women of the United States are the equals of men politically and urge them to go in a body to the polls next November and cast their ballots not only as a right, but as a duty to assist in the selection of the best person in the choice of a republican government."

Paraphrasing her *Crowning Constitutional Argument*, she drew a scattering of applause as she emphasized her logical evidence:

> *"Franchise was not a provision of the Constitution, but a conceded part of it. That caused a clause to be inserted prohibiting any state from making laws in conflict. It does not say man's franchise or woman's franchise. To be a voter there must be citizenship. To be a citizen carries with it the right to vote. All citizens should enjoy the rights of 'Life, Liberty, and the Pursuit of Happiness.' These the Constitution guarantees."*

The crowd, mostly women, stamped their feet in approval when Mary lectured,

> *"President Woodrow Wilson is too good a lawyer*
> *not to know that women have always had the*
> *franchise from the United States Constitution."*

Old and wise she was. Senile and stupid she was not. Her mental agility surprised most of her opponents even at this late stage of her life

⸎⸙⸎

Between her infrequent trips to Washington, Dr. Mary was most often found at the family homestead in Oswego. She encouraged visitors whose curiosity made her home a mini-tourist attraction.

Haunted by recollections of her parents and siblings, all deceased, she managed her affairs amid her cherished antiques and the myriad of memorabilia she'd gathered over the years. She delighted in showing guests the original family heirlooms she had inherited from her aunts: handsome furniture, fireplace equipment, foot warmers, and the like.

There were countless Indian relics collected early on, when Oswego was still surrounded by red men. But her favorite pastime was pointing out her souvenirs of the rich and famous.

Possessed of a remarkable memory for detail, she joyfully expounded on the occasions at which she had been presented with every item in her collection.

Carefully preserved were such wonders as a piece of material from the couch that comforted the final hours of Queen Victoria's beloved consort, Prince Albert; the linen collar worn by President Garfield's assassin, Charles Guiteau, the night before he was hanged; a personalized picture of Florence Nightingale; a gold chain that a grateful Hawaiian Queen, Lilioukalani, had presented to her after Mary's impassioned defense of the queen's civil rights. Dozens of autographs of noted personages of the 19th century were carefully preserved.

She treasured her artifacts from the Civil War, especially a ring made for her by soldiers of the 52nd Ohio. There was a hunk of the Confederate blockade wall at Charleston, her medicine kits, and a small coin purse she'd secreted on her person while at Castle Thunder.

A small closet she called her torture chamber contained a display of corsets, hoop skirts, high-heeled shoes, and voluminous gowns.

One of her most valuable possessions was a chair that had been used by George Washington, John Adams, Thomas Jefferson, James Madison, James Monroe, and John Quincy Adams. She thought of it as her 'Seat of the Mighty,' and indeed it was.

And, of course, she flaunted her most cherished prize, her Medal of Honor for Meritorious Service. Actually, there were two medals; the first was pinned to her breast in 1865 by President Andrew Johnson at the Congressional testimonial. The Army sent her the second, a modified design, in 1907. This duplicate she wore for every day, saving the original for special occasions. When the situation warranted, she wore both of them.

Formal to a fault, Mary dressed for the time of day. Her morning clothes consisted of soft flannel shirts and trousers, while her farm clothes were of more sturdy fabric. Whenever she expected guests, she quickly donned her usual costume, changing the color of the neck scarf to suit her whim of the day.

Still spry in her eighties and still sharp as a tack mentally, she ran her farm with meager help. She was an accomplished manipulator when it came to getting visitors to do her bidding. Her wit and cleverness saved her many repair dollars that she could ill afford. If things needed mending, she 'allowed' men callers to do the fixing. When the chore was accomplished she always exclaimed, "Tea and cakes in the parlor. Won't be a moment."

Many reporters who interviewed her miscast her as an army nurse. She wrote scathing letters to the editors to "get it right. It's Doctor Walker. I am a surgeon."

But, neither corrected titles, nor the profuse laurels of her fellow soldiers who extolled her bravery and sacrifice, could erase the humiliation and disillusionment experienced by a dumbfounded Dr. Mary when she was dealt the most devastating blow of her life.

CHAPTER SEVENTY

OSWEGO, NEW YORK/WASHINGTON

WITH THE STROKE of a retired general's pen, Dr. Mary Walker's name was deleted from the prestigious list of Medal of Honor recipients.

The Medal itself had been adopted (retroactive to the start of the Civil War) in 1862 by Congressional resolution "as a means of recognizing the deeds of American soldiers and sailors who were distinguishing themselves in the fighting."

The resolution provided that the medal be presented to officers and enlisted men for "gallantry in action and other soldier-like qualities."

In early June, 1916, after years of research, a board of retired military officers advised the Senate that the regulations pursuant to the medal's presentation were much too ambiguous and should be narrowed to "action involving actual conflict with an enemy, distinguished by conspicuous gallantry or intrepidity, at the risk of life, above and beyond the call of duty." Any application or recommendation for the Medal must be proven with "official documents describing the deed involved."

The panel also recommended that prior awards be investigated along such parameters in order to protect the valiant few who genuinely deserved the honor.

Consequently, all 2,625 awards were reviewed. 911 names were stricken as undeserving, including Dr. Mary, 'Buffalo Bill' Cody, and more than eight hundred members of the Maine contingent to whom President Lincoln had personally issued the medal in 1863–the same contingent who ultimately served as escort to his funeral cortege.

Notification was forwarded to Mary with the quote that the board "could find nothing in the records to show the specific acts for which the decoration was originally awarded and that her service does not appear to have been distinguished in action or otherwise."

The letter also contained the admonition that to continue to wear the Medal was considered a crime against the government.

Dr. Mary, stunned beyond comprehension, crumpled the document as she collapsed into her mother's old wooden rocker, shedding tears of frustration dredged up from her shattered soul.

Hours passed while she sat with numbed fingers locked around her precious Medal, her thumb caressing the familiar rough surface, an old habit that had comforted her through miserable disappointments. It was the one solid thing in her life that gave credence to her unquestionable worth to her beloved country.

Memories of battlefields swam before her flooded eyes. Broken bodies she'd helped to repair and broken spirits to whom she had given hope lay like lead in her chest. She shivered at the memory of the excruciating cold on the icy Rappahannock riverbank and inhaled again the rusty smell of pitiful, bloody corpses, remnants of the slaughter at Chickamauga.

Lonely trails through the southern countryside superimposed the faces of simple country folk she'd treated.

She recalled the dangerous, black eyes and terrifying grin of Confederate General 'Champ' Ferguson; and that ugly worm, Ezra Philbert, who tried so hard to humiliate her on the road to Castle Thunder. Suddenly, she wondered what had happened to her gallant mount, Thomasina, stolen at Castle Thunder.

Oh, yes, she rode where men dared not go, secretly garnering what information she could for the Generals, and got herself captured for her pains.

God, those prison days were awful. Poor, sick Alonzo Devereaux came to mind, and she remembered his gift of the little fan with the American flag that had probably saved her sanity. Those deplorable conditions that had sapped her robust health and ruined her eyesight were unspeakable reminders of that terrible place.

All the long-repressed incidents percolated up from her subconscious. Mountains of little details; minutiae when added together formed a network of sacrifices she had endured for her country.

Where was the grateful government now that the war was a distant memory, the bloodshed scarcely remembered?

Her head pounded with tension, her throat ached as if she had swallowed sheets of coarse sandpaper, and her heart seemed to hemorrhage in her chest.

"How could they?" she wailed, over and over. "The award was by Act of Congress, and the President himself gave me the Medal."

Heartbroken and nearly beaten, she rocked and rocked.

When she was all cried out, her fertile mind went to work. Who could help her? She counted off her old supporters.

President Johnson was no longer alive. General Thomas and General Burnside had been dead for years. So was The Big Man, himself, General Sherman, whose backside she had saved. Returning from one of her solo forays, she'd reported, "They're lying in wait for you, Sir. You're walking into a Confederate trap."

Sadly, she had outlived everyone of note who could exert any political pressure in her favor.

Her only recourse was to lobby Congress for re-instatement. She pinned the medal to her breast and vowed to wear it until the day she died. No arbitrary act could deny her the privilege she'd earned. They could carry her kicking and screaming to the gallows, but she would fight any and all who tried to take her prize away from her.

"They shall have my Medal back over my dead body," she vowed.

Enough! She had no more time for self-pity. She would fight for what was rightfully hers.

She drew a long deep sigh. One more tedious battle with those pompous asses in Washington, she thought. Dear God, would it never end?

Strangely enough, the letter Mary wrote to the Adjutant General's Office in Washington did not detail her good works on the battlefield, nor did it enumerate any tactical information her watchful eyes and ears had gleaned. In her mind, her covert actions would ever be secret.

Instead, she wrote:

> *"The special valor was for going into the enemy's grounds when the inhabitants were suffering for professional service, and sent to our lines to beg for assistance, and no man surgeon was willing to respond for fear of being taken prisoner, and by my doing it, the people were won over to the Union. We could not be ordered out of our lines without our consent, and the dental, obstetrical, surgical and medical distress were such that I consented to respond. I was eventually captured by a Texan who did not understand the situation, while the beneficiaries of my services were very much incensed. I expect my case will have to be made special, as I have two medals"*

Despite letters and several trips to Congress Mary's status remained the same. She was no longer a Medal of Honor winner.

While Dr. Mary was fighting for her just due, another battle was heating up over seas.

President Wilson's Neutrality Proclamation of 1914 was losing favor with the American people who stood on the side of England and the Allies.

By the time Germany declared that the English Channel and surrounding waters a war zone, the United States issued a protest. The Lusitania was torpedoed and 114 Americans sank to their frigid, watery graves.

President Wilson demanded that Germany cease and desist or face severance of diplomatic relations. In defiance, the French vessel, *Sussex*, was torpedoed and followed the Lusitania to the ocean depths.

America's National Defense Act of 1916 increased the Army to 220,000 soldiers and the National Guard to 425,000 active members.

Wilson won re-election against opponent Supreme Court Justice Hughes, and Mary was certain war was inevitable.

She was dead right. Merchant Marine ships were armed in March of 1917, and the Declaration of War was signed on April 6th.

She had to do something. It was unthinkable that American blood be shed again on foreign shores.

In a daring move, she composed a cable to Kaiser Wilhelm, praying that he would be as reasonable and empathetic as Chancellor Otto von Bismarck had been years before when he and Mary had chatted together in Berlin.

She wrote and requested that the Kaiser choose representatives to a peace conference to be held at her farm as soon as a truce was arranged. She promised to gather together all manner of office equipment and services necessary for promoting a business atmosphere. Besides all that, she would provide meals for the lot of them.

She offered an escort to meet him at the docks in New York and drive him by automobile to her home at Bunker Hill. No answer was ever received, but the gesture indicates how far Dr. Mary would go to protect young American men from the ravages of war.

CHAPTER SEVENTY-ONE

WASHINGTON/OSWEGO, NEW YORK

ARGUMENTS WITH THE SOLONS about her Medal of Honor brought no satisfaction for Dr. Mary. She was treated to political rhetoric or a plain old run-around every time she broached the subject to one of them.

"We cannot interfere with the military."

"It's not our province." Or, "Go see this man."

"Go visit that office." Or, "You should try writing to so-and-so."

Excuses, excuses, excuses.

The powers that be had spoken, and no one was going to take up her cause.

Dr. Mary's trip to Washington in the winter of 1917 would prove her final undoing.

Upon leaving the Capitol after a last ditch effort to restore her Medal, she stepped out into the cold, blustery day, her overcoat buttoned high against the wind, a scarf tied around her ears, gloved hands clutching her dilapidated top hat.

In the blink of an eye she tumbled headlong down the stone steps. She lay at the bottom in a crumpled heap, dazed and semi-conscious. Her heavy garments probably saved her old bones, but the shock to her system left her nauseous as passers-by helped her to her feet.

"I'm fine, I'm fine," she insisted, as she took back her creaky stovepipe hat retrieved by a helpful bystander. She retied her scarf and clapped the chapeau atop her scraggly gray hair.

Too proud to admit that an old lady fell over her own feet, she advised onlookers, and later her friends, "The wind blew me over, that's all."

She limped away under her own steam, but from that day forward, her health began its downward spiral.

Friends accompanied her back to Oswego. She was never to visit her beloved Washington, again.

Grieving for her lost standing in Congress and her lost freedom of mobility, she spent all of her time on Bunker Hill. That didn't mean, however, that she had abandoned her causes.

She followed the Great War's progression as if every soldier were her own child. Poor as she was, she bought a Liberty Bond for $50.00, truly a patriotic sacrifice.

She was sorely distressed to discover that American infantrymen facing enemy fire were distracted by severe bouts of belly cramps and itching skin. How could they face their perilous duties under such adverse conditions?

She thought of the poor Union troops of the 52nd Ohio who had faced similar problems so many years before.

She launched a campaign to improve the diet of the beleaguered doughboys. Explicit instructions were forwarded to President Wilson describing her cost-effective remedy.

In order to ensure that her letter gained proper notice, she forwarded copies of it to the editors of prominent newspapers suggesting healthy diets and treatment for cramps and crotch itch.

The body of the letter also contained statistics to support her contention that too much sugar was being wasted by the tobacco industry. Besides, she maintained, tuberculosis sufferers desperately needed wheat and sugar to return to robust health. Therefore, such products should not be exported when other goods would serve the Army in better stead.

The newspapers ran with the story. One headline read,

"WE ARE SURPRISED AT DR. MARY WALKER'S FEAR OF A LITTLE THING LIKE CRAMPS AND BODY ITCH."

Bully for them, Mary thought, it's not their bellies that are screaming, and they aren't scratching their armpits and crotches till they're raw and bleeding.

A Medal for Dr. Mary

❦

In the early summer of 1918, the newspapers reported that there would be too little coal to stoke the home fires in the coming winter.

Dr. Mary had a solution for that problem, too.

Her plan was unique, but it smacked of her vehement antipathy to capital punishment. She proposed that governors excuse condemned criminals from execution and, instead, sentence them to hard labor in the coalmines.

The cost to export the death row inmates to the mines would be no more than the expense of housing and hanging or electrocuting them.

Besides, the mothers of the criminals could be proud that their sons (still loved despite their sins) were at least productive instead of dead. These poor parents would not have to keep hiding their faces in shame.

It was no surprise to Dr. Mary that executions continued to happen, and the coal shortage remained acute. Men in positions of power did not take kindly to advice from a mere non-voting woman.

❦

By August, fellow Oswegans–watching from the sidelines–began to fear for Mary's well-being. She remained cloistered, more helpless as the weeks passed. Her dire financial straits made proper food a luxury, and there was no money for nursing care.

Finally, at the behest of concerned neighbors, the town fathers appeared on her doorstep and entered without so much as a by-your-leave. After much powerful palaver, they convinced their most illustrious citizen that she should let them take her to the General Military Hospital at Fort Ontario.

"It is your right to go there, after all," they argued. "We cannot let you stay here on your own, any longer."

Too miserable to disagree, and perhaps a little frightened, as well, she allowed herself to be transported to the facility. *The Palladium* reported that Colonel H. D. Thompson's aide described Dr. Mary's condition as 'precarious.' The aide went on to explain that the patient had been weakened by her advanced age, and that her deprived living conditions were insufficient for a woman at her stage of life.

In late summer, her old friend, Nellie van Slingerland, visited the hospital and once again succumbed to Mary's pleading. "Get me out of this damnable place."

She arranged for the patient to be taken back to Bunker Hill to the home she loved. The officer in charge assured Nellie that he would find a suitable companion who could see to Mary's needs.

Despite the man's promises, no one came to her aid. Relatives and friends were contacted, but all declined. Her pitiable state wore her down. I'm a troglodyte, she thought, hidden away from the world amid a house full of antiques and memorabilia I can no longer enjoy.

A quote from the grand old lady summed up the substance of her life: "I remember when I could get anything I wanted in this or any other city in the Union. Doors opened to me everywhere. Presidents and Cabinet Ministers and great Generals were glad to meet and listen to me. I was younger, then, and working for our soldier boys. But I am alone now, with the infirmities of age fast weighing me down and practically penniless, and no one wants to be bothered with me. But it is the same story and the same experience that have come to others. Why should I complain?"

Though her relatives were unwilling to come running when she called, they were not averse to coercing her into deeding over her unencumbered property that she'd paid off long before. Sister Vesta's son, Byron Worden, inveigled her into signing over the homestead and her government checks, as well. Because of these actions, Mary thought her nephew would care for her until the end. He walked away without fulfilling his promise.

At least, he did not evict her from her home, but, now, she no longer had her meager income, either. Her twenty-dollar a month pension had been consigned to her greedy nephew, and she never saw another sou.

Her independent spirit was revolted by the indignity of it all.

Fall came blustering in, and with the departing Indian summer went the remainder of Mary's strength. Mostly bedridden and desperately lonely, she watched the dying leaves form a carpet of red and gold across the neighboring fields she once galloped in joyful abandon. She was cold all the time, now. Attempts to keep the stove going wore her out.

But Mary had one steadfast friend.

Frankie Dwyer, the ten-year-old son of her neighbors, Frank and Missy Dwyer, took it upon himself to stop by before and after school each day. He did what he could for the patient, fetching her hot soup and stoking the fires. But he knew it was never enough. A plan formed in his sympathetic, young heart—a plan that might save his old friend.

He approached his father after dinner one windy night as a raging Arctic Express whipped heavy waves across a pewter-colored Lake Ontario with such fury the Dwyer's house shuddered in its wake.

"I'm afraid she'll freeze to death over there in that freezing house," the child cried. "We need to bring her back here to take better care of her."

"That's not possible," said Mr. Dwyer. "We have barely enough room for ourselves, and your mama has so much to do as it is."

"I'll help, I promise I will," the child begged.

Day after day, the boy pleaded Mary's case, until finally the Dwyers gave in to their son.

Dr. Mary was wrapped in blankets and lifted into the back of their wagon for the short drive to the Dwyer's small house. Silent tears slid down her wrinkled cheeks as she watched her clapboard home disappear beyond the tailgate. I'll never see it again, she thought.

∽◦◉◦∽

January: Mary's weight fell away, while her appetite became non-existent.

February blustered in. Mary lived with constant pain, her inflamed joints screaming in rebellion every time she moved her fleshless body. Feeble now, in and out of consciousness, her fevered brain conjured up the past.

Cynthia was there. Sometimes her confused mind saw her sister on the sick bed with Mary in attendance. Sometimes, it was Cynthia who was the caretaker.

She wept with shame over her failed marriage that never should have happened in the first place. Albert Miller had been cruel and sadistic–trying too hard to control a free spirit who could not bow down if her life depended on it. She realized she would not have changed her decision to divorce, no matter how her life had played out.

Sometimes, she was back at Syracuse Medical School with Edwin–handsome, decent, loving Edwin whose memory was ever young and fresh in her heart. Had he not already been spoken for how different her life might have been. Papa's face drifted in and out. Mama called her name.

At four o'clock on Friday afternoon, when young Frankie hurried in from school, his mother shook her head, tears brimming, her face a study in sadness. He hurried to his bedroom where his old friend had suffered for the past three months. Suddenly shy, he hesitated in the doorway.

When Mary held her frail arms out to him, he stepped close to her side and patted her pillow. Her blue eyes, now faded with age, gazed steadily at him from beneath silver brows.

With a supreme effort she raised a trembling hand and placed her fingers against his rosy cheek still chilled and damp from the February snow outside.

"Thank you, child," she whispered so quietly he strained to hear, then her hand fell back to the coverlet. Her sad eyes closed slowly as if the weight of the lids was too much to bear.

It was Dr. Mary's last conscious act.

At eight o'clock, on February 21st, 1919, the brave old warrior escaped from the world that had treated her so badly for most of her adult life.

Dr. Mary was entitled to all the pomp and ceremony of a full military funeral and burial in Arlington Cemetery, but that was not to be.

Gentle women washed her corpse and lovingly dressed her in her shabby clothes, kinder to her in death than in life. Her ravaged body was carried to her dining room table, and, finally, Mary was alone in her shuttered, unheated house from Saturday until Monday.

Her little polished boots pointed heavenward, her liver-spotted hands lay folded against her waist and her careworn face was peaceful, at last.

Her cherished Medal of Honor was pinned above her heart along with several other awards.

Early Monday Morning, a cheap wooden coffin, big enough for a child, was carried in. Mary's tiny, fragile body was tenderly lifted into it. Before the lid was nailed down, her Medals were removed for safekeeping. The country would be better served if her most famous treasures were preserved for future generations.

Finally, Mary's flag was draped across the wooden cover.

Monday afternoon the weather was freezing cold and spitting snow. Few people attended the simple two o'clock funeral in the Walker homestead. Following Mary's wishes, there were no hymns or extended eulogies.

Fewer trekked the two miles over a winding road to hear Methodist minister, the Reverend Alonzo Hand, deliver the graveside prayers beside the Walker family plot in Rural Cemetery. Her nephews, Byron Worden; Luna's sons, Charles and Orla Griswold; and a cousin, N. G. Thompson, acted as pallbearers. It was the least they could do for an aunt and cousin they had all but abandoned in life.

At the end of the service the undertaker proceeded to remove Mary's flag from the coffin, but Frank Dwyer interfered. He remembered the words of her old poem:

> "When I am buried 'neath the ground,
> Wrap the flag my corpse around,
> Plant that flag above my grave,
> Then let it wave! Let it Wave!"

"She loved that flag with all her heart," Dwyer protested, brushing roughly at his tears. "She wanted it buried with her."

Others voiced the same opinion, and the flag was interred with its faithful owner.

The grave lies in the section called The Old Acre in Rural Cemetery far from the main highway. The Walker plot shelters the remains of

Alvah, Vesta, Cynthia, and Mary. There is a small granite headstone on the scraggly lot inscribed, 'Father, Mother, Sister.' Another is inscribed, 'Mary,' and sports a wrought iron standard placed by the G. A. R. Its small, faded flag fights bravely against the constant wind, even as Dr. Mary Walker fought against impossible odds in order to make her country a better place.

Newspapers all over the world published obituaries, finally speaking kindly of Mary now that she was no longer able to read their comments.

The Palladium:

"The doctor's passing marks the end of one of the most remarkable characters that ever resided in Oswego, in fact, in the country. Small and frail, she nevertheless had wonderful energy and vitality—no task was too great for her to attempt. Her nervous energy kept her on the move, physically and mentally. Dr. Walker is gone, but it will be a long time before she is forgotten."

The New York Herald:

"A woman who was all her life a sensible champion of women's cause, deserves something better in the way of remembrance than to be identified with a whim (dress reform). A later generation of advocates of woman's rights, with most of those rights established, may well spare a tribute to this earnest, if eccentric, pioneer in their field. Her contribution to the health and happiness of the human race should

banish sartorial eccentricities from the mind of any unprejudiced historian."

The New York Sun:

"This unusual character is remembered, probably always will be remembered as long as her memory lives at all, by the fact that she wore men's clothes. The trousers, frock coat, starched shirt and collar in which she chose to attire her little body effectually overshadowed all the work she ever did."

The Palladium reported that Dr. Mary Walker left little of value, but that was far from the truth. Her rare antiques, many over one hundred years old, her china, artifacts, and treasures, utensils and farm equipment accounted for a goodly portion of her wealth.

Her nephew lost no time in cataloguing and selling the belongings and adding the proceeds to what he had already cheated from his aunt.

On Tuesday, April 27th, an auction was held, and all of Dr. Mary's worldly goods were pored over, bid upon, and carried away.

How she would have hated it!

The Walker homestead no longer exists. It was demolished by fire in the early 1940s. The famous old landmark has disappeared from the planet along with its unappreciated owner.

> *"I am forgotten as a dead man out of mind."*
> *Psalm 31:12*

Thus endeth the chronicles of Dr. Mary Edwards Walker, a courageous and selfless woman.

But there is one final chapter left to complete this fascinating tale

EPILOGUE

D R. MARY'S grand niece, Helen Hay Wilson, fought long and hard for the restoration of her aunt's Medal of Honor. Her diligence finally paid off.

In the spring of 1976, both the Common Council of the City of Oswego and the New York State Assembly unanimously passed resolutions stating that the matter of revocation of Dr. Mary Edwards Walker's honors must be reconsidered. Both resolutions were forwarded to the United States Congress urging reinstatement of the Medal to their prestigious citizen.

The matter was funneled by Congressman McEwen through the Committee on Armed Services then presented to the 2nd Session of the 94th Congress.

The House Bill #925 that directed President James Earl Carter, Jr. to act in favor quickly followed:

"JOINT RESOLUTION

Restoring the Medal of Honor to Dr. Mary Edwards Walker.
WHEREAS, Dr. Mary Edwards Walker was one of the first women to become a doctor;
WHEREAS, Doctor Walker fulfilled many other roles including teaching, writing, and lecturing as an outspoken advocate of women's rights, urging women's suffrage and other reforms;
WHEREAS, while in the service of the Union Army during the Civil War, Doctor Walker became

the first woman commissioned as an assistant
surgeon and was later awarded the Medal of Honor
by President Andrew Johnson for her patriotic zeal
in attending sick and wounded soldiers;
WHEREAS, the name of Dr. Walker, the only
woman ever to receive this Nation's highest award
for valor, was stricken from the official Medal of
Honor list in 1917 allegedly because specific acts of
valor for which the Medal of Honor was awarded
could not be found: Now, therefore, be it resolved by
the Senate and House of Representatives of the
United States of America in Congress Assembled,
That the President shall restore to Dr. Mary
Edwards Walker the Congressional Medal of
Honor, which was awarded on November 11,
1865, and which was revoked when her name was
stricken from the official Medal of Honor list in
1917."

Massachusetts Senator Edward W. Brooke, a black politician who knew a great deal about discrimination, introduced the Resolution in the Senate. He was quoted in a news release:

"Dr. Mary Edwards Walker earned it on the
battlefields of the Civil War, only to lose it 52 years
later for the simple reason that she was a woman.
The Army's action rightfully restores our highest
medal to a true American heroine There was more
than enough evidence to prove that Dr. Walker
served as an unsalaried physician in the Union
Army during which time she treated soldiers in
battle. At the risk of capture she crossed enemy lines
to care for destitute civilians This brave and
wonderful woman later endured four months in a

Confederate prison, where she continued her medical mission of mercy by attending to ailing inmates to the detriment of her own health. It is only fitting that we restore to Dr. Walker what was rightfully hers, and, in so doing, pay tribute to one of America's finest women." The country loved it. Helen Wilson, in deference to her country, was forced to veto the idea of replicating the Medal of Honor on a T-shirt. However, she thought one with a good picture of Mary might be appropriate. Still, that was not the end of the saga.

June 10, 1982: A COMMEMORATIVE STAMP honoring the fifth anniversary of Dr. Walker's reinstatement to the roster of Medal of Honor winners was officially introduced to the appreciative citizens of Oswego at their diminutive United States Post Office.

The stamp is done in vertical format with an oval of Dr. Mary centered on an ivory background. Its beautiful cameo portrait, fashioned on antique ivory by the noted painter of miniatures, Glenora Case Richards, depicts a young Mary, a pensive look about her amazing blue eyes, a firm set to her closed lips and gently curving jaw line. Her black, curly hair, parted in the middle, is held away from her serene face by a narrow blue ribbon.

A white, lacy fichu pinned with a tiny blue flower relieves the starkness of her black tunic. Her Medal of Honor on her left shoulder is painted in bronze with a blue and white ribbon. The total effect has captured the lovely persona of a completely feminine, extremely intelligent young woman.

Above the picture is the heavy black caption, DR. MARY WALKER. Blue lettering just below her name reads ARMY SURGEON. Beneath the oval in stark black is MEDAL OF HONOR, and below that the cost, a mere 20c, repeats in blue.

But honors did not stop there. On the 9th of May, 2012, a six-foot bronze statue of the intrepid little doctor was installed in front of the Oswego Town Hall.

Her quote about having to die before she is recognized is inscribed on the side of the lectern before which she stands.

Dr. Mary would have been very pleased!

⊷⊶❀⊷⊶

Thus the valiant lady whose life span embraced twenty-two incumbent presidents, several wars, including the Civil War and the Great War to end all wars, was finally vindicated.

In Dr. Mary's own words:

> *"I am the original new woman. I have made it possible for the bicycle girl to wear the abbreviated skirt, and I have prepared the way for the girl in knickerbockers. I have got to die before people will know what I have done. It is a shame that people who lead reforms in this world are not appreciated until after they are dead. I would be thankful if people would treat me decently now, instead of erecting great piles of stone over me when I am gone."*

> *In spite of being blessed with the right to vote and be heard, with legal protections from male oppression, with high-powered jobs, fast automobiles and comfortable trouser outfits, few modern women give a second thought to the desperately fought battles that prepared the way. Perhaps these Walker chronicles will remind them one courageous woman sacrificed everything to make that easier road possible.*

That, after all, was Dr. Mary Edwards Walker's fondest dream.

End.

Author's Note:

In 1995, when my research began for Dr. Mary, southern libraries had a dearth of information about northern heroines. Then I discovered that Dr. Mary's commemorative stamp, issued in 1982, bears a remarkable resemblance to my High School graduation photograph. Eerily, there were many times in my writing as I strove to make her human that I knew exactly what Dr. Mary would say or how she would react.

My journey took me to the **Oswego Historical Society Archives** in Oswego, NY. where I was allowed to copy letters and articles and handle precious memorabilia, including her Medal of Honor.

Although Syracuse University is not connected to Dr. Mary's Syracuse Medical School, the archives at the **Department of Special Collections** in the **Syracuse University Library** contains boxes of Walker's letters, clippings and memorabilia.

Next I visited **Allegheny University of Health and Sciences Archives and Special Collections on Women in Medicine** to pore over their files of letters, clippings, etc.

A Microfilm Publication from the **National Military Archives in Washington, DC** contains copies of letters to, from and about Dr. Mary. There are missives from military personnel such as Generals Sherman, Burnside and McCook as well as letters to and from President Lincoln.

The **Encyclopedia of the Civil War** contains descriptions of all the military personnel mentioned.

Extensive reading on the Suffragettes with whom Dr. Mary had a running disagreement followed. Every historical character in the book was researched as were political activities, medical practices, costumes, vehicles, etc covering her eighty-seven years.

Dr. Mary's *Crowning Constitutional Argument* acclaimed at the time by senators and judges as well as her controversial books, *Hit* and *Unmasked: The Science of Immorality* all contributed to this history.

CPSIA information can be obtained at www.ICGtesting.com
Printed in the USA
LVOW080849031212

309774LV00001B/4/P